"Evocative,
enticing, erotic..."
—J. R. Ward,
bestselling author of
Lover Unbound

Midnight
Awakening

LARA ADRIAN

Nationally Bestselling Author of *Kiss of Crimson*

Also by Lara Adrian

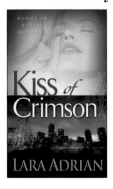

Available from Dell

COMING SOON!

ISBN 978-0-553-58939-9

US $6.99/ $9.99 CAN

50699

"What happened to you tonight, Elise? Did someone hurt you out there? Were you attacked before the Rogues discovered you in the alley?"

Her answer was long in coming. "No. I wasn't attacked."

"You want to explain all that blood on your coat over there?"

She held her head in her hands, her voice a rough whisper. "I don't want to explain anything. Please, Tegan. I wish you hadn't come here. Just, please . . . you have to leave now."

He exhaled a sharp laugh. "I just saved your sweet little ass, female. I don't think it's too much to ask that you tell me why I had to."

"I didn't mean to be out past dark. I know the dangers. Things just took . . . a little longer than I anticipated."

"Things," he repeated, not liking where this seemed to be heading. "We're not talking about shopping or coffee with friends, are we?"

Tegan's gaze went back to the kitchen counter, to the familiar design of the cell phone that lay there.

"Where'd you get this, Elise?"

"I think you know," she replied, her voice quiet but defiant.

He turned to face her. "You took it off a Minion? By yourself? Jesus Christ . . . how?"

She shrugged, rubbing the side of her head as if it pained her. "I tracked him from the train station. I followed him, and when the chance was there, I killed him."

It wasn't often that Tegan was taken by surprise, but hearing those words coming out of the petite female hit him like a brick to the back of his head. "You can't be serious."

But she was. The level look she gave him left no doubt whatsoever.

Tegan dropped his ass onto the futon and raked his fingers through his hair. "Holy hell, woman. Have you lost your mind?"

Also by Lara Adrian

KISS OF MIDNIGHT

KISS OF CRIMSON

Midnight
Awakening

MIDNIGHT BREED SERIES
BOOK THREE

LARA ADRIAN

A DELL BOOK

MIDNIGHT AWAKENING
A Dell Book / December 2007

Published by Bantam Dell
A Division of Random House, Inc.
New York, New York

Dell is a registered trademark of Random House, Inc.,
and the colophon is a trademark of Random House, Inc.

ISBN 978-0-553-58939-9

Printed in the United States of America
Published simultaneously in Canada

www.bantamdell.com

OPM 10 9 8 7 6 5 4 3 2 1

To my readers, with deep appreciation for all the enthusiasm and support you've shown for my books. Thank you so much!

And to my husband, my true north, and proof positive that "happily ever after" really does exist outside the written page. You'll always be my hero!

Acknowledgments

With thanks to my agent and everyone at Bantam Dell for the continued belief in me, and for the wonderful attention given to each of my books. Thanks also to my copyeditors, proofreaders, and other folks working behind the scenes. (Hi, Destiny and Jeremy!)

Big hugs to my writer pals for tolerating prolonged bouts of radio silence on my end, yet still being available for last-minute sanity checks and encouragement. Thank you especially to Kayla Gray, Jaci Burton, Larissa Ione, and Stephanie Tyler for simply being awesome.

Additional gratitude goes out to three immensely talented bands whose music brought much of this story to life in my imagination. Inspiration (and a continuing daily addiction) is due to the artistry of Collide, H.I.M., and Black Lab.

Midnight Awakening

CHAPTER
One

She walked among them undetected, just another after-noon rush-hour commuter trudging through the fresh February snowfall on her way to the train station. No one paid any mind at all to the petite female in the hooded oversized parka, her scarf concealing her face to just be-low her eyes, which watched the crowds of human pedes-trians with keen interest. Too keen, she knew, but she couldn't help it.

She was anxious being out among them, and impa-tient to find her prey.

Her head rang with the pound of rock music blaring in through the tiny earbuds of a portable MP3 player. It wasn't hers. It had belonged to her teenage son—to

Camden. Sweet Cam, who'd died just four months ago, a victim of the underworld war that Elise herself was now a part of as well. He was the reason she was here, prowling Boston's crowded streets with a dagger in her coat pocket and a titanium-edged blade strapped to her thigh.

More than ever now, Camden was the reason she lived.

His death could not go unavenged.

Elise crossed at a traffic light and moved up the road toward the station. She could see people talking as she passed them, their lips moving silently, their words—more important, their thoughts—drowned out by the aggressive lyrics, screaming guitars, and pulsing throb of bass that filled her ears and vibrated in her bones. She didn't know precisely what she was listening to, nor did it matter. All she needed was the noise, played loud enough and long enough to get her into place for the hunt.

She entered the building, just one more person in a river of moving humanity. Harsh light spilled down from fluorescent tubes in the ceiling. The odor of street filth and dampness and too many bodies assailed her nose through her scarf. Elise walked farther inside, coming to a slow pause in the center of the station. Forced to divide around her, the flowing crowd passed on either side, many bumping into her, jostling her in their haste to make the next train. More than one glared as they passed, mouthing obscenities over her abrupt halt in the middle of their path.

God, how she despised all of this contact, but it was necessary. She took a steadying breath, then reached into her pocket and turned off the music. The din of the station rushed upon her like a wave, engulfing her with the racket of voices, shuffling feet, the traffic outside, and the metallic grate and rumble of the incoming train. But these noises were nothing compared to the others that swamped her now.

Ugly thoughts, bad intentions, secret sins, open hatreds—all of it churned around her like a black tempest, human corruption seeking her out and hammering into her senses. It staggered her, as always, that first rush of ill wind nearly overwhelming her. Elise swayed on her feet. She fought the nausea that rose within her and tried her best to weather the psychic assault.

—*Such a bitch, I hope they fire her ass*—

—*Goddamn hick tourists, why don't you go back where you belong*—

—*Idiot! Outta my way, or I'll friggin' knock you flat*—

—*So what if she's my wife's sister? Not like she wasn't after me all this time*—

Elise's breath was coming faster with each second, a headache blooming in her temples. The voices in her mind blended into ceaseless, almost indistinguishable chatter, but she held on, bracing herself as the train arrived and its doors opened to let a new sea of people pour out onto the platform. They spilled around her, more voices added to the cacophony that was shredding her from the inside.

—*Panhandling losers ought to put the same effort into getting a damn job*—

—*I swear, he puts his hand on me one more time, I'ma kill the sumbitch*—

—*Run, cattle! Run back to your pens! Pathetic creatures, my Master is right, you do deserve to be enslaved*—

Elise's eyes snapped wide. Her blood turned to ice in her veins the instant the words registered in her mind. This was the one voice she waited to hear.

The one she came here to hunt.

She didn't know the name of her prey, or even what he looked like, but she knew what he was: a Minion. Like the others of his kind, he had been human once, but now he was something less than that. His humanity had been bled away by the one he called Master, a powerful vampire and the leader of the Rogues. It was because of them—the Rogues and the evil one guiding them in a growing war within the vampire race—that Elise's only son was dead.

After being widowed five years ago, Camden was all she'd had left, all that mattered in her life. With his loss, she'd found a new purpose. An unwavering resolve. It was that resolve she leaned upon now, commanding her feet to move through the thick crowd, searching for the one she'd make pay for Camden's death this time.

Her head spun with the continued bombardment of painful, ugly thoughts, but finally she managed to single out the Minion. He stalked ahead of her by several yards, his head covered by a black knit cap, his body draped in a tattered, faded green camouflage jacket. Animosity poured out of him like acid. His corruption was so total, Elise could taste it like bile in the back of her throat. And she had no choice but to stick close to him, waiting for her chance to make her move.

The Minion exited the station and headed up the sidewalk at a fast clip. Elise followed, her fingers wrapped tightly around the dagger in her pocket. Outside with fewer people, the psychic blare had lessened, but the pain of overload in the station was still present, boring into her skull like a steel spike. Elise kept her eyes trained on her quarry, picking up her speed as he ducked into a business off the street. She came up to the glass door and peered past the painted FedEx logo to see the Minion waiting in line for the counter.

"Excuse me, miss," someone said from behind her, startling her with the sound of a true voice, and not the buzz of words that were still filling her head. "You going inside or what, lady?"

The man behind her pushed open the door as he said it, holding it for her expectantly. She hadn't intended to go in, but now everyone was looking at her—the Minion included—and it would draw more attention to herself if she refused. Elise strode into the brightly lit business and immediately feigned interest in a display of shipping boxes in the front window.

From her periphery, she watched as the Minion waited his turn in line. He was edgy and violent-minded, his thoughts berating the customers ahead of him. Finally he approached the counter, ignoring the clerk's greeting.

"Pickup for Raines."

The attendant typed something into a computer, then hesitated a second. "Hang on." He headed to a back room, only to return a moment later shaking his head. "It hasn't arrived yet. Sorry 'bout that."

Fury rolled off the Minion, tightening like a vise around Elise's temples. "What do you mean, 'it hasn't arrived'?"

"Most of New York got hit with a big snowstorm last night, so a lot of today's shipments have been delayed—"

"This shit's supposed to be guaranteed," the Minion snarled.

"Yeah, it is. You can get your money back, but you have to fill out a claim—"

"Fuck the claim, you moron! I need that package. Now!"

My Master will have my ass if I don't turn up with this delivery, and if my ass goes in a sling, I'm going to come back here and rip your goddamn lungs out.

Elise drew in her breath at the virulence of the unspoken threat. She knew the Minions lived only to serve the one who made them, but it was always a shock to hear the terrible depth of their allegiance. Nothing was sacred to their kind. Lives meant nothing, be they human or Breed. Minions were nearly as awful as the Rogues, the bloodthirsty, criminal faction of the vampire nation.

The Minion leaned over the counter, fists braced on either side of him. "I need that package, asshole. I'm not leaving without it."

The clerk backed away, his expression suddenly gone wary. He grabbed the phone. "Look, man, as I've explained to you, there's nothing more I can do for you on this. You're gonna have to come back tomorrow. Right now, you need to leave before I call the police."

Useless piece of shit, the Minion growled inwardly. *I'll come back tomorrow all right. Just you wait 'til I come back for you!*

"Is there a problem here, Joey?" An older man came out from the back, all business.

"I tried to tell him that his stuff ain't here yet on account of the storm, but he won't give it up. Like maybe I'm supposed to pull it out of my a—"

"Sir?" the manager said, cutting off his employee and pinning the Minion with a serious look. "I'm going to ask you politely to leave now. You need to go, or the police will be called to escort you out of here."

The Minion growled something indistinguishable but nasty. He slammed his fist down on the countertop, then whirled around and started stalking away. As he neared the door where Elise stood, he swept over a floor display, sending rolls of tape and bubble packs scattering to the floor. Although Elise stepped back, the Minion was coming too hard toward her. He glared down at her with vacant, inhuman eyes.

"Get out of my way, cow!"

She'd barely moved before he barreled past her and out the door, pushing so hard the glass panes rattled like they were going to shatter.

"Asshole," one of the patrons still in line muttered once the Minion had gone.

Elise felt the wave of relief wash over the other customers at his departure. Part of her was relieved too, glad that no one met with harm. She wanted to wait for a while in the momentary calm in the store, but it was an indulgence she couldn't afford. The Minion was storming across the street now, and dusk was coming fast.

She only had half an hour at best before darkness fell and the Rogues came out to feed. If what she did was dangerous in the daytime, at night it was nothing short of suicide. She could slay a Minion with stealth and steel—already had, in fact, more than once—but like any other human, female or not, she stood no chance against the blood-addicted strength of the Rogues.

Girding herself for what she had to do, Elise slipped out the door and followed the Minion up the street. He was angry and walking brusquely, slamming into other pedestrians and snarling curses at them as he passed. A barrage of mental pain filled her head as more voices joined the din already clanging in her mind, but Elise kept pace with her target. She hung a few yards behind, her eyes trained on the pale green bulk of his jacket through the light flurry of fresh snow. He swung left around the corner of a building and into a narrow alley. Elise hurried now, desperate not to lose him.

Midway down the side street, he yanked open a battered steel door and disappeared. She crept up to the windowless slab of metal, palms sweating despite the chill in the air. His violent thoughts filled her head—murderous thoughts, all the grisly things he would do out of deference to his Master.

Elise reached into her pocket to withdraw her dagger. She held it close to her side, poised to strike, but concealed behind the long drape of her coat. With her free hand, she grasped the latch and pulled open the unlocked door. Snowflakes swirled ahead of her into the gloomy vestibule that reeked of mildew and old cigarette smoke. The Minion stood near a bank of mail slots, one shoulder leaning against the wall as he flipped open a cell phone like the ones they all carried—the Minions' direct line to their vampire Master.

"Shut the fucking door, bitch!" he snapped, soulless eyes glinting. His brows dropped into a scowl as Elise moved toward him with swift, deadly purpose. "What the hell is th—"

She drove the dagger hard into his chest, knowing that the element of surprise was one of her best advantages. His anger hit her like a physical blow, pushing her backward. His corruption seeped into her mind like acid, burning her senses. Elise struggled through the psychic pain, coming back to strike him again with the blade, ignoring the sudden wet heat of his blood spilling onto her hand.

The Minion sputtered, grasping out for her as he fell against her. His wound was mortal, so much blood she nearly lost her stomach at the sight and smell of it. Elise twisted out of the Minion's heavy lean and leaped out of the way as he fell to the floor. Her breath was sawing out of her lungs, her heart racing, her head splitting in agony as the mental barrage of his rage continued in her mind.

The Minion thrashed and hissed as death overtook him. Then, finally, he stilled.

Finally, there was silence.

With trembling fingers, Elise retrieved the cell phone from where it lay at her feet and slipped it into her pocket. The slaying had drained her, the combined physical and psychic exertion almost too much to bear. Each time seemed to weigh more heavily on her, take longer for her to recover. She wondered if the day would come that she might slide so deep into the abyss that she'd not rebound at all. Probably, she guessed, but not today. And she would keep fighting so long as she had breath in her body and the pain of loss in her heart.

"For Camden," she whispered, staring down at the dead Minion as she clicked on the MP3 player in preparation of her return home. Music blared from the tiny earbuds, muting the gift that gave her the power to hear the darkest secrets of a human's soul.

She'd heard enough for now.

Her day's sober mission complete, Elise pivoted around and fled the carnage she'd wrought.

CHAPTER
Two

The scent of blood carried on the thin, wintry breeze. It was faint, fresh, a coppery tickle in the nostrils of the vampire warrior who leaped soundlessly from the roof of one dusk-shadowed building to another. Snowflakes fell around him like floating white ash, blanketing the city that spread out beneath him some six stories down.

Tegan crouched at the ledge and surveyed the tangle of bustling streets and alleyways. As one of the Order—a small cadre of Breed vampires engaged in war against their savage brethren, the Rogues—Tegan's primary nightly objective was dealing death to his enemies. It was something he did with a cold efficiency, a skill perfected during his more than seven centuries of existence. But down to his marrow, he was Breed, and there were none among his kind who could ignore the call of newly spilled human blood.

He curled back his lips and dragged the cold air in through his teeth. His gums tingled, an ache blooming where his canines began to stretch into fangs. His vision sharpened beyond its preternatural acuity, pupils narrowing into thin vertical slits in the center of his green eyes. The urge to hunt—to feed—rose up in him swiftly. It was an automatic response that even he, with his disciplined, iron self-control, could do little to suppress.

All the worse for him, being of the first generation of vampires spawned on Earth. Gen One appetites—physical, carnal, and otherwise—burned the strongest.

Tegan crept along the edge of the building, then leaped down onto the roof of another, his eyes rooted on the movement of people below, searching for the weak member in the herd. But he didn't comb the crowds merely to satisfy his own needs: find a human with an open flesh wound, and he knew for a fact that any Rogues within a mile radius would not be far behind.

Except now that he was zeroing in on the source of the blood scent, he realized that what he smelled had an increasingly stale edge to it. It was spilled blood. Not fresh at all, but several minutes old.

Following the metallic odor, Tegan's gaze lit on a short, slight figure in a long hooded parka who was hurrying up the main thoroughfare, past the train station. There was an anxious clip to the person's gait, an obvious desire not to be noticed in the low tilt of the head as it cut away from a crowd of pedestrians and headed for an empty side street.

"What the hell have you been up to?" Tegan murmured under his breath as he tracked the individual.

Male or female, he couldn't be sure under all that dark, quilted down. Either way, the human was about to get some very unwanted company.

Tegan saw the Rogue an instant before it came out of hiding near a Dumpster several yards ahead of the human. He couldn't hear the words being said, but he could tell by the vampire's swagger and glowing amber eyes that it was taunting the person—just having a little fun before it made its move. Two more Rogues came around the corner from behind now, hemming the human in.

"Damn it," Tegan growled, rubbing a hand over his jaw.

He'd never had much use for the shiny brand of honor that demanded his kind act as unsung saviors to the humans who inhabited the planet with them. Even half-human himself, as was all of the Breed, Tegan had long ago given up needing to be the hero. He'd seen too much bloodshed, too much senseless slaughter and tragic waste from both sides.

His purpose now and for the past five hundred years— since the brutal torture and death of the only woman he'd ever loved—was simple enough: take out as many Rogues as possible, or die trying. He didn't really give a shit which came first.

But there was an ancient part of him that still bristled at the thought of grossly unfair odds, like the situation taking place on the street below.

The human in the bloodstained parka was being surrounded. Like sharks moving in for a kill, the Rogues started closing ranks. The hooded head came up suddenly, pivoted around to note the threat closing in from behind. Too late, though. No human stood a chance against one Bloodlusting suckhead, let alone a pack of three.

With a curse, Tegan advanced his position and jumped to a lower rooftop above the alleyway.

Just as the Rogue in front of the human lunged into action.

Tegan heard a sharp intake of breath—a female gasp of terror—as the Rogue grabbed for its prey. It seized the front of the woman's hood and threw her down on the snow-covered pavement, letting loose a howl of savage amusement as she took the hard fall.

"Jesus Christ," Tegan hissed, already drawing a large blade from the sheath at his hip.

With a running leap, he dropped down from the ledge of the building, landing smoothly on the ground in a low crouch. The two Rogues nearest him split up, one taking cover while the other shouted that they were under attack. Tegan silenced the warning in mid-sentence, slicing his length of titanium-edged steel across the suckhead's throat.

A few yards ahead of him in the alleyway, the female was on her stomach, scrabbling to get away from her assailant. She had a weapon too, Tegan was surprised to see, but the Rogue noticed it at the same time and kicked it out of her hand. The Rogue planted the heavy sole of his boot on the center of her back, pinning her to the ground with his heel jammed hard into her spine.

Tegan was on him at once. He threw the Rogue off the woman, driving the snarling vampire into the side of the brick building and holding it there with his forearm wedged under the suckhead's chin.

"Get out of here!" he shouted to the human as she started to drag herself up off the ground. "Run!"

She flung a frightened look over her shoulder—the first glimpse Tegan got of her face. His gaze locked on to a pair of huge, pale lavender eyes. The woman stared at him from over the top of a dark knit scarf that could hardly disguise the delicate beauty beneath it.

Holy shit.

He knew her.

And she wasn't just a random human female; she was a Breedmate. A young widow from one of the vampire nation's Darkhaven sanctuaries in the city. Tegan didn't know her well. He hadn't seen her for several months, not since the night he'd taken her home from the Order's compound after she'd learned her only son had gone Rogue.

It was the last he had seen of her, but it hadn't been the last time he'd thought about her.

Elise.

What the hell was she doing here?

Tegan's flat stare held Elise transfixed for a moment that seemed to stretch out endlessly. She saw a flash of recognition in the warrior's unblinking gaze, felt the cold blast of his fury emanating toward her across the distance that separated them.

"Tegan," she whispered, astonished to see that it was him coming to her rescue. She'd first met the terrifying warrior around the time that her son had gone missing. Tegan had been the one to take her home from the Order's compound after she'd learned Camden had fallen in with the Rogues. He'd shown her kindness in that late night ride back to her Darkhaven home, and although she hadn't seen the warrior in the four months since, she hadn't forgotten his unexpected compassion.

But none of that was present in him now. Battle rage had fully transformed his face to that of his true nature—a Breed vampire, with gleaming fangs and fierce eyes that were no longer their usual gem-green, but swamped with bright, glowing amber that burned like twin flames in his skull.

"Run!" he shouted, the deep, otherworldly growl of his voice cutting through the blare of music still pouring into her head from the earbuds she wore. "Get out of here—now!"

That brief inattention cost him. The Rogue he had pinned to the bricks in front of him twisted its big head, jaws wide, huge fangs dripping saliva. It bit down hard on Tegan's forearm, ripping into the warrior's muscled flesh. Without a sound of pain or anger, only chillingly swift efficiency, Tegan brought his other hand up and buried a blade in the Rogue's neck. The diseased vampire dropped, lifeless, its corpse sizzling from the titanium that poisoned its corrupt bloodstream.

Tegan whirled around, his breath sawing out from between his lips, clouding in the chill air. "Goddamn it, woman—go!" he roared, just as the remaining Rogue vaulted into a further attack on him.

Elise jolted into movement.

She sped out of the alleyway and onto another street, running as fast as her legs would carry her. The small apartment she rented wasn't far, just a few long blocks from the train station, but it seemed like miles. She was exhausted from her own ordeal that day, shaking from the violence she'd just witnessed in the alley.

She was worried for Tegan too, even though she was certain he didn't need her concern. He was a member of the Order, probably the most lethal of them all, if his reputation was anything to go by. He was a killing machine according to all who knew his name. Seeing him here in action for herself, Elise didn't doubt it for a second.

And now that she'd been discovered alone in the city, she could only hope that the warrior would take no interest in what she was doing. She couldn't allow herself to be pushed back into the Darkhavens, not even by a male as fearsome as Tegan.

Elise ran the last block to her apartment and raced up the concrete steps. The main door used to be keyed access, but someone broke the lock five weeks ago and the building super hadn't gotten around to fixing it yet. Elise pushed the door open and dashed down the first floor hallway to her unit. She unlocked the dead bolt and slipped inside, immediately flipping on all the lights.

The stereo and television went on next—tuned to nothing in particular, but both playing loudly. Elise pulled off the MP3 player and set it down on the chipped yellow kitchen counter, along with the dead Minion's cell phone. She ditched her ruined parka on the floor next to her treadmill, her stomach turning as the bare bulb hanging from the combination dining-living room ceiling washed over the dark red stains from the Minion's blood. It was on her hands too; her fingers were sticky with gore.

And her head was still pounding, the usual vicious migraine that came in the wake of any prolonged period of using her skill. It wasn't as bad right now as it would be soon. She still had time to clean up and try to get herself to bed before the worst of it hit her.

Elise dragged herself into the bathroom and turned on the shower. Her fingers were trembling as she unfastened the leather knife sheath from her thigh and placed it on the sink. The sheath was empty. She'd lost the titanium blade in the snow when the Rogue kicked it out of her grasp. She had others to replace it. A lot of the money she'd left the Darkhavens with had gone into weapons and training equipment—things she had never wanted to know anything about but now considered necessities.

Lord, how drastically her life had changed in just four months.

She could never go back to what she was. In her heart, she knew there could be no going back now. The person she had been all the time she'd lived under the protection of the Breed was gone now—dead, like her beloved mate and her son. The pain of those losses had been a furnace that devoured her old life, reduced it to cinder. She was what was left—the phoenix that rose out of the ash.

Elise glanced up into the fogging mirror and met her own haunted gaze in the glass. Blood smeared her cheek and chin, grime smudged her brow, all of it like warpaint. There was a feral glint in the weary eyes staring back at her.

God, she was tired . . . so tired. But so long as she could stand, she could fight. So long as her heart still ached for vengeance, she would use the psychic gift that had for so long been her greatest weakness. She would endure any hardship, face any risk. She would sell her everlasting soul if she must. Whatever it took to have justice.

CHAPTER
Three

Tegan wiped his bloodied blade on the dead Rogue's jacket and idly observed the swift disintegration of the last body in the alley. The postmortem cleanup was courtesy of Tegan's titanium weapons, a metal that acted as poisonous acid to the diseased cellular makeup of Breed vampires gone Rogue. The three bodies dissolved in the snow, reducing flesh, bone, and clothing to nothing but dark spots of ash against the pristine white.

Tegan blew out a curse, his senses still quivering with the heat of combat. Battle-sharpened eyes lit on the knife Elise had lost in her struggle with the Rogue who'd attacked her. Tegan walked over and retrieved the weapon.

"Christ," he muttered, picking the blade up from the

snow. It wasn't some dainty dagger a lady might carry for protection but a serious-looking bit of hardware. Seven inches long, serrated near the upward jut of the tip, and, unless he missed his guess, the metal was not your basic carbide steel but Rogue-eating titanium.

Which only begged the question again: what the hell was the Darkhaven female doing out on the streets alone, covered in blood, and toting warrior-grade weapons on her person?

Tegan lifted his head and sniffed at the air, searching for her scent. It didn't take long to find it. His senses were always sharp, predatorially acute; combat lit them up like laser beams. He pulled the heather-and-roses scent of the Breedmate into his lungs, and let it guide him deeper into the city.

The scent trailed off at a shit-hole apartment building in one of the seedier sections of the low-rent area of town. Not at all the kind of place he'd expect to find a genteel Darkhaven-raised female like Elise. But without a doubt, she was inside the graffiti-tagged, brick-and-concrete eyesore; he was certain of that.

He stalked up the steps and scowled at the feeble door with its broken lock. Inside the vestibule his boots scuffed on ratty, stained carpeting that reeked of urine, filth, and decades of neglect. A battered wooden staircase rose to the left of him, but Elise's scent was coming from the door at the end of the first-floor hall.

Tegan moved past another apartment door on his right, the thump of music vibrating the floor and walls. He could hear a television too, a deafening barrage of background noise that seemed to swell as he neared Elise's place. He rapped on the door and waited.

No response.

He knocked again, dropping his knuckles hard on the scarred metal. Nothing. Not that she could hear anything inside the place with all the racket going on in there.

Maybe he shouldn't be there, shouldn't get involved in whatever it was that brought the female to this place in her life. Tegan knew she'd had a rough time since the disappearance and later death of her son. The Order had learned that Camden was killed by Elise's brother-in-law, Sterling Chase, when the kid showed up at the Darkhaven in full-on Bloodlust. From the account Tegan heard, Camden had been about to attack Elise when Chase gunned him down with several titanium rounds—right in front of her.

God only knew what witnessing her son's death might have done to the female.

Not his concern, though.

Yeah, not his fucking problem at all. So why was he standing in this rank tenement house with his dick in his hand, waiting for her to come around and let him in?

Tegan eyed the array of locks on the apartment door. At least these were in working order and she'd had the good sense to set them once she got inside. But for a Breed vampire of Tegan's power and lineage, tripping the locks with his mind took all of two seconds.

He slipped inside the apartment and closed the door behind him. The decibel level in the small studio was enough to make his head shatter. He glanced around the place with narrowed eyes, taking in the odd decor. The only furniture was a futon and a bookcase, which housed a quality stereo system and a small flat-panel television—both on and blaring.

Next to the futon, in a space that might have held a table and chairs, was a treadmill and a resistance-training machine. Elise's bloodstained parka lay on the floor there, and on the sorry-looking yellow kitchen counter was a cell phone and an MP3 player. Elise's decorating style left a lot to be desired, but it was her choice of wall covering that Tegan found most peculiar.

Crudely nailed to all four walls of the one-room living space were acoustic foam panels—soundproofing material. Yards of the stuff, covering every square inch of the walls, windows, and the back of the door too.

"What the fu—"

In the adjacent bathroom, there was a metallic squeak as the shower abruptly cut off. Tegan turned to face the door as it opened a moment later. Elise was pulling a thick white terry-cloth robe around herself as she glanced up and met his gaze. She gasped, startled, one slender hand coming up near her throat.

"Tegan." Her voice was barely audible over the din of the music and TV. She made no move to turn them down, just came out of the bathroom and stood as far away from him as was possible in the cramped apartment. "What are you doing here?"

"I could ask you the same thing." Tegan let his eyes drift around the meager living quarters, if only to quit looking at her in her state of near undress. "Shitty place you have here. Who's your decorator?"

She didn't answer him. Her pale amethyst eyes stayed fixed on him as though she didn't quite trust him, nervous to find herself alone with him. And who could blame her?

Tegan knew that by and large Darkhaven residents held little affection for members of the Order. He'd been called a stone-cold killer by more than one of the sheltered class of civilians that Elise was a part of—not that he cared. His personal reputation was simply stated fact. But while he could give a shit what others thought of him, it irked him that Elise looked at him now in fear. The last time he'd seen the female, he'd shown her nothing but kindness, deference paid the young Darkhaven widow out of respect for what she was going through. It hadn't hurt that she was a breathtaking beauty, as fragile as a frost flower.

Some of that fragility was gone now, Tegan noted, seeing the lines of muscle definition in her bare calves and arms. Her face remained lovely, but not as full as he remembered. Her eyes were still alive with intelligence but their sheen was somehow brittle, a characteristic made more pronounced by the trace shadows beneath the generous fringe of her lashes.

And her hair . . . Jesus, she'd shorn off the long blond waves. The cascade of pale spun gold that used to fall to her hips was now a crown of thick, silky spikes that rose around her head in pixie-like disarray and framed the lean oval of her face.

She was still stunning, but in an entirely different way than Tegan ever would have imagined.

"You forgot something back in the alley." He held out the wicked hunting blade. When she moved to take it from him, he drew it back out of her reach. "What were you doing out there tonight, Elise?"

She shook her head, said something too softly to be heard over the din filling the apartment. Impatient, Tegan mentally shut the stereo down. He glanced to the television, about to silence that device as well.

"No!" Elise shook her head, wincing, her fingers clutching her temple. "Wait—leave it on, please. I need . . . the noise soothes me."

Tegan scowled his doubt, but left the TV alone. "What happened to you tonight, Elise?"

She blinked, shuttering her gaze and tipping her head down in silence.

"Did someone hurt you out there? Were you attacked before the Rogues discovered you in the alley?"

Her answer was long in coming. "No. I wasn't attacked."

"You want to explain all that blood on your coat over there? Or why you're living in a part of town where you feel the need to carry around this kind of hardware?"

She held her head in her hands, her voice a rough whisper. "I don't want to explain anything. Please, Tegan. I wish you hadn't come here. Just, please . . . you have to leave now."

He exhaled a sharp laugh. "I just saved your sweet little ass, female. I don't think it's too much to ask that you tell me why I had to."

"It was a mistake. I didn't mean to be out past dark. I know the dangers." She looked up, gave a vague lift of her slim shoulder. "Things just took . . . a little longer than I anticipated."

"Things," he repeated, not liking where this seemed to be heading. "We're not talking about shopping or coffee with friends, are we?"

Tegan's gaze went back to the kitchen counter, to the familiar design of the cell phone that lay there. He scowled, suspicion coiling in his gut as he walked over and picked it up. He'd seen dozens of these things lately. The phone was one of those disposable jobs, the kind favored by humans in league with the Rogues. He flipped it over and disabled the built-in GPS chip.

Tegan knew if he took the cell phone into the compound lab, Gideon would find it contained just one number, super-encrypted and impossible to break. This particular phone was spattered with human blood, the same shit that soaked the front of Elise's coat.

"Where'd you get this, Elise?"

"I think you know," she replied, her voice quiet but defiant.

He turned to face her. "You took it off a Minion? By yourself? Jesus Christ . . . how?"

She shrugged, rubbing the side of her head as if it pained her. "I tracked him from the train station. I followed him, and when the chance was there, I killed him."

It wasn't often that Tegan was taken by surprise, but hearing those words coming out of the petite female hit him like a brick to the back of his head. "You can't be serious."

But she was. The level look she gave him left no doubt whatsoever.

Behind her, the television screen flashed with a live breaking-news bulletin. A reporter came on, delivering word that a stabbing victim had been discovered a few minutes before:

" . . . the deceased was found just two blocks away from the train station, yet another killing in what authorities are beginning to suspect is a string of related murders . . ."

As the report continued, and Elise calmly stared at him from across the room, Tegan's blood ran cold with understanding.

"You?" he asked, already knowing the answer, incredible as it seemed.

When Elise didn't respond, Tegan stalked over to a footlocker on the floor near the futon. He yanked it open and swore as his eyes lit on a large assortment of blades, guns, and ammunition. A lot of it was still brand-new, but others had been used and had the wear to show for it.

"How long, Elise? When did you start this insanity?"

She stared at him, her slender jaw held rigid. "My son is dead because of the Rogues. Everything I loved is gone because of them," she said finally. "I couldn't sit around doing nothing. I *won't* sit back and do nothing."

Tegan heard the resolve in her voice, but that didn't make him any less pissed off about what was going on here. "How many?"

Tonight wasn't the first, obviously.

"How many times have you done this, Elise?"

She said nothing for a very long time. Then she slowly walked over to the bookcase and knelt down to pull out a lidded crate from the bottom shelf. Her gaze on Tegan, she lifted the top and calmly set it aside.

In the bin were more Minion cell phones.

At least a dozen of the damned things.

Tegan dropped his ass onto the futon and raked his fingers through his hair. "Holy hell, woman. Have you lost your goddamn mind?"

Elise rubbed her palm over her forehead, trying to ease some of the throbbing that was battering her from within. The migraine was coming on fast, bearing down hard. She closed her eyes, hoping to stave the worst of it off. Bad enough she'd been discovered tonight; she didn't need the humiliation of a psychic meltdown that would leave her unable to function, let alone deal with the Breed warrior in her living room.

"Do you have any idea what you're doing?" Tegan's

voice, though level and without a hint of anything beyond basic disbelief, boomed into Elise's head like can-
non fire. With the box of cell phones in hand, he started
pacing off somewhere behind her in the small studio, the
sound of his heavy boots on the worn, grubby, low-pile
carpet grating in her ears. "What the hell are you trying
to do, woman, get yourself killed?"

"You don't understand," she murmured through the
drumming of pain behind her eyes. "You couldn't . . .
could not possibly understand."

"Try me." The words were curt, sharp. A command
issued from a powerful male who expected to be obeyed.

Elise slowly got up from her kneel beside the shelving
unit and moved to the other side of the room. Each step
was a chore she worked hard to disguise, relief coming
only when she was able to lean her spine into the wall for
some much-needed support. She practically sagged into
the acoustic-padded plasterboard, wishing Tegan was
gone so she could collapse in private.

"This is my own business," she said, knowing he probably heard her shortness of breath, which she was unable
to fully conceal. "It's personal."

"For crissake, Elise. It's fucking suicide."

She flinched at the warrior's profanity, unaccustomed
to hearing rough language. Quentin had never uttered
anything harsher than an occasional *damn* in her presence, and then only when he was in the worst of states
over frustration with the Agency or restrictive Darkhaven
policies. He'd been a perfect gentleman in all ways, gentle even though she knew that as one of the Breed, his
strength was immeasurable.

Tegan was a crude, deadly contrast to her departed
mate—one she'd been raised to fear growing up as a

ward of the Darkhavens from the time she was a young girl. To Quentin and the Enforcement Agency he'd been a part of, Tegan and the rest of the Order were considered dangerous vigilantes. To many in the Darkhavens, the warriors were simply a cadre of savage, medieval-minded thugs who'd long outserved their purpose as defenders of the vampire nation. They were merciless—some would say lawless—and even though Tegan had saved her life tonight, Elise couldn't help feeling wary of him, as if there was a wild animal loose in her home.

She watched him thrust his big hand into the box of Minion communication devices, heard the clatter and slide of plastic and polished metal as he inspected the collection.

"The GPS chips on these are already disabled." He leveled a narrow, dubious look at her. "You knew to shut them off?"

She gave a faint nod. "I have a teenage son," she replied, then winced as the words left her lips. Lord, it was still so automatic to think of him alive, especially at times like this, when her body was weakened from psychic fatigue. "I *had* a teenage son," she corrected quietly. "Camden didn't like me being able to keep tabs on him, so he used to turn off his cell phone's GPS when he went out. I learned how to reactivate it, but he always found me out and shut it back off."

Tegan made a noise in the back of his throat, something low and indistinct. "If you hadn't crippled these tracking devices, there's a real good chance you'd be dead by now. Better than good—it's a fucking certainty. The one who made the Minions you've been hunting would have found you, and you don't want to know what he is capable of."

"I'm not afraid of dying—"

"Dying," Tegan scoffed, cutting her off with a sharp, exhaled curse. "Dying would be the least of your worries, female, trust me. You may have gotten lucky with a few careless Minions, but this is war, and you're way out of your league. What happened tonight should be evidence enough of that."

"What happened tonight was a mistake I won't make again. I went out too late in the day and took too long. Next time I'll be sure I'm finished and home before nightfall."

"Next time." Tegan pinned her with a sharp scowl. "Jesus Christ, you really mean that."

For a long while, the warrior only stared at her. His steady gem-green eyes were unreadable, unemotional. The schooled lines of his face gave no indication of his thoughts. Finally, he gave a shake of his tawny head and pivoted away from her to gather up the collection of Minion cell phones. He stuffed them into the pockets of his coat, his rough movements flashing a staggering array of weaponry that he wore beneath the folds of the black leather.

"What are you going to do?" Elise asked as the last of the devices disappeared into a deep inside pocket. "You're not going to turn me in, are you?"

"I damn well should." His flinty gaze raked her dismissively. "But what you do isn't any of my concern so long as you keep your ass out of my way. And don't expect the Order to ride to your rescue the next time you get in over your head."

"I won't. I don't . . . expect anything, I mean." She watched him head for the door, feeling awash in relief that she would soon be alone to contend with the tidal wave of pain that was roaring up on her swiftly. As the warrior opened the door and stepped out into the ratty hallway, Elise summoned what remained of her voice. "Tegan, thank you. This is just . . . something I have to do."

She fell silent, thinking of Camden, and all the other Darkhaven youths who'd been lost to the poison of the Rogues. Even Quentin's life had been cut short by a diseased member of the Breed who'd gone Rogue and attacked while in custody of the Agency.

Elise couldn't bring any of the lost lives back; she knew that. But each day that she hunted, each Minion she eliminated meant one less weapon in the Rogues' arsenal. The pain she suffered for the task was nothing compared to what her son and the others must have endured. True death for her would be in being forced to sit within the shelter of the Darkhaven and do nothing while the streets ran red with the blood of the innocent.

That, she couldn't bear.

"This is important to me, Tegan. I made a promise. I mean to uphold it."

He paused, slid a flat glance over his shoulder. "It's your funeral," he said, and pulled the door closed behind him.

CHAPTER
Four

Tegan threw the last of Elise's hunting souvenirs into an isolated stretch of the Charles River and watched as the dark water rippled out and the cell phone vanished into the drink. Like all the rest that he and the other warriors had confiscated on their patrols, the encrypted cell phones would be of no use to the Order. And he sure as hell wasn't about to leave them with Elise, GPS chips disabled or not.

Christ, he could not believe what the woman had been up to. Even more incredible was the fact that she'd been carrying out her lunatic vendetta for what had to be weeks, maybe even months. Obviously her brother-by-marriage had no idea, or the by-the-book ex–Darkhaven

Enforcement Agent would have put a swift stop to it. Everyone in the Order knew that Sterling Chase had once had feelings for his brother's widow—probably still did. Not that it was any of Tegan's business. Nor was Elise's apparent death wish.

Shoving his hands into the pockets of his unbuttoned coat, Tegan stalked back to the street, his breath rolling between his lips in a cloud of misting steam. It was snowing again in Boston. A blustery curtain of fine white flakes fell onto a city already frozen from weeks of an unusually frigid winter. Tegan knew it had to be pushing single digits with the windchill, but he didn't feel the cold. He could hardly remember the last time he'd felt discomfort of any kind. Longer still, the last time he'd felt pleasure.

Hell, when was the last time he'd felt anything at all?

He remembered pain.

He remembered loss, the anger that had once consumed him . . . long, long ago.

He remembered Sorcha and how much he'd loved her. How sweetly innocent she was and how completely she had trusted him to keep her safe and protected.

God, how he'd failed her. He would never forget what had been done to her, how savagely she'd been abused. To survive the blow of her death, he had learned to detach from his grief, from his raw fury. But he could never forget. Would never forgive.

More than five hundred years of slaying Rogues, and he wasn't even close to calling things square.

He'd seen some of that same grief and fury in Elise's eyes tonight. Something she cherished had been taken from her, and she wanted justice. What she would get was death. If her dealings with the Rogues and their human mind slaves didn't kill her, the weakness of her body surely would. She had tried to hide her fatigue from him, but Tegan hadn't missed it. The weariness he saw in her went deeper than mere physical need, although he could tell from a glance at her gaunt frame that she'd been neglecting herself since she'd left the Darkhaven—maybe longer than that. And what was the deal with all that acoustical foam nailed to the walls of her place?

Shit. Whatever.

It really was none of his concern, he reminded himself as he hoofed it toward the secret compound that housed the Order, just outside the city. The brick-and-limestone mansion and its multi-acred estate were surrounded by tall, high-voltage fencing and a massive iron gate rigged with cameras and laser-tripped, motion-sensor alarms. Not that anyone had ever come close to breaking in.

Very few of the entire Breed population knew the precise location, and those who did were well aware the property was held by the Order and were wise enough to stay away unless expressly invited. As for humankind, fourteen thousand volts of electricity was enough to discourage the curious from getting too close; those of the stupider variety woke up parboiled from a taste of the juice or nursing a killer hangover from a thorough mind scrub delivered by the warriors—neither one of those options being particularly pleasant. But they were effective.

Tegan keyed his access code into the concealed security panel near the gate, then slipped inside as the heavy iron parted to let him in.

Once admitted, he veered off the long, paved drive and let the wooded grounds envelop him. Up ahead some few hundred feet, he could see the faint glow of the mansion's lights through the thick cover of snow-dusted pines. Even though the Order's true headquarters were housed in a subterranean compound beneath the Gothic manse, it wasn't unusual to find one or more of the warriors and their mates using the house in the evenings for dinners or entertaining.

But whoever was there tonight wasn't enjoying any kind of pleasant recreation.

As Tegan neared the building, he heard a fierce animal roar, followed by the crash of shattering glass.

"What the—"

Another loud crash sounded, more violent than the first, coming from the mansion's opulent foyer. Like something—or some*body*—big was tearing the place apart. Tegan leaped up the marble steps to the front door and threw open the aged slab of black-lacquered wood, a blade gripped hard in his hand. As he stepped inside, his boots crunched in a chaos of broken porcelain and glass.

"Jesus," he muttered, taking in the source of the destruction.

One of the warriors stood at an antique sideboard in the center of the tiled entryway, his scarred olive-dark hands braced on the carved edges of the piece as if that was all that kept him upright. He was soaking wet and naked from the waist up, wearing only loose-fitting gray cotton sweats that looked like they'd been yanked on just seconds before. His dark head hung low, long espresso-brown waves sleek with water and drooping over his face. The *dermaglyphs* that tracked up his bare chest and over his shoulders were livid with color, the intricate pattern of Breed skin markings pulsing with furious life.

Tegan brought his weapon down, the blade concealed

by his hand until he'd sheathed it again. "How we doing, Rio?"

The warrior grunted low in the back of his throat, less acknowledgment than aftershock of his rage. Water sluiced off him to pool around his bare feet and the scattered shards of a priceless Limoges bowl he'd swept off the sideboard. Polished glass littered the surface of the mahogany cabinet; above, the wall mirror and its ornate gilt frame were smashed to bits by the bloodied knuckles of Rio's right hand.

"Doing some late-night home improvements, my man?" Tegan walked closer to him, keeping his eyes trained on the tight coil of the warrior's bulk. "For what it's worth, I never had any use for that froufrou French shit either."

Rio exhaled a rough, shuddering breath, then swiveled his head to look at Tegan. Topaz eyes still held a trace of glowing amber; the light from them sliced through the dark fall of his hair, throwing off the heat of a lingering madness. The bone-white glint of fangs shone behind the vampire's parted lips as he dragged in air through his teeth.

Tegan knew it wasn't Bloodlust that called up the warrior's savage side. It was fury. And remorse. The gunmetal tang of it filled the air, pouring off Rio in heated waves.

"I might have killed her," he rasped in a voice that was sharp gravel and anguish, not the Spaniard's usual rolling baritone. "Had to get out of there, *pronto*. Something inside me just fucking . . . snapped." He sucked in air around a feral-sounding snarl. "Shit, Tegan . . . I wanted to—*needed to*—hurt somebody."

Someone else might have known a current of alarm at

those words, but Tegan absorbed them with calm observation, narrowing his eyes on the burn-scarred, shrapnel-
ruined left side of Rio's face that wasn't quite concealed
by the wet spikes of his hair. There wasn't much left of
the handsome, sophisticated male who'd once been the
most laid-back member of the Order, always quick with
a joke or an easy smile. The explosion he'd survived last
summer had taken most of his looks; the revelation that
his own Breedmate, Eva, had betrayed him into the
deadly ambush had taken away everything else.

"*Madre de Dios*," Rio whispered roughly. "No one
should be near me. I'm losing my goddamn mind! What
if I . . . *Cristo*, what if I did something to her? Tegan,
what if I hurt her?"

Alarm tripped Tegan's senses. The warrior wasn't
talking about Eva. She'd died by her own hand the day
her treachery had been discovered. The only other female who had any regular contact with Rio now was
Tess, Dante's Breedmate. Since her arrival at the compound a few months ago, Tess had been working with
Rio, using her healing touch to mend what she could of
his broken body and trying to help him rehabilitate from
both the physical and the mental wreckage left in the
wake of his ordeal.

Ah, fuck.

If the warrior had harmed her, accidentally or not,
there would be some serious hell to pay. Dante loved his
woman with an intensity that had surprised everyone at
the compound. Once the reckless bad boy, Dante was
wrapped around Tess's slender finger and didn't care
who knew it. He'd kill Rio with his bare hands if anything happened to his mate.

Tegan hissed a curse. "What did you do, Rio? Where is Tess now?"

Rio gave a miserable shake of his head and gestured vaguely toward the back wing of the sprawling mansion. Tegan was about to take off in that direction when urgent footsteps sounded on the long corridor that led from the general area of the estate's indoor pool. The soft smack of a light, barefoot gait drew nearer, followed by a female's voice raised in concern.

"Rio? Rio, where are y—"

Tess rounded the corner in a squeaking skid, wearing black workout pants over a wet baby-blue tank swimsuit. The look was pure sports therapy business, but any male with eyes in his head and red blood in his veins would be crazy not to notice how beautifully she filled out all that nylon and Lycra. Her honey-brown hair was swept back in a long ponytail, the ends damp and curling from the pool. Peach-polished toenails stopped dead at the edge of the field of broken porcelain in the foyer.

"Oh, my God. Rio . . . are you all right?"

"He's okay," Tegan told her flatly. "What about you?"

Tess's hand went up reflexively to her neck, but she nodded her head. "I'm fine. Rio, look at me, please. It's okay. You can see that I'm perfectly fine."

But something had gone down a few minutes ago; that much was obvious. "What happened?"

"We had some setbacks in today's session, nothing major."

"Tell him what I did to you," Rio muttered. "Tell him how I blacked out in the pool and came to only to find my hands wrapped around your throat."

"Jesus." Tegan scowled, and now that Tess moved her

fingers away from her neck he could see the fading out-line of a bruising grip. "You sure you're all right?"

She nodded. "He didn't mean it, and he let go the in-stant he realized what he was doing. I'm fine, really. He will be too. You know that, right, Rio?"

Tess cautiously stepped forward, avoiding the shards at her feet yet keeping a healthy distance from Tegan like he was more of a threat to her general safety than the feral wreck that was Rio.

Tegan wasn't offended. He preferred his solitary exis-tence and worked hard to maintain it. He watched Tess move slowly toward Rio's stiff stance at the sideboard.

She gently placed her hand on the warrior's scarred shoulder. "Tomorrow will be better, I'm sure. Every day there are small improvements."

"I'm not getting better," Rio muttered, in what could have sounded like self-pity but seemed more a bleak un-derstanding. He shook off Tess's touch with a snarl. "I should be put down. It would be a blessing . . . to every-one, especially me. I am useless. This body—my mind—it's all fucking useless!"

Rio slammed his fist down on the sideboard, rattling the broken mirror glass and putting a tremor in the two-hundred-year-old mahogany beneath it.

Tess flinched, but there was an unwavering resolve in her blue-green eyes. "You are *not* useless. Healing takes time, that's all. You can't give up."

Rio growled something nasty under his breath, his hooded eyes throwing off amber light in warning. But not even a half-mad vampire's ferocious bluster was go-ing to dissuade Tess from helping him if she could. No doubt she'd seen this sort of snarling behavior before from Rio—and possibly even her own mate—and hadn't run away in terror.

Tegan watched Tess stand firm, calm, steady, tenacious. It wasn't hard to imagine why Dante adored her so much. But Tegan could see that Rio was in a particularly unstable, volatile state. He may not mean anyone harm—least of all, Tess, whose extraordinary healing skills had nursed him out of near psychosis—but rage and anguish made for one powerful emotional cocktail. Tegan knew that fact firsthand; he'd lived it once, long ago. Add to that the lingering aftereffects of a traumatic brain injury like Rio had suffered, and the warrior was a lit powder keg just waiting to go off.

"Let me," Tegan said when Tess started to move toward Rio again. "I'll take him down to the compound. I'm heading below anyway."

She gave him a wary smile. "Okay, thanks."

Tegan approached Rio with deliberate movements and carefully guided him away from the female and out of the field of debris around their feet. The big male's steps were heavy, lacking the grace that used to come so naturally to him. Rio leaned heavily on Tegan's shoulder and arm, his bare chest heaving with every deep breath he hauled into his lungs.

"That's it, nice and easy," Tegan coached him. "We good now, *amigo*?"

The dark head bobbed awkwardly.

Tegan glanced to Tess as she knelt down and began collecting the shattered glass and porcelain from the foyer tiles. "Have you seen Chase around tonight?"

"Not for a while," she said. "He and Dante are still out on patrol."

Tegan smirked. Four months ago, the two males had

been ready to tear out each other's throats. They'd been tossed together by Lucan as unwilling partners when Darkhaven agent Sterling Chase showed up at the compound with info about a dangerous club drug called Crimson and to solicit help from the Order in getting the shit off the streets. Now he and Dante were almost inseparable in the field, had been ever since Chase left the Darkhavens and came on board officially as a member of the Order. "The pair of them are a regular Mutt and Jeff, eh?"

Tess's eyes held a trace of humor as she looked up from the mess in front of her. "More like Larry and Curly, if you ask me."

Tegan exhaled a wry laugh as he steered Rio into the hallway. He brought him to the mansion's elevator, walked him inside, then pushed the code to begin the journey down to the underground headquarters of the Order.

After dropping Rio off in the warrior's compound apartments, Tegan headed back to the tech lab to check in. Gideon was at his post, as usual, the blond vampire rolling back and forth on a wheeled office chair, working his magic on no less than four computers at the same time. A wireless cell phone headset curled around his ear and he was giving a string of coordinates over the small mic that arced toward his cheek.

The consummate multitasker, Gideon looked up as Tegan entered the lab, gestured him over, and brought up a set of satellite stills on one of the monitors. "Niko's got a possible lead on that Crimson lab," he informed Tegan, then went back to his conversation as his fingers flew over the keyboard of another machine. "Right. I'm running a check right now."

Tegan stared at the images Gideon had called up on the screen. Some were known Rogue lairs—most of them former lairs, due to the efforts of the Order—and others showed Rogues and Minions coming and going from various locations in and around the city. One face caught Tegan's eye more than the rest. It was the human Crimson dealer, Ben Sullivan.

Although Dante had taken the bastard out last November, the whereabouts of his manufacturing lab were yet unknown. Problems with the drug had simmered down in the months since the Order got involved, but so long as the Rogues possessed the means to manufacture more of the shit, the threat of a resurgence in Crimson use among the Breed still existed.

"Hold up. I'm getting a match on a location out in Revere," Gideon was saying now. "Yeah, whaddaya know, I think it's a legit lead. You guys wanna do a drive-by down by the Chelsea River, see what you find?"

Tegan zeroed in on the photo of Ben Sullivan's grinning, busted-up face. The human had killed a lot of young vampires with his drug, including Camden Chase, Elise's teenage son. If not for Crimson, that kid would never have turned Rogue and had to be put down. And a gently bred female like Elise wouldn't be holed up in that slum apartment downtown, out of her head with grief and anger, and hell-bent on some maternal brand of vengeance that was probably going to get her killed too.

A weight settled on Tegan as he considered all the bloodshed, the centuries he and the others like him had been fighting this battle against the savage side of the Breed. There were peaks and lulls, of course, times of relative peace, but the unrest was always there, burrowed deep within the race. Festering and corrupting.

"It's fucking never going to end, is it?"

"Sorry?"

Tegan didn't realize he'd spoken until he glanced over and saw Gideon looking at him over the rims of his pale blue shades. Tegan shook his head. "Nothing."

He stalked away from the computers, his thoughts gone dark and churning as Gideon swung back to his monitors and sent his fingers clacking over a keyboard. Another satellite image filled the screen, this one showing an old industrial lot not far from the riverfront.

Tegan knew the location. He didn't need anything more.

"Yeah, Niko," Gideon said into the mouthpiece. "Right. Sounds good. If things look hot over there, yell for backup. Dante and Chase are less than an hour away and Tegan's right . . . here . . ."

But Tegan wasn't there anymore.

He was stalking purposefully up the corridor outside the tech lab now, where he heard Gideon's voice trail off as the lab's glass door hissed shut.

CHAPTER
Five

This is it. Hang a left up here at the stop sign," Nikolai said from the backseat of the Order's black SUV. He was busy reloading the weapons that he and the two new warrior recruits accompanying him tonight had put to good use on the city's east side. The custom rounds he'd made were his favorite Rogue-blasting numbers—kick-ass hollowpoints filled with powdered titanium. One taste of that metal meant certain death to the blood-addicted members of the vampire race. Niko slapped the clip into the tricked-out Beretta 92FS he'd converted to full auto, then shoved the weapon into its holster under his coat.

"Park behind that piece of shit pickup truck," he told the warrior doing the driving. This part of Revere was tight with houses and run-down businesses, thick clusters of humanity clinging to the outskirts of Boston and a briny stretch of the Chelsea River. "We'll hoof it the rest of the way. Go in nice and quiet so we can get a good look around."

"You got it." Brock, a towering nightmare of a fighter recruited out of Detroit, was as smooth behind the wheel as he was with the ladies. He swept the vehicle over to the side of the snowy curb and killed the engine.

Next to Brock in the front seat, Niko's other trainee pivoted around and held out his hand for the refreshed weapon. Kade's wolflike silver eyes were still glowing from the night's earlier action, his black hair spiky and wet with melted snow. "Think we're gonna find something out here?"

Niko grinned. "I sure as hell hope so." He handed pistols and fresh clips to both of them, then pulled a couple of silencers out of the leather duffel bag at his feet and slapped them into the warriors' palms. When Brock arched a brow on his dark forehead, Niko said, "I'm all for cooking a bunch of Rogues with some 9mm high-test, but there's no need to wake the neighbors."

"Nah," Kade added, flashing the tips of his pearly white fangs, "that would be just plain rude."

Nikolai grabbed the rest of his gear and zipped the duffel shut. "Let's go sniff around for some Crimson."

They climbed out of the Range Rover and skirted the residential area on foot, all three of them keeping to the shadows as they navigated back to the old warehouse lot where Niko's tip had led them.

The building looked like shit from the outside—a 1970s industrial eyesore of concrete, wood, and glass. Steel posts from what had once been part of a chain-link fence poked out of the perimeter lot at various angles, not a single one of them straight, not that it mattered. The place had a derelict, keep-out quality about it, even amid the snowglobe flurries that were filling the night sky.

Niko and the guys stepped onto the loose gravel of the empty lot, their boot heels cushioned by the fresh fall of snow. As they neared the building, Niko spotted a dark ash trail on the ground. The large, irregular shape was still visible, still smoldering and hissing as the delicate white flakes fell on it and melted on contact. He gestured to the pile of disintegrating remains as Brock and Kade came closer.

"Someone smoked a Rogue," he told them, his voice low as a whisper. "Still fresh too."

Gideon hadn't mentioned sending in backup, so they'd be wise to be cautious of what else they might find. Rogues were basically savages, and it wasn't unheard of that they took one another out over turf or petty disagreements. It was all good as far as the Order was concerned; saved the warriors time and effort when the Bloodlusting bastards lost their cool and offed their own.

Another suckhead had taken a lethal hit of titanium near the entrance of the building. A large padlock lay in the cellular goo, and Brock motioned toward the battered steel door. It was slightly ajar, just a thin wedge of darkness behind it.

Kade shot Niko a look of question, waiting for the signal to act.

Nikolai shook his head, uncertain.

Something wasn't right here.

He heard a faint rumble from somewhere deep inside the place, a rumble he felt as a slight vibration in the soles of his feet. On the night's soft chill, he caught a whiff of something sweetly cloying, chemical. It was . . . kerosene?

The rumble got deeper, stronger. Like gathering thunder.

"What the fuck is that?" Kade hissed.

Niko smelled the tang of hot metal—

"Oh, shit." He glanced at the other two warriors. "Go! Move it! Go, go, go!"

They all sprang into a dead run, hauling ass across the lot as the rumble became a roar. There was a deep percussion—sharp, violent—as the explosion erupted from within the bowels of the old building. Glass blew out from the top floor windows, shooting flames and thick black smoke in its wake.

And as the three of them watched in awe, the front door of the place banged open, tearing clean off its hinges. Not by the force of the blast, but by the will of a single individual.

Rolling orange fire silhouetted him from behind, backlighting the warrior's broad shoulders and casual, longlegged stride. As he strolled away from the inferno, the ends of his loose black coat winged out behind him like a cape befitting the prince of darkness himself.

"Holy hell," Brock murmured. "Tegan."

Niko shook his head, chuckling at the blatant awe in the newbies' faces. Not that it wasn't deserved. They didn't come much more impressive than Tegan, and this display was going to go down as legend, he was sure. Behind him now, the warehouse was engulfed in flames, throwing off heat like hell's own furnace. It was incredible, really, a thing of roaring, violent beauty. By the blasé flatness of Tegan's expression as he approached, he might as well have just come back from taking a piss.

"Everything good in there, T?" Niko quipped. "You need backup or anything? Bag of marshmallows to roast over that little campfire you just started?"

"It's handled."

"No shit," Niko replied, he and the other two warriors watching sparks erupt from the burning warehouse, a plume of fire reaching high into the night sky.

Tegan strode past them as cool as could be, giving neither excuse nor explanation. But then it was always that way with him. He was the ghost you never saw coming, death breathing down your neck before you even realized you were in the crosshairs.

He was never less than thorough in combat, but the annihilation he'd delivered to the Crimson lab was beyond anything Niko had ever seen the warrior do before. Based on the intel he had on this place, it was probably manned by half a dozen Rogues—all of them dead at Tegan's hand and a building that would be nothing but smoldering rubble in a couple of hours. If Niko didn't know better, he'd be tempted to call it personal.

"Glad we could be of assistance to you, man," Niko called after him, exhaling a wry curse.

"Damn, that dude is cold," Brock remarked as Tegan disappeared into the darkness and the scattering flurry of snow.

"He's ice," Niko said, glad as hell that the Gen One warrior was on their side. "Come on, let's roll before the place starts swarming with humans."

Tegan walked back into the city alone, the scream of sirens wailing in the distance behind him. He didn't have to turn around to know that a fiery glow lit the night down near the Chelsea. He smirked into the darkness. No matter how much water the Revere FD threw on the old warehouse, there would be no saving it. Tegan had made sure there would be nothing left once the smoke finally cleared. He'd wanted the place torched, with a ferocity he hadn't felt in years.

Shit, it had been more than years since he'd known the kind of savagery that ran through his veins tonight. Centuries was more like it.

And the kicker was, it had felt damned good.

Tegan flexed his hands in the wintry bite of the evening air. He was still able to feel the pain he'd delivered on the Rogues tonight—the delicious horror that swamped the hearts of each one he had killed in the Crimson lab. He'd indulged in their anguish as the titanium sped through their blood, cooking them from the inside out.

Where he'd long ago learned to disengage his own emotions, the psychic power he possessed was beyond his control. Like all of the Breed, he had, in addition to the vampiric traits of his father, certain unique extrasensory abilities passed down from the human female who bore him. For Tegan, he had only to brush against another individual—be it human or vampire—and he knew what they were feeling. Touch someone, and he absorbed the emotions into himself, feeding from the connection like a leech to an open wound.

The gift had been both weapon and curse to him throughout his life; now it was his private vice. He used it as infrequently as possible, but when he did, it was with deliberate, sadistic relish. Better that he siphon enjoyment out of others' pain and fear than let his own feelings rise up to rule him as they had before.

But tonight he'd felt the kindling of some inner satisfaction as he dealt death to the Rogues and the couple of Minions who'd evidently been recruited to continue the manufacture of Crimson. And after none of them were left breathing, the concrete floor of the old warehouse running red with blood and stinking with the cellular meltdown of the Rogues he'd offed with blades and bullets, Tegan had needed something more.

For reasons he had no interest in examining even now, he had stood in the center of the carnage he'd wrought, wanting nothing less than complete obliteration.

Fire and cinder, smoldering rubble. He had wanted the Crimson lab erased from existence, nothing but a scar of black ash on the empty lot where it stood.

And whether he wanted to acknowledge it or not, he knew that his want for destruction had more than a passing connection to Elise. It had been her face he'd seen in his mind as he lit the place up. It had been the thought of her grief that made him savor each of the Rogue deaths he delivered tonight.

Shoving his hands into the pockets of his coat, Tegan headed against the wind and cut down a South End side alley. He wasn't sure where he was going, although he supposed he should have known. He recognized Elise's shitty neighborhood even before he turned onto the street that would eventually dump him onto her block.

Tegan still couldn't fathom her living in such squalid conditions. As the widow of a high-ranking Breed government official, Elise had to be more than financially set. She could have lived in any of the Darkhavens, wanting for nothing, whether or not she chose to take a new mate. That she had chosen to leave her old life to exist topside among basic humankind was surprising. She'd seemed so sheltered and fragile when he met her some four months ago. He couldn't have been more shocked to find her earlier tonight, awash in Minion blood and armed like one of the Order.

But for all her defiance and resolve, Tegan had not missed Elise's weariness. She'd appeared bone-tired and exhausted, in a way that seemed to go deeper than just plain fatigue. He supposed that was why he found himself outside her apartment again now.

He wasn't about to go to the front door. It was late, she was probably asleep, and so long as it was dark outside, his priority one was the Order.

When he rightly should have kept on walking, Tegan instead slipped between Elise's building and the one next to it, heading around to the back. The interior of her first-floor unit appeared dark as pitch from outside, but the acoustic foam covering the windows would have blocked out nearly any light. Even with the soundproofing in place, Tegan could hear the heavy bass of her stereo and the competing chatter of the TV. He ran a hand through his snow-dampened hair, then pivoted around and paced three long strides into the strip of backyard behind the place.

Forget about her and just walk away.

Yeah, that was damn well what he should do, all right. Put the heartbroken, beautiful female with the apparent death wish out of his head and walk the fuck away.

Except . . .

He crept closer to the building, scowling at the blocked glass of the windows. He didn't hear anything other than music and television noise, but that was the thing that pricked his warrior's senses onto alert.

That, and the faint tickle of a blood scent coming from

within the apartment. Elise's blood. His nose registered a subtle heather-and-roses sweetness that could only be the Breedmate inside. She was bleeding—perhaps not a lot by the trace scent of it, but it was impossible to tell much with brick and glass and three-inch-thick foam in the way.

Tegan opened the sash lock on the window with his mind—the second time he'd perpetrated a B&E on her place in one night—and lifted the heavy pane from outside. There was no screen, and it took all of a second to push away the acoustic panel and peer inside.

There were no lights on, but his vision was even sharper in the dark. Elise was there, on the futon, curled up in a tight, fetal ball, and still wearing the white terry robe from her shower several hours ago. Her arms were wrapped around her head in a protective cage, the short crown of silky blond hair mashed and spiked in complete disarray from her sleep.

She didn't even stir as Tegan hoisted himself over the windowsill and swung himself inside, although he moved in silence and the audio racket in her place was deafening. Tegan willed the stereo and television to mute—and that's when she suddenly shot straight up, not quite awake but jolted into a semiconscious panic.

"It's okay, Elise. You're all right."

She didn't seem to hear him. Her lavender eyes were wide, but out of focus, and not just from the lack of light in the apartment. She moaned as if in pain and flopped off the futon in a clumsy sprawl, her hands casting about frantically for the remote near her feet. She grappled for the device and began pushing the buttons in a frenzy. "Come on, turn on, damn it, turn on!"

"Elise." Tegan walked over to her and knelt down beside her. He scented more blood on her and when he lifted her chin with the edge of his hand, he saw that her nose was bleeding. Scarlet droplets stained the bright white lapel of her bathrobe, some fresh, and some from an earlier bleed. "Jesus . . ."

"Turn it on!" she howled, then she glanced over and saw the open window, the loose acoustic foam hanging askew. "Oh, God. Who moved that panel? Who would do something like that!"

She pushed herself to her feet and hurried over to re-pair the breach, slamming the window closed and throw-ing the lock. Her hands moved restlessly over the soundproofing as she tried to wedge the material back into place over the glass.

"Elise."

No response, just a deepening sense of anxiety radiat-ing out from her petite form under the white terry robe. With a keening moan, Elise gripped her temples in both hands and slowly sank to the floor below the window, as if her legs just gave out beneath her. Huddled tight on her folded knees, she leaned forward, rocking herself back and forth.

"Make it stop," she whispered brokenly. "Please . . . just . . . *make it stop.*"

Tegan approached her slowly, not wanting to upset her any further. With a curse, he crouched down, and carefully put his hand on the delicate arch of her spine. Fingers spanned wide, his senses open to the connection, Elise's pain shot into him like an electrical current.

He felt the splintering agony of the migraine that gripped her, felt the hard thud of her heartbeat ringing in his ears as if it were his own. He tasted acid on his tongue, his teeth aching from the force with which she clenched her jaw to combat the torment that was riding her.

And he heard the voices.

Nasty, corrosive, terrible voices that were traveling on the air around them, silent to all but the psychically sensitive Breedmate crumpled before him on the floor.

In his mind—through the connection he held with Elise—Tegan registered the belittling argument of a couple down the hall. Across the way, a man was lusting for his own daughter. In the apartment above Elise's, a junkie was shooting a month's worth of child support into her vein while her hungry baby wailed, utterly ignored, in the other room.

Every negative, destructive human thought and experience within a radius Tegan could only guess at seemed to home in on Elise's mind, pecking away at her like vultures on carrion.

It was hell on Earth, and Elise was living it every waking moment. Maybe even while she was asleep. Now he understood the foam panels and the audio racket. She'd been trying to drown out the input with other noise—the stereo, television, and even the MP3 player that lay in a tangle of wires on the kitchen counter.

She was deluding herself if she thought she could cope like this in the human world. To say nothing of the insanity of her intent to pursue vengeance on the Rogues and their Minions.

"Please," she murmured, her soft voice vibrating against his open palm, "I need it to stop now."

Tegan broke the contact and expelled a curse through gritted teeth.

This was no good. He couldn't leave her like this. He should turn her over to the Darkhavens. Maybe he would. But right now she needed relief from the pain she was feeling. Even he wasn't cold enough to sit back and watch her suffer.

"It's okay," he said. "Relax now, Elise. You're okay."

He gathered her up into his arms and carried her back to the futon. She was so light, too light, he thought. Elise was a petite woman, but she felt as weightless as a child against his chest. When was the last time she'd fed? Holding her this close, Tegan couldn't help noticing the sharp angle of her cheekbones, the frailty of her jawline.

She needed blood. A good dose of Breed red cells would give her strength and quiet some of her psychic pain, though far be it from Tegan to volunteer. Elise was a Breedmate, one of those rare human females born genetically compatible with members of the vampire race. Feeding her from his vein would revitalize her in many ways, but putting his blood into her body would also create an unbreakable bond between them. That kind of link was reserved for mated pairs, the most sacred of Breed vows. Only death could break a blood bond, so there were few among the race who approached it lightly, or out of charity.

Elise was widowed, and the several years she'd obviously gone without a male's blood—not to mention the damage she was inflicting on herself every day she lived among humankind—were starting to take a heavy toll on her. Tegan carefully laid her down on the bulky futon mattress.

He was slow and easy as he stretched out her lean legs and arranged her in what he hoped was a comfortable sleeping position. The terry-cloth robe she had on gaped from thigh to sternum, the belt at her waist having come undone and hanging loosely. He had to work to pull the ends of the sash out from under her, all the while trying his damnedest not to notice the wedge of creamy white skin that was exposed to him in the process. It was impossible to pretend he was blind to the feminine curves, or to the buoyant swell of her small, perfect breasts. But it was the sudden flash of a gorgeous thigh that sucked most of the air out of Tegan's lungs.

There, on the inner side of her right leg, was the tiny teardrop-and-crescent-moon birthmark that all Breedmates bore somewhere on their bodies. Elise's rested at the most tempting part of her thigh, just beneath the downy triangle of her sex.

"Ah, fuck." Tegan reeled back, saliva surging into his mouth at the instant, swelling urge to taste that sweet spot.

Off limits, man, he told himself harshly. *And way the hell out of your league.*

His movements were quick now, his breath sawing past the tips of his emerging fangs as he tugged the ends of her robe around the nakedness of her body. Her nose had begun to bleed again from her migraine. The trickle of bright scarlet smudged the soft white skin of her cheek. He dabbed away the blood with the hem of his black tee-shirt, trying to ignore the sweet fragrance that called to everything in him that was Breed. Her fluttering pulse was like a drumbeat in his ears, the rapid little ticking of her carotid drawing his eyes to the graceful line of her neck.

Damn, he thought, mentally wrenching his gaze away. His own appetite sharpened just to be near her. He hungered now, fiercely, even though it hadn't been that long since his last hunt. Not that the street-weary, foul humans he took his nourishment from could compare to the tender beauty spread out before him now.

Elise winced behind her closed eyelids, moaning softly, still in pain. She was so vulnerable right now, so defenseless against the psychic anguish.

And at the moment, he was all she had.

Tegan reached out to her and smoothed his fingers over her cool, damp forehead. He gently pressed his palm over her closed eyes.

"Sleep," he told her, putting her in a light trance.

When her breathing slowed to something close to normal, and the tension eased out of her body, Tegan sat back and watched her slide into a calm, restful slumber.

CHAPTER
Six

$\underset{\text{\Large}}{\sim}$

Elise woke up slowly, feeling as though her consciousness had been transported somewhere far away and tranquil, only to be returned to her body like a feather carried gently on the breeze. Maybe it was a dream. A long, sweet dream . . . a peace she hadn't known for months. She stretched a little on the futon, her bare legs rasping against the terry-cloth of her bathrobe and the soft crush of a blanket that covered her from chin to toe. She snuggled deeper into the pleasant warmth, sighing, and the sound of her own breath startled her.

No noise.

No blaring music or chattering television, even though she couldn't sleep—could hardly function—without them.

Her eyes snapped open and she waited for the psychic assault to hit her. But there was only silence. Dear Lord. Seconds passed, then a full minute or more . . . and there was only blessed, wondrous silence.

"Sleep well?"

The deep male voice carried from across the studio apartment somewhere. She smelled toast browning, and the buttery scent of eggs sizzling in a fry pan. Tegan was standing in her meager kitchen, apparently cooking breakfast. Which only made the surrealism of the morning that much more complete.

"What happened?" Her voice was a soft croak in her throat. She cleared it and tried again. "What are you doing here?"

Oh, God. He didn't have to answer because she remembered as soon as the words left her lips. She recalled the migraine that had laid her low, and the unexpected return of Tegan some hours after he'd found her following her run-in with the Rogues. He'd come back and broken into her apartment for some reason. Had muted the cushioning noise that she needed so badly.

Elise remembered waking in agony. In a flood of humiliation, she remembered collapsing in a blind hysteria near the window, trying to fix the soundproofing—which was all neatly back in place now, she noticed.

And she also remembered the sensation of being soothed into a calming state of numbness . . .

By Tegan?

Holding her robe in place, Elise moved aside the blanket and carefully eased herself into a sitting position on the futon. She still didn't trust her surroundings, certain the blast of mental anguish was going to hit her at any moment.

"What did you do to me last night?"

"You needed help, so I helped you."

He made it sound like an accusation as he leaned back against the counter near the stove, watching her with a look of cool detachment. He was dressed in night battle clothes: a black knit tee-shirt and black fatigues; his leather gun holster and belt of terrible-looking blades lay on the counter across from him.

Elise met the sharp, measuring gaze that was fixed on her from across the room. "You knocked me out somehow?"

"Just a mild trance so you could sleep."

She clutched the lapels of her bathrobe in her fist, suddenly very aware of the fact that she didn't have anything on beneath the loose drape of the terry-cloth. And last night, this warrior had put her in a forced doze, leaving her totally at his mercy? A tremor of alarm ran through her at the thought.

Tegan must have read the look in her eyes because he scoffed a bit, low under his breath. "So, you Darkhaven folks see the Order not only as cold-blooded killers but rapists as well? Or is that distinction reserved primarily for me alone?"

"You've never hurt me," Elise said, feeling bad that she'd let her ingrained biases doubt him. "If you wanted to do anything harmful to me, I think you would have by now."

He smirked. "Such a ringing declaration of faith. I suppose I should be flattered."

"And I really should be thanking you, Tegan. You helped me twice last night. And I never thanked you for your kindness a few months ago either, when you gave me a ride home from the Order's compound."

"Forget it," he said, shrugging one broad shoulder as if the topic were closed before she'd even had a chance to crack it open.

That November evening was never far from Elise's mind. After viewing Camden on video surveillance captured by the Order, Elise had dissolved in one of the compound's many corridors. Bereft, in shock and denial, it had been Tegan who'd found her. Incredibly, it had been Tegan who took her out of the compound and drove her to her Darkhaven home in the waning hours before dawn.

She had embarrassed herself with tears that wouldn't end, but he'd let her spill them all. He'd let her weep, and even more astonishingly, he'd let her crumble against him, holding her through her grief in silence. With his strong arms wrapped around her, he held her together when she felt like she was being torn into pieces by her anguish.

He couldn't have known he'd been her rock that night. Maybe it had meant nothing to him, but she would never forget his unexpected tenderness. When she'd finally found the strength to remove herself from the car, Tegan had merely watched her go, then drove away from the curb and out of her life . . . until last night in that alleyway when he'd saved her from the Rogues.

"The trance I put you in last night is still active," Tegan said, evidently deciding to change the subject. "That's why your talent is muted now. The block will hold so long as I'm here to keep it in place."

He crossed his arms over his chest, drawing her eye down to the elaborate pattern of *dermaglyphs* that tracked up his forearms and disappeared under the short sleeves of his shirt. Where *glyphs* served as emotional barometers on members of the Breed, Tegan's were only a shade darker than his golden skin tone at the moment, giving away nothing of the warrior's mood.

Elise had seen his impressive Breed skin markings once before, when she'd first spoken with him at the Order's compound a few months ago. She didn't want to stare, but it was hard not to marvel at the swirling arcs and elegant, interlocking geometric designs that distinguished Tegan as one of the oldest of the race. He was of the Breed's first generation; if the depth of his powers didn't out him as such, the prevalence and complexity of his *glyphs* certainly did.

But the fact that he was Gen One also made him most vulnerable to things like sunlight, which, at the current hour of morning, was a very real concern.

"It's past nine A.M.," she said, in case he hadn't noticed. "You stayed here all night."

Tegan merely turned away to spoon up a plateful of scrambled eggs. He turned off the electric burner, then popped the toaster and added the slice of bread to the plate. "Come over here and eat while it's warm."

Elise didn't realize how hungry she was until she reached the counter and took her first bite of food. There was nothing she could do to hold back her little moan of pleasure as she chewed. "Oh, this is wonderful."

"That's because you're starving."

Tegan went to the mini refrigerator and came back with a protein shake in a plastic bottle. Aside from the eggs, yogurt, and a couple of apples, there wasn't much more to be found in there. She'd been living on meager sustenance, not because of the cost, but because it was hard to think about eating when her migraines were so severe. Which was a daily occurrence since she'd left the

Darkhaven—worse each day she ventured out among humankind to hunt Minions.

"You're not going to last, you know. Not like this." Tegan placed the shake down in front of her, then went back to his post against the opposite counter. "I know what it's doing to you, living here among the humans. I know how hard the psychic input hits you, Elise. You have no control over it, and that's a dangerous thing. It can destroy you. I felt what it does to you, when I pulled you up off the floor a few hours ago."

She recalled her initial encounters with Tegan, how his touch had made her feel somehow exposed to him. The first time she experienced the warrior's touch had been when he and Dante had shown up at the Darkhaven looking for her brother-in-law. The warriors had confronted Sterling in front of the residence, and when Elise ran out at the commotion, it was Tegan who grabbed her and held her away from the fray.

Now, after last night, he understood the flaw that had kept her prisoner in the Darkhavens all her life. Judging from the dispassionate look he trained on her, she wondered if he intended to see her put back in that cage again.

"Your body is weakening from the strain you're putting it through, Elise. You're not equipped to handle what you're doing."

She shook the plastic bottle he'd given her, then cracked the seal. "I'm coping well enough."

"Yeah, I see that." He shot a meaningful glance at all of the soundproofing she'd tacked onto the walls in an effort to damper her ability. "Looked to me like you were coping real well last night."

"You didn't have to help me."

"I know," he said, no expression in his tone or in his face.

"Why did you? How come you came back here?"

He lifted one thick shoulder in a shrug. "I thought you might like to know that the Order took out the Crimson lab. The lab, the manufacturing supplies, the individuals running the facility . . . all of it is ash now."

"Oh, thank God."

Relief washed over her like a balm. Elise closed her eyes, feeling hot tears well up behind her lids. At least the insidious drug that stole Camden couldn't harm any other woman's son now. It took her a moment to compose herself enough to look at Tegan again, and when she did, she found that gem-green gaze fixed hard on her.

She wiped at the tears that streaked her cheeks, embarrassed that the warrior should see her break down. "I'm sorry. I don't mean to be so emotional. There's just this . . . *hole* . . . in my heart, ever since Quentin died. Then, when I lost my son . . ." She trailed off, unable to describe how empty she felt. "I just . . . *ache*."

"It will pass." His voice was crisp and flat, like a slap to the face.

"How can you say that?"

"Because it's true. Grief is a useless emotion. The sooner you figure that out, the better off you'll be."

Elise gaped at him, appalled. "What about love?"

"What about it?"

"Haven't you ever lost someone you loved? Or do males like you, who live for killing and destruction, even know what it is to love?"

He didn't so much as blink at her angry outburst, just held her in a steady, unflappable stare that made her want to launch across the counter and strike him.

"Finish your breakfast," he told her with aggravating civility. "You should rest while you can. As soon as the sun sets, I'm out of here, and you'll be back to your own defenses. Such as they are."

He walked over to the long black trench coat that was draped neatly over the treadmill and coolly fished out his cell phone. As he began to dial, Elise had the sudden absurd urge to pick up the plate in front of her and hurl it at him, just to get some kind of reaction out of the stony warrior.

But while she listened to him call in to the Order's compound, that deep voice of his so matter-of-fact and unreadable, Elise realized that she didn't so much dislike him as she envied him. How did he manage to keep himself so cold and disengaged? His psychic gift was not so different from her own. Last night, he had experienced her torment through his touch but it hadn't laid him low like it did to her. How was it he could withstand the pain?

Perhaps it was his Gen One strength that made him so impenetrable, so totally aloof. But perhaps it was training. If it was something he'd learned, then it could be taught.

"Show me how you do it," Elise said as he ended his call and flipped the phone shut.

"Show you what?"

"You say I need to learn some control over my mind's powers, so show me what I need to do. Teach me. I want to be like you."

"No, you don't."

She walked around the edge of the counter to where he stood. "Tegan, show me. I can be an asset to you and to the Order. I want to help. I need to help, do you understand?"

"Forget it." He started to stalk away from her.

"Why, because I'm female?"

In a move so fast it stole her breath, Tegan wheeled around on her and pinned her with his fierce predator's eyes. "Because you're motivated by pain, and that's a fatal weakness right out of the gate. You're too raw. You're too swamped in your own self-pity to be of use to anyone."

Fire flashed in his gaze, then banked as quickly as it had risen. Elise swallowed hard as she registered his cutting words. The assessment stung, but it was true. She blinked slowly, then gave an admitting nod of her head.

"The best place for you is in the Darkhavens, Elise. Out here, like you are, you're a liability—to yourself especially. I'm not saying it to be cruel."

"No, of course you aren't," she agreed softly. "Because even cruelty would imply some kind of feeling, wouldn't it?"

She didn't say another word. Didn't so much as look at him as she retrieved her plate from the counter and walked it to the sink.

"What do you mean, it's gone?" The leader of the Rogues sat forward in his leather chair, planting his elbows on the surface of a large mahogany desk and steepling his fingers as the voice of a nervous Minion cracked over the speaker phone.

"The call came in to the firehouse late last night, sire. There was an explosion. Whole friggin' warehouse went up like a Roman candle. No saving it, according to the guys who responded to the call. Initial reports say there appears to have been a gas leak—"

With a snarl, Marek jabbed the *End* button, cutting off his human servant's useless report.

There was no way in hell the Crimson lab was destroyed by chance or faulty utilities. This bit of infuriating news had the Order written all over it. The only thing that surprised him was that it had taken this long for his brother Lucan and the warriors who fought alongside him to make their move on the place. But then, Marek had been keeping them busy fighting Rogues in the streets since last summer.

Which was exactly where he wanted the Order's focus to remain.

Hold them off with one hand so the other could do the real work unnoticed and undisturbed.

It was the reason he'd come to Boston in the first place. The reason this particular city was experiencing an increased Rogue problem. All just part of his plan to create havoc while he pursued a bigger prize. If he could take out the warriors in the process, so much the better, but keeping them distracted would serve him just as well. Once his true goal was achieved, even the Order would be powerless against him.

And as much as the loss of the Crimson lab infuriated him, the even greater irritation was the fact that one of his other Minions had failed to report in as instructed. Marek was waiting on information—vital information—and his patience was thin even in the best of situations.

It didn't bode well that his Minion was late. The human he'd recruited for this particular job was volatile and arrogant, but he was also reliable. All Minions were. Drained to within a bare inch of life, the human mind slaves were under the complete control of the vampire who made them. Only the most powerful among the vampire race could create Minions, and Breed law had long prohibited the practice as barbaric.

Marek scoffed with contempt at the self-imposed, bureaucratic castration of his kind.

Just one more example of why the vampire realm was overdue for change. They needed strong new leadership to usher in a new age.

The new age that would belong to him.

CHAPTER
Seven

He had pissed her off, probably hurt her, and even though an apology perched at the tip of his tongue most of the day, Tegan held it back. He had nothing to be sorry about, after all. He didn't owe the female anything, least of all explanations or excuses for why he came off like the callous bastard everyone knew him to be.

And he wasn't about to give so much as a second's consideration to her request that he help her bring her psychic gift to heel. She'd surprised him with the suggestion. The idea that any female, particularly a sheltered Darkhaven widow like her, would think to put herself in his care for any reason was beyond his comprehension. As if he could be trusted for something like that.

Yeah. Not fucking likely.

Elise made it easy for him to avoid the issue. In the hours since he'd shut her down, she hadn't uttered another word to him. She busied herself around the apartment, making up the futon, washing the breakfast dishes, dusting the bookshelves, going thirty minutes on the treadmill, and generally keeping as far away from him as seemed possible in the cramped quarters.

He'd heard her in the shower a while ago and had allowed himself a few minutes' sleep where he sat on the floor, but the water was off now and he was awake, listening to Elise getting dressed behind the closed door. She came out in blue jeans and a hooded Harvard sweatshirt that fell halfway down her thighs. Her short blond hair was towel-dried and as shiny as gold, setting off the pale lavender of her eyes.

Eyes that slid to him in a chilly glare as she went to the closet in the hallway and pulled a white down vest off a hanger. She bent into the closet and took out a pair of tan suede boots.

"What are you doing?" Tegan asked her as she silently suited up for the outdoors.

"I have to go out." She closed the closet door and zipped up the thick vest. "You probably noticed my refrigerator is practically empty. I'm hungry. I need to eat, and I need to pick up a few things."

Tegan stood up, aware that he was scowling. "The trance won't hold if you leave, you know."

"Then I'll just have to try to manage without it."

Elise coolly walked over to the counter and picked up the MP3 player that lay there. She tucked the slim black case into the front pocket of her jeans, then threaded the earbuds under her sweatshirt and let them dangle down the front of her chest. She didn't pick up the blade that had been left on the counter from her Minion hunting of the night before, and Tegan didn't detect that she had any other weapons on her person either.

She wouldn't look at him as she pulled the hood of her sweatshirt up over her head. "I don't know how long I'll be. If you leave before I get back, I'd appreciate it if you locked up. I have my keys."

Damn it. She might be hungry like she said, but he could tell by the rigid line of her spine that the female had a point to prove here.

"Elise," he said, moving toward her as she reached for the apartment door. If he wanted to stop her, all it would take was a thought. He knew it, and by the look on her face as she turned to look at him now, so did she. "I know you're angry about what I said earlier, but it's the truth. You're in no shape to go on like this."

When he took another step, concluding he might as well tell her that he'd decided to turn her over to the Darkhaven for her own safety, she closed her hand around the doorknob and sharply twisted it open.

She couldn't have chosen a more effective weapon against him.

Bright afternoon sunlight streamed in from the vestibule and hall, driving Tegan back with a hiss. He leaped out of the path of the searing daylight, and from under the shielding arm he held up over his eyes, he watched as Elise's pointed stare held him and she calmly strode out, closing the door behind her.

Elise took her time walking to the corner market and shopping for a few basic groceries. With a small bag of items in hand, she strolled up the sidewalk, away from her neighborhood block. The chill air was bracing against her cheeks, but she needed the cold to help clear her head.

Tegan had been right about his trance wearing off once she was gone from her apartment. Beneath the au- dial grate of electric guitars and screaming rock lyrics pouring into her ears from Camden's iPod, she could feel the hum of voices, the acid growl of human corruption and abuse that was her constant companion since she'd embarked on this dark journey beyond the sanctuary of the Darkhavens.

She had to admit, Tegan's psychic intervention had been a welcome gift. Even though he'd infuriated her— insulted her—the hours she'd spent cocooned within the trance he'd put her under had been so very needed. The break had given her a chance to think, to focus, and in her mind's calm, under the spray of a long, hot shower, she remembered a specific detail about the Minion she'd hunted yesterday.

He had been attempting to pick up an overnight pack- age for the one he called Master. The Minion—Raines, she thought he'd said his name was—had been quite out- raged to learn that the delivery had not arrived as ex- pected. What could be so important to him? More to the point, what could be so important to the vampire who'd made the Minion?

Elise intended to find out.

She'd been itching to leave her apartment since the moment she recalled the intriguing detail, but a rather immense, rather arrogant Breed warrior stood in her way. As Tegan didn't think she had anything to con- tribute in the fight against the Rogues, Elise saw no reason to bother him with her information until she was certain what it might mean.

It took several minutes to reach the FedEx store near the train station. Elise loitered outside for a while, formulating a loose plan and waiting for the handful of customers inside to complete their transactions and leave. As the last one came toward the exit, Elise tugged her earbuds free and walked up to the counter.

The clerk on duty was the same kid who had been working yesterday. He nodded a vague greeting at her as she approached, but thankfully he didn't seem to recognize her.

"Can I help you?"

Elise took a deep, calming breath, fighting hard to work through the cacophony that was building in her mind now that her crutch of blaring music was gone. She wouldn't have long before she was overwhelmed.

"I need to pick up a package, please. It was due here yesterday but got delayed because of the storm."

"Name?"

"Um, Raines," she replied, and attempted a smile.

The young man glanced up at her as he typed something on the computer. "Yeah, it's in. Can I see some ID?"

"Excuse me?"

"Driver's license, credit card . . . gotta have signature and ID for the pickup."

"I don't have any of those things. Not with me, I mean."

The clerk shook his head. "Can't release without some form of ID. Sorry. It's policy and I can't afford to lose this job. No matter how bad it sucks."

"Please," Elise said. "This is very important. My . . . husband was here yesterday to pick it up, and he was very upset that it was delayed."

She weathered the clerk's answering rush of animosity toward the Minion. He was thinking of baseball bats, dark alleys, and broken bones. "No offense, lady, but your husband is a dick."

Elise knew she looked anxious, but it would only serve her all the better at this moment. "He's not going to be happy with me if I come home without that shipment today. Really, I must have it."

"Not without ID." The kid looked at her for a long moment, then ran his palm over his chin and the little triangular growth of whiskers below his lower lip. "Course if I happen to leave it on the counter and go back for a smoke break, there's a good chance that box might sprout legs and walk off while I'm gone. Shit does go missing from time to time . . ."

Elise held the kid's cagey stare. "You would do that?"

"Not for nothing, I won't." He glanced at the earbuds dangling from the collar of her sweatshirt. "That the new model? The one with video?"

"Oh, this isn't . . ."

Elise started to shake her head in refusal, ready to tell the clerk that the device belonged to her son and it wasn't hers to give away. Besides, she needed it, she thought desperately, even while reason told her she had the means to buy a hundred new ones. But this one was Camden's. Her only tangible link to him now, through the music he'd been listening to in the days—the hours, in fact—before he left home for the very last time.

"Hey, whatever," the clerk said, shrugging now and pulling the box back off the counter. "I shouldn't be messing around anyway—"

"Okay," Elise blurted before she could change her mind. "Yes, okay. It's yours. You can have it."

She pulled the wires out from under her sweatshirt, then wound them around the iPod and set the sleek black case down in front of the clerk. It took her a while to remove her hand from the top of the device. When she did, it was with a wince of deep regret.

And rigid resolve.

"I'll take the package now."

CHAPTER
Eight

Tegan came out of a brief, light doze, fully recharged, as footsteps approached the apartment door from outside. He knew the sound of Elise's soft but determined gait even before a key slid into the lock announcing her arrival.

She'd been gone almost two hours. Another two and the sun would finally be gone, and he'd be free to get the hell out of there, back to his business as usual.

Seated on the floor with his elbows resting on his knees, his back against the foam-padded wall, he watched as the door opened cautiously and Elise slipped inside. She didn't seem as eager to singe him with the waning light from the hall; now she was focused on her own movements, as if it took most of her concentration just to remove the key and carefully close the door behind her. A lumpy plastic grocery bag swung from her tightly fisted left hand.

"Find what you needed?" he asked her as she rested a moment with her forehead pressed against the door. Her weak nod was her only reply. "Another headache coming on?"

"I'm fine," she answered quietly. As if marshaling her strength, she pivoted around and with her right hand up at her temple, she headed for the kitchen. "It's not one of the bad ones . . . I wasn't out very long, so it will ease soon."

Without dropping her grocery bag or shedding her down vest, she walked past the treadmill into the narrow galley. She was out of his line of vision now, but Tegan heard the tap running, water filling a glass. He got up and moved so that he could see her, debating whether to offer her the comfort of the trance again. God knew, she looked like she needed it.

Elise drank the water greedily, her delicate throat working with every swallow. There was something fiercely basic about her thirst, her need so primal it struck him as absurdly erotic. Tegan considered how long she'd gone without blood from one of the Breed. Five years at least. Her body had begun to show the lack, muscle groups going leaner, skin less pink than pale. She would be able to better cope with her talent if she was nourished by Breed blood, but she had to know that, having lived among the vampire race for any length of time.

She drank more water, and after her third full glass, Tegan saw some of the tension drain from her shoulders. "The stereo, please . . . will you turn it on?"

Tegan sent a mental command across the room and music soared to fill the quiet. It wasn't blaring like she preferred, but it seemed to help her take the edge off a bit. After a moment, Elise began putting away the supplies she'd brought home. With each second that passed, her strength renewed before his eyes. She was right; this wasn't nearly as bad as what he'd walked in on last night.

"It's worse when you get close to the Minions," he observed aloud. "Being exposed to that level of evil—having to get close enough to touch it—is what brings on your migraines, and the nosebleeds."

She didn't try to deny it. "I do what I must. I'm making a difference. And before you tell me that I'm of no use to the Order in this fight, you might be interested to know that the Minion I killed last night was in the middle of an errand for the vampire who made him."

Tegan froze, eyes narrowing on the petite female as she turned to look at him at last. "What kind of errand? What do you know?"

"I tracked him from the train station to a FedEx store. He was there to pick something up."

Tegan's brain went into instant recon mode. He started firing questions at her one after the other. "Do you know what it was? Or where it came from? What exactly did the Minion say or do? Anything you can remember might be—"

"Helpful?" Elise suggested, her tone nothing but pleasant even though her eyes flashed with the spark of challenge.

Tegan chose to ignore the slight goad. She may want to grind that tired axe with him from the morning, but this shit was too critical. He didn't have the time or interest for playing games with the female. "Tell me everything you recall, Elise. Assume that no detail is insignificant."

She went through a basic recap of what she observed about the Minion she'd hunted the night before, and damn if the female didn't make an excellent tracker. She'd even gotten the Minion's name, which might prove useful if Tegan decided to locate the dead human's residence and dig around for further information.

"What will you do?" Elise asked as he formulated his plan for the night.

"Wait for nightfall. Hit the FedEx store. Grab that goddamn package and hope it gives up some answers."

"It won't be dark for a couple more hours. What if the Rogues send someone to get it before you have the chance?"

Yeah, he'd thought of that too. Damn it.

Elise cocked her head at him, like she was measuring him somehow. "They might already have it. And because you are Breed, you're stuck here waiting for the sun to set."

Tegan didn't appreciate the reminder, but she was right. Fuck it. He needed to act now, because the odds were good there wouldn't be a later.

"What street is the delivery place on?" he asked her, flipping open his cell phone and dialing 411.

Elise gave him the location and Tegan recited it to the computerized prompts on the other end of the line. As the call connected to the FedEx store, he prepared to hit whoever answered with a little mental persuasion, level the playing field while he had the chance. The line picked up on the fifth ring and the voice of a young male who announced himself as Joey offered a disinterested greeting.

Tegan latched on to the vulnerable human mind like a viper, so focused on wringing information out of the man he hardly noticed Elise coming toward him from the kitchen. Without a word, she dropped a weighted plastic grocery bag down in front of him, a rectangular box at the bottom of it clopping on the counter.

Through the yellow smiley face "Thank You" logo stamped on the bag, Tegan saw an airbill addressed to one Sheldon Raines— the same Minion that Elise had killed the day before.

Holy hell.

She couldn't have—

He released the FedEx clerk's mind at once and cut off the call, genuinely astonished. "You went back for this today?"

Those pale violet eyes holding his surprised gaze were clear and keen. "I thought it might be useful, and in case it was, I didn't want to risk letting the Rogues have it."

God. Damn.

Although she didn't say it, Tegan could tell that Elise's Darkhaven-bred propriety was the only thing keeping her from reminding him how not a few hours before he'd assured her there was nothing she could do to help the Order in this war. And whether it was stubborn defiance or courageous savvy that sent her out today, he had to admit—at least to himself—that the female was nothing if not surprising.

He was glad for the interception, whatever it might prove to yield, but if the Rogues—particularly their leader, Marek—were expecting the package, then it must be of some value to them. The question remained, why?

Tegan pulled the box out and sliced open the tape seals with one of the daggers at his hip. The return address appeared to be one of those shared-office corporate types. Probably bogus at that. Gideon could verify that fact, but Tegan was betting that Marek wouldn't be so careless as to leave a legitimate paper trail.

He tipped the box and the contents—a thin, leatherbound book sealed in bubble wrap—slid into his hand. Peeling the cushioned plastic away from the antique, he scowled, perplexed. It was just an unremarkable, half-empty book. A diary of some sort. Handwritten passages scrawled in what appeared to be a mixture of German and Latin covered a few of the pages; the rest were blank except for crude symbols doodled here and there into the margins.

"How did you manage to get this, Elise? Did you have to sign for it, or leave your name, anything?"

"No. The clerk on duty wanted identification, but I don't have any. There was never a need for anything like that when I was living in the Darkhaven."

Tegan fanned the yellowed pages of the book, seeing more than one reference to a family called Odolf. The name wasn't familiar, but he was willing to bet it was Breed. And most of the entries were just repetitions of some kind of poem or verse. What would Marek want with an obscure chronicle like this one? There had to be a reason.

"Did you give the delivery station any information that might identify you at all?" he asked Elise.

"No. I, um . . . I traded for it. The clerk agreed to give the box to me in exchange for Camden's iPod."

Tegan glanced up at her, realizing just now that she'd made the trip back to her apartment without the aid of music to block her talent. No wonder she had seemed out of it when she came in. But not anymore. If she felt any lingering discomfort, she didn't let it show. Elise leaned forward to inspect the book, focused wholly on the task at hand with the same interest as him, her mind totally engaged.

"Do you think the book might be important?" she asked him, her eyes scanning the page that lay open on the counter. "What could it mean to the Rogues?"

"I don't know. But it sure as hell means something to the one leading them."

"He's not a stranger to you, is he."

Tegan thought about denying it, but allowed a vague shake of his head. "No, he isn't a stranger. I know him. His name is Marek. He's Lucan's elder brother."

"A warrior?"

"At one time he was. Lucan and I both rode into many battles with Marek at our side. We trusted him with our lives and would have given our own for him."

"And now?"

"Now Marek has proven himself to be a traitor and a murderer. He's our enemy—not only the Order's, but all of the Breed's as well. They just don't know it yet. With any luck, we'll take him out before he has a chance to make whatever move it is he's been planning."

"What if the Order fails?"

Tegan turned a hard stare on her. "Pray we don't."

In the answering silence, he flipped through more of the journal pages. Marek wanted the book for some reason, so there had to be a clue of some sort secreted in the damn thing somewhere.

"Wait a second. Go back," Elise said suddenly. "Is that a *glyph*?"

Tegan had noticed it at the same time. He turned to the small symbol scribbled onto one of the pages near the back of the slim volume. The pattern of interlocking geometric arches and flourishes might have appeared merely decorative to an untrained eye, but Elise was right. They were *dermaglyphic* symbols.

"Shit," Tegan muttered, staring at what he knew to be the mark of a very old Breed line. It didn't belong to anyone called Odolf, but to those of another Breed name. One that had lived—and died out completely—a long time ago.

So what reason could Marek have for digging up the ancient past?

Screams carried into the drawing room of an opulent Berkshires estate, the howls of anguish emanating down from a windowed attic room on the third floor of the manor house. The chamber boasted a wraparound wall of windows with unobstructed views of the wooded valley below.

No doubt the scenery was breathtaking, bathed in the day's last searing rays of sunlight.

The vampire being held upstairs by Minion guards certainly sounded impressed. He'd been treated to a front row seat of the UV spectacle for the past twenty-seven minutes and counting. More screams poured down the central staircase, agony giving way to the weariness of sobs.

With a bored sigh, Marek rose from a fine Louis XVI wing chair and crossed the room to the double doors of his dimly lit private suite. Other than the attic interrogation room, the rest of the mansion's windows were shaded for the day by sun-blocking electronic blinds.

Marek moved freely into the hall outside and summoned one of his Minion attendants who waited to serve him. At Marek's nod, the human dashed up the staircase to instruct the others that their Master was on the way and to ensure the windows were covered for his arrival.

It took only a moment for the captive vampire's bleating to dry up. Marek climbed the wide marble steps, up and around to the second floor, then up and around again, to the smaller flight of stairs that rose to the attic. As he progressed, fury kindled to life in him again.

This was only one of several frustratingly exhaustive interrogations of the vampire in his custody the past couple of weeks. Torture was amusing, but rarely effective.

There was little amusing about the day's developments back in Boston. The Minion courier dispatched to obtain an important overnight delivery for him had instead turned up at the city morgue—a John Doe stabbing victim, according to Marek's contact in the coroner's office. As he was killed in broad daylight, that ruled out the Order or any other Breed intervention, but Marek still had his suspicions.

And he was very interested to learn that the package he'd been expecting had gone missing from the FedEx store that very day. The loss was serious, but he intended to reclaim it. When he did, he would take great pleasure in personally questioning the thief who had it.

Up ahead, at the top of the attic stairwell, one of the Minions on guard opened the door to permit Marek entry into the now-darkened room. The vampire was naked, strapped to a chair by chain links and steel shackles at each ankle and wrist. His skin was smoking from head-to-toe burns, emitting the sickly sweet odors of sweat and badly seared flesh.

"Enjoy the view?" Marek asked as he strolled in and

looked on the male with revulsion. "A pity it's still winter. I understand the colors up here are amazing in the fall."

The vampire's head was dropped low on his chest, and when he tried to speak, the sound was nothing more than a sputtered rasp in the back of his throat.

"Are you ready to tell me what I need to know?"

A pitiful moan slipped past the male's blistered, swollen lips.

Marek crouched down before his captive, offended by both the stench and sight of him. "No one would know that you broke. I can give you that, if you cooperate with me now. I can send you away to heal, ensure your protection. That's easily within my power. Do you understand?"

The vampire whimpered, and Marek sensed a possible teetering of conviction in the pained sound. He had no intention of making good on the lies he fed his captive. They were merely tools meant to bend him where torture and suffering had not.

"Speak it, and be free of this," he coaxed, his tone quiet and unhurried despite the urgent greed swimming in him to have the answer. "Tell me where he is."

There was an audible click of the prisoner's throat as he attempted to swallow, a vague tremor in his head as he struggled to lift it from its slump on his ravaged chest. Marek waited, eager with hope and uncaring that the Minions standing around him could probably feel that hope vibrating off him.

"Tell me now. You don't need to carry this burden any longer."

A hiss began to leak from between the vampire's lips, a drawn-out, rattling exhalation. A shudder overtook him, but he gathered himself and tried again, expelling the start of his confession at last.

Marek felt his eyes widen in anticipation, his own breath ceasing as he waited for the words that would begin his destiny.

"Ffff . . ." One eye peeled open just a crack behind the vampire's seared lids. The iris was bright amber from the prolonged suffering, the pupil a thin slit of black that found Marek's own gaze and burned into him with hatred. The captive drew in a breath, then spat it out on a low growl. *"Fff . . . fuck . . . you."*

With an utter calm that belied the storm of rage that swept instantly to life inside him, Marek rose and began a deliberate stroll toward the attic stairs.

"Open the blinds," he instructed the Minion guards. "Leave this worthless offal to the sun. If he doesn't perish by the time it sets, let him bake up here with the dawn."

Marek quit the room, not so much as flinching when the first terrorized screams cranked up again in his wake.

CHAPTER
Nine

$\sim$

As the last few minutes of day passed into dusk, Tegan gathered up the book and his weapons, then reached for his dark coat. Elise had spent the past hour or more—since the moment she'd handed the FedEx package over to him—watching him pore intensely over every page of the text while she worked up the nerve to ask him again about helping her become more involved in the war against the Rogues. Now, as he shrugged into the black leather trench coat, she sensed it was her final chance.

"Tegan . . . I hope the book proves useful."

"It will." Striking green eyes flicked to her, but she could see that his mind was churning on the new information in his hands. He blinked and it was as if he had dismissed her entirely now, was itching to get away from her. "You have the Order's gratitude for this."

"What about yours?"

"Mine?"

When he paused, scowling, Elise said, "It's not so much to ask, is it? You're the only one who can help me deal with this . . . flaw of mine. Teach me how to mute it, how not to feel. I can be an asset to you and to the Order. I want to help."

His answering look scathed her with its sharp edge. "I work alone. And you don't know what you're asking for. Besides, we've already covered this ground."

"I can learn. I want to learn. Please, Tegan. I *need* to learn."

"And you think I'm the one to help you?"

"I think you're my only hope."

He scoffed at that, shaking his head. When he moved away from her, Elise marched toward him, undaunted, as if she could physically keep him from leaving. She caught herself a mere hairbreadth from contact, and let her hand fall to her side. "Don't you think I'd go to someone else—anyone else—if I could?"

He was silent for a moment, considering, she hoped. But then he exhaled a curse and reached for the door. "I gave you my answer."

"And I gave you that journal. That's worth something, isn't it?"

He barked out a cutting laugh and whirled back on her. "You seem to think we're negotiating here. We are not."

"If that book contains insight into current dealings with the Rogues, I'm sure the Darkhavens would be just as interested in it as you are. All it would take is a single call to any of my husband's Enforcement Agency connections and I could have the Order's compound swamped with agents within the hour."

It was true. Quentin's rank within the Agency had been at the highest level, and as his widow, Elise's own political status was considerable. She personally knew a great deal of influential Darkhaven individuals. Quentin's name alone would open ten times as many doors if she felt the need to use it.

Tegan didn't need her to explain that fact. Anger flared in his normally icy gaze, the first hint of emotion she'd seen in him.

"Now you're threatening me." His brittle chuckle put a knot of fear in her throat. "Female, I give you fair warning: you are playing with fire."

Elise's skin went tight with anxiety, but she couldn't back down. For too long, she had been kept in a neat little box, coddled and protected. And if it meant stoking the temper of a warrior—even a lethal Gen One like Tegan—in order to help her break out of that box, then she would simply have to brave it and pray she would come out the other side in one piece.

"Whether you approve or not, I am part of this war. I didn't go looking for it; the Rogues brought it to my door when Camden died. All I'm asking is that you show me how to be more effective. I should think the Order would welcome any allies they can get."

"This isn't about the Order and you know it. This is about revenge, an eye for an eye. Your emotions have been on a hard boil ever since you watched your Rogue son get smoked in front of your eyes."

Tegan's harsh words cut into her like glass, the reality of what he said like acid poured into the wounds.

"It's about justice," she told him sharply. "I need to make this right! Damn it, Tegan, do I have to beg you?"

She shouldn't have touched him. She'd been so desperate to make her point that before she could stop herself, she had reached out and put her hand on his arm. Tegan's hard muscles flexed beneath her fingertips, going as tense as the expression on his unreadable face.

He didn't snatch his arm away from her touch, but his cold green eyes flicked past her to the stereo that was playing in the background. It went silent on his mental command. In the resulting quiet, the dark stirrings of Elise's psychic talent began to wake.

Voices swelled in her mind, and from the piercing glint of Tegan's gaze, which fixed on her now in stony, watchful purpose, she knew that he was reading every nuance of her distress. He was absorbing it, she realized, feeling him siphon in her reaction through the point where their skin touched.

Elise fought the awful storm that battered her mind, but the voices were growing louder. She nearly staggered from the obscenity and corruption that filled her head.

Tegan merely watched her as he might study an insect under glass.

Damn him, but he was enjoying this, driving home his point with each passing second of emotional assault that she tried to endure. As their eyes locked, Elise began to understand that he was somehow controlling the painful barrage that was beating at her skull. He was amplifying the input in much the same way that he was able to mute the music and television.

"My God," she gasped. "You are so cruel."

He didn't even try to deny it. Expressionless, maddeningly stoic, he broke contact with her and stood in silent contemplation as she backed away from him, more wounded than she cared to let him see.

"Lesson number one," he murmured coldly. "Don't count on me for anything. I will only let you down."

He was a prick and a bastard, but it would have been less than honest of him to let Elise think any differently. Leaving her looking at him from across the small apartment, her gaze stung and despising, Tegan headed out into the hallway to make his escape.

Maybe he should feel guilty for treating her so roughly but he frankly didn't need the hassle. And she was far better off looking to someone else for whatever she needed. He hoped to hell she would.

With the book held against him under his coat, Tegan's pace was brisk as he walked out into the dark night. Curiosity made him cut along a side street, then up onto the one that would take him past the FedEx store. Elise's description of the Minion and all that had transpired there had been informative, but part of him wondered if he'd find out anything more if he went by and questioned the clerk himself.

Not a hundred feet from the place, he realized he wasn't the only one interested in checking things out, and he'd gotten there too late.

Tegan smelled fresh spilled blood. A lot of it. The store was dark inside, but Tegan could see the motionless body of a clerk lying behind the counter. The Rogues had already been there. On a closed-circuit monitor in the corner, a single frame from a video feed was frozen onscreen. It was a blurry but recognizable shot of Elise, caught in mid-motion, the package in her hands.

Damn it.

And right about now, the Rogues who'd been there were no doubt scouring the area looking for her.

Tegan turned around and hauled ass back to her apartment building, using all the preternatural speed at his disposal. He banged on her door, cursing the blare of music likely drowning him out.

"Elise! Open the door."

He was just about to throw the locks and barge inside when he heard her on the other side. She opened the door only a crack, glaring at him. Before she could tell him to fuck off like he deserved, he pushed her back inside with the bulk of his body and slammed the door shut.

"Get your coat and boots. Now."

"What?"

"Do it!"

She flinched at his barked command, but she held her ground. "If you think I'm going to let you send me back—"

"Rogues, Elise." He saw no reason to pretty the situation up for her. "They just killed the clerk at the FedEx store. Now they're looking for you. We don't have much time. Get your things."

She blanched white at the news, but blinked at him like she didn't quite trust him—which made good sense, since he'd given her no reason to think she could. Especially after what he did to her not a few minutes ago.

"I have to get you out of here," he told her when she hesitated another second. "Now."

She nodded, grave acceptance in the pale amethyst of her eyes. "Okay."

It took her no time to grab a wool coat and shove her

feet into a pair of boots. On her way to the door with him, she suddenly doubled back. "Wait. I'm going to need a weapon."

Tegan took two strides in and caught her by the wrist. "I'll protect you. Come on."

They hurried out of the apartment—only to find a Rogue peering through the glass of the building entrance, its feral eyes glowing amber as it locked on to them in the narrow hallway. It curled back bloodstained lips and snarled something over its thick shoulder, no doubt calling in reinforcements from the street.

"Oh, my God," Elise gasped. "Tegan—"

"Get back inside." He pushed the book he was carrying into her hands and shoved her back toward her apartment. "Stay in there until I come for you. Bolt the door."

She obeyed him at once, her footsteps retreating fast, the door shutting tight as the Rogue outside shouldered his way into the building. Another followed, both suckheads leering psychotically through their elongated fangs, both big vampires armed for bear.

They started coming for him, and Tegan went on the offensive, springing from his stance near Elise's door. He plowed into the one in front, driving that Rogue into the one behind him. The Rogue who would have been at the bottom of the pile feinted left at the last second, dodging the fall as Tegan took his companion down in a killing grip.

The commotion brought one of the building's residents into the hallway, but the human took one look at the confrontation and wisely decided to butt out. "Oh, shit!" he squeaked, then immediately spun back into his unit, slammed the door, and threw all the locks.

Totally unfazed, Tegan pounced fast and hard on the

Rogue he held on the floor, ripping one of his blades across the suckhead's throat. It roared and sputtered under the swift poison of the dagger's titanium edge, oozing gore as its body began a rapid meltdown.

"Your turn," Tegan told the other one as it attempted to scramble out of the way.

The vampire threw its arm out, swiping at Tegan with its blade, but it was a careless move, even for a Rogue. When it had the chance to come at him, it hesitated, started inching to the side, drawing things out. Distracting him, Tegan realized in that next instant, when he heard the sudden crash of breaking glass coming from Elise's apartment.

"Son of a bitch," he growled as the female's scream shot through the walls.

The Rogue chose that second to fly at him, but Tegan was ready for the attack. He leaped out of the suckhead's path, landing in a low crouch behind it and coming up fast with his blade. He skewered the bastard in a split-second's move and was gunning for Elise's door before the dead bulk of the Rogue hit the floor.

Using mental will and brute force, Tegan smashed the apartment door off its hinges and stormed inside. Elise was on the floor, facedown, her spine trapped beneath the heavy boot of the Rogue who'd come in through the window. She held the journal tight to her chest, protecting it with her body.

Jesus Christ.

She'd been cut somehow in the struggle; a gash on her upper arm was bright red, slick with fresh blood. And the scent and sight of it had sent her Rogue attacker into a slavering fit of Bloodlust. Instead of going for the book, which the trio had no doubt been dispatched to do, the

Rogue on Elise seemed rooted on just one thing—slaking its unquenchable thirst.

"Tegan!" she cried as her stricken gaze lit on him. She started scrambling to push the journal out from under her now, like she meant to pass it to him even though her life was hanging in the balance. "Don't let them have it. Take the book, Tegan!"

Fuck that, he thought, his temples pounding with the need to spill more Rogue blood. He went after the suckhead on Elise, knocking the Rogue off with a fierce strike of his mind. Without touching the bastard, using only his will and a flaring, savage anger, Tegan threw the Rogue against the far wall and held him there, two-hundred-and-fifty pounds of thrashing, feral vampire suspended three feet off the ground.

He saw the hunger in the Rogue's eyes, those slitted pupils fixed on Elise, even though Tegan was tightening his mental hold around the suckhead's throat, killing him by degrees. The long fangs were dripping saliva, the mind inside the huge skull no longer capable of any thought besides feeding the thirst. Tegan despised this element of his kind—knew it better than most, enough to know that extermination was the only solution for vampires lost to the disease.

But it wasn't duty or cool logic that made him draw his blade and drive it into the Rogue's heart. It was the heather-and-roses scent of Elise's spilled blood, the bitter tang of her fear, which clung to the air like a mist. This bastard had injured her, an innocent female, and that was something Tegan could not abide.

He let the dead Rogue crumble to the floor, instantly forgotten.

"Are you all right?" he asked Elise, turning to see her coming to her feet behind him.

She nodded. "I'm okay."

"Then let's get out of here."

As they hit the street, Tegan flipped his cell phone open and speed-dialed the compound. "I need pickup," he told Gideon when the warrior came on the line. "Send it fast."

There was a fractional hesitation, no doubt because Tegan, ever the loner, never called for backup. "You hit?"

"Nah, I'm good. But I'm not alone." He glanced at Elise's wound and ground out a curse. "I'm with a female from the Darkhaven. She's bleeding, and I just smoked three Rogues downtown. Got a feeling there's going to be more real quick."

And if so, he and Elise might be able to shake their pursuers temporarily, but so long as they were leaving a blood scent trail, the Rogues would track them like hounds.

"Ah, shit," Gideon breathed, understanding that fact the same as Tegan did. "Where are you at right now?"

Still running, Elise hurrying alongside him, Tegan gave his location and the direction he was heading.

"Yep, I got ya right here," Gideon said over a clacking rush in the background as he typed something on a keyboard at the compound. "Tracking GPS on the others now to see who's closest . . . Okay, looks like Dante and Chase are on patrol just north of you about fifteen minutes out."

"Tell them they'd better get here in five. And, Gideon?"

"Yeah."

"Let them know that the injured female who's with me . . . let them know it's Elise."

"Fuck, T. You serious?" Gideon's voice dropped low, incredulous. "What the hell are you doing with that female?"

Tegan heard the edge of wary suspicion in the vampire's tone, but he ignored it. "Just tell Dante to haul ass."

CHAPTER
Ten

Elise fought to keep pace with Tegan as they cut down one dark street, then another. She knew he was slowed by her; no human was any match for the incredible speed that those of the Breed possessed. The Rogue who was fresh on their trail was deadly fast too. No sooner did Tegan end his call to the compound than he spotted the new threat on their heels.

"This way," he said, grabbing for her hand and pulling her onto a narrow lane between two Colonial-era buildings.

Behind them, Elise heard heavy boot falls, then sudden, empty silence, followed a second later by a hard metallic clank. She threw a glance over her shoulder and saw that another Rogue was onto them now. The large vampire had gone airborne, leaping up and landing on a metal fire escape that clung to the side of the old brick structure. It leaped again, then swung up onto the roof to track them from above.

"Tegan—up there!"

"I know."

His voice was grim, his hand clamped firmly around hers as they neared the end of the lane. That grip was solid as iron, an unspoken promise that he was not about to let go of her. Elise drew from his strength, forcing her legs to work harder, ignoring her screaming lungs and the burn in her arm where the Rogue who attacked her had laced her open.

As they cleared the lane and spilled out onto the adjacent street, a dark SUV came roaring up from the traffic light and pulled a hard, skidding stop in front of them at the slushy curb. The back door flew open.

"Get in."

Tegan let go only to push her into the vehicle, and Elise scrambled onto the leather bench seat, her heart pounding in her chest. In a move so fast it hardly registered to her, he pivoted around, drew a dagger, and let it fly down the alleyway. From somewhere in the darkness came a shout of pain, then the low, anguished howl of a Rogue meeting its demise at the end of Tegan's titanium blade.

Tegan dived into the SUV next to Elise and slammed the back door shut. "Make us gone, Dante. There's more on the way. Coming at us from above—"

At that instant something heavy hit the roof of the vehicle. In a peal of screeching tires, Dante threw the SUV into reverse, dislodging the Rogue onto the hood. A fast zigzagging maneuver threw it off the car completely, and as the feral vampire came up from its roll on the street, the leather-clad warrior in the passenger seat leaned out his open window and filled the Rogue with a merciless hail of bullets. The warrior squeezing the trigger shouted a coarse battle cry as a seemingly endless blast of gunfire ripped like thunder into the night.

When it finally ceased, Dante exhaled a wry oath. "Just a tad excessive there, buddy. But I think the suck-head got your point."

There was no answering humor from the grim one seated next to Dante, only the cold metallic clack and grate of a weapon being reloaded.

"You okay?" Tegan asked from beside Elise, drawing her attention away from the violence.

She nodded, breathing too hard to speak, fear still making her heart race within her breast. She was too aware of Tegan's body next to her, the heat of him an odd comfort. His muscled thigh pressed alongside hers, his arm slung casually over the back of the bench seat behind her. Elise knew that propriety demanded she put space between them, but she was too shaken to make herself move.

And as the SUV sped into the night, her mind absorbed the din of the city's corruption, her talent cracking her wide open.

"Come here," Tegan murmured. He pressed his palm lightly to her brow, trancing her with a touch and silencing her pain before it could really begin. His hands were gentle on her, even though his face was dispassionately cool. "Is that better?"

She couldn't hold back her relieved sigh. "Yes, much better."

It took him a moment to draw his hand away. When he did, Elise felt a pair of eyes fixed on her from the front passenger side of the vehicle. She glanced up and met the measuring stare of the warrior seated there. The blue gaze was intense beneath the light brows and black knit cap, but not quite friendly.

Dear Lord.

"Sterling," she whispered, astonished.

He said nothing, the silence stretching interminably.

She hadn't seen him for four months—not since Camden's death that terrible night outside their home. Sterling had walked off alone that night, the last anyone at the Darkhavens had heard from him. Elise knew he blamed himself for taking Camden's life—she had too. That blame was misplaced, however, and seeing him so unexpectedly now made her heart ache to tell him how sorry she was . . . for everything.

But the eyes that once looked at her with noble compassion, even affection, now dismissed her with a slow blink and a turn of his head. Sterling Chase was no longer her brother-by-marriage. He was a warrior, and if she hoped to reclaim him as her ally—as her last remaining kin—that hope bled away as the SUV roared out of the city, toward the Order's headquarters.

"Is Lucan still topside?" Tegan asked as Gideon met him and the others upon their arrival at the compound.

"He came in from patrol about twenty minutes ago. Decided to stick around after you called in."

"Good. I need to see him. The tech lab?"

Gideon shook his head. "He's in his quarters with Gabrielle. What the hell is going on, T?"

"See that she gets medical help for that wound," he said instead of answering, gesturing to Elise's bloodied arm and already heading off with the book she'd intercepted, down the corridor toward Lucan's private apartments in the compound.

He found the Gen One leader of the Order in the room his Breedmate favored most: the library study that was lined with floor-to-ceiling bookcases and a hand-crafted tapestry depicting Lucan himself in chain mail armor and astride a rearing medieval warhorse beneath a cloud-streaked crescent moon. There was a hilltop castle burning in the background, its parapet smoking and under siege—a declaration of war instigated by Lucan.

Tegan remembered the night represented in the intricately rendered needlework. He remembered the carnage that had come before. And afterward. He'd been there with Lucan when the Order was conceived in blood and fury—the two of them and six others banding together in a pledge to fight for the future of their race, the Breed.

Jesus, that had been a lifetime ago. Several lifetimes ago.

A lot of death had followed the Order to this moment, both within their ranks and without. Most of the original warriors were lost to time and combat. Only Tegan, Lucan, and Lucan's elder brother Marek—now their most dangerous adversary, having recently resurfaced to anoint himself leader of the Rogues—had survived of the original cadre of eight.

As Tegan paused in the open doorway of the library, Lucan looked up from an array of color photographs that Gabrielle spread out before him on the squat table in the center of the room. She had a gift that extended be-

yond her artist's eye for beauty: Gabrielle's camera lens
was often drawn to vampire locations, both Breed and
Rogue. It was in part how she and Lucan met the past
summer; now it wasn't unusual for the Breedmate to return from occasional daytime outings to the city and sub-
urbs with pictures that proved useful to the Order's recon
efforts topside.

But this particular collection was something different.

Even from a distance, Tegan's eye was drawn to vibrant, sunlit images of the mansion's winter grounds and
gardens. Ice glistened on branches like diamonds, and in
one of the shots a red cardinal was captured close-up, a
blast of shocking color amid a field of fresh white snow. A
few of the pictures were taken in the city, some showing
children in one of the area parks, bundled up in bright
snowsuits, rolling large snowballs for a family of snow-
men that stood half-completed nearby.

All things that those of the Breed didn't often get a
chance to see, the warriors especially.

Lucan's woman had taken the photos simply for his
pleasure, bringing him images of a vivid daylight world
that existed just out of his reach.

Tegan glanced away from the pictures with a mental
shrug; it didn't feel right for him to share in this joy. It
didn't belong to him, and he sure as hell hadn't come
here looking for warm fuzzies.

"Not like you to call in the cavalry, Tegan," Lucan
drawled. There had been a smile lingering in the formidable warrior's gray eyes as he met Tegan's gaze from
across the room, but he sobered instantly. "We have new
trouble coming our way?"

"It could be."

The Gen One leader of the Order nodded gravely,

understanding from a single exchanged look that the night was about to head south.

Way south, Tegan thought. He held the curious journal under his arm, but ancient protocol made him hesitant to discuss potentially disturbing Order business in front of a female. It did not escape his notice that instead of getting up from the room or requesting privacy from Gabrielle, Lucan reached out to take her hand in his. The slight nod he gave her as she sat back down beside him was one of respect and solidarity.

The statement was clear: they were a unit, and while Lucan would walk through fire to protect her, the venerable warrior kept no secrets from her. No doubt the female would have it no other way.

It had been like that between the couple from the day she arrived at the compound as Lucan's mate. The same could be said of Gideon and Savannah, who were paired more than thirty years and an equally solid match. Dante and Tess were two halves of one whole as well, though they had only been together a few short months.

Breedmates had their freedoms, even those bonded to members of the Order, but there wasn't a male among the entire vampire nation who would stand by and condone what Elise had been doing the past few months she'd been living topside. What she intended to keep on doing, even if it killed her.

"Tell me what this is about," Lucan said, indicating for Tegan to come into the library chamber. "Gideon said you phoned in that you were with an injured Darkhaven female."

Tegan arched a brow in acknowledgment. "Elise Chase. No longer of the Darkhavens, as it turns out."

"She left?"

"After the death of her son. She's been living in the city by herself."

"Jesus. What happened to her tonight?"

Tegan smirked, still disbelieving the woman's tenacity. "She attracted some unwanted attention from the Rogues. They came gunning for her at her apartment."

He left out the fact that one of the bastards got to her before he could stop it. The thought still burned in him, self-directed anger seething beneath his cool veneer.

Gabrielle frowned. "What would they want with Elise?"

"This." Tegan held the book out and Lucan took it, scowling as he touched the faded tooling on the aged cover, then flipped through some of the yellowed pages. "It was waiting for overnight pickup by a Minion. Somebody was in a big rush to have it."

Lucan's look was grave. No question as to who the somebody was.

"And the Darkhaven woman?"

"She intercepted it."

"Christ. What about Marek's human mule?"

"The Minion is dead," Tegan stated simply. "Marek must have gotten wind of that fact and unleashed his hounds to retrieve the book. It would have been easy enough to track down Elise from the store's closed-circuit feed."

"What is it, some kind of diary?" Gabrielle asked, peering past Lucan at the fanning pages.

"Appears to be," Tegan said. "Apparently it belonged to a family named Odolf. You ever hear of them, Lucan?"

The vampire shook his dark head as he ran through the journal again. Before Tegan could direct him to the disturbing symbol at the back of the text, Lucan flipped to the page himself. As soon as his eye lit upon the hand-drawn *dermaglyphic* marking, he muttered a curse. "Holy hell. Is this what I think it is?"

Tegan gave a grim nod. "No doubt you recognize the pattern."

"Dragos," Lucan said, a dark weight hanging on that one word.

"Who is Dragos?" Gabrielle asked, peering past Lucan at the *glyph* scrawled onto the page.

"Dragos is a very old Breed name," Lucan explained. "He was one of the original members of the Order—a first generation vampire. Like Tegan and me, Dragos was sired by one of the ancient creatures who began the vampire race as we know it. Dragos fought alongside us when the Order declared war on our alien fathers."

Gabrielle nodded, showing no surprise or confusion. Evidently Lucan had already filled her in on the other-worldly origins of the Breed, as well as the bloody war that arose within the Breed during the fourteenth century of the human era.

It was a tumultuous time, rife with treachery and vio-lence—most of it carried out by the long-lived, savage creatures from a distant planet who prowled the night and fed without discretion, sometimes wiping out entire villages of humankind. The Ancients were ravenous and brutal, supremely powerful. Without the Order to inter-vene, they'd been a bloodthirsty pestilence that made even the worst Rogue look like a misbehaving frat boy.

Gabrielle's gaze went from Lucan to Tegan. "What happened to Dragos?"

"Killed in battle a few years into the war with the Ancients," Tegan supplied.

"Can you be sure of that?" she asked. "Until last summer, everyone believed that Marek was dead too . . ."

Lucan gave a firm nod. "Dragos is dead, love. I saw his body with my own eyes. None of the Breed can resurrect when their head is taken."

Tegan recalled that night as well. It was a moment that marked many losses, starting with Dragos's Breedmate, who took her own life upon hearing the news of his death. Kassia had been a good, caring woman, as close as a sister to Sorcha. It wasn't long after Kassia's death that Tegan lost Sorcha as well. Dark times that he preferred not to think on, even now. He'd learned to suppress the pain, but he still had so many memories . . .

Tegan sharply cleared his throat. "Which brings us back to the name Odolf. Who is it? And what can it mean to Marek?"

"Maybe Gideon can turn something up in the IID," Lucan suggested, handing the book back to Tegan as he got to his feet. "The database isn't a complete record, but it's all we've got."

"You two run your search," Gabrielle interjected when they reached the corridor outside. "I'm going to check in on Elise. It sounds like she's been through a lot tonight. Maybe she could use some company and something to eat."

Lucan's eyes darkened as he held his woman's gaze. He whispered something low in her ear, then pressed a kiss to her lips. There was a faint pink tint to her cheeks as she broke the embrace.

Tegan glanced away from the exchange and started the trek toward Gideon's lab. Lucan was behind him in no time, Gabrielle heading in the opposite direction to look for Elise.

It was impossible not to notice the calm that enveloped the warrior whenever he was around his Breedmate. Not that long ago, Lucan had been a powder keg just looking for an open flame. He'd pretended an iron control, but Tegan knew him longer than any of the others at the compound, and he knew that Lucan had been only a few steps away from total disaster.

Bloodlust was the fatal flaw of all the Breed—a tipping point that could push even the most stable vampire over the edge into a permanent addiction. All of the Breed needed to consume blood to survive, but some took it too far. Some turned Rogue, and it had stunned Tegan to discover that Lucan was teetering on the very knife-edge of that abyss. He'd been nearly lost.

Until Gabrielle.

She grounded him somehow, gave Lucan what he needed through their blood bond, yet trusted him not to fall. She'd saved the warrior, and it was clear that she continued to do so every moment they shared together.

"You're well mated," Tegan said as Lucan caught up to him and strode along at his side in the corridor.

He'd meant it in praise, but it came out sounding harsh, almost an accusation. Lucan didn't seem surprised by the rough tone, but he didn't rise to the bait like he might have at one time either. "I think about you and Sorcha sometimes, when I look at Gabrielle and imagine what my life would be like without her. It's sure as hell not a place I like to visit often. How you ever got through it—"

"It passes," Tegan murmured, a bit too tightly even to his own ears. "And the only ghost I'm interested in talking about right now is Dragos."

Lucan dropped the subject as the two of them entered

the tech lab. Gideon was at his usual post behind the long console, keying something into one of the many computers. "What've you got?" he asked the moment they strode in, his eyes and fingers never leaving his task.

Tegan put the airbill and journal down on the table. "Need you to check the origin of this package, but first run a search of the IID records for the name Odolf."

"You got it." The vampire grabbed a wireless keyboard, dropped it into his lap, and started typing. "Am I looking for criminal records, birth records, death records . . . ?"

"Any of the above," Tegan said, watching the monitor screen fill with a scrolling list of data. It kept running and running, turning up zilch. Then one record stuck at the top of the screen while the program scrolled for more results. "You got one?"

"Deceased," Gideon replied. "A one Reinhardt Odolf, of the Munich Darkhaven. Went Rogue in May 1946. Deceased the following year by solar suicide. Another entry, this one for Alfred Odolf, lost to Bloodlust in 1981. Hans Odolf, Bloodlust, 1993. A couple of missing persons on record . . . here's one more for you: Petrov Odolf, Berlin Darkhaven."

Lucan moved in to get a better look at the computer. "Also deceased?"

"Actually no. Not yet, anyway. Petrov Odolf, institutionalized for rehabilitation. According to the record, this boy's been Rogue for the past few years and a ward of the Enforcement Agency in Germany."

"Is he coherent?" Tegan demanded. "Can he be questioned? More importantly, can his answers be trusted to be valid?"

Gideon shook his head. "The record's not complete

about his current condition, other than he's breathing and under the supervision of the institution in Berlin."

"Berlin, eh?" Lucan turned a questioning look on Tegan. "Think you can call in any favors over there?"

Tegan turned away from the monitor and pulled out his cell phone. "Guess it's as good a time as any to find out."

CHAPTER
Eleven

Elise looked down at the healed wound on her left arm, then over at Tess, whose gifted hands had erased all traces of the bleeding cut and mended the torn flesh with just a touch. "This is incredible. How long have you had this talent?"

"Pretty much all my life, I suppose." Tess pushed a curling lock of honey-blond hair behind her ear and gave a small shrug. "For a long time, I didn't use it. I just wished it would go away, you know? So I could be . . . normal."

Elise nodded, understanding completely. "You're lucky, though, Tess. Your ability is one of strength. It works for the good."

Shadows seemed to crowd the Breedmate's aqua eyes. "Now it does, yes. Thanks mostly to Dante, that is. Before I met him, I had no idea why I was so different from other women. I treated my talent like a curse. Now I wish it went deeper. There is so much more I wish I could do—like with Rio, for instance."

Elise knew the warrior Tess referred to. She'd seen him in one of the other infirmary rooms when she was led down here by Gideon. As they passed his open door, Rio had looked up from where he lay on a hospital bed, one side of his face distorted by old burns, the muscles of his bare chest and torso riddled with shrapnel scars and healed gouges that indicated some very severe injuries. His topaz-colored eyes had been dull beneath the fall of his overlong, dark brown hair. Elise hadn't wanted to stare, but the anguish she saw in his face was arresting— even more so than the ravaged condition of his person.

"I can't take away old wounds and scars," Tess said. "And some of the worst ones a person bears are on the inside. Rio is a good man, but he's damaged in ways he may never recover from, and there is no Breedmate talent that can erase those kinds of hurts."

"Maybe love?" Elise suggested hopefully.

Tess shook her head as she ran her hands under the counter tap and scrubbed up. "Love betrayed him once. That's what left him the way he is now. I don't think he'll let anyone get that close again. All he's living for is to get back out in the field with the other warriors. Dante and I are trying to convince him to take things slowly, but when you try to slow Rio down, he only pushes harder."

In some small way, Elise could relate to the warrior's determined need to take action, even if only in the name of revenge. She was driven by a similar need and, like Rio, hearing others advise her to step back didn't make the need burn any less.

From outside the infirmary room came the soft gait of female footsteps, accompanied by the quick, rhythmic click of a four-footed companion. Savannah and a perky brown terrier appeared in the doorway. Gideon's pretty Breedmate offered Elise a warm smile. "All set here?"

"We've just wrapped up," Tess said, drying her hands with a paper towel and bending down to scratch the chin of the little dog who quite obviously adored her. The mutt jumped all over her, showering Tess with wet kisses.

Savannah came in and carefully ran her fingers over Elise's healed arm. "Good as new. Amazing, isn't she?"

"You're all amazing," Elise answered, meaning it totally.

She'd met Savannah and Gabrielle a short while before, when both women had come down to check on her soon after her arrival at the compound. Savannah with her gorgeous mocha complexion and velvet brown eyes, had instantly made Elise feel at home with her gentle, caring demeanor. Gabrielle was sweet as well, a ginger-haired beauty who seemed wise beyond her years. And then there was pretty, quiet Tess, who'd taken care of Elise as compassionately as she might her own kin.

Elise felt humbled before them all. Having been raised in the Darkhavens, where the warriors of the Order were considered at best to be an antiquated, dangerous faction within the vampire race—at worst, a deadly gang exercising vigilante justice—it was surprising to meet the intelligent, kind women who'd taken members of the Order as their mates. She couldn't see any one of these women binding herself to anything less than a male of honor and integrity. They were too smart for that, too confident in themselves.

Surprisingly, they seemed so pleasant and warm, not unlike the Darkhaven females Elise considered her friends.

"Since you're finished here, why don't both of you come with me?" Savannah said, breaking into Elise's thoughts. "Gabrielle and I just made some sandwiches and a fruit salad. You must be hungry, Elise."

"I am . . . or at least, I should be," she admitted quietly. It had been several hours since she'd eaten and her body felt depleted, in need of nourishment, but the idea of food held little appeal. Everything tasted bland, even the things she used to enjoy when Quentin was alive.

"How long has it been for you, Elise?" Savannah's tone was cautious, concerned. "I've heard that you lost your mate about five years ago . . ."

She knew what the woman was asking, of course. Had she gone so long without blood? In the Darkhavens it would be considered rude to ask questions about another female's blood bond with her mate—even worse to question a widow about whether or not she drew sustenance from another in her mate's absence—but here, among these women, there seemed no reason to hide the truth.

"Quentin was killed by a Rogue in the line of duty five years and two months ago. I haven't turned to anyone else for my needs—not any of them. Nor will I."

"Five years without Breed blood in you is a long time," Savannah acknowledged. Thankfully she didn't bring up the other implication in Elise's confession: that she hadn't taken another lover in all that time either.

"Your body is aging," Tess said, a look of curiosity in

her eyes, maybe sadness. "If you don't take another male as your mate—"

"Eventually I will die," Elise answered. "Yes, I know. Without Breed blood to sustain me in a state of perfect health, I need to work my muscles and keep fit, just like any other human. And, like any other human, my body will start to progress in years—it already has. In time, like any other human, I will succumb to old age."

Savannah's dark eyes were sympathetic. "That doesn't bother you, the thought of dying?"

"Only when I think that I might go to my grave without having made a difference in this world. That's why I . . ." She glanced down, still finding it difficult to speak about the thing that motivated her to leave the Darkhaven and begin another life. "I lost my son four months ago. He got involved with Crimson, and the drug turned him Rogue."

"Yes," Savannah said, reaching out to softly touch her shoulder. "We heard what happened. And how he died. I'm so sorry."

"So am I," Tess added. "At least the Crimson lab has been destroyed. Tegan saw to it personally."

Elise's head shot up in surprise. "What do you mean, personally?"

"He razed the place," Tess said. "It's all that Nikolai, Kade, and Brock have been talking about since they got back. Evidently Tegan went in by himself and single-handedly shut the operation down before the others had even arrived on scene. Then he burned the building to the ground."

"Tegan did that?" Elise was astonished. And she was fairly certain he'd implied the Order was responsible for shutting the lab down, not him personally. Why would he let her believe that if he had been the one responsible?

"Niko said Tegan came out of that burning warehouse like something out of a nightmare," Tess went on. "Then he walked off into the night without any explanation."

And from there he went to her apartment to look in on her, Elise realized now.

"Come on, let's talk some more while you eat. Gabrielle's waiting for us in the dining room upstairs."

The three women left the infirmary, Tess's little dog trotting after them, and walked a confusing maze of corridors into the heart of the Order's subterranean compound. They were nearly to an elevator when a glass door whisked open somewhere nearby and deep male voices filled the area. Elise recognized Sterling's voice among them, but he sounded rougher than normal, talking about night patrols and racking up his tally of Rogue kills like it was some kind of sport for him.

The other male's voice rolled with an exotic accent, making Elise picture turquoise ocean waves and golden sunsets. It was Dante, she realized, as the two armed warriors rounded the corner and the one walking with Sterling moved in to sweep Tess into a tight embrace.

"Hello, angel," he drawled and nuzzled his mouth against her neck while she laughed at the sudden amorous assault. His eyes flashed amber with the spark of his desire for his woman, emotion he didn't even attempt to hide.

"I missed you," she whispered, stroking his dark hair. "I always miss you."

"Well, I'm home now." The words were a deep rasp as he reached down and twined his fingers through hers.

Elise could see the tips of his fangs when he gave his Breedmate a slow, crooked smile. "And I'm thirsty for you, Tess."

The female's smile was full of longing. "I was just on my way to have a bite with my friends."

Savannah laughed. "I think you found something better. We'll save you a sandwich. Lord knows, you're probably going to need it."

Tess beamed over her shoulder as Dante led her away. The couple strode off together, leaving no one in the room in doubt of what would soon transpire privately between them.

When Tess's little terrier started barking as Dante led her away, Savannah bent down to pick up the dog. "Come on, you darling beast. I'll find something for you too." She glanced over at Elise. "I'm just going to go see what Gideon's up to in the lab. I'll be right back, okay?"

Elise nodded. And when she turned her head away from Dante and Tess's retreat, it was to find Sterling staring at her from across the corridor. His eyes scathed her, taking in her appearance—from the top of her shorn hair to her bloodstained shirt, pants, and damp winter boots. There was disapproval in his eyes, even worse than Tegan's initial reaction to her. She saw Sterling's gaze drift down to her hands, to her fingers, which were twisting anxiously at the hem of her shirt. He stared at her wedding band, a muscle ticking in his beard-shadowed jaw.

"Aren't you going to even say hello to me?" she asked him in the unbearable silence. "We have to talk to each other sometime, don't we?"

But Sterling didn't say a word.

With a vague shake of his head, he simply turned and strode away, leaving her alone in the long corridor.

Tegan tensed up as the lights flicked on over the estate's indoor pool. He'd gone there after making his call to the Berlin Darkhaven, looking for solitude and means of working off some excess steam. He was pissed but not surprised that Gideon hadn't been able to get a legitimate origin for Marek's FedEx shipment. The vampire's network of Minions had to be extensive. That journal had probably been handed off like a relay baton at half a dozen stops before arriving in Boston, just to muddy its trail.

As for the book itself, not even Savannah's impressive psychic ability to read the emotional history of an object had proved helpful there. All Gideon's Breedmate could cull from the journal was the deep madness—the mind-eating Bloodlust—of the one who had written on its pages.

Frustrated by it all, Tegan had swum a few laps, and now sat in the corner of the vaulted space, bare legs straddling a teakwood chaise, his hair and the brief black trunks clinging to his groin still damp from the water. He'd been enjoying the alone time and the darkness—or had been, until the rows of domed lights above the pool blinked on like interrogation room high beams.

He stood up, expecting to see Rio limp in with Tess for a round of therapy. But it wasn't either of them who came out of the shower room into the pool area.

It was Elise.

She didn't see him as she padded in barefoot, wearing a snow-white swimsuit that was sliced up the sides and held together by delicate bronze rings. The front of it plunged low, another ring centered between the perfect swell of her breasts. The daring suit was almost as big of a surprise as seeing her here; Tegan would never have guessed the reserved Darkhaven widow to look so right in such immodest clothing.

And goddamn, did she ever look right.

A deep, primal awareness stirred in him as he watched her draw away the spa towel she had slung around her neck. She let it fall to the tiles at the water's edge, then stepped down onto the first submerged step at the shallow end of the pool.

Soundlessly, Tegan inched his way back into the corner, hardly breathing in the thin shadows that concealed him. Even though it was clear that her body was leaner than it should be from want of fortifying Breed blood, Elise was lovely. She was beautifully formed, from the grace of her long legs and the gentle flare of her hips, to the slender curves of her waist, breasts, and delicate shoulders.

He had seen hints of her figure when she'd come out of the shower in her apartment last night, and when she'd lain unconscious on the futon, but the thick robe had hidden more than it revealed. The scrap of elastic white material she wore now only accentuated her assets. In a big way.

She strode down into the water, then began a slow swim toward the center of the pool. Abruptly, she dove under, disappearing from his view until she reemerged at the far end to come up for air. As her face broke the surface of the water, she opened her eyes and spotted him. Her little gasp echoed in the cavernous room.

"Tegan." She brought her arm up to hold on to the

edge of the pool, but kept her body submerged as if the water could shield her from his intrusive gaze. "I thought I was alone in here."

"So did I." He walked out under the lights, and didn't miss the flush of color in her cheeks as she quickly averted her eyes from his near nakedness.

He drew closer to the edge and smirked a bit as she moved away, going toward the center of the pool. "Your arm looks better."

"Tess took care of my wound," she said. "Gabrielle and Savannah fed me and gave me some fresh clothes. Savannah said it would be all right if I came up here for a swim . . ."

Tegan shrugged, watching her tread water, lithe arms and legs moving sinuously beneath the surface. "Do what you want. You don't need to explain anything to me."

She held his gaze across the pool. "Then why do you make me feel like I do?"

"Do I?"

Instead of answering, she pivoted and started swimming at an easy pace, putting more distance between them. "Were you able to find out anything about the journal?"

"Looking to change the subject, are you?" He watched her retreat toward the deep end, and for some absurd reason, it took every ounce of impulse control for him to not dive in and follow her. "We might have a lead on something in Berlin. I'm heading there tomorrow night."

"Berlin?" She reached for the lip of the pool and turned a frown on him. "What's in Berlin?"

"Someone we might be able to persuade into giving us information. Unfortunately, our best lead right now is a

Rogue. He's been cooling his jets in a holding tank for the past few years."

"A rehabilitation facility?" Elise asked. At Tegan's nod, she said, "Those places are controlled by the Enforcement Agency."

"So?"

"So, what makes you think they'll permit you inside? I'm sure you are aware that the Order doesn't have a lot of admirers in the Darkhavens. They have never approved of your methods when it comes to dealing with the problem of Breed vampires going Rogue."

He had to give the female credit: she was up on her politics, and she was right about the Enforcement Agency intending to block the Order's access to the captive Rogue. Tegan's call to his old ally in Berlin, Andreas Reichen, had only confirmed what he and Lucan expected. The only way they were getting near Petrov Odolf was through a lot of red tape and bureaucratic bullshit.

Assuming Reichen could get Tegan an audience at all.

Elise knew that too. "I have connections in the Agency. Maybe if I went with you . . ."

Tegan scoffed. "No way."

"Why not? Are you so stubborn that you would refuse my help even in something like this?"

"I work alone, that's why."

"Even if it means banging your head against a wall?" Now she laughed, stunning him with her open mockery. "I would have thought you were smarter than that, Tegan."

Anger pricked at him, but he held it back, refusing to let her bait him. With a shake of her head, Elise pivoted around and headed back for the shallow end, swimming with determined strokes. "I should leave," she murmured.

Tegan kept time with her, strolling along the edge of the pool. "Don't let me interrupt your swim. I was just on my way out anyway."

"I mean, I should leave the compound. It's obvious I don't belong here."

"You can't go back to your apartment now," he informed her curtly. "The Rogues will have turned the place inside out. Marek will have his spies embedded all over the neighborhood, looking for you."

"I know that." Her slim body glided through the water, nearly to the end of the pool. "I'm not foolish enough to think I can return there."

Tegan chuckled, satisfied that maybe she had come to her senses at last. "Then I guess Harvard has convinced you to go back to the Darkhaven?"

"Harvard? Is that what Sterling goes by now that he's one of you?"

"One of us," Tegan said, hearing the accusation in her clipped tone.

Not that she tried to conceal it.

She swam to the steps and came out of the water, evidently too piqued to care that Tegan was staring openly at her wet body. His eyes homed in on the birthmark riding the inner edge of her thigh, drawn there unerringly like a heat-seeking missile locked on target.

Saliva surged into his mouth as he watched rivulets of water slide down her smooth, bare thighs. His skin felt tight all over, heat moving in his veins, and in the *dermaglyph* markings that covered his body and declared him one of the Breed. His gums ached with the sudden press of his fangs. He clamped his jaws together, curbing the startling jolt of hunger.

He didn't want to look at the female, but damned if he could tear his eyes away from her now.

"Sterling hasn't convinced me of anything," she said as she grabbed her towel and covered herself with it. "He won't even speak to me, if you want to know the truth. I think he must hate me after what happened last fall."

Tegan studied her smart lavender eyes. "Is that really what you think—that he hates you?"

"Sterling was my mate's brother—by marriage, he is my brother. It would be completely improper—"

Tegan scoffed. "Men have gone to war with their own brothers for want of the same woman. Desire could give a damn about propriety."

Elise held the towel closed between her breasts and paced from him. "I don't like where this conversation is heading."

"Do you have feelings for him?"

"Of course not." She looked at Tegan, clearly, rightfully, appalled. "And what right have you to ask me that?"

None at all, but suddenly it was important to him that he know. He stood there, deliberately blocking her path if she even thought to duck away from him. "He desires you. He would take you into his bed if you'd let him. Hell, maybe he wouldn't even need your permission."

"Now you're just being rude."

"I'm only stating the truth. Don't tell me you weren't aware that Chase burns for you. Anyone with eyes in his head can see that."

"But only you would be coarse enough to speak it."

That pale purple gaze flashed with outrage and for a second he wondered if he was about to get slapped. He rather hoped he would. He wanted her angry. Wanted her hating him, especially now, when the scent of her warm, wet skin was drilling into his senses. Every curve of her petite body branding itself into his mind's eye.

He was close enough to take her in his hands. Too close, because at this intimate range, he could see the flutter of her pulse drumming frantically at her throat, and he was all too aware that there would be no one to stop him if he pulled her into his arms and took a forbidden taste of her.

"You hang your callousness on the excuse of truth," she said, a fierceness creeping into her voice. "So maybe you can tell me why you found it necessary to lie to me about what happened with the Crimson lab."

Tegan narrowed a hard look on her, the question raising some kind of alarm within him. "I didn't lie to you about anything."

She didn't flinch under his glare, only held his gaze steadier, challenging him. "It was you who destroyed the lab, not the Order. You personally, Tegan. No one else. I heard all about it."

A low hiss leaked out of him. He drew back, knowing he was the one retreating now, but unable to stop his hedging backward momentum. Elise moved with him, her wet, nearly naked body too close. Too goddamn tempting.

"Why would you do something like that, Tegan? I can't believe that you had any kind of personal stake in seeing the lab razed. So tell me. Why? Did you do it for me?"

He said nothing, incapable of speech and edging dangerously close to an emotion he did not want to feel.

She stared up at him fiercely. The silence was heavy, immovable. "Where's your truth now, warrior?"

Tegan forced a scoff, hearing the humorless laugh scrape in his throat. "I've warned you once, female. You're toying with fire. I won't be gentleman enough to warn you again."

Elise closed her eyes as Tegan snarled a curse and stalked away from her. She didn't dare move, hardly drew a breath in the moments Tegan's swift footsteps carried him to the pool's exit. She heard him leave. Only then did she allow herself to sag in relief.

What on earth was she thinking? Had she completely lost her mind, provoking a warrior like him toward anger?

And it was anger she saw in his expression. An unmistakable, smoldering fury had lit his bright green eyes as he'd stared at her, probably no less than an instant away from lashing out at her. Was she suicidal, like he'd accused her last night? Because if his ruthless reputation was anything to go by, pushing him like she had was liable to get her killed.

Except it wasn't anger she'd been looking for just now. She had wanted to see some kind of feeling in him . . .

Feelings he might have toward her.

Which was utterly foolish.

Still, she wondered. Had been wondering, ever since that early November night when Tegan had taken her home from the compound. Elise didn't want to think there was anything between them. Lord knew, she didn't need a complication like that in her life right now.

But in the tense moments before Tegan left the room, something had indeed been there.

Despite his cool demeanor, color had risen in his Gen

One *dermaglyphs.* The beautiful markings had swirled like elaborate, changeable tattoos across Tegan's muscular chest, arms, and torso . . . and down, beneath the tight black swimsuit that blatantly accentuated his profane sexuality.

And as she'd stood before him, close enough to feel his breath skate hotly across her skin, those incredible *glyphs* had begun to pulse in shades of burgundy, indigo, and gold—the colors of awakening desire.

CHAPTER
Twelve

Hey, T. Looks like you're Berlin bound tomorrow night," Gideon said as Tegan entered the tech lab. He scrubbed a hand through his spiky blond hair, disheveling it even worse than it had been before and amping up his usual geeky-genius look. "We just got FAA clearance for our private jet. The pilot will be waiting for you at Logan's corporate terminal at dusk. You'll have to stop to refuel in Paris, but you'll arrive in Berlin with about an hour to spare before dawn the following day."

Tegan acknowledged the news with a vague nod. It had been a couple of hours since his encounter with Elise at the pool, and his blood was still drumming in his temples, his body still alive with a tingling sense of aware-ness that was frankly starting to annoy him.

At least he had an escape plan. Tomorrow night he would be on his way out of the country, putting several thousand miles between him and the woman who was driving him to a very uncharacteristic distraction. It didn't look like his mission in Berlin was going to be easy; he would probably be gone for at least a week, maybe longer. Plenty of time for him to put Elise out of his mind.

Yeah, just like he'd done so effectively in the four months since he'd first met the female.

Taking her home that night from the compound had been a mistake. Stupid impulse—something he rarely in-dulged in, and, on the occasions he did, generally lived to regret. The way he reacted to her earlier tonight only drove that point home like the sharp edge of a blade.

He hungered for her, and he couldn't delude himself with the hope that she hadn't seen ample evidence of that fact. He hadn't been able to curb the transformation of his *glyphs* in her presence, let alone suppress his unwill-ing arousal just from being near her.

Jesus Christ, he needed to be gone, and gone soon.

Across the lab, Dante and Chase were going over tac-tics with Niko and the new recruits. A couple of heads lifted as Tegan strolled inside and dropped into a chair next to Gideon at the bank of computers and compound surveillance monitors.

"You all right?" Gideon asked, glancing at him from under an arched brow. "You're throwing off heat like a radiator."

"Never better." Tegan punched the speaker key on the telephone near his elbow. "Let's give Reichen the flight details and see if he's been able to get anywhere with the suits in charge of the containment facility."

Tegan dialed the private line of the Berlin Darkhaven and was immediately put through to Andreas Reichen.

"Everything is in order," he told the German vampire, not bothering with the pleasant hi-how-are-yas in his impatience to get the mission underway. "Expected arrival at Tegel Airport is two days from now just before sunrise. Think you can get me to your place before I go crispy?"

Reichen chuckled. "Of course. I will have a car waiting to retrieve you." His deep, accented voice rolled through the speaker. "It has been too long, Tegan. I have not forgotten my debt to you for your assistance with our little . . . problem over here a while ago."

Tegan remembered that time. The Berlin Darkhaven's *little problem* had entailed a string of Rogue attacks on its residents, several ending in grisly killings. Tegan had gone in as a one-man commando unit, tracking the Rogue cell into the thick forests of Grunewald then wiping out the Bloodlusting predators who'd been terrorizing the region. That had been, shit . . . almost two hundred years ago.

"We'll be square if you can get me inside that Enforcement Agency facility," he told Reichen.

"Ah, that is resolved, my friend. The head of security phoned only moments before you called. The Director of the Agency here in Berlin gave specific license for access to the facility. There is no issue with permitting your emissary into the facility to question Petrov Odolf."

"My emissary . . ."

As the words left his mouth and suspicion started to simmer in his blood, Tegan heard the soft whisk of the tech lab's glass doors as they slid open to let someone inside. He knew who that someone was, even before he saw Chase's jaw go tight across the room. Tegan pivoted around in his wheeled chair and found Elise standing there, looking guilty as sin.

"What the hell have you done?"

"It wasn't my doing," Reichen said over the speaker. "I assumed it was something you initiated . . ."

The German leader of the Berlin Darkhaven was still talking but Tegan wasn't hearing a word. Elise walked forward, her steps a bit halting. One of the other Breedmates had given her a change of clothes. The purple knit tunic and dark blue jeans were an improvement over the havoc of the revealing swimsuit, but it still didn't totally conceal her petite, feminine lines.

Which only pissed Tegan off more.

"Whatever you think you're doing, forget it. I told you, I work alone."

"Not this time. The arrangements are already in place with the Agency and the containment facility. They are expecting me."

"This must be a fucking joke."

"I'm completely serious. I'm going with you."

Tegan dismissed her with a brief look and went back to his call with Reichen. "There will be no Darkhaven emissary accompanying me. Just me alone, Andreas, and we're still getting in to see that Rogue, even if we have to break into—"

"Tegan, I think you misunderstand." Elise's voice was unwavering behind him and dangerously bold. "I wasn't asking for your permission."

He froze, stunned at the woman's nerve. "I'll be in touch," he told Reichen, then severed the connection with an overzealous punch of the keypad.

"I'm the one who delivered the journal to the Order," Elise said as he turned a glare on her. "Without me, you wouldn't have known anything about the individual you mean to question. Without me, you won't be permitted to get within viewing range of him, let alone speak to him. I am going with you."

Tegan vaulted out of his chair. Elise leaped back, startled—the first show of good sense he'd seen in her since she walked into the lab. He pinned her with a narrow stare that swept with scathing, deliberate slowness from her flushing cheeks to the tips of her borrowed shoes. "You're in no condition for travel. Look at you— you're weak, little more than skin and bones. We won't even talk about the fact that you can hardly be near humans without inviting vicious migraines and nosebleeds."

"I will manage."

He scoffed. "How?"

She frowned, dropping her gaze as Tegan's voice boomed around them.

"What are you going to do between now and then— solicit the vein of a vampire to bolster your strength? Because that's what it would take."

Her cheeks went suddenly awash in color.

"Maybe one of them will offer to service you," Tegan said, ruthless now, indicating the other warriors who were watching the exchange in tense silence.

"Shit, Tegan," Gideon cautioned beside him. "Lighten up, for crissake."

Tegan tuned out everything but the Darkhaven female's shocked expression. "That's what it would take, Elise—Breed blood coursing through your body. Nothing less. Without it, your talent will continue to rule you, as it does now. You'll only be a liability."

He saw the outrage spark in her eyes, but it was her humiliation that struck him like a blow to the gut. It was considered crass in the extreme to speak publicly of the blood bonds between a female and her mate—even worse, to speak of it in mixed company.

To suggest that an unbonded Breedmate take a male for sustenance alone was beyond profane.

"I am a widow," she said quietly. "I am in mourning—"

"Five years," Tegan reminded her, his voice sounding tight even to his own ears. "Where will you be in another five? Or ten? You're letting yourself die on your feet and you know it. Don't ask me to help you get there faster."

She stared up at him mutely, her delicate throat working as she swallowed what was likely a sob. Maybe a curse that he go straight to hell, which was probably where he was heading even before this ugly display.

"You're right, Tegan," she whispered, not a trace of weakness or any hitch in her voice. "You are right . . . and I concede that you've made your point."

With squared shoulders, she pivoted around and walked calmly out of the lab, a vision of stoic dignity. Tegan felt like an ass, watching her leave in rigid silence. After she disappeared from view, he exhaled a sharp curse.

"What the fuck are you looking at?" he barked to Chase, who had risen from the table he'd been seated at. The ex-Darkhaven agent had his hand curled around the butt of a handgun that was holstered across his chest. His expression was nothing short of murderous.

"Screw this," Tegan growled. "I'm outta here."

Not surprisingly, Chase was right on his heels. He gave Tegan's shoulder a hard shove as the two of them exited to the corridor outside the lab.

"You son of a bitch. She didn't deserve that kind of treatment—least of all from someone like you."

No, she didn't. But it was necessary. There was no way in hell he was going to put himself in close quarters again with Elise, let alone make her his accomplice on this mission to Berlin. He'd needed to shut her down, and shut her down hard. So what if he'd made himself into a bigger asshole for doing it publicly. He'd only fortified what everyone already thought of him.

Tegan met Chase's furious look and affected a callous smile. "You care so much about the female, Harvard? Why don't you go console her like you're burning to do. Just do us all a favor and keep her the fuck away from me."

Chase got up in his face, blue eyes flashing raw anger. "You're a real dick, you know that?"

"Yeah?" Tegan shrugged. "Last time I checked, I wasn't campaigning for any Mr. Congeniality awards."

"Arrogant motherf—"

Parting his lips, Tegan hissed through his lengthening fangs as he bore down on Chase, cutting off the further round of insult. He half hoped the irate vampire would push him into a fight. Part of him craved to know Chase's feelings of torment and rage, and as torqued as he was right now, he wouldn't turn down a chance to bruise his knuckles in a little hand-to-hand.

But Dante smoothly intervened, coming out of the lab at that very second to grab Chase's arm and physically pull the warrior out of Tegan's path. "Shit, Harvard. Don't go getting yourself killed now that I've almost got you trained. What a friggin' waste that would be, eh?"

After a few seconds of interference, Chase simmered down, but his eyes were still hot on Tegan even as Dante tugged him up the corridor. In the lab, Gideon was back at his keyboard. Nikolai, Brock, and Kade got back to business too, all of them acting as though Tegan hadn't just come off like a heartless bastard in front of a defenseless female.

Tegan cursed low under his breath. He had to get the hell out of there, and the way things were going, tomorrow night's flight to Berlin wasn't going to be soon enough.

He had somewhere he could go—the place he always went when shit started bearing down on him. Sometimes he'd disappear there for nights on end; none of his brethren in the Order had ever been there. It was his own private hell, a forsaken, hollow place, filled with death. Right about now, it sounded like a fucking holiday.

Elise stood in the center of a large, mostly vacant chamber in the compound, feeling as if she'd had the wind knocked out of her. She was still shaking from her confrontation with Tegan, but whether it was from humiliation or anger, she wasn't sure. What he'd done to her in front of his brethren was inexcusable, incredibly cold. He had to know that what he suggested was blasphemous and profanely insulting—not just to her, but to the warriors who'd been in the room to hear it. Only the lowest females living among the Breed would engage in a blood bond without a solemn commitment and a deeply shared love.

The blood bond was the most sacred communion between a Breedmate and the male she chose as her own. The ultimate intimacy, it was very often a sexual act, and one never entered into lightly. To use a vampire's blood only to further one's longevity and strength was simply not done. Not by anyone Elise knew.

But she couldn't deny that Tegan's observations of her had been the truth.

What he'd said was cruel and crude . . . and utterly accurate. She was willingly wasting away, which was her prerogative as a widowed Breedmate. But she wanted to have an active part in thwarting the Rogues, and it was foolish of her to think she could do so if she continued on as she was.

Elise glanced at the barren room around her. The white, windowless walls contained no color at all—no pleasing art or photographs, like she'd seen in the rest of the compound. No sofa, no electronic equipment or computers, no books. Nothing of personal expression at all.

Near the far wall stood a tall black cabinet, and a black wooden bench beside it, underneath which was two pairs of large black leather boots, arranged with military precision. There was a large bed in the adjacent room, but even that wasn't particularly inviting. Just gunmetal gray sheets and a coal-colored blanket folded neatly at the foot of the king-sized mattress. Elise had never seen a soldiers' barracks, but she imagined they'd look like this . . . maybe not this cold and impersonal.

She knew where she was, of course. She'd known where she was heading when she navigated the labyrinth of corridors after removing herself from the embarrassment she'd endured in the Order's control room.

She knew what she was about to do now, but that didn't make her heart skip any less frantically when she heard Tegan's hard gait approaching from outside the open door of his private quarters.

That long-legged stride slowed, then ceased altogether

as the air stirred coldly, announcing his arrival. His immense body filled the door frame, muscular arms crossed
over his chest, his powerful, denim-clad thighs spread in a
battle stance. He didn't speak at first, but there was no
need for words when his emerald-green eyes narrowed
on her, as sharp as gemstones and as cold as a glacier.

"Tegan—"

"If you're looking for an apology, you can forget it."

Elise held that menacing gaze as she forced herself to
approach him. "I'm not here for that," she told him, surprised there was no tremor in her voice for the way her
pulse was skittering in her veins. "I came here to tell you
that you were right back there. I do need the strength of a
blood bond, but I'm not looking for a mate. I need an
uncomplicated arrangement, with someone who isn't
going to care what I do, or when I walk away . . . so I
choose you."

CHAPTER
Thirteen

Every smartass, apathetic reply that might have sprung to his lips fled, along with all the blood in his brain. Tegan stood there in the doorway of his private apartments, struck stupid with shock at what he just heard.

He sure as hell never saw this coming.

And although all good sense told him to deny Elise's proposal—shut the goddamn idea down before another second passed—his mouth didn't seem capable of speech. An erotic mental image burned instantly into his mind: Elise's lips pressed against his skin, her sweet pink tongue lapping at him, her mouth drawing deeply from his vein.

He wanted that, he realized in a flash of disbelief.

Wanted it so bad he shuddered with the force of it.

"Jesus Christ," he muttered, finding his voice at last. "You're insane. And I'm leaving. I only came to grab a few of my things and I'm out of here."

When he stalked forward, meaning to dismiss her and her ludicrous suggestion without another word, Elise moved into his way. He glared down at her, but she didn't so much as flinch under the deadly look that would have withered warriors and Rogues alike.

"What are you running from, Tegan?" Soft lavender eyes fixed on him in defiant challenge. "I'm sure it can't be me scaring you off."

He scoffed at the idea, refusing to let her see how close to the mark she might be. "Do you know what you're asking for? If you take my blood, a part of you will be linked to me for as long as I'm alive. It's an unbreakable connection."

"I know very well what the blood bond entails. All of it."

Her sudden flush seemed to indicate that she was also aware of the sexual nature of the act. Vampire blood had a highly aphrodisiac quality. In females without the Breedmate mark, the effect was often a rush of fierce desire; in females like Elise, who were capable of bearing Breed offspring, the drinking of Breed blood nearly always sent them into a heated sexual hunger that demanded to be slaked.

"I'm not what you're used to," he told her sternly, the only warning he could think of now. "Don't think that I'll be gentle with you. I wouldn't show you any mercy."

Her little smile was mocking. "I'd hardly expect that you would."

With that, she turned and strode away from him, her

spine impeccably erect as she went into his bedroom to await him. Tegan raked his fingers through his hair, knowing he had about two seconds to get a grip on himself and walk away from this certain disaster. Any longer for him to think about it, and he didn't know if he'd have the will to refuse her.

In the adjacent room, he heard the soft clop of Elise's shoes hitting the rug as she took them off. If he thought he could scare her out of going through with this, apparently all he'd done was fortify her resolve. She'd thrown a gauntlet here, and he had never been the kind of male to back down from a challenge.

Even now, when every survival instinct he possessed was clamoring for him to turn tail and run from a situation that had catastrophe written all over it.

Long moments ticked by.

And still she waited.

Tegan growled a dark oath.

Then, with hardly a conscious thought to command it, he brought the door to his apartments closed with the will of his mind and headed for the bedroom after her.

Some of Elise's resolve wavered as Tegan came in behind her to his bedroom. There was a savage intensity in his slow steady stride and in the unblinking gaze trained on her. Suddenly she felt as if she were standing before a predator while it measured its options, preparing to close in for the kill.

"How do you want . . ." She let the words trail off, uncertain how to proceed now that she actually had him here. "Where shall I . . . ?"

"The bed," came his flat reply.

He began pulling off his black knit shirt, baring his *glyph*-marked torso. Their normal henna hue was deepening now, no longer the neutral shade indicating a placid mood, but blushing darker, the patterns beginning to saturate. Elise sat down on the very edge of the mattress and turned her head to avert her eyes from him. She heard the crush of fabric as Tegan set the shirt aside and came nearer to the bed.

"You're overdressed," he said, his warm breath tickling the side of her bare neck.

His presence so close to her was almost as startling as his words. Elise turned an anxious glance on him. "You mean for me to disrobe? I don't see why I sh—"

"You will," he said, leaving no room for argument. "If I were a cultured Darkhaven male and not the crude warrior that I am, I doubt you'd expect me to receive you fully clothed."

It was true. Respect for the act of blood-bonding between vampire and Breedmate demanded that both parties come to each other without concealment, coercion, or reservation. Naked in body, commitment, and intent.

Tegan reached down to unfasten the zipper on his low-slung blue jeans.

As they sagged on his trim pelvis, Elise's eyes fell unwillingly to the ridges of taut muscle that defined him, and to the trailing pattern of *dermaglyphs* that quite obviously continued all the way down to his naked, swelling groin. He wore nothing beneath, she realized in a state of instant panic.

"Please," she gasped. "Tegan, please. Will you . . . leave them on?"

He didn't reply, but he slowly pulled the denim back together and dragged the zipper up. She couldn't help noticing that the button at the top stayed undone, baring a small vee of his smooth tawny skin.

"That's the only request you get tonight," he said in a deep rasp. "You still have time to reconsider. But not much. Now disrobe, or ask me nicely to let you leave."

He was testing her. She knew he was deliberately pushing her now, probably so sure that he could make her change her mind with a few menacing words.

Really, she should be afraid. Not just of being alone with a warrior like Tegan, but also of the intimate, sacred act she was about to defile by drinking from a male she had no intention of taking as her mate. Truly, she degraded them both by asking Tegan to service her like this, and if he was disgusted by the thought—or by her—she could hardly blame him.

"What's it going to be, Elise?"

She stood up, too aware of him watching her, waiting for her to bolt. With only the slightest tremble in her fingers, she began to lift the hem of her tunic and drew it up over her head.

Tegan's warm breath ceased. He went utterly still beside her, but she could feel heat rolling off him as she set her top down on the bed.

She crossed her arms over the modest white cotton bra she wore, and turned a questioning look on him.

When Tegan finally spoke, his voice was thick, obstructed by the points of his gleaming white fangs. "Your pants too. You can keep the rest on for now."

She stripped out of her jeans as quickly as she could, then sat back down on the edge of the bed.

"Move to the middle, and face me sitting on your knees."

As she scooted to the center of the king-sized mattress,

Tegan came up onto the bed as well. He prowled forward on his knees, until only a foot of space separated them. The pupils in the heart of his green irises began to thin, narrowing down by degrees into vertical slits. When he parted his lips to speak, his fangs seemed enormous.

"Last chance, Elise."

She gave a shake of her head, incapable of talk now. Tegan snarled something nasty under his breath, then brought his wrist up to his mouth. With his eyes on hers, he bared his fangs and sank them into the flesh below his palm.

Dark red blood dripped from the wound, falling softly, steadily, onto the gray sheets.

"Come here," he said, holding his arm out to her, his lips stained crimson from his bite.

With her eyes closed, heart stuttering in her breast, Elise leaned forward. She put her hands under his thick forearm and carefully lifted his bleeding punctures to her mouth. There, she hesitated, knowing there would be no turning back. With one taste, she would be bound to this deadly male. Aware of him always, like a living warmth buzzing in her veins, until the time should come that one or the other of them would die.

But she would be stronger too.

Her psychic torment would be lessened, far easier to manage. Her body would rejuvenate, require less work to keep it fit and healthy.

Her promise to Camden wouldn't feel so hollow once she had some of Tegan's power coursing through her veins.

But to use him like this?

She glanced up and found him staring down at her, his lips peeled back and glistening, his breath raking coarsely through his teeth. His *dermaglyphs* were livid with color now, strikingly beautiful on so much sculpted muscle and golden skin.

"Do it," he snarled, that fierce gaze daring her to take him to her mouth . . . damning her for it.

Elise bent down over his wrist and carefully opened her mouth to receive him. The instant her lips touched his skin, Tegan hissed, arcing sharply. Elise drew gently, using her tongue to lap at the twin openings in his skin. His blood was hot and tingly as it slid down her throat, filling her with a heat that soon became a roar of swelling, compounding power.

It hit her so fast, she moaned from the intensity, feeling instantly overwhelmed. Warmth boiled through her limbs and into her core, pulsing hard, rolling like a tide.

She hadn't been prepared for such a swift, stunning reaction. Inside she was molten, going liquid and boneless . . . wanton.

When she tried to pull away, Tegan placed his palm on the back of her head. His large fingers spanned her skull, burrowing through her hair. There was no denying his strength, yet the pressure he held her with was light. But it was also unyielding.

Elise glanced up at him, anxious now. Maybe this wasn't a good idea at all. Maybe she'd been wrong.

Tegan's eyes glittered, pupils swamped by fiery amber.

"You shouldn't have started if you weren't prepared to finish." His face was starkly serious, unforgiving. "Take more. You know you need it."

Her breath sawed out of her at his invitation. God help her, but she did need more. Already she could feel Tegan's blood mixing with her own, pounding in her temples. She licked her lips, savoring the wild, powerful taste of him on her tongue.

Tegan's jaw went visibly rigid.

"Christ," he ground out tightly. His fingers were a searing presence across her nape and up along the back of her head. He could have pushed her down so easily, but he only held her there, tender beneath all that coiled Breed power. "Take more of me, Elise."

Panting now, every nerve ending firing off inside her like a hail of sensory explosions, she lowered her head and latched on to him once more.

Tegan sucked in a sharp breath as Elise fastened her mouth to his wrist and took another long pull from his opened veins. She moaned as she swallowed more and more of him. Her hunger was rising. Greed for more made her pull harder, deeper, even as she quenched herself on him. Her tongue was a moist, hot demand against his skin, but it was the light scrape of her teeth that made Tegan's sex surge even harder than it already was.

He knew he wasn't alone in his arousal. He could feel her body's response; he absorbed her thoughts and emotions through his fingertips, which were buried in the silky layers of her short blond hair, resting against the warmth of her nape. He indulged in a brief few strokes of her soft skin, then drew his hand away when the sensations became too intense.

Jesus, she was on fire with need—both the physical thirst and the carnal one that Breed blood inspired in females bearing the teardrop-and-crescent-moon birthmark.

Absurdly, Tegan fought to distance himself from the

gravity of what was happening. He tried to occupy his mind with a clinical mental inventory of her features— anything to dull the erotic movements of her mouth on him—but it was no use. Elise was too real, too damn hot, the way her spine arched and snaked with each long draw of her mouth. Her breath heaved, rapid and deep, and her lips were making deliciously wet noises in the quiet of the room.

Her eyelids flicked open as if to beg permission and Tegan was struck by the lovely amethyst color of her irises now that hunger and desire had darkened them. Her cheeks were pinkening already from his blood in her system, her lips stained a glossy, beautiful red where they held fast to his wrist.

"Finish it," he told her, his tongue thick, his own mouth dry as bone. "Take your fill."

With a throaty groan, Elise pushed him down onto his back and followed him there, never breaking contact as she crawled alongside him on the bed, his arm raised to accommodate her continued feeding.

Even though he was hard as granite in his jeans, Tegan wanted to remain detached from the entire catastrophe playing out before him. He needed to tune out the incredibly desirable woman who was now writhing against him in nothing but a modest cotton bra and panties, throwing off erotic heat like a furnace.

And her emotion was swamping him. Her need was so raw, so honest.

Christ, he had forgotten what that felt like. He didn't want to think about how long it had been since he'd lain with a woman. Didn't want to acknowledge how empty— how willfully chaste, physically and emotionally—his life had been for the past five centuries.

He didn't want to think about Sorcha. . . .

He couldn't think about her, not when Elise was driving him to the edge with every moan and sigh and catlike slide of her body next to him. To his surprise, he wanted very much to touch her—not to flex his psychic talent a little more, but to just touch her.

Reaching over with his free hand, Tegan traced his fingers along the smooth line of her shoulder and upper arm. A spray of gooseflesh rose along the trail he'd made on her skin. Beneath the thin white cotton of her bra, her nipples tightened into hard pearls. He brushed his thumb over one pebbled bud, his breath catching in the back of his throat as she arched into him uninhibited, the blood fever from her feeding making her know no shame.

He could take her, Tegan knew. She probably expected it, since it was rare that the act of blood-drinking with a Breedmate would end without sex to relieve a female of her need.

But he'd told her no mercy, and a cruel part of him wanted to make good on that promise.

Especially since he was the one being used in this scenario.

Elise's legs flexed and scissored as he continued his tactile exploration of her body. He traced his fingers along the dip of her flat stomach, then up the graceful flare of her hip. She was liquid in her movements, undulating and arching as her suckling at his wrist became more urgent. With a low, breathy moan, she opened her legs for him and moved his hand down where she wanted him. She clamped her thighs together, holding him to her and grinding when he hesitated to touch her on his own.

It was too much to resist, even for him.

He brushed his fingers along the moist cleft shielded

by her panties and she jerked as if he touched her with an open flame. He stroked her again, with more purpose, feeling her need ratchet tighter with every slide of his fingers.

"Tegan," she gasped, turning her head aside to look at him with dazed, brilliant eyes, "Tegan . . . please . . . do something."

She put her hand down on his, but he was already in motion. He slid his fingers beneath the scrap of damp cotton between her legs. Flossy curls were drenched and slick, the petals of her sex giving way easily as he glided his thumb along the delicate valley between them.

God, she was so soft. Like velvet and satin.

And the scent of her . . .

The fragrance of her arousal was a shattering combination of heather and roses and fresh spring rain.

"Please," she whispered, forcing him into an urgent rhythm when he might have taken his time to savor her.

But her need was too far gone. He'd threatened no mercy, and while he knew he was a coldhearted bastard, he couldn't deny her relief.

"Drink some more," he said, his voice reduced to coarse gravel in his throat. "I'll take care of the rest."

Elise obeyed him, fastening onto his wrist as Tegan stroked her toward a shattering release. She came apart in wave after wave of shuddering pleasure, her blunt human teeth biting down hard on him as her climax rippled through her body.

By the time it was over, Tegan's fangs were throbbing, his cock straining to be freed and buried deep inside the wet, hot core of Elise's body. He drew his hand away from her, his senses swamped with the intoxicating perfume of sex and blood and warm, languid woman.

He wanted to spread her legs wide and mount her like an animal. Wanted it so badly his head was pounding with the urge to rip away the denim she'd made him keep on and fall on her in a savage, lustful fury.

Oh, yeah.

That's just what he needed to do to really take this bad situation and send it straight into a goddamn nuclear-grade disaster.

What he really needed was to get the fuck out of there.

Too bad he hadn't done that before she'd managed to goad him into giving her his vein.

With a growl of frustration, Tegan eased his arm out from under Elise's slack mouth and brought the wounds to his lips. He sealed the punctures with his tongue, licking away the last of the blood and trying not to taste Elise on his skin. He even failed at that.

"I have to go," he said, unwilling to look at her and be tempted into more idiocy in one night. He moved to the far edge of the bed and swung his feet down onto the floor. He grabbed his shirt and yanked it over his head. "If you insist on going with me to Berlin, be ready tomorrow night. We leave promptly at dusk."

CHAPTER
Fourteen

The wait until the following evening seemed unending to Elise. She'd gotten dressed and crept out of Tegan's quarters in absolute shame immediately after he left her there, somehow managing to find her way to the room Gabrielle had prepared for her elsewhere in the compound without being seen. Once inside the comfortable suite, she had holed up like a hermit, feigning a headache so that she could take her meals in privacy and not have to face scrutiny from the other women—or, God forbid, any of the warriors—for anything they may know about what had transpired between Tegan and her.

Not that Tegan would have spoken of what they'd done.

She had most certainly disgusted him, if not by her use of him as her blood Host, then most definitely by her humiliatingly base reaction during the event. She could hardly stand to think on it now, and she didn't suppose an apology to Tegan would be enough to excuse her behavior.

Supposing he would even give her a chance to attempt one.

In the nearly twenty hours that he'd been gone, it didn't appear that anyone had heard from him at all. He hadn't said where he was going—just put on his clothes and a pair of black combat boots, then left Elise alone in his quarters like he couldn't bear to be near her for another second. Understandable, of course. She had embarrassed them both.

Part of her considered abandoning the idea of going with him to Berlin—to save what was left of her pride, if nothing else. But she had already taken things this far, and it was a little late to turn back now.

She could feel Tegan's blood inside her, the low hum of power that beat in her temples and in each of her pulse points. Five years without Breed blood in her body had sapped her of more than she realized, but drinking from Tegan was a revelation. She felt him flowing through her muscles, bones, and cells, giving her a vitality she had almost forgotten was possible. Even her senses were tuning up, becoming more acute, just after that one taste from the warrior's Gen One veins.

And because of that blood connection to him, she felt the precise moment when Tegan entered the compound. He was there, somewhere, his arrival like a light blinking on in a shadowed corner of her mind.

This was the connection she could never break with him now—this bone-deep awareness of him. She would always be drawn to Tegan, conscious of him on an elemental level, until the day that one or the other of them died.

God, what had she done?

Elise paced the living room of her guest quarters, anxious now that the time was coming that she would be leaving with Tegan for Berlin. Maybe she should venture out into the compound to find him and make sure that he didn't intend to depart without her. Maybe she should wait for him to come to her?

She heaved a sigh and started for the door—

At the very second a knock sounded on the other side.

It wasn't Tegan; her senses told her that much. Elise opened the door and was stunned to find a familiar face outside.

"Oh." She glanced down, surprised and shamed. "Hello, Sterling."

She couldn't look at him now, especially when he was standing there with genuine concern in his eyes.

"I heard you weren't feeling well. Savannah said you've been in here alone all day, so I . . . I wanted to check and make sure you're all right."

Elise nodded. "I'm fine. Just a headache. To be honest, I needed some time alone."

"Of course." Sterling's voice was schooled, almost awkwardly so. He let a long moment pass before he spoke again. "I cannot believe what he did to you in the lab, why he felt the need to say what he did—"

"No, don't. Don't feel sorry for me. There is no need, Sterling."

He exhaled sharply, anger radiating from his stiff stance in the doorway. "Tegan was way out of line. He had no right to speak to you like that. I don't expect him to have honor enough to apologize for what he subjected you to, so I've come to do it for him."

"You don't have to," she said, looking up into those familiar, flinty blue eyes.

"Yes, I do," he insisted. "And not just for Tegan's behavior, but for my own as well. Ah, Christ, Elise. What happened to Camden that night outside the Darkhaven . . . I'm so sorry. I'm so damned sorry for everything that happened. If I could have traded places with him—if it could have been me who'd gone Rogue . . . me in front of that gun when the trigger was pulled . . ."

"I know." She reached out to her brother-in-law, and gently squeezed his muscled forearm. "I'm sorry too."

He gave her a grim look, tried to dismiss her regret with a stiff shake of his head.

But she couldn't let the rest go unsaid now.

"Yes, hear me out, please. I blamed you for Camden's death, Sterling, and that was wrong of me. You did everything you could to save him. I know what it cost you. I am the one owing an apology. You felt responsible for him . . . for me . . . and I let you shoulder that burden when I shouldn't have. It wasn't fair to you."

Something tender moved across his features. "You were never a burden."

"Not yours, certainly," she said, as gentle as she could be. "It was wrong of me that I never pointed that fact out to you. I should have made sure you understood how I felt."

He went rigid at the words, his jaw going tight.

"Sterling, I never meant to hurt you, or to make you think we might in any way, at any time—"

"You were never anything but proper, Elise."

His clipped, careful tone was brittle to her ears. "But I still hurt you."

He slowly shook his head. "All of my decisions have been my own. You've done nothing to regret."

"Don't be so certain of that," she murmured, thinking on all her past mistakes, not the least of which would probably prove to be the blasphemy of a blood bond she'd instigated with Tegan.

She felt the warrior's presence getting stronger within her, and knew that wherever he was in the compound now, he was coming closer. She could feel him in the warmth skating along her limbs, and in the prickle of the fine hairs at the back of her neck.

"I appreciate your concern, Sterling, truly. But everything is fine. I'm fine."

His light brown brows were knit together in a scowl. "You don't look fine. You look flushed. You have goose bumps on your arms."

"It's nothing."

He stared at her face, which was probably pink with color from both the recent nourishment of Tegan's blood and the sudden flood of embarrassment that Sterling would soon guess the cause of her discomfort for himself.

That dawning came over him instantly. It was evident in the fall of his expression, then the glowering rage that filled his eyes with indigo fire.

"What did he do to you?"

"Nothing," she said, awash in humiliation but through no fault of Tegan's.

"You drank from him."

It was an accusation that Elise could not deny. "It's nothing. Don't worry about me—"

"Did he belittle you into thinking you had to do this? Did he . . . *seduce you* into drinking from him?" Sterling hissed an oath, his fangs emerging in his rage. "I'll fucking kill him. If he forced you, I swear to you, that bastard will pay—"

"Tegan didn't force me to do anything. I went to him. It was my choice. I asked him to let me use him. It was my doing, Sterling. Not any of his."

"You went to him?" He looked at her as if she'd slapped him. "You drank from him by choice. Jesus, Elise . . . *why?* "

"Because I made a promise to Camden that I'd do whatever I could to make sure no one else was hurt by the Rogues or those who serve them. I made a vow, but I can't live up to it if my body isn't strong. Tegan was right. I needed Breed blood, and he gave it to me."

Sterling raked his hand through his hair, then over his face. When he reached out to take hold of her shoulders, his eyes were wild with pain, his fingers gripping her hard.

"You didn't have to demean yourself with a stranger, Elise. Goddamn it, you could have come to me. You should have come to me!"

She jumped at the harsh spike in his voice, and at the ferocity of his handsome face. When she tried to slip out of his strong grasp, he only held tighter.

"I would have taken care of you. I would have treated you right. Don't you know that?"

"Sterling, please let go of me. You're hurting me."

"I'd do as the lady asks, Harvard."

The cool command issued from just a few feet away in the corridor. Tegan stood there, garbed in a graphite-colored sweater and black pants. His arms were crossed, one thick shoulder leaning against the white marble wall.

Everything about his stance said he couldn't be both-ered with the little conflict playing out between Elise and her deceased mate's brother, but Tegan's eyes told a different story. His stare was locked on Sterling, unblinking. Threatening in its steady hold on the other male.

Elise brought her hands up to touch the ones still gripping her like a vise. "Sterling, please . . ."

He looked at her, stricken, and let go at once. "I'm sorry. Now I'm the one who's overstepped my bounds. This won't happen again, I promise you."

"Damn right it won't," Tegan said, his tone oddly protective even though he hadn't moved from his position across the corridor. As Sterling backed off, clearly distressed by his uncharacteristic display, Tegan finally glanced away from him to look at Elise. "The plane is ready. Are you coming or not?"

Elise swallowed, and gave a wobbly nod of her head. "I am."

Awkwardly, she inched away from Sterling. She felt his eyes on her as she slipped out into the hallway. The weight of her brother-in-law's sullen stare remained with her as she fell in beside Tegan and walked the length of the corridor at his side.

Chase stood in the hallway long after Elise and Tegan disappeared from view. He couldn't pretend he was surprised that Elise rejected him. That hurt had been a long time coming, and one he knew he'd brought upon himself.

She had never been his, no matter how he had wished things to be different. She had belonged to his brother. In her heart she probably still did, even though she'd finally traded her mourning widow's whites for street clothes.

And now a part of her belonged irrevocably to Tegan.

That was the truth that stunned him most. Tegan, the deadliest of the Order, the coldest. The one with the least regard for life—his own, or anyone else's.

Yet in her need, Elise had turned to him.

Had Tegan bedded her in the process? Chase refused to consider that likelihood, although it would be virtually unheard of for a Breed vampire to put a female to his vein and not be overcome with the sexual impulse to take her body in return. Tegan wasn't one to brag about his conquests—in all the months Chase had been among the Order, he'd never once heard a single boast of any kind from the warrior—but the many nights Tegan spent unaccounted for outside the compound left little doubt that the warrior had his own private itches to scratch. A sheltered female like Elise was probably no more than a moment's amusement to an icy individual like Tegan.

"Goddamn it," Chase muttered, pounding the corridor wall with his fist. It was a futile exercise that only brought him more pain. But right now, he welcomed the hurt. He wanted to bleed. So much the better if he could take out a few Rogues in the process.

He stalked up the hallway and found Dante hanging outside the tech lab with Niko, Brock, and Kade. All of them were armed like Chase, suited up for the night's patrol topside.

Dante gave him a cautious nod of greeting as he approached, his whiskey-colored eyes narrowing thoughtfully. "They're gone," he said, as if Chase ought to be relieved to hear it. "You okay, Harvard?"

"Do I look like I need a fucking group hug?" he snapped. "I'll be a hell of a lot better once my feet are on pavement and my hand's stained with Rogue blood.

Anyone game to smoke some suckheads tonight, or would you all rather stand around here thinking about it?"

He didn't wait for an answer, just headed off for the compound's elevator with dark, deadly purpose, the other warriors falling in behind him.

CHAPTER
Fifteen

Elise dozed most of the nine hours in flight to Berlin. Tegan, however, remained awake. He'd never particularly enjoyed the modern modes of transportation, and while he could appreciate the efficiency of jet travel, propelling himself more than thirty thousand feet above ground at five hundred miles an hour while trapped inside several tons of metal ranked about dead last on his list of favorite things to do.

He was relieved to feel the private jet begin its gradual descent once they reached Berlin's Tegel Airport. A few minutes later, the sleek aircraft's wheels touched down on terra firma.

"We're here," he told Elise when the soft bump of the landing roused her awake.

She stretched demurely, hiding a yawn behind her hand. "Was I asleep all this time?"

Tegan shrugged. "You needed the rest. Your body is still adjusting to the blood you consumed. It can take a day or two to level out."

She blushed a shade much deeper than the pink color that had come back into her cheeks from her feeding the night before. Turning her face as if to hide her reaction from him, she lifted the shade on the small oval window beside her and looked out over the predawn cityscape below.

"It's beautiful," she said, her voice pleasingly rough from sleep. "I've never been to Berlin. Have you?"

"Once. It was a long time ago."

She shot him a half-smile of acknowledgment from across the minimalist elegance of the fuselage, then glanced away again. They hadn't spoken of what happened between them, and Tegan had zero interest in cracking open the topic himself. Bad enough he'd been unable to get the sight of her—the incredibly silken feel of her—out of his head in the time he'd been gone from the compound. He'd been hoping like hell she'd back out of the Berlin trip, and he'd even considered a change of plans that would leave her behind.

He didn't want to think about why he'd been compelled to go looking for her, and then intervene when he found Chase and her together in the corridor. The jolt of protectiveness he'd felt seeing the other male's hands on her had come up on him fast. He'd like to blame it on the power of the blood bond, but the problem there was that the connection was only half-complete. He hadn't taken any of Elise's blood, so he shouldn't be feeling possessive of her at all.

For several long centuries, he'd been perfecting his general state of apathy like armor that had long since meshed into his own skin, so unless he willed it, he shouldn't feel a goddamn thing.

But he did.

Just looking at Elise triggered off a storm of unwanted feelings, not the least of which being a lust that tightened every inch of his skin and made his cock stir to aching life. He could hardly reconcile his want of the woman. Seeing her come undone while she suckled at his wrist had only amplified the desire that was already there. Now he craved her with a need that was bound to prove disastrous.

Because if he ever had her naked beneath him, there would be no stopping him from taking her tender Breedmate vein at the same time.

She caught him staring as she suddenly turned away from the window. "A long black Rolls-Royce just pulled up next to us on the tarmac."

"That'll be Reichen."

"Who?"

"Andreas Reichen." Tegan stood up as the aircraft eased to a stop. "He oversees the largest of the area Darkhavens here. We'll be staying with him at his estate outside the city."

The door to the plane's cockpit opened and the two uniformed pilots came out to give Tegan a nod of greeting as they prepared to disembark. They were both human, both topclass, and available 24/7 by private retainment of the Order. So far as the pilots knew, they worked for a very private, very wealthy corporation that demanded anonymity and absolute loyalty in exchange for a healthy paycheck.

For most humans, that was enough. For the few who proved less than trustworthy, they were rewarded with a thorough mind scrub and a swift kick to the curb.

"Enjoy your stay in Berlin, Mr. Smith," said the captain as he opened the door of the jet onto the waiting flight of stairs that had been placed beside the aircraft. He gave Elise a courteous smile as she stepped past him to exit the plane. "Miss Smith," he said politely. "A pleasure to serve you. Have a pleasant day."

On the tarmac below, a suited driver got out of the black Rolls limousine and opened the door for his passenger in the back of the vehicle. Andreas Reichen climbed out as Tegan and Elise came off the last stair and walked toward the car.

He looked more the wealthy executive than the libertine Tegan knew him to be, his gray shirt and black trousers sporting barely a wrinkle beneath the fall of his tailored overcoat. Only his dark hair gave his hedonist side away: he wore it long and loose, the thick chestnut waves lifting in the wintry breeze that came in off the pavement.

"Welcome, friends," he said, his accented baritone voice just as rich and cultured as Tegan remembered it. The vampire hadn't changed much at all in the many decades since Tegan had last seen him—not only in his movie star looks, which were an unapologetic source of pride for him, but also in his blatant appreciation for feminine beauty.

"Andreas Reichen," he purred, offering Elise his hand.

"I am Elise Chase," she replied. "It's nice to meet you."

When she reached out to accept his greeting, Reichen

smoothly captured her fingers and brought them to his
lips for a chaste kiss, bowing his dark head over her hand.
"Enchanted. And I am honored to welcome you to my
domain."

Elise gave him a shy smile. "Thank you, Herr Reichen."

The German frowned as if wounded by her formality.
"You must call me Andreas, please."

"Very well. If you will call me Elise."

"With honor, Elise." It took him a moment before he
finally broke away to acknowledge Tegan. "Very good to
see you again, my friend, and so much the better that it is
under more pleasant circumstances than before."

"That remains to be seen," Tegan said, not particularly caring that his grim attitude might put a damper on
the pleasantries. "Is everything still a go for the containment facility visit?"

"Yes, all is in order." Reichen indicated the idling
vehicle. "Shall we be on our way? Klaus will see to your
bags."

"This is it," Tegan said, holding up a black leather
duffel that contained his combat gear and a few extra
weapons. "We won't be here more than a couple of days.
It can't take that long to get what we need out of the
Odolf Rogue."

Reichen's chiseled cheeks showed twin dimples with
his answering smile. "I'm not surprised that you are all
business, Tegan, but what about the lady?"

Elise shook her head. "This trip came up so abruptly, I
didn't have much chance to prepare—"

"No matter," Reichen said. "I will take care of it. I
have accounts at several designer houses on the
Ku'damm. I'll call from the car and have them bring
some selections to the estate today for both of you."

He flipped out his cell phone and began talking even before they were all seated in the limousine. Tegan understood a bit of German from the Old Times, when all of the Breed existed primarily in Europe—enough to know that Reichen was ordering up pricey gowns and shoes in a range of what he guessed to be Elise's petite sizes.

When he dialed another store and requested a men's tailor to come out for a custom fitting within the hour, Tegan shot him a threatening look. "What the hell's going on, Reichen?"

"A reception, of course. I'll be hosting it at the estate this evening. It's not often the Berlin Darkhavens get to receive such esteemed company. There are people within the Enforcement Agency in particular who insisted they be allowed to greet you properly."

"I'll bet." Tegan scoffed. "I have no interest in being paraded around like a tuxedoed monkey in front of a bunch of Darkhaven bureaucrats. So, no offense to you, Reichen, but the rest of your stuffed-shirt pals can kiss my—"

The German pointedly cleared his throat as if to remind Tegan that a lady was present and to mind his tongue. Frigging Darkhaven sophisticate and his flawless manners. A rusty old part of Tegan acknowledged that Elise probably didn't need to hear him go off on the society that had raised her. It wasn't that long ago that she was very much a part of that world—still would be, if not for the deaths of her mate and her only son.

Reichen smiled, arching a dark brow as Tegan bit back the rest of his ripe thoughts.

But there was some spark of satisfaction gleaming in

Reichen's dark eyes that had little to do with his silver spoon upbringing. It was humor, wry amusement.

"Actually, Tegan, the reception has been arranged in honor of your lovely companion. Perhaps you were not aware that Quentin Chase was one of the most respected figures in the Enforcement Agency, in the States and abroad." Reichen gallantly inclined his head in Elise's direction. "It is a great honor for us to receive the late Director Chase's widow for however long she chooses to stay with us."

Tegan scowled in the dimly lit vehicle, stealing a glance at Elise. She seemed less surprised than resigned at the announcement, like she was used to the sort of attention Reichen described. Like she lived that kind of rarefied society fuss all the time.

Shit.

She hadn't been kidding when she said she could bring the entire Enforcement Agency down on the Order with a single phone call. He knew her mate had been well connected, but he'd had no idea how high up the Darkhaven food chain Elise was herself.

"Your hospitality overwhelms me, Herr Reichen . . . Andreas," she corrected demurely. "Thank you for welcoming us so graciously."

Tegan stared hard at her now, seeing how easily she fell into the role of diplomat with Reichen. She hadn't been so gratingly proper with him last night at the compound. No, with him she'd been wanton and demanding, perfectly willing to use him to get what she needed.

And why the hell not?

He knew how the Darkhavens viewed the Order. With the exception of a few current generation males who'd been impressed by the warriors' destruction of the

Boston-area Rogue lair the summer before, most of vampire society regarded the Order on a par with feral pit bulls. Those within the Enforcement Agency, the group whose policies of capture and rehabilitation operated in direct opposition to the Order's bag-and-tag methods of dealing with deadly Rogues, were the most vocal in their contempt.

Little wonder that Elise, as the Breedmate of one of their highest ranking officials, would think of Tegan as nothing more than a means to an end.

That he'd let her drink from him burned Tegan like a lick of midday sunlight on his skin. The fact that he craved the woman—even a little bit—made him want to leap out of the moving car and run until he hit the dawn.

Yeah, it was a damn good thing he was seeing her clearly now. Before he allowed himself to do anything even more stupid with the female.

CHAPTER
Sixteen

Elise skimmed her hands over the yards of glistening indigo silk that covered her. The sleeveless designer gown was breathtaking, one of more than a dozen couture pieces that Andreas Reichen had arranged to be brought in earlier that day from the city for her selection. She chose the simplest dress in the least dramatic color, wishing she didn't have to attend the evening's reception at all.

She'd been treated like a queen all day, and even after a restful bit of sleep, she wasn't much in the frame of mind for the hours of socializing that awaited her in the lakeside estate's grand ballroom downstairs. But years of practice on Quentin's arm had taught her what was expected of a member of the Chase family: *duty first*. That had been his personal credo, and one Elise had learned to embrace as well. So, after a quick shower in her guest suite, she had put on the form-fitting dark purple gown and a pair of gem-encrusted sandals, then arranged her short hair into some semblance of a style and headed out of her room ready to act her part.

Or at least, she thought she had been ready.

As soon as she descended the curving stairwell from the expansive wing of living quarters above, the din of voices and elegant music made her pause.

This would be the first public reception she'd attended since Quentin's death. Until she'd left the Darkhaven four months ago, she had kept herself in mourning, wearing the long white tunic and scarlet sash that declared a Breedmate a widow. As such, she'd been able to sequester herself in her home, seeing only those people she wished to, and neatly avoiding the sympathetic stares and whispers that would only remind her of Quentin's absence all the more.

There would be no more avoiding it, she realized, seeing Andreas Reichen striding toward her across the marble foyer from the direction of the crowded ballroom. He was stunning in a black tuxedo and crisp white shirt. His dark hair was pulled back off his face into a loose queue at his nape, showcasing those razor-sharp cheekbones and his strong square jaw. The handsome German's warm smile put her somewhat at ease immediately as he approached.

"A perfect choice. You look exquisite," he said, his dark eyes taking her in from head to toe as he took her hand and lifted her fingers to his mouth. His brief kiss of greeting was whisper soft and warm as velvet. He released her with a slight bow of his head, and when his gaze reached her face, he frowned. "Something is wrong? Is anything not to your liking?"

"Everything is fine," she assured him. "It's just . . . I haven't done this in a very long time. Been out in public, that is. For the past five years, I've been in mourning—"

Reichen's frown deepened in understanding. "In mourning, all this time?"

"Yes."

"Ah, God. You must pardon me, but I didn't know. I am sorry. You need only say the word and I will send everyone away. They don't need to know why."

"No." Elise shook her head. "No, I would never ask you to do that, Andreas. You've gone to so much trouble, and it's just a pleasant gathering, after all. I can get through this. I *will* get through it."

She couldn't help looking around Reichen's broad shoulders, searching for the one face she knew. Even though Tegan could hardly be considered friendly, he was familiar, and gruff or not, his strength would be a comfort to her. By the low current in her veins, she could feel him somewhere in the mansion, nearby, yet out of her line of sight.

"Have you seen Tegan?" she asked, trying to sound only passingly interested in the answer.

"Not since we arrived this morning." Reichen chuckled as he led her away from the sweeping staircase, toward the ballroom. "We won't see him anywhere near the reception, I'm sure. He never was one for social gatherings."

No, she didn't suppose he was. "Do you know him well?"

"Oh, not particularly. But then I doubt few can claim

to know that warrior well. Personally, I know all I need to know to consider him a friend."

Elise was curious. "How so?"

"Tegan came to my aid some time ago, when the area was having a sudden, but persistent problem with a group of Rogues. This was ages ago, in the early 1800s . . . 1809, the height of summer."

Two hundred years would seem a very long time to human ears, but Elise herself had been living among the Breed for more than a century, after being rescued from Boston's slums by the Chase family when she was a young child. The Breed's Darkhaven communities had been in existence in various parts of Europe and the United States for much longer than that. "Things must have been very different for you then."

Reichen grunted as if remembering those times. "Things were different, yes. The Darkhavens weren't nearly as secure as they are now. No electronic fences, no motion sensors, no cameras to warn of breaches. Normally, our problems with Rogues were isolated incidents—one or two weak-willed vampires succumbing to Bloodlust and wreaking a bit of havoc on the human population before they were captured and contained. But this was different. These Rogues had begun attacking humans and Breed alike. They had banded together in their hunting, doing it for sport, it seemed. They managed to infiltrate one of our Darkhavens. Before the first night had ended, they'd violated and killed a number of women and slaughtered several Breed males as well."

Elise winced, imagining the terror that must have cut through the hearts of the area's residents at such an episode of violence. "How did Tegan help you?"

"He'd evidently been roaming the countryside when

he entered the Grunewald and came across an injured Darkhaven male from my community. When Tegan heard what was going on, he showed up on my doorstep with an offer to assist us. We would have paid him anything, of course, but he would accept no fee in exchange. I don't know how he did it, but he hunted down every one of those Rogues and killed them all."

"How many were there?"

Reichen's expression was nothing short of awe. "Sixteen of the diseased savages."

"My God," Elise gasped, beyond astonished. "So many . . ."

"The Berlin Darkhaven you see today might have been wiped out of existence if not for Tegan all those years ago. He tracked and killed all sixteen Rogues single-handedly, then simply went on his way. I didn't hear from him again until many years later, after he'd settled in Boston with the few remaining members of the Order."

Elise had no words for what she'd just been told. Part of her was stunned by Reichen's account of Tegan's heroics, but another part of her was suddenly awash in a deep chill of dread that made her shudder. She knew Tegan was a skilled warrior—an extremely lethal individual—but she truly had no idea what violence he was capable of doing.

And to think she had forced herself on him the other night. Goaded him into the profanity of a blood bond she'd initiated with him. How she must have insulted him, and yet by some miracle, he hadn't lashed out at her even though he had every right to despise her for using him.

Good Lord.

If all the hideous things she'd been raised to believe

about the Order's members were even remotely true, she probably wouldn't be standing here. As it was, her legs felt a bit weak beneath her. The buzzing in her temples was increasing, distracting her like a swarm of gnats circling her ears.

"Andreas, I think I . . . I could really use a drink now."

"Of course." Reichen offered her his arm and she gladly took it. "Come, I'll present you to the gathering and make sure you have whatever you like."

Tegan waited until they were gone before he descended from the upper floor landing of the mansion. He took the stairs, even though he could have just as easily vaulted over the side of the carved mahogany railing to the marble foyer three floors below.

After a day of being cooped up in the mansion awaiting nightfall, he'd been on his way out to hunt for blood and Rogues when the sound of Elise's voice stopped him in his tracks upstairs. He peered over just in time to see Reichen sweep in on her, full of his usual dark charm as he kissed Elise's hand for the second time since meeting her. He'd called her exquisite and by God, she was.

The indigo dress she wore hugged her petite figure in all the right places, an architectural wonder of crisscrossing silk layers and flowing, filmy skirts. Her bare shoulders and short blond hair accentuated the graceful line of her throat, which drew Tegan's eye like a beacon. Her pulse ticked frantically below her ear, a beat that echoed in his own veins, even now that she was gone from view.

Damn, he needed to feed.

The sooner the better.

Garbed in combat gear, Tegan headed straight for the

mansion's front vestibule, eager to get the fuck out of the place. He strode past the wide-open double doors of the grand ballroom, ignoring the soaring whine of the string quartet and the chaotic buzz of the many conversations underway inside the reception.

He tried to ignore the sight of Elise on Reichen's arm as the suave German brought her before the crowd of their peers. She looked so elegant and refined amid the glitter of the gathering, fitting in perfectly with the Darkhavens' elite.

This was her world; there could be no mistaking that fact now that he saw her enveloped within it. She belonged here, and his place was out on the streets, staining his hands with the blood of his enemies.

Yeah, he thought, feeling a surge of anger run through him. *He belonged anywhere but here.*

As she strolled farther into the ballroom on Reichen's arm, Elise scanned the crowd of fifty or more, recognizing several faces from events she'd attended with Quentin in the past. Everyone was staring at her—had been since the instant she entered the room. Conversations paused, heads turned. The string quartet played on near the other side of the room, falling into a soft whisper of music as Andreas Reichen presented her to the gathering.

He introduced her to one person after another, a dizzying line of names and faces that eventually began to blur together in her mind. She accepted the offers of condolence for Quentin's passing and listened with not a little pride as many of the area's Enforcement Agency representatives recounted their dealings with her respected mate. More than one person asked about the nature of her business in Berlin, but she dodged the questions as artfully as she could. It didn't seem prudent to discuss the Order's business in such a public arena, and it would be next to impossible to mention her association with the warriors without explaining how she'd come to know them in the first place.

How shocked and appalled would these politic Darkhaven males be to learn that she had been out on Boston's streets hunting Minions just a few days before?

Some rebellious part of her almost wished she could blurt that truth out, if only to watch the stuffy civilians balk. Instead, Elise merely sipped the wine Reichen had fetched for her soon after they arrived, her attention only partially focused on the Enforcement Agent who had been bending her ear for about fifteen minutes straight.

Looking slightly down his aquiline nose at her, the imposing blond vampire was quick to impress upon her how he had served the Agency most of his life—racking up more than a hundred years of self-aggrandizing war stories that he seemed compelled to describe to her in great detail. She nodded along and smiled at the appropriate moments, wondering how long it would take her to hit the bottom of her wineglass.

About three seconds, she decided, casually draining the last of the fine French wine.

"Your years of service are commendable, Agent Waldemar," she said, already extricating herself from the conversation. "Will you excuse me, please? I'm afraid this wine has gone straight to my head."

The arrogant agent sputtered something about the fact that she hadn't yet heard about the time he required a full twenty stitches after a run-in with a Rogue outside

Tiergarten, but Elise just gave him a polite smile as she slipped into the thickest knot of the crowd.

In the middle of the perfumed, silk-clad bodies, a female hand reached out to clasp her own. "Elise? Oh, my goodness, it's so nice to see you!"

She was swept into a tight, warm hug. When she drew back, a flood of delight filled her to see the face of an old, dear friend. "Anna, hello. You look well."

"I am. And you—how many years has it been since we've seen each other? The boys were so young then. Were they even six years old the last time we were all together?"

"They were seven," Elise said, hit with an instant blast of memory. Camden and Anna's son Tomás had been fast friends, spending an entire summer together before the Agency reassigned Anna's mate overseas.

"I can't believe how time flies," the other Breedmate exclaimed, then took Elise's hand in both of hers. "We heard what happened to Quentin, of course. I'm so sorry for your loss."

Elise attempted a smile. "Thank you. It was . . . a difficult time. But I'm adjusting to life without him as best I can."

Anna clucked her tongue. "And poor Camden. I can only imagine how hard it's been for him too, losing his father when he could have barely been into his teens. How is he holding up? Did he come with you to Berlin? I know Tomás would be thrilled to see him."

All the blood seemed to drain out of her head at the well-meaning questions. The pain in her heart was still raw from this more recent loss. So raw, she could hardly find her voice to speak. "Camden is . . . well, he's not here, actually. There was an incident a few months ago in Boston. He, um . . . he ran into some trouble, and he . . ." She had to take a breath and push the words out of her mouth. "Camden was killed."

Anna went white with shock. "Oh, Elise! Forgive me, I had no idea—"

"I know you didn't. It's all right. Cam's death was sudden, and not many people know."

"Oh, my dear friend. You've been through so much tragedy, haven't you? You must be the strongest woman I know. To lose so much in so short a time . . . it would have destroyed me, I'm sure. I think I would have curled up and simply faded away."

Elise might have too. Lord knew, she wanted to do that very thing at first. But anger pulled her through the initial suffering.

Vengeance would take her the rest of the way.

"You do what you must in order to survive it," she heard herself say to the stricken female who looked at her with so much pity it stung. "You just do . . . whatever it takes."

"Of course," Anna replied. She smiled, but it was a wobbly effort that didn't quite mask her discomfort with the conversation's awkward turn. "How long will you be in town? Perhaps if you have time, I could show you around the city. We have some lovely parks and museums . . ."

"Perhaps." Elise glanced at her wineglass as if she just recalled it was empty. "Will you excuse me? I think I'll take a little walk and refresh my drink."

"Yes," Anna said, sympathy still softening her eyes. "It was good to see you, Elise. Truly."

Elise gave her friend's hand a gentle squeeze. "You too."

As she started to walk away, a low rumble of conversation carried through the crowd. Elise hardly had to turn to see what caused it; she felt the disturbance deep within her bones, and in the warm prickle of awareness that settled in her breast.

"For God's sake," Agent Waldemar muttered from a few feet away from her. He and several of his cronies were gaping in open contempt toward the entrance of the ballroom. "You'd think he'd at least have the decency to dress accordingly for a function like this. Despicable savages, every last one of them."

Elise swiveled her head and saw Tegan making his way into the gathering. He was a startlingly grim vision, dressed in full combat gear and dripping with weapons. His overlong tawny hair was wild around his head and broad, leather-clad shoulders, and there was a lethal sharpness to his green-eyed gaze as he casually scanned the crowd.

He had to know how nightmarish he must look to these pampered civilians, but he only sneered at those few individuals who dared to stare at him as he strode into their midst.

"Just look at that uncouth Gen One barbarian," Waldemar chortled, much to his Agency companions' smirking amusement. "The younger generations may be impressed by the Order's violent methods—particularly after that bit of spectacle last summer in Boston—but they need only take a hard look at this one to see the warriors for what they truly are: uncivilized hoodlums who have long outlived their purpose."

The group of them chuckled, so pompous in their silk tuxedos, their arrogance rolling off them like a sour wind.

Elise hated how the Darkhaven males were looking at Tegan. And in a small, shamed corner of her conscience, she knew that she had been guilty of the same thing at one time. She'd been raised in an Agency family nearly from infancy, taught to believe that the Order was exactly what this man claimed them to be.

And when it came to Tegan himself, Elise had to acknowledge that she'd been judging him most unfairly of all.

"Tell me, Agent Waldemar," Elise said, putting herself squarely in front of the Breed male and staring up into his surprised expression. "Have you lived in the Berlin Darkhaven for long?"

He puffed out his chest with pride. "One hundred and thirty-two years, my dear lady. As I mentioned, most of them spent in service with the Agency. Why do you ask?"

"Because it occurs to me that while you and your friends stand around at fancy parties, patting yourselves on the back and condemning the Order as obsolete, the warriors are on the streets risking their lives each and every night to protect a nation that hasn't bothered to so much as thank them for their trouble in the past few hundred years."

Waldemar blanched, but then his feathery blond brows lowered dangerously. "You are Quentin Chase's widow, so I'll be kind and not burden you with the facts about just how brutal those thugs can be. But I assure you, madam, they are soulless killers, each and every one of them. Especially that one," he said, his voice low and conspiratorial. "He would slit your throat in your sleep if he felt like it, you mark my words."

"That one," Elise said, knowing that Tegan was coming closer all the time. Her veins were lit up like live wires, her temples buzzing. But she was furious and getting more incensed by the second. "That warrior you would insult so freely is the main reason any of you are standing here tonight."

"Indeed," Waldemar scoffed, clearly incredulous.

"Is the historical memory so short in this area that you have forgotten about the band of Rogues who descended on your Darkhaven two hundred years ago, killing many of your citizens? It was that warrior who took it upon himself to hunt the Rogues down. He saved your community single-handedly, and he asked for nothing in return. I don't think a little respect for him now would be misplaced."

None of the Darkhaven males said a word as she finished her diatribe and waited for their reaction. They were looking past her now, Agent Waldemar the palest of them all. As the group of them slowly shrank back into the crush of milling bodies, Elise turned around and found herself standing less than an inch away from Tegan. He glared down at her, looking about as mad as she'd ever seen him before.

"What the hell do you think you're doing?"

CHAPTER
Seventeen

Tegan had known it was a mistake to walk into the reception. He'd been half a mile away from the mansion on foot when the urge suddenly struck him to go back and make his presence known to all of the Darkhaven idiots who thought they were better than him.

Or maybe he just wanted to make his presence known to the woman who had been turning his head inside out since the moment he first met her. Some masochistic part of him wanted to stake a claim here, even though he fully expected her to be appalled by his presence—much like everyone else who saw him strolling into their pleasant little party dressed for war.

What he never expected was to hear Elise rising to his

defense as if he needed to be protected from a bunch of blowhards in tuxedos and bow ties. He couldn't remember the last time he felt the sting of humiliation, but he felt it now, left standing alone with Elise as the rest of the crowd shrank back.

"Excuse me," she said, ignoring his demand that she explain herself. Without waiting for him to speak, she simply walked away. Tegan stood there, following her with his eyes as she deposited her empty wineglass on a server's tray and headed for the wall of glass doors that looked out over the estate's lakefront back lawn and gardens. When she slipped outside alone, Tegan snarled a curse and went after her.

She was halfway to the water by the time he reached her, the frozen grass crunching under the slender heels of her shoes.

Tegan grabbed her arm and pulled her to a stop. "You want to explain to me what that was about back there?"

She shrugged. "I didn't like what I was hearing. Those self-righteous 'stuffed shirts' as you call them were wrong, and they needed to hear it."

Tegan exhaled sharply, his breath misting in the chill air. "Look, I don't need anyone coming to my defense—especially not with a bunch of assholes like that. I fight my own battles. Next time, spare me the concern."

Her eyes narrowed in the dark as she stared up at him. "No, you can't accept even the smallest kindness from anyone, can you, Tegan?"

"Last time I checked, I was doing just fine on my own."

She laughed at him. Threw her pretty head back and really laughed, right in his face. "You're unbelievable! You can take on an army of Rogues all by yourself, but you're scared to death that someone might actually care for you. Or even worse, that you might be tempted to care for someone else."

"You don't know the first thing about me."

"Does anyone?" She yanked her arm out of his light hold. Her face seemed stark in the moonlight, her soft features drawn tight. "Go away, Tegan. I'm tired and I just . . . I really want to be left alone right now."

He watched her lift her long indigo skirt above her pale ankles as she began another trek farther out toward the dark lake glistening at the end of the lavish grounds. She paused in the shadows of an old stone boathouse at the shoreline, her arms wrapped around herself.

Tegan considered doing as she asked, just turning around and letting her have her space. But now he was pissed off and he wasn't about to let Elise deliver him a verbal slap in the face and simply walk away.

He was fully prepared to lace into her for presuming to know anything of what he'd been through or for thinking she could possibly know how he felt, but as he came up behind her he saw that she was trembling. Not just shuddering from the cold, but really shaking.

Jesus Christ, was she crying?

"Elise . . ."

She shook her head and pivoted to move farther up the lawn, out of his reach. "I said go away!"

Tegan went right after her, moving faster than her human eyes would be able to track him. He stopped in front of her, blocking her path. Pale, tear-filled eyes lifted and widened before she pivoted to get around him. She didn't make it even a single step. He reached out, holding her still, his fingers wrapped over her trembling bare shoulders.

Her grief sliced through him the instant his hands made contact. He hadn't helped the situation any, but most of what she was feeling was something bleaker than the anger he stoked in her. Tegan felt her emotions seep in through his fingertips, registering the cold ache of loss. It was fresh again, like a wound ripped open before it had fully healed.

"What happened in there?"

"Nothing," she lied, her voice thick with sorrow. "It will pass, right?"

The very words he'd said to her at her apartment when he'd callously dismissed her bereavement. She threw them back at him now, her flashing lavender eyes daring him to say something kind, or to so much as think he might offer her comfort.

He wanted to offer that to her. The realization hit him hard, squarely in the center of his chest. He didn't want to see her in pain.

He wanted . . . God, he didn't even know what to want when it came to this woman.

"I know what you're going through," he admitted quietly. "I understand loss, Elise. I've been there too."

Ah, hell.

What was he doing? Some ancient part of him roused in a defensive panic as soon as the words left his tongue. He hadn't aired out his bleak history in ages. He knew he was exposing the soft belly of a long-sleeping beast, but it was too late to call the admission back.

Elise's expression muted from distress to tender surprise. A sympathy he wasn't sure he was ready to accept. "Who did you lose, Tegan?"

He cast his gaze out over the moonlit water and the twinkle of lights shining across the way, thinking back on a night he'd relived a thousand times in his mind. More than five hundred years of imagined alternate scenarios— endless things that he could have, would have, should have done differently—but the outcome never changed. "Her name was Sorcha. She was my Breedmate a very long time ago, when the Order was new. She was abducted by Rogues one night when I was out on patrol."

"Oh, Tegan," Elise whispered. "Did they . . . hurt her?"

"She's dead," he replied, simple stated fact.

He didn't think she'd want to know the horrific details of how her captors had sent her back to him, abused and violated, a broken shell of who she had been. God knew, he didn't want to talk about the guilt and rage that had torn at him when Sorcha had come back alive—but only barely, drained of her blood and her humanity. To his horror, she'd come back to him a Minion.

Tegan had lost his mind, certainly lost his self-control, in those dark days following his Breedmate's abduction and return. He'd fallen into the grip of Bloodlust, and had come deadly close to going Rogue.

All for nothing.

Death, when it finally came for Sorcha, had been a mercy.

"I can't bring her back, and I can't take away what happened."

"No," Elise said softly. "Would that we could. But how long does it take before we stop blaming ourselves for everything we wish we'd done differently?"

He looked back at her now, unused to this feeling of affinity. But it was the regret in her eyes that made something inside him thaw just a little. "You didn't give your son the drug that corrupted him, Elise. You didn't push him over that edge."

"Didn't I? I thought I was protecting him, but I held him too close all the time. He rebelled. He wanted to be a man—he *was* a man—but I couldn't bear to lose my child because he was all I had left. The more I tried to keep him close, the harder he pulled away."

"Every kid goes through that. It doesn't mean you caused his death—"

"We argued the last night I saw him," she blurted out. "Camden wanted to go to some kind of party—a rave, I think he called it. There had already been a few Darkhaven youths who'd gone missing, so I was worried something might happen to him. I forbade him to go. I told him that if he did, he shouldn't come back home. It was just an empty threat. I didn't mean it . . ."

"Jesus," Tegan muttered. "We all say things we regret, Elise. You were only trying to keep him safe."

"Instead I killed him."

"No. Bloodlust killed him. Marek and the human he paid to create Crimson killed your son. Not you."

She crossed her arms over herself and gave a mute shake of her head. He didn't miss the sudden flood of tears that filled her eyes.

"You're shivering." Tegan shrugged out of his heavy leather coat and draped it around her before she could refuse him. "It's too cold. You shouldn't be out here."

Not with him, he thought, so very tempted to touch her now.

Before he could stop himself, he was raising his hand to her cheek and smoothing away the wetness that streaked down her fair skin. He caressed her face, letting his thumb brush across her lips. It was all too easy to re-call how sweet her mouth had been, pressed against his wrist. How heated her tongue had been when she lapped at him, drawing strength from his blood.

How the feel of her body, hungry and writhing next to his, had inflamed him.

He wanted that again, with a ferocity that stunned him.

"Tegan, please . . . don't." Elise sighed, closing her eyes as if she knew the direction of his thoughts. "Don't do this if you don't mean it. Don't touch me like that if you don't . . . if you don't feel it."

He lifted her chin, tenderly sweeping his fingertips over her petal-soft eyelids, compelling her to see him. They opened slowly, dark lashes framing pools of beautiful light amethyst.

"Look at me, Elise. Tell me what you think I'm feeling," he murmured, then bent his head to hers and pressed his mouth to her parted lips.

The warmth of her kiss was like a flame, kindling the cold space in his chest. He let his fingers thread into the short, silky hair at her nape, holding her against him as he slid his tongue along the seam of her lips. She parted for him on a gasp, trembling in his arms as he tasted the wet velvet of her mouth.

When her hands came up to touch him, Tegan was the one to tremble, shocked by the sensation of being held, astonished by how much he needed it—how much he needed her. It had been so long since he'd allowed himself this kind of intimacy. The centuries of solitude had been their own comfort to him, but this . . .

The craving for this woman seared him with its intensity. His gums throbbed with the emergence of his fangs. Even behind his closed eyelids he could tell his irises were throwing off amber light, evidence of his desire for Elise.

His skin was tight, his *dermaglyphs* prickling with the sudden rush of blood that would deepen their color to vivid shades of indigo, burgundy, and gold. He knew she had to feel the hard ridge of his cock, which was wedged between their bodies, pushing against her abdomen.

Elise had to be aware of all his body's responses to her—she had to know what it meant—yet she didn't shove him away. Her fingers curled deeper into his shoulders, holding him with an intensity he could hardly fathom.

He was the one to pull back, breaking contact on a low, muttered curse. When he glanced up at the mansion, he saw several faces near the glass, Elise's Darkhaven peers staring out at them in open disdain.

Elise saw them too. She followed his gaze up the frozen lawn and gardens, but when she turned back to Tegan, there wasn't so much as a trace of shame in her expression. Only soft regard, and the lingering heat of desire in her eyes.

"Let them stare," she said, stroking his jaw before their disapproving audience. "I don't care what they think."

"You should. That's your world up there on the other side of that glass." She sure as hell couldn't stay out here with him any longer, not when their kiss was still setting fire to his blood. "You should go back inside."

She glanced back up toward the golden light spilling out of the ballroom and slowly shook her head. "I can't go back in there. I look at them and all I see is a beautiful cage. It makes me want to run before the trap closes on me again."

Tegan was surprised at the frank admission. "You weren't happy in the Darkhaven?"

"It's all I've known. Quentin was all I'd known. His

family took me in as a baby and raised me as one of their own soon after I arrived at the Darkhaven. I owe them everything for the life they afforded me."

Tegan grunted. "That sounds like gratitude to me. Nothing wrong with it, but what I asked was if you were happy there."

She turned a thoughtful look on him. "I was mostly, yes. Especially after Camden came along."

"You said you felt caged."

She nodded lightly. "I was never very strong, physically. My gift made it difficult for me to leave the Darkhavens for any length of time, and Quentin thought it unwise for me to go anywhere by myself. He only meant to protect me, I'm sure, but at times it was . . . stifling. Then there were all the Agency obligations and the impossible expectations that came with being a member of the Chase family. It was a fine line that had to be walked at all times—allegiance to the Agency no matter what, know your place and keep it, never dare to speak out of turn. I can't tell you how often I wanted to scream, just to prove to myself that I could. Most days, I still want to."

"So, what's stopping you?"

She threw him a frown over her shoulder. "What?"

"Go ahead. Scream right now if you want to. I won't stop you."

Elise laughed. She glanced up at the mansion behind them. "That would really make their tongues wag, wouldn't it? Can you imagine the tales they'd tell tomorrow about how you terrorized a defenseless civilian female? Your reputation would never recover."

He shrugged. "All the more reason to do it, if you ask me."

Elise exhaled a long sigh, her breath steaming the chill air. When she turned back to look at him once more, there was a pleading light glimmering in her wide lavender eyes. "I can't go back in there tonight. Will you stay with me out here, Tegan . . . just for a little while?"

Marek's vision burned red with fury as he scanned the flight plan one of his Minions had procured from the Boston airport a few hours before. A private jet had scheduled a last minute evening trip to Berlin last night, carrying two passengers—one of which was certain to be a member of the Order.

Tegan, no doubt, based on the visual description provided by Marek's mole. But the female accompanying him was a mystery. Tegan was the consummate loner, and try as he might, Marek couldn't imagine what would compel the stoic, deadly warrior to tolerate a woman's presence for more than a few necessary minutes.

He hadn't always been like that, however. Marek recalled well the warrior's utter devotion to the female he'd taken as his mate—Jesus, could it be some five hundred years ago? She was pretty, Marek remembered, with dark gypsy looks and a sweet, trusting smile.

Tegan had been devoted to her. It had nearly destroyed him to lose her so savagely.

Pity it didn't take him all the way.

The fact that Tegan was in Berlin now was troubling news. Couple that with the journal Marek lost—a journal that had taken him a long time to find—and he was looking at a fucking disaster in the making. The Order had the journal now, Marek had no doubt.

How long would it take them to put all the pieces in

place? He would have to work fast if he meant to stay ahead of them.

Unfortunately for him, it was daytime and unless he wanted to risk a lethal suntan at thirty thousand feet too close to the sun, he'd have to wait until dark before he could get overseas and take control of the situation personally.

Until then, he would have to call out a few Minion eyes and ears in his place.

CHAPTER
Eighteen

Tegan opened the door of the stone-and-timber boat-house that hugged the shoreline of the lake and led Elise inside. She couldn't see well in the dark, but Tegan's hand was firm around hers, his steps sure where she walked gingerly over the wide plank floor in her high heels.

The space for a large boat was empty for the winter, the water partially frozen where it came into the base of the building.

"There should be a loft up here," Tegan said, guiding her toward a wooden staircase.

"How do you know?"

"This was the warden's cottage when I was here last. Guess there's not much need for gamekeepers anymore, so Reichen's had it converted to house one of his many toys."

Elise lifted the ends of her skirt and Tegan's oversized leather coat and climbed up the stairs with him. At the top of the steps he opened a door that revealed a wide post-and-beam space above. It was rustic, but welcoming. Moonlight poured in through an A-shaped window that overlooked the lake. Big leather club chairs flanked a sofa positioned for the best views of the water, and set into the eastern wall was a fireplace built out of thick stone.

"Knowing Reichen, there's got to be electricity out here," Tegan said from somewhere behind her. A second later, a table lamp went on across the room, activated by his will.

"Actually, if you don't mind, I think I prefer the dark. It's peaceful."

The light blinked off, replaced once more by the cool pale wash of moonglow. Elise felt Tegan's eyes on her as she walked toward the window and gazed out into the night. Her heels sank into a plush white rug—sheepskin, she realized, glancing down at the fluffy, irregular shape of the floor covering. On impulse, she kicked off the elegant sandals and let her toes burrow in the luxuriously thick pelt.

Some of her anxiety faded at once. She gave herself over to the tranquil movement of the water outside, and the quiet darkness of the loft. The stress of the reception was ebbing away, but her pulse still thrummed from Tegan's kiss. She hadn't expected him to be so tender with her, or to open up like he had and share any part of his past.

She hadn't expected his desire.

He wanted her, and she wanted him too.

The space around them practically throbbed with that awareness, the air thick with all that was unspoken between them.

"This is a bad idea," Tegan murmured as he came up beside her, his low, growling voice setting off a vibration deep in her bones. "You shouldn't be alone with me right now."

Elise turned to look at him and was struck to see the dim glow of amber in his eyes. It hadn't faded since their kiss outside. Nor had the heat of his body. She could feel it radiating toward her, permeating the leather of the coat that draped her.

Tegan bared his teeth and fangs in a pained-looking smile. "In case you're not sure, that's your cue to make a quick retreat."

She didn't move. She had absolutely no wish to leave right now, even though she knew Tegan wouldn't be the type to allow second chances. Holding his intense gaze, she watched as he came toward her and drew the coat from her shoulders. He set it down on the chair behind her. As he straightened, he skimmed his fingers over the bare curve of her arm. His touch was searing hot and yet she trembled from it.

Desire coiled within her. She wanted him to touch her, needed it so badly it wrung a soft moan from her throat.

Tegan scowled, his tawny brows lowering over the glowing embers of his eyes. He retracted his hand with a glare. "No," he said thickly. "No, this is a very bad idea. I'll take more from you than you're willing to give."

When he turned as if he meant to walk away, Elise moved toward him and lifted her hand to the side of his rigid jaw. "Tegan, wait. I don't want you to go."

She went closer to him, until their bodies brushed together in the dark. She heard his sharp intake of breath hiss through his teeth and fangs as she rose up on her toes in front of him. She felt the rush of heat roll off every coiled muscle of his body in that instant before she pressed her lips to his. She tasted the ferocity of his hunger in the way he wrapped his arms around her and dragged her deeper into his embrace, his mouth demanding as he took her tentative kiss and turned it into something fevered and dark.

He groaned, and Elise felt the long tips of his fangs rasp against her lips as he traced his tongue along the seam of her mouth. She let him in, reveling in the erotic invasion, unable to bite back her mewled complaint when he abruptly drew back.

His chest was heaving with every rough breath he dragged into his lungs. He stared at her from under low brows, the green of his eyes swamped completely by amber light, his pupils thinned to slivers in the center of all that fiery gold. Even in the dark, shrouded by his black combat gear, she could see that he was fully aroused. She'd felt the thick ridge of his sex pressing insistently against her in that moment before he pulled away. She knew that if she peeled off his weapons and fitted black knit shirt, she'd see his Gen One *dermaglyphs* churning with livid color.

He'd never looked more predatory than he did in that moment—a massive, powerful Breed male who could have her beneath him in an instant.

Faster than that, if he willed it.

Perhaps she should fear him, now more than ever. But it wasn't fear that was making her knees feel boneless under her. It wasn't fear sending her heart into a frantic drum in her breast.

Nor was it fear that made her fingers tremble as she slowly reached behind her to find the zipper of her confining bodice and begin to tug it down.

Before the tiny teeth had parted more than an inch, Tegan's large hand closed around hers, stilling her. He held her there, her arm gently trapped behind her as he brought his free hand up between their bodies. His fingers moved over the detail of her gown's low neckline, skimming the edge of dark silk that framed the tops of her breasts. There was a delicious possessiveness in his touch, in the way he restrained her while his other hand roamed freely over her body.

When he kissed her now, it was blatantly carnal, a deep claiming of her mouth that mimicked the hard thrust of his hips where they pressed against her. The hand at her back pulled her forward as his eyes snapped open on her stunned gaze, those twin amber coals commanding her to understand how close she was to the ledge of a very steep fall.

If she tumbled down with him now, there would be no coming back. He would take her body, and he would take her blood. There was no mistaking that feral promise in his eyes.

As if to drive home his point, Tegan smoothed the flat of his hand higher, up the slope of her throat. He bared her neck and bent down over her, dragging his tongue along the path of her carotid. His fangs were a subtle, but unmistakable, abrasion as his mouth moved to a tender spot just below her ear.

A tremor of uncertainty rippled through her at the

thought of where this was heading, more swiftly than she'd been prepared for.

She really shouldn't be here.

Shouldn't be doing this . . .

Tegan's chuckle sounded cruel, darkly satisfied. He released her at once, practically pushing her out of his reach.

"Go on," he said, his voice so deep she hardly recognized it. "Get out of here before we do something we'll both regret."

She brought her hand up to the side of her neck, where she could still feel the lingering heat of his mouth. Her pulse was hammering now, so loud it was audible to her own ears. When she drew her fingers away from her neck, she saw that the tips bore trace stains of blood.

Dear God, had he been so close to biting her?

Tegan's hungry gaze tracked her every movement, and he looked savage enough to pounce if she hesitated so much as a second longer.

"What are you waiting for? I said get the fuck out of here!" he bellowed, the animal snarl jolting her into action.

Elise grabbed her sandals from the floor beside her and ran out of the boathouse as fast as her feet would carry her.

Tegan dropped into the nearest chair as soon as he heard the boathouse door bang shut on Elise's heels.

He was physically shaking from need of her, all of his Breed senses torqued off the charts with the depth of his hunger for the female.

Jesus Christ, he'd been just a fraction of a second away from sinking his fangs into her.

That unintentional graze of her skin, which brought only the faintest taste of her blood to his tongue, had practically laid him out. He shuddered from the heather-and-roses sweetness that still lingered in his mouth. His fangs throbbed, along with another part of his anatomy, both equally ravenous. Both damning him for letting Elise get away.

The only thing that had snapped him back to his wits was her sudden flood of anxiety. Through the connection of touch, he felt the jolt of fear override her desire—and not a moment too soon. She'd been too pliant, too accepting, even when he was deliberately pushing, wanting her to understand just where he wanted to take things.

Where he still wanted to take things with her.

Yeah, straight to hell, with him leading the way.

He gripped the leather arms of the club chair, digging his fingers into the supple hide to keep from vaulting to his feet and going out after her. Which was the very thing he ached to do.

The part of him that was more savage than human railed at being forced to heel. He was a predator at heart, and he never felt it more than he did in that moment, with his vampire eyes reflecting back at him from the glass of the boathouse window, his fangs stretched long and sharp as razors.

Every dark instinct in him was tuned on one thing: Elise.

Barely a taste of her and he was on fire with the need for more. How lost would he be if he ever got the chance to fill his mouth with that lush nectar running through her tender veins?

Ah, fuck. He was in seriously bad shape.

And he needed to feed.

Not for sustenance so much as distraction. Because if he didn't slake at least one of the hungers sticking its talons into him, he was going to have the luscious Elise flat on her back beneath him before the night was through.

Elise didn't stop running until she had circled the mansion and found the front entrance. She knew she should go inside. It was late and she was cold. Her bare feet were wet and freezing, her body trembling from the wintry night air. She knew how close she'd come to disaster with Tegan; she should be grateful that he gave her the opportunity to escape what could only prove to be a heartbreaking mistake in the end.

And yet . . .

She stood on the wide marble steps that led up to safety, and her hand refused to reach for the door. The fear she'd felt moments ago in the boathouse had muted into something else—something that still unsettled her in many ways, but the sharp edge of it was gone.

She'd felt anxious, apprehensive in those passionate few minutes with Tegan. All too aware of his hunger for her, and stunned to realize how his hunger enflamed her. Now, having fled him like a coward, she felt . . . empty.

Elise backed away from the elegant manor house.

This wasn't what she wanted.

As soon as her soles hit the cold grass, she lifted her damp skirt and dashed back around the corner of the mansion. She cut across the long yard and gardens, breathless as she reached the dark brick-and-timber

building near the water. She threw open the door and ran
up the stairs to the loft, ready to let Tegan take whatever
he wanted from her.

But the boathouse was empty.

He was already gone.

Tegan hoofed it back into the city, moving with the preternatural speed that made the Breed all but invisible to
human eyes. He was glad for the long run from Reichen's
lakeshore Darkhaven. He was glad for the chill snap in
the air that helped clear his head after the near catastrophe with Elise.

But he was glad most of all for the thick clot of humanity that was prowling the darkened streets of
Lichtenberg in Berlin's depressed Eastern District. Row
upon row of twenty-story concrete high-rise eyesores
towered over this former East Berlin sector, which only
added to the general malaise of the place. There were
few tourists here at this hour of night. Only grim-faced
locals hurrying from late-shift jobs or the grimy
brewhauses that catered to the working-class poor—folks
who weren't leaving the GDR in this lifetime, wall or
no wall.

Tegan scanned his surroundings with a hunter's eye. He
was hardwired to look for Rogues, but he could tell at a
glance there were no suckheads in the vicinity. While
Boston had been practically overrun with the Bloodlusting
bastards courtesy of Marek's recent reappearance, Berlin
and most other major cities had been reporting only mini-
mal Rogue activity for years.

And damn if that didn't suck ass.

Because right now, Tegan would have welcomed a

good hard fight with his enemies—several, if he had his choice about it.

He had to force his aggression to heel as he stalked down one of the desolate streets that would lead him deeper into the district. He watched for his night's prey, ignoring a pair of human women who gave him the once-over as they stumbled out of a bar and into his path. He walked around them with an annoyed snarl.

He wouldn't feed from a female.

He hadn't in all this time . . . not since Sorcha's death.

It was his choice, something he'd adopted as self-imposed punishment for failing the innocent girl who had been so wrong in trusting him to keep her safe from his enemies. But somewhere along the way, Tegan's aversion to drinking from females, let alone binding himself to another Breedmate, had become an act of desperation.

It had become an act of plain survival.

His hungers ran too deep. And he knew from experience how easy it was to lose control. He'd tasted Bloodlust once before, and he could never allow himself to get close to it again.

That he'd been so tempted by Elise tonight had rattled him hard. He'd never wanted to take a female—to his mouth or to his bed—in a long span of time that had somehow become centuries. He'd been alone by his own will, bonded to nothing but his mission to wipe out the Rogues.

But now . . . ?

"Fuck," he ground out savagely from between clamped teeth and fangs.

Now he was about two seconds away from hauling ass

back to the Darkhaven where Elise was probably cowering in terror from what he might have done to her—to them both—if he'd given in to the impulse to drink from her.

Instead, he plowed forward, his sights locking on to a trio of skinheads in black leather and chains. The white laces on their jackboots practically glowed in the scant light shed by the intermittent streetlamps overhead. They hooted at an elderly woman in a headscarf who was coming toward them up the sidewalk. Her dark eyes dropped to avoid facing the threat, and when she started to cross the street to get out of their way, the gang of neo-Nazis loped after her, taunting her with ugly racial slurs. They shoved her into the alcove of a nearby building, and one of them made a grab for her purse. The woman screamed and held on, and suddenly she was being dragged into the adjacent alley where the situation was sure to escalate.

Tegan moved in quickly, feeling battle rage transform him.

The first skinhead didn't know what hit him until he was thrown several yards into the street. Wisely, he got up, took one look at Tegan, and started running in the opposite direction. His companions took a bit more convincing. While one pulled the old woman farther into the alley by her purse strap, the other one drew a switchblade and made a jab at Tegan.

He missed.

But then it's damn hard to hit a target that's standing in front of you one second, then suddenly behind you the next, wrenching your arm out of its socket. The skinhead howled in agony, dropping the blade as he crumbled to his knees on the pavement.

Tegan's breath rolled out of his mouth in cloudy plumes, and his hands itched to finish the asshole, but the one who really needed killing was the one pounding his fists into a defenseless old woman a few yards away.

"Get the fuck out of my sight," he snarled down at the whimpering human, peeling his lips back from his fangs to make sure the kid got a good eyeful of the hell he'd be dealing with if he decided to stick around.

"Ah, shit!" the human gasped, reading Tegan loud and clear. He scrambled to his feet and took off running, his dislocated arm dangling uselessly at his side.

Tegan wheeled around and stalked into the alleyway where the last of the skinheads had finally wrestled the purse away from the old lady. He dug through the leather bag, dumping out the scant contents. He tore out the lining and let it fall to the ground.

"Where's your cash, bitch? You've got to be hiding something in here to hold on as tight as you did!"

The woman crawled forward to retrieve a small framed photo from the slushy pavement. "My photograph," she wailed, her German tinged with an Arabic accent. "It's all I have left of my husband. You've ruined it!"

The skinhead laughed. "Oh, my heart is breaking for you. Nasty foreign scum."

Tegan came up on the guy like a ghost. He clamped his hand around the back of the skinhead's neck and steered him away from the woman. In his periphery, he saw her collect her meager belongings and hurry out of the alley.

"Hey, *ubermensch*," Tegan hissed about an inch away from the human's ear. "You ever get tired of terrorizing old women? Maybe you wanna hit a hospital next, eh?

Bet you could really do some damage on the children's ward. Or would the cancer wing be more your speed?"

"Fuck you," the thug seethed back at him in English. "Maybe I show you the morgue, asshole."

Tegan smiled, flashing his fangs. "Funny. That's exactly where you're headed."

The human hardly had a chance to scream before Tegan tore into his throat and began to feed.

CHAPTER
Nineteen

Tegan managed to avoid her the entire next day. Elise didn't know where he'd gone the night before, or where he spent the hours before dusk, when the time of their appointment at the Enforcement Agency's containment facility drew near. He didn't speak to her—hardly did so much as look at her—the whole forty-five minutes in the car as Reichen's driver took the three of them south of the city to the location where the Odolf Rogue was housed.

The entrance was gated and manned by an auto-mated security system. There was no sign to indicate what lay on the other side of the tall, solid iron gates, but it was clear from the high-voltage, fortresslike perimeter wall that whatever was held inside was meant to stay there. As the car approached, Elise saw a thin red stream of light sweep through the vehicle from one of the mounted electronic devices that flanked the entrance. A moment later, the wall of iron parted in front of them.

Reichen's driver eased the car inside, only to pause before another set of tall gates. A quartet of armed Breed guards approached from either side of the vehicle and opened the doors. Elise didn't miss Tegan's deep-throated growl as they all climbed out, practically held at gunpoint.

Another Breed male came forward now, having come out of a windowless door built into the interior gate of the complex. He looked serious and distinguished in his dark gray suit and black turtleneck, his reddish brown beard trimmed into a precise goatee.

"Madam Chase," he said, greeting her with a curt nod. "Welcome. I am Heinrich Kuhn, director of this facility. If you are ready, we will escort you inside now." He looked to the two males with her, barely affording Tegan a glance. "Your, er . . . companions may await you here, if you please."

"Absolutely not." Tegan's deep voice, the first he'd spoken since leaving Reichen's estate, sliced through the air like a sword. Ignoring the sudden clack of shifting metal as the guards raised their weapons on him, he stepped toward Elise, placing himself between the facility head and her in an unmistakably protective stance. "She's not going in there alone."

"It will be perfectly safe," the director said, pointedly addressing Elise rather than Tegan, as if the warrior did not warrant a direct explanation. "The patient will be restrained, of course, and he has also been sedated for his feeding, which should be finished any moment now. There will be no danger from him, I can assure—"

"I don't care if you have that suckhead bricked up behind ten feet of solid stone," Tegan snarled, his green eyes flashing. "She doesn't go inside that Rogue holding tank without me."

Two of the guards flicked nervous glances at the director, as if they waited for his order to move in yet dreaded the idea of tangling with the Gen One warrior with a widely accepted lethal reputation.

And well they should hesitate. Elise had no doubt that if things escalated here, it was going to take a lot more than a Darkhaven-trained security detail to handle Tegan. Andreas Reichen seemed to understand that too, and the German evidently found the idea mildly amusing, smiling as he stood back and watched the suited civilian squirm.

"Madam, if you please," said the director in a patently false diplomatic tone. "Facility visitations are rarely granted to anyone due to the stress it tends to cause the residents in treatment. At the pleasure of the Enforcement Agency's Chief Director, we have made an exception for you with this interview, but I am loath to think what the mere sight of a warrior inside the clinic could do to my patient's progress. You must be aware that his kind revels in agitating the afflicted among our race. We practice mercy here, not malice."

Tegan scoffed. "I'm going in with her. It wasn't a question."

Even though he kept his narrowed gaze trained on the containment facility director, Elise knew that Tegan had already sized up the four guards and dismissed them as any kind of true threat. Underneath the long coat he wore, the warrior was also armed with a nasty-looking handgun and several deadly blades sheathed across his torso and at his hip. He made no move to reach for any of his weapons, but Elise knew from seeing him in action that it would take less than a second for him to turn the contained stretch of pavement into a blood-soaked graveyard.

"I would like Tegan to accompany me inside," she said, taking control of the situation. She saw Tegan's eyes slide her way for an instant, before he turned his icy stare back on the director.

"Madam, I really don't think—"

"Tegan comes with me." Elise removed her jacket and draped it over her arm. She smiled politely, but her gaze was as unwavering as her tone. "I'm afraid I must insist, Director Kuhn."

Elise's handling of the self-important facility director was impressive. She knew Darkhaven and Enforcement Agency protocol and understood just how far she could bend both. Her station as Quentin Chase's widow brought her a lot of pull, which she didn't hesitate to put to use.

The fact that she'd sided with Tegan when she could have just as well left him to fight his way inside to interrogate the Odolf Rogue—and would have been within her rights to do just that, after how things ended between them last night—impressed him even more. Elise was cool under pressure, a consummate lady and a level-headed tactician.

She was, he had to admit if only to himself, a damn valuable asset.

The fact that he could hardly take his eyes off her in the sexy, all-business navy trousers and crisp white blouse she wore only amplified his appreciation of her. The evidence of that rousing appreciation was a hard, heavy presence behind the zipper of his black fatigues as he left Reichen to wait behind with the driver and followed the graceful sway of Elise's hips through the second set of gates, toward the containment facility ahead.

Tegan ignored the gaping of the clinic employees he passed. He vaguely registered the hasty scrambling of civilian feet all around him—both the ones getting the hell out of his way and those few daring souls who came out from behind their monitoring stations or meeting-room doors to have a look at the dark, dangerous stranger stalking through their midst.

The facility director led Tegan and Elise deeper into the place, through one after another set of secured doors. Finally, they turned down a long concrete hallway and stopped in front of a heavy steel door marked *Treatment Center*. The director punched a code into a wall-mounted keypad, then put his face in front of a scanner and waited as a light took a quick read of his retinas.

"This way," he said, sniffing almost imperceptibly down the length of his nose as he held the door open for Elise and Tegan to enter yet another hallway.

The space inside was dimly lit and quiet except for intermittent moans and feral-sounding growls not quite masked by the soft classical music piped in through overhead speakers. Closed doors lined either side of the hallway, some with small windows that looked in over the room's occupant. A few of the rooms were empty, but others held Rogues in various stages of consciousness, all of them strapped into full body restraints. Heavy steel bars equipped with electronic locks held the doors closed, sealing the patients inside their rooms.

Tegan glanced into one of the windows as he passed, taking in the pathetic sight of a drooling, blood-addicted Breed vampire, its limp body stuffed into a soiled white jumpsuit, head shaved bald and still sporting tiny contact pads from a recent bout of electroshock therapy. The Rogue's fiery amber eyes were at half-mast, rolled back into its skull from whatever sedative it had been given.

"So, this is the Darkhavens' version of Betty Ford, eh?" Tegan gave a humorless chuckle. "And you people have the balls to say the Order has no mercy."

Elise shot him a quelling look, but Kuhn ignored the jab completely. He walked them toward the last of the holding cells, pausing to enter an access code. As the admittance light blinked green above the door, the director said, "Since the feeding is still under way, we will have to wait in the observation room until they finish. It should only be another few minutes."

Tegan followed Elise inside the vestibule, and was there to hold her steady as she physically recoiled the instant she got her first glimpse of the procedure taking place on the other side of the shaded one-way glass.

"Good Lord," she gasped, one hand coming up to her mouth.

In the adjacent room, the Rogue named Petrov Odolf was strapped down on a custom-rigged examination table like a specimen under a scope. He was naked except for the multiple sets of thick metal clamps that held him at each limb, around the torso and neck, and across the width of his brow. His shaved head was wrapped in a leather-and-wire-mesh mask that held his jaw and massive fangs stationary for the tube that was running fresh blood into his mouth from the Host who had the unpleasant task of feeding him. The Rogue had pissed himself at some point during the procedure, leaving a puddle of urine beneath the table that only added to the degradation of the whole thing.

And then there was the woman.

Tegan exhaled a ripe curse as his gaze followed the blood-filled tube running from the Rogue's mouth to the inner forearm of a young woman lying on another exam table a few feet away from him. Garbed in a white clinic jumpsuit without sleeves, she lay very still on her back, calmly in fact, but her freckled cheeks were stained with tears.

"You sent a female in there with that beast?"

"She's his Breedmate," Kuhn replied. "They'd been together for many years before he succumbed to Bloodlust and turned Rogue. She's been coming in every week to feed him, and to take her own nourishment from him as well. She must keep her own health and longevity in order to continue to care for him. Truly, he's lucky to have her devotion. Most of our other patients have no Breedmate to look after them, so they must be fed from human donors."

Elise inched closer to the glass now, obviously as transfixed by what she was seeing as she was repulsed. "How do you find those other donors, Director Kuhn?"

He shrugged when she glanced back at him over her shoulder. "We never have to look far. University students willing to join medical studies for a little money, prostitutes, the homeless . . . drug addicts, if we're desperate."

"Well, shit," Tegan drawled, full of sarcasm. "This is a real class operation you got here."

"No harm done to anyone, generally speaking," Kuhn

said with an annoyed smile. "The procedures are very closely monitored and none of our recruited Hosts maintain a single memory afterward. We simply return them to their lives with a little cash in their pocket that they wouldn't have had otherwise. A little time spent here is the best thing to happen to some of the unfortunates we collect as donors."

Tegan was ready to spit a cutting remark at the pompous Darkhaven male, but it had been less than twenty-four hours since he himself had been hunting for blood on Berlin's darkened streets. He'd killed, even though he could justify it with the knowledge that there was one less human criminal around to violate a defenseless woman. But that didn't make him a saint by any stretch. At heart, all of the Breed were self-serving, ruthless predators. Some just attempted to hide the fact behind sterile white walls and a fleet of clinical equipment.

"There now," the facility director announced when a small beep sounded on the console near the viewing window. "The feeding procedure is complete. As soon as the patient is alone and resting, we can go in."

They waited as Odolf was disconnected from his feeding tube. The vampire fought the removal, his insatiable blood addiction making him snap and growl behind the wire-mesh face mask as the attendants cut off his supply. He struggled against his body restraints, but the effort was sluggish and ineffective, no doubt from the sedatives Kuhn had mentioned earlier.

The Rogue's *dermaglyphs* were still seething from deep purples to red to black, the colors of ferocious hunger traveling along the pattern of markings that ran up his bare chest and over his shoulders.

His huge fangs flashed bone white with his sudden

roar of protest. His pupils were fixed into vertical slits, the irises throwing off a blast of amber light every time he tried to raise his big head up off the table. Even though he was drugged, the taste of blood had inflamed him to the point of madness—as it did all Rogues.

Tegan ought to know. He'd lived a similar thirsting, angry as hell himself. He hadn't progressed as far Rogue as this male, thankfully, but he'd come damn close. Seeing this blood-addicted male up close was a strong reminder of what those dark months Tegan had fought to shake off his own weakness had been like.

As Petrov Odolf rattled his bonds in futility, his Breedmate got up off the table beside him and cautiously approached where he lay. She kept her hands at her sides, even though it was clear from the anguish in her eyes that she longed to touch her mate. She said something too quiet to be heard over the cell's audio monitors, then she turned away and walked toward the door of the observation room, wiping tears from her freckled cheeks.

Kuhn opened the door for her, and she seemed startled to see that she'd had an audience. Her face flamed red, and her downcast gaze said it was in shame. "Pardon me," she murmured, trying to make a beeline for the outside hallway.

"Are you all right?" Elise asked gently.

The Breedmate gave a wobbly nod. A sob hitched in her throat, broken and raw. "Will you excuse me, please?"

"This way," Director Kuhn said as the Rogue's female slipped out of their company and headed down the corridor. "I can permit you no more than ten minutes with him, Madam Chase. And I must reiterate that I think it best if the warrior—"

"Actually," Elise said, her voice full of confident authority, "I would like Tegan to conduct the interview without me."

"Wha— Without you?" Kuhn's brows crashed together furiously. "That was not the term of our arrangement at all."

"It is now. I'm not about to let that poor woman leave here in such a state of distress," she said, then glanced at Tegan. "Tegan will speak with Petrov Odolf. I trust him in this, Director Kuhn, and you can too."

She didn't wait to hear the facility head sputter his disagreement, just strode out of the observation room and went after Odolf's distraught Breedmate like a guided missile in a designer suit and stilettos.

Tegan was tempted to smile, but instead he turned a flat gaze on Kuhn.

"After you," he said, daring the director to try to keep him out of that containment cell.

CHAPTER
Twenty

Elise found the Breedmate just a short way down the corridor. The woman was seated on a cushioned bench, her face pressed into her hands. She was weeping quietly, but her contained sobs shook her entire body.

"I'm very sorry," Elise murmured, unsure if she should intrude on such a private moment, yet too moved by what she had seen to simply let the Breedmate suffer alone. She fished a small package of tissues out of her bag and held them out as she walked closer to the female. "Would you like these?"

Red-rimmed light brown eyes lifted to meet Elise's gaze. "Yes, thank you. I always think I'll be strong for him, but it's so hard. It never gets easier, seeing him like he is."

"Of course," Elise said, taking a seat beside her. "I'm Elise, by the way."

"Irina," she answered softly. "Petrov is my mate."

"Yes, I know. The facility director told us."

She glanced down as she took out one of the folded tissues. "You're from America?"

"Boston."

"So far away. Director Kuhn informed me that some people were coming to see my mate, but he couldn't tell me why. What is it that you want with Petrov?"

"We just need to ask him some questions, Irina. That's all."

There was a worried glint in the female's sidelong look. "That male you're with—he's not Darkhaven Breed."

"No. Tegan is one of the Order. He's a warrior."

"A warrior?" Irina went visibly rigid, her brow creasing. "But Petrov has hurt no one. He is a good man. He has done nothing wrong—"

"It's all right," Elise assured her, placing her hand over the anxious woman's trembling fingers. "Tegan is not here to harm him, I promise you. Only to talk to him."

"About what?"

"We need some information about your mate's family line. We need to talk to him, and see if he recognizes a particular *dermaglyphic* symbol."

Irina sighed and gave a small shake of her head. "He hardly recognizes me anymore. I don't think he will be much help to you."

Elise smiled, sympathetic. "We have to try. It's very important."

"You give me your word that no harm will come to him?"

"Yes. I give you my word, Irina."

The Breedmate stared at Elise for a long moment, those warm brown eyes searching, divining the truth. "Yes," she said at last. "I believe you. I trust what you are telling me."

Elise squeezed the woman's hand. "How long have you and Petrov been blood-bonded?"

"It will be fifty-seven years this summer." There was pride in the statement, and love. But sadness crept into her voice as she went on. "He has been in this . . . *this place* . . . for the last three of those years."

"I'm very sorry," Elise said.

"I thought he would be stronger than the weakness that plagued his father and his brothers—I thought my love might be enough, you know? But he was haunted by demons I never understood. Three years ago, in the weeks before I lost him to his disease, he was a different man."

"How so?" Elise asked the question carefully, not wanting to pry into what had been such a painful time for the woman.

"He changed in so many ways after his older brother went Rogue and died. I think maybe Petrov knew the day was coming that he would fall too. It was as if a terrible burden had been heaped upon him. He withdrew from everything—from me as well. He became secretive, writing for hours in his study, only to burn his papers to a cinder. I managed to retrieve a page, but it was filled with nonsense, just a lot of crazed ramblings that he couldn't—or wouldn't—explain to me." She shrugged, her head hung low. "Petrov started going on feeding binges late at night, while I slept. He went quite mad in time. He attacked me one night in a fit of Bloodlust, and I realized it was time for us to part."

"It must have been so difficult for you, Irina."

"Yes," she whispered. "Bloodlust is a terribly seductive thing. I know Petrov will never come home. They rarely do come home from this place. But still, I hope."

The Breedmate waved her hand as a fresh round of tears welled in her eyes. "Listen to me going on like this. I need to change out of this awful feeding garment and get myself home. Thank you for talking to me. And thank you for these," she said, pulling out another tissue and dabbing her moist eyes.

"You're very welcome."

Elise stood with Irina, and gave her a brief hug as the other woman gathered herself to leave. Once she was gone, Elise walked back up the corridor to Petrov Odolf's containment cell. Tegan was just coming out, and he didn't look pleased. Director Kuhn was right behind him, sputtering something about *ensuring the patient's comfort* and *perfectly acceptable doses.*

"What's going on?"

Tegan raked a hand over his scalp. "Odolf is so medicated he's practically catatonic. We won't get anything out of him in this condition."

"Additional sedatives are always required for a feeding procedure, for the safety of the patient and his blood Host," Kuhn declared, indignant.

"And the other half a dozen drugs you've pumped into him?" Tegan challenged.

"Just our normal protocol for making certain our patients are comfortable at all times."

"You weren't able to talk to him at all?" Elise asked, ignoring Kuhn's bluster to focus on Tegan.

"A minute after I got in there, he was barely conscious. We've got shit so far."

"Then we'll come back tomorrow." Elise turned to the facility head. "I'm sure Director Kuhn can see to it that he's more lucid when we return. Won't you, Director?"

"To reduce a patient's medication is an enormous risk. We won't be responsible for any harm that comes to either of you if that is your request."

Elise glanced to Tegan, who gave her a nod of agreement. "That's fine. Expect us tomorrow evening at this time, and have Petrov Odolf awake and clearheaded when we arrive."

Kuhn's mouth went tight, but he inclined his head in compliance. "As you wish, madam."

Although Tegan was quiet, she felt his eyes on her the entire time as they left the treatment center and were escorted back out to where Reichen's car and driver waited. Whatever had passed between them last night in the boathouse, and the heavy awareness that had remained in the hours since, was still present now. Just being near him, her body thrummed with a disquieting heat.

She knew part of it was the link she shared with him through his blood, but there was another part of her that responded to him as well. It was that latter part—the elemental, feminine stirring—that troubled her the most, because after the way he'd left her last night, it seemed that she was alone in her desire.

Tegan was stoic and silent with her, stepping aside as Reichen's driver opened the back door of the Rolls-Royce to her as they approached the car. She glanced into the vehicle as she began to climb inside and was surprised to find it empty.

"Where is Andreas?"

The driver gave a polite little bow of his bald head. "With regrets, madam, he was called away briefly to attend a personal matter in the city. He asked that I contact him once you and the gentleman had completed your meeting here. We'll go retrieve him now."

"Oh. All right, Klaus. Thank you."

Elise slid into the private passenger area of the luxurious sedan limousine. Tegan followed, seating himself across from her, one muscled arm slung over the back of the sumptuous leather bench seat. His thighs were spread indecently wide as he slouched back and stared at her under a hank of his thick tawny hair. He was considering her in that maddening silence of his, those bright green eyes fixed on her for so long she could hardly bear the weight of his unreadable scrutiny.

The few minutes it took to reach the center of Berlin felt like an hour. And even worse, the farther they drove into the heart of all that humanity, Elise's temples began to pound with the incoming chatter of hundreds of dark thoughts and ugly voices hissing their corrupt impulses into her ears. She turned her face toward the tinted glass of the car window, feeling the crush of her psychic gift squeezing all the air out of the vehicle.

Lord, just let the drive be over soon. All she wanted was to crawl into bed and put the past few nights behind her.

". . . handled it well."

Tegan's deep voice roused her out of her mounting panic. She'd been so distracted, she hadn't realized he'd finally started speaking to her. "I'm sorry?"

"Back there at the containment facility. You were good, the way you handled Kuhn . . . and all the rest of it. I'm impressed."

The praise warmed her, mostly because she knew how rare it was, coming from Tegan. He wasn't the type to coddle, or to dole out kind words unless he meant them. "I wish we'd had better luck with Odolf."

"We'll get what we need from him tomorrow."

"I hope so."

Idly, she rubbed at her throbbing temple, a move Tegan followed with his eyes. "Are you all right?"

"Fine," she said, wincing a bit as the car stopped at a traffic light in the center of a crowded intersection downtown. Pedestrians crossed in front of them, a thick knot of people whose thoughts rattled Elise's head like a long roll of thunder. "I'll be fine once we're out of the city."

Tegan stared at her.

"You need more blood," he said, not sounding very happy about the idea. "After so long without, feeding just one time isn't going to hold you."

"I'm okay," she insisted, wishing it were true. "I'm not going to take anything more from you, Tegan."

"I wasn't offering."

Humiliation flooded her at his grim statement of fact. "You weren't offering that first time either, were you? I forced your hand that night at the compound, Tegan. I'm sorry."

"Forget it. I'll live."

Well, he certainly closed the door on that subject. Actually, he seemed preoccupied and edgy, even more than usual. Elise had seen how appalled Tegan had been by the containment facility's practices.

She'd also seen the way he'd looked at Petrov Odolf, restrained and feverish from the Bloodlust that had robbed him of his sanity and, probably, his soul. Tegan, who was normally so detached and unmovable, had felt a degree of sympathy for the Rogue being held in that cell. Incredibly, it had seemed as though Tegan might even relate to the vampire's pitiful condition.

Elise could hardly imagine that, seeing how rigidly the warrior clung to his self-control. Or maybe he held on so tightly because he knew what it was like to lose his grasp . . .

She might have pondered that in more depth, but a fresh wave of nausea assailed her as another large group of people filed past the car while it waited for the light.

In a fluid move, Tegan came over onto the seat next to her. "Come here. I'll trance you."

"No." She drew away from him, not wanting any of his pity. "No, I need to deal with this myself. It's my problem, like you've said. I want to manage it on my own."

Thankfully the vehicle was moving again, turning a corner onto a side street off the exclusive main thoroughfare with its bright boutique lights and milling crowds. It was better here, but still a struggle to hold it together under the constant battering of her mind. Her mind was like a broken radio receiver, intercepting only the worst feeds, bombarding her with countless inputs until the cacophony seemed to consume her.

"Find one that you can focus on," Tegan said from beside her. His breath was warm, his fingers tender but commanding as he took hold of her hand. His thumb swept over her skin, gentling her. Grounding her. "All you need is one, Elise. One voice that you can deal with on its own. Separate it from the others. Let the rest go. Let them fall away."

His deep voice was almost hypnotic, coaching her further into the pain of her gift so that she could learn to harness it. With eyes closed, she followed his direction, sifting through the terrible din to find something she could grasp ahold of. Slowly, bit by bit, she peeled away the worst of the voices in her mind until she heard one that hurt the least.

"Focus on the one," Tegan murmured, still holding her hand, still guiding her with his words and the protective warmth of his touch. "Pull one voice closer, even as the others begin to drift around you. They can't touch you. You're stronger than your gift, Elise. Your power is in you, in your own will."

She felt everything he was saying. She knew it was true. With his fingers wrapped around hers, his voice a low purr near her ear, she believed that she was strong. She believed that she could do this . . .

"Feel your strength, Elise," Tegan coached her. "There is no panic here, only calm. Your gift does not own you . . . you are in control."

And so she was, she realized only now—knowing that what Tegan was showing her was just a glimmer of the control she was capable of. He was opening a door in her subconscious, and wherever it was that her Breedmate gift originated within her, Tegan was guiding her inside that place, letting her see the power of her own potential.

It was a revelation. Her temples still pounded from the onslaught of psychic pain, but it was a dull, manageable throb now that she was focusing, honing her skill. She wanted to keep working it, to keep pushing herself, but the exercise was also exhausting. The one voice she clung to began to slip out of her grasp, blending back into the din.

Outside her body and her mind, she felt the car slow to a stop. Footsteps approached, two pairs of them, joined by the efficient shuffle of the driver's quick gait as he ran around the vehicle to get the door.

As soon as it opened, Tegan's touch was gone.

Elise blinked, lifting her gaze to find Reichen outside the car, giving a beautiful raven-haired woman a brief kiss on the mouth. She was wrapped in a silvery fur coat—and from what Elise could tell, little else beneath it. On the side of her graceful throat was a pink bloom of color, only a fading rosebud mark to indicate the place where Reichen had no doubt fed from her just a short while ago.

"A pleasure as always, my darling Helene," he said as the two of them parted. "You spoil me so well."

Evidently the Darkhaven male's personal business was of a very personal nature.

The woman's glossy mouth curved into a catlike smile at his charm. She didn't wait at the car for him to leave, but pivoted on staggeringly tall silver stiletto heels and sauntered back into a red, unmarked door of the building where Reichen's car sat idling.

"My thanks for the curb service," the German said as he crawled into the limousine and took a seat opposite Tegan and Elise. "Not to imply I don't enjoy your company, but I rather hoped you might be longer at your appointment. You finished quickly."

Tegan smirked. "So did you, from the looks of it."

Reichen chuckled, unabashed as he lounged back in the seat and the car took off. He smelled like expensive perfume, blood, and sex. Not that he cared, Elise thought as she considered him. His broad, sated grin said he couldn't be in a happier, more familiar state.

Andreas Reichen was a very attractive male, mysterious and sophisticated, but even his smoldering sensuality paled next to Tegan's raw appeal. Elise practically burned from the heat of Tegan's thigh where it pressed unassumingly against hers. His head was tilted down, eyes hooded beneath the thick fringe of his eyelashes.

He kept his arms crossed over his chest now, and she missed the warm feel of his touch. She craved it, especially as the limousine navigated through the busy city streets and her Breedmate gift continued to buffet her senses. Instead she tried to use the brief lesson he'd given her, taking what he'd shown her and wielding it against the crush of her psychic pain.

More than anything, she wanted to grab Tegan's hand again and feel his calming strength.

But he only put a measure of distance between them. He moved away from her on the seat, a subtle shift of his thigh that left a gap of space in its place. When they arrived a short while later at the lakeshore Darkhaven, Tegan leaped out of the car almost as soon as Klaus slowed to a stop on the front driveway.

"I have to report in to the compound," he said, keeping his gaze averted. He stalked off before either Elise or Reichen could get out of the car.

"All business, that one," Reichen remarked with a shake of his head. "May I get you something to eat in the house, Elise? You must be hungry."

She was famished, actually, having last eaten around noon. "That would be lovely, thank you."

Elise let Reichen help her out of the vehicle, and took his proffered arm as they walked up to the main entrance of the estate. But all the while, her thoughts were fixed on Tegan, and on quelling the strong—evidently one-sided—desire he stirred in her.

CHAPTER
Twenty-one

Tegan closed his cell phone after reporting in to the compound and leaned back on the ridiculously froufrou velvet settee in his private room of the Darkhaven. He was pissed off that the night had resulted in a stalemate with Petrov Odolf, and more rattled than he cared to admit by the Bloodlust reality check he'd gotten at the facility. Seeing Odolf and the other Rogues was a damn good reminder of the fire he'd walked through after Sorcha's death.

He'd managed to beat his Bloodlust all those years ago, but the fight had been brutal. And the hunger was always with him, even when he was trying his hardest to deny it.

Being near Elise only magnified his craving. Damn, but that female put his blood on a slow, rising boil.

That moment alone with her in Reichen's car—touching her, walking her through her psychic distress—had been a colossal mistake. It only made him realize how deeply he wanted to help her. That he didn't want to see her in pain.

That despite centuries of religiously honed apathy, he was starting to care. He was genuinely beginning to have feelings for her, a bold and complicated Darkhaven beauty who could have her choice of any male, Breed or otherwise. He truly cared about Elise. He wanted her . . . and he knew that it was only a matter of time before he went after her like the predator he was.

Touching her soft skin had made him recall how good it had been to feel her body pressed against him, how delicious her mouth fit his own . . . how sweet even the smallest taste of her blood had been on the tip of his tongue.

Christ.

He hadn't been able to bolt out of the car fast enough. And the hour he'd spent alone up here in his guest room hadn't done much to cool the need that urged him to go downstairs and find Elise. Sate himself with her the way Reichen had so freely been able to do with the woman in the city.

The fire Elise had stoked in him from nearly the moment he set eyes on her was banked, but still burning.

Maybe he could douse it, Tegan thought, stalking into the bathroom to turn on the shower. God knew he wanted to get the feel of the containment facility off his skin as well. Seeing those incarcerated, mostly catatonic Rogues had pulled him back to an ugly time in his own life—one he had no desire to relive, even in passing memory. That part of him was buried deep, where it belonged.

He stripped off his shirt and weapons and dropped the lot of it on a chair beside the settee. His fingers were working the zipper of his black fatigues when a knock sounded on the closed door to the hall. He ignored it, wondering if it might be Reichen looking to drag him into a few hours of sin back in the city. Part of him was tempted by the thought—anything to slake the coiling hunger he had for Elise.

The knock came again, and this time Tegan threw open the door without a thought.

As the panel swung wide, he was surprised—and not a little furious—to see the subject of his frustration standing there. Just what he didn't need right now. Gorgeous as ever, still wearing the proper navy pantsuit she had on at the clinic, the sight of Elise was a major dose of gasoline tossed on his fire.

"What the hell are you doing up here?" His voice was harsh, more rough than he intended.

Elise didn't so much as flinch. "I thought we might talk."

"What happened to Reichen finding you some dinner downstairs?"

"He did. That was almost an hour ago. I . . . waited for a while to see if you might come out of your room, but when you didn't, I decided to come to you."

He stared at her for a minute, then mentally cut the shower off and turned to grab his shirt and weapons holster. "I was just on my way out."

"Oh." She didn't look like she was buying it. "What could be so urgent all of a sudden?"

"Just a little thing called duty, sweetheart. I'm not used to spending my nights sitting on my ass when I could be outside killing something." He said it deliberately to shock her, and he probably took a bit too much satisfaction at the disturbed frown that creased her forehead. "I need to get out of this place for a while. I should be in the city, on the streets, where I'm useful. Not wasting my fucking time sitting around here."

He expected her to give him space and be glad he was leaving. His cold attitude had scared away countless Breed males, even among the Order, so he didn't expect this female to linger for long.

For a second, he really thought she was going to retreat like he'd intended her to do.

But then she strode right over the threshold and into his room.

"You're not going anywhere tonight," she said, soft but resolute. There was apprehension in her expression, but damn if she didn't close the door behind her and keep coming toward him. "Tonight we need to talk. I need to know where things stand. Where *we* stand, Tegan."

He glared. "You think it's wise to shut yourself in here with me? It won't take long for Reichen and the rest of this house to figure out where you are and think the worst. He may be discreet when needed, but the others who live here—"

"I don't care what anyone else thinks. I just need to know what you think."

He scoffed, a grating sound that held more mockery than he'd intended. "I think you're out of your fucking head."

She glanced down, gave a little nod. "I'm confused, I'll give you that. I don't know if you . . . I don't know what to make of you, Tegan. Not from day one. I don't know how to play this game that we seem to be playing together."

"I don't play games," he said, deadly serious. "I don't have the interest or the time—"

"Bullshit!"

He arched a brow at her unexpected blurt of profanity. He was ready to push again—seething with the compulsion to shove her away hard, before she got any closer to the truth of what he was feeling. But the glint of anger in her eyes gave him pause.

She crossed her arms over her breasts and took a couple of paces nearer to him, making it clear that if he pushed now, she was sure as hell going to push back.

"What do you call it when you're tender with me one moment, then cold as ice the next? You kiss me, only to push away a minute later." She drew a breath, letting it out on a frustrated-sounding sigh. "Sometimes you look at me as if you might really feel something for me, but then . . . then you blink and it's like the feeling was never there in the first place. What is that, if not your twisted idea of fun?"

Since she wasn't about to stand down, he pivoted away from her on a snarl and went for the duffel bag that held more of his gear and weapons, ignoring her attempt to goad him. He reached in and blindly grabbed for a cache of combat supplies. He pulled out a sheathed blade, then a clip of titanium rounds for his 9mm— anything to keep his hands moving and his focus trained on something other than the maddening awareness of the woman who was slowly walking up behind him.

Incredibly, his fingers were shaking as he put his gear down on the settee's velvet cushions. His vision was going sharp, his field of sight taking on a hard edge as his pupils narrowed and a flood of amber fire bathed everything in a hunter's light. His gums ached with the emergence of his fangs, his mouth watering with the hunger he'd barely been able to stave off before Elise arrived in his room.

Now that she was here, provoking him with her mere presence, he didn't know how long he could hold the beast at bay. It had been snapping at its leash since the moment he first laid eyes on her.

Behind him, he heard the thick Persian rug crush with the subtle movement of her feet. He closed his eyes, his senses flooded with awareness of her.

With the keen, aching want of her.

"You say you don't play games, but you're a master at it, Tegan. In fact, I think you've been playing at them for so long you can't remember how to be real anymore."

He was hardly aware of his own movements as he whirled back on her with a furious roar. Distance closed in fractional seconds—a blink of time between the moment he'd been turned away from Elise and the next, when he was bearing down on her like a train in motion, pushing her with both the force of his will and his body until they both slammed up against the closed door.

He pinned her there, between the hard, unyielding length of him and the thick plank of oak at her back.

"Is this real enough for you, sweetheart?"

He hissed the words at her, his lips curled back from his fangs. Desire had him livid, fully transformed into the savage side of his nature. With a growl, he bent his head and took her mouth in a hot, demanding kiss.

She cried out, startled, her hands coming up to brace defensively against his shoulders. He only kissed her harder, thrusting his tongue past her teeth as she gasped to take a breath.

Christ, she was sweet. So warm and lush against his mouth.

So soft against the scorching rigidity of his body.

He didn't want to feel this arousal. Wanted like hell to reject this consuming need. But he was burning up with it, and there would be no denying it now.

No stopping the pound of his blood as everything Breed in him—everything elementally male—awakened to the delicious taste of Elise.

When he broke their kiss, she was panting. He was too. His whole body heaved with the force of his hunger, his every pulse point pounding with a beat he felt echoing in Elise as well.

"Last night in the boathouse, I felt your fear," he whispered fiercely, holding her wide gaze, pressing the front of his body deeper into hers. His cock was rigid, growing harder just at the feel of her. "I let you go instead of taking what I wanted. I'm not going to be forgiving this time. So, fear me if you will, Elise, but don't expect me to fucking care—"

"I went back last night." A breathless little sound curled up from her throat, but when she spoke her voice was steady. "I wasn't afraid of you, Tegan. I went back for you."

The words sank into his brain slowly, stilling him as he registered what he was hearing.

"Last night, after you told me to leave you . . . I had gotten as far as the main house and I realized that I didn't want to leave. I wanted to be with you."

She stared up at him without the slightest tremor of uncertainty now. Where his hands held her arms, he felt only pliant acceptance, knowing surrender. Through the connection of his touch, he read her desire. Felt it radiating out to him, seeping into him.

"I wanted to be naked with you, Tegan. I wanted you inside me, so I went back. But you were already gone."

Holy hell.

He knew he should probably say something, but he had no voice. Only a dumbshit muteness like he'd never known before. His weight settled back on his heels, and the urge to shove her away from him in defense—remove her from his reach—was nearly overwhelming.

But he found he couldn't let go of her.

He couldn't stop looking into the clear lavender pools of her eyes. The unwavering honesty—the guileless need—that he saw in their depths floored him.

"I want to be with you now, Tegan . . . so if you want me, even a little bit—"

He pulled her close and silenced her doubt with another kiss. She put her arms around him and held him to her, parting her lips and taking his tongue as he swept inside her mouth the way he intended to be inside her body. He guided her around, away from the door and toward the waiting bed, their lips never parting. Hands roaming, clutching, trembling.

Clothing was stripped away quickly under the force of their need. Tegan drew off Elise's jacket and made fast work of the white silk blouse beneath it, slipping free what seemed like a hundred tiny buttons until he had unveiled her satin-and-lace-covered breasts. He ran his hands over the gossamer white fabric, watching with a hungry gaze as her nipples rose to his touch.

Easing her back onto the bed, he unfastened her tailored navy trousers and slid them down her pale, slender legs. Her sex was hidden behind a small scrap of white satin. Tegan followed the line of thin triangle with his fingers, softly stroking the warm velvet of her hip and inner thigh. His thumb traced beneath the satin to something even more silky. The slick, wet heat of her made him groan, compelled him to delve deeper into that searing, moist cleft.

Elise sucked in her breath as he stroked the dewy petals and the tight little nub nestled at the top of her sex.

He pushed her legs apart and his hungry gaze settled on the tiny birthmark that rode the inside of her right thigh. Tegan smiled, amused that she bore it on such a delectable part of her body. He'd been wanting to taste that tender spot on her from the first time he saw it. Now he kissed the little teardrop-and-crescent-moon, nipping her gently as he came back up to look at her.

God, she was beautiful. Pure and decadent at the same time.

He wanted to feast on her slowly, but need was stronger—his own, and hers as well. He could feel Elise's hunger in every questing brush of his fingers, and knew her want was as strong as his, a sexual need coiling to the point of pain.

Tegan shucked his fatigues with hasty impatience, kicking them aside as he pushed Elise farther up on the bed. He drew off her panties and climbed over her, bracing his arms on either side of her head. His cock hung down between them, engorged and ruddy, a thick spear of hard flesh that weeped a drop of moisture into the cradle of her belly. The Gen One *glyphs* that covered him from shoulder to mid-thigh were pulsing with color, the pattern alive with lust's variegating shades of indigo, gold, and wine.

"Is this too real for you, Elise?" His voice was reduced to a bestial growl, speech made difficult for the presence of his fangs, which were fully extended in response to his desire for her. "Jesus Christ . . . I think it's too goddamn real for me."

If she had given the slightest indication that she was unsure about what they were about to do, he might have found the strength to back off.

He would have forced himself to heel, even though he was nearly out of his head with the need to possess her. Despite all his hard-ass threats, he knew, looking down into her gentle gaze, that he would have shown her mercy. Some panicked part of him hoped to hell she would want out.

But Elise didn't tremble at the feral beast poised over her. She reached up and put her hand around the back of his neck. Firmly, she guided him down to her, her eyes wide open and fixed on his, and pressed his mouth to hers.

Tegan crushed her beneath him as he claimed her lips in a heated kiss. God help him, but she met his every thrust and parry, driving him wild when he felt the un-gentle prod of her tongue slipping inside his mouth, tracing the length of his fangs.

Without breaking contact with her lips, he reared back on his knees and took himself in hand, guiding his thick erection between her parted thighs. She arched up to meet him, a tremor rocking her as he played the head of his penis along the wet core of her body.

The tease was too much to bear, and he was too far gone to be patient. He tilted his hips back, then thrust into her moist sheath with one long, filling stroke.

Elise gasped near his ear as he came down over her

and seated himself to the hilt. Her body was small beneath his, her sex tight and hot, a molten vise around his cock.

Everything he thought he knew about being inside a woman—everything he thought he remembered—was obliterated by the incredible feel of Elise wrapped around him. This was unlike anything he'd known before, more powerful than he ever could have imagined. He was connected to her, mind and body, feeling her pleasure pour into him everywhere their bodies touched. Elise was vibrant and strong, consuming. After centuries of exile from touch, from feeling, Tegan looked into Elise's beautiful face and gave himself up to the warm, wet bliss of her.

He couldn't stop his hips from pumping, couldn't stanch the escalating urge to lose himself inside her. His shaft swelled with the rise of his orgasm, and he knew he was just a few desperate seconds from exploding.

He grunted, going deep as the coil wound tighter. His voice was a raw scrape in his throat. "Ah, Christ—Elise!"

He couldn't hold it back. With a hard surge, he drove his hips into hers and came like a breaking storm. He shouted with the force of his release, thrusting as wave after searing wave shuddered out of him.

And still it wasn't enough. He was still erect, still hungry for her.

Still pumping into the velvety glove of Elise's exquisite body.

He stared down into her dusky eyes as he filled her, needing to see her as he gave her some of the same pleasure she was giving him.

"I was greedy," he murmured, bending down to kiss her in apology. He didn't dare get close to her luscious throat, not when his fangs were throbbing with another need that was raging to be sated. "If you want, we can take it slower now."

"Don't you dare," she said, wrapping her legs around his thighs to make her point.

Tegan chuckled, and some distant part of him wondered when the last time was that he'd actually felt humor. When was the last time he'd felt anything close to what Elise roused in him?

He didn't want to explore the place she seemed to have breached inside him. All he wanted right now was this.

"It's been a long time for me," Elise whispered. "And you feel so good . . . "

Her words trailed off on a moan as Tegan pushed as deep as she could take him. He withdrew and thrust again, feeling the walls of her channel grip and contract around him.

"My God," he rasped, hissing with the pleasure of it.

Already another orgasm was ratcheting up within him.

Elise's climax was swiftly building too. She took him deeper with every furious pound of their meeting flesh, clutching at his shoulders and panting as her body's need overtook her.

Tegan could feel her pleasure in each stroke of his fingers on her flesh, each silken caress of her core. Her emotion seeped into him from every point of contact, swamping him with a surfeit of sensation. He absorbed everything she gave him, all his focus on bringing her toward a shattering release.

He kissed her passionately, with tongue and teeth and fang. Elise met him every inch of the way, and when he felt the sharp nip of her blunt human teeth sink into the flesh of his lower lip, he bucked wildly, groaning as her tongue lapped at the small wound she'd made. She sucked a little harder and he was totally lost, fevered with the desire to have her at his vein.

Before he could think better of it, Tegan reared back and punctured his wrist with his fangs. Blood dripped in steady rivulets onto her bare breasts and throat as he offered the gift to her and gently pressed his arm to her mouth.

"Take it," he said. "I want to feed you."

With her eyes locked on his, she sealed her lips around his flesh. She drank him down, pulse after pulse, her tongue creating a mesmerizing, erotic suction. And all the while, Tegan thrust into her, taking carnal delight in every gasp and shudder of her body as she spiraled closer to release. Her fingernails scored his skin where she gripped his arm, holding him fast against her mouth, pulling hard at his vein as her orgasm seized her.

She broke apart on a violent tremor, crying out as Tegan drove in a relentless rhythm, chasing his own fierce climax now too. He plunged deep, felt the rush of hot seed jetting up his shaft, erupting from him in a gushing wave as Elise's sex milked him like a hot, wet fist.

"Ah, fuck," he gasped, rolling away from her, spent but not sated.

Not even close.

The scent of blood and sex was ripe in the room, a potent fragrance that only reminded him of the savage side of his nature. The part that had once ruled him . . . had almost destroyed him.

Beside him on the bed, Elise crept closer. Her naked breasts pressed against his shoulder as she leaned over him. Her fingers were tender as she stroked the side of his face and smoothed his sweat-dampened hair off his brow.

"You didn't finish."

He scoffed weakly, still weathering the aftershocks of his release. "You obviously weren't paying attention."

"No, Tegan. I mean . . . you didn't finish."

Her arm came around him, hovering in front of his mouth. Alarm arrowed into his brain, overriding the hard-core impulse that made him want to fall on her like the beast he was and fill his mouth with the sweet heather-and-roses taste of her blood.

He got up like he'd been spurred in the ass, vaulting to his feet next to the bed. He licked the wound at his wrist, sealing up the punctures with an efficient sweep of his tongue.

"You won't drink from me?"

"No," he said, forcing the word past his tongue. "I can't do that."

"I thought maybe you wanted to—"

"You thought wrong," he snapped.

His denied hunger made his voice take on an even sharper edge. He cast a glance at his discarded clothes and weapons, wondering how fast he could pull them on and get the hell out of the room. He had to go, before he gave in to the temptation Elise presented, sitting naked and beautiful in his bed, cradling in her lap the delicate wrist he had so callously refused.

Tegan's breath sawed out of him as it passed over his fangs. "Shit," he said, his voice rough gravel, harsh and otherworldly. "This is going too damn far. I need to . . . ah, fuck." He raked a shaky hand over his face. "I need to get out of here."

"Don't bother." Elise crawled off the bed. "It's your room. I'll go." She hastily gathered up her clothes, yanking on her blouse and pulling the navy jacket over the top of it, buttoning it with sure, steady fingers. She grabbed her pants and stepped into them, fastening them as she headed for the door. "This was a mistake. Another one, where you're concerned. You win, Tegan. I'm finally giving up."

She ran out, and he forced himself to let her go.

CHAPTER
Twenty-two

Elise closed the door of her guest room behind her and sagged against the carved oak panel.

She felt like an utter fool.

Bad enough she'd thrown herself at Tegan like some kind of wanton idiot, but she had to top it off by offering her blood to him. Blood that he rejected.

Of course, it didn't surprise her that he had refused. To drink from her would irrevocably complete their blasphemy of a blood bond, a fact that Elise had been willing to accept in those heated moments of passion in his bed. At least Tegan had the good sense—the levelheaded self-control—to avoid that kind of disaster.

His obvious horror at the idea of bonding himself to

her, even without any of the vows that true mated couples shared, had come to Elise as no surprise at all.

But God, it hurt.

Especially when her veins were alive with the powerful roar of his blood within her, and her body was still thrumming and boneless from the intensity of his lovemaking.

She was a naïve fool, because some hopeful part of her had actually thought they shared something more than just an unwanted, yet undeniable, physical attraction. When Tegan touched her tonight—when he kissed her so hungrily, then scored his own wrist to let her drink from him—she really believed that she meant something more to him than mere conquest. She had thought he might truly care for her.

Worse than that, she'd hoped he did.

After five years of being alone, thinking she could never feel anything for another male, she had finally allowed her heart to open.

To a warrior, she thought grimly. There was no small amount of irony in the idea that she would let herself fall for one of the dark, dangerous members of the Order—especially after being taught all her life that they were heartless savages, never to be trusted.

And for her to care anything for Tegan, likely the coldest of them all . . .

Well, that went beyond foolish.

She'd been asking for this kind of hurt from that very first night all those months ago, when she let him drive her home from the compound. Tonight he'd done her a favor—spared her from making an enormous mistake she could never call back.

She should be grateful for that small mercy, particularly in a man who claimed to possess none at all.

Tegan was a heartbreak she didn't need.

Yet as she crossed the room to the adjoining bath and turned on the water in the shower, she couldn't help reliving the moments she had spent with him in his bed. She stripped off her clothes and stepped under the warm spray, feeling his hands on her, their bodies melded together, burning with pleasure.

She ached for him, even now.

Would be drawn to him always, the pull of his blood within her binding her to him with unseen chains.

But as much as she wanted to blame her feelings for Tegan on the unfortunate fact that she'd drunk from him—twice now—she knew that the problem went even deeper than that.

Yes, God help her. It was far, far worse than that.

She was falling in love with him.

Perhaps she already had.

Tegan spent a good long time under a punishing ice-cold shower, and still his body was inflamed with thoughts of Elise. His skin was tight all over, *dermaglyphs* pulsing under the chilly pummel of the water. He braced his fists on the marbled tile wall in front of him, struggling against the urge that compelled him to stalk Elise into her guest room and finish what they'd started.

Christ, did he ever want to finish it.

His vision was still sharp from the dual hungers that both centered on one woman alone, his fangs throbbing, the long points not yet receded. He dropped his head with a deep, ragged sigh. This need for Elise was only getting worse, becoming a fever in his veins.

How long before his control snapped its flimsy tether and he sealed their sham of a blood bond? And if he allowed himself to have a taste of something as sweet as Elise, how could he be sure his thirst wouldn't rise up to rule him again?

It was that much harder to resist, knowing that Elise would so willingly offer herself to him, even without the promises of love and devotion that any male would be privileged to give her. She had been ready to let him take so much for so little in return. It humbled him.

It shamed him, because he had been so damn close to taking her pretty wrist in his teeth . . .

With a roar, Tegan hauled his arm back and let his fist fly at the unyielding marble tile of the shower. The smooth polished square shattered on impact, breaking apart and crumbling down around his bare feet. Pain splintered into his hand and wrist, but he soaked it all in with relish, watching as droplets of his blood swirled down the shower drain.

No. Damn it, no.

He was stronger than this animal need he felt for Elise. He could resist it. He had to.

He'd only really known Elise for a handful of days and she was somehow under his skin, had somehow managed to break down some of the protective walls it had taken him several lifetimes to construct. He could not permit things to escalate between them.

And he wouldn't.

Even if he had to spend every spare moment out of her sight for the rest of their short stay in Berlin.

Tegan lifted his head and cut the water off with a curt

flick of his mind. He stepped out of the shower and wrapped one of the thick black towels around his hips. As he entered his suite, he saw the message light blinking on his cell phone. He dialed in, hoping like hell he was going to hear orders from the compound that he was needed in Boston and had to return there without delay.

No such luck. Not that he should expect good fortune to provide him with any kind of assist. Fate had turned its back on him a long time ago.

Gideon's message played on speaker, grim and concise: he'd gotten word that there was an inquiry made on the Order's flight logs out of Logan airport. There was no mistaking that Marek was involved, probably soon to be in Berlin himself or, at the very least, tapping local contacts or sending out feelers to determine how much the Order knew, and what they intended to do with the knowledge.

Shit.

Now more than ever, Tegan was certain they were onto something big with Petrov Odolf and the journal Elise had intercepted from Marek's courier. He didn't need any more excuse than that to quickly towel off and get dressed for a few hours' patrol of the city. With weapons strapped to his hips, thigh, and ankle, he grabbed his coat and headed down the estate's main staircase.

Reichen was just strolling out of a mahogany-paneled study with a young Darkhaven couple as Tegan neared the foyer. The youthful male was blushing fiercely under a floppy lock of strawberry-blond hair, murmuring his thanks to Reichen for some favor recently granted, while his pretty redheaded Breedmate was beaming, her hands placed lovingly atop a very prominent pregnant belly.

"Congratulations to you both," Reichen said in

German. "I look forward to welcoming your fine, strong son once he arrives."

"Thank you for agreeing to be godfather," said the young woman. "You honor us well."

She went up on her toes to place a kiss on Reichen's cheek, then took her mate's hand and the two of them hurried off, gazing at each other as if the world outside them didn't exist.

"Ah, love," Reichen said, glancing over at Tegan with a broad grin once the happy pair had departed. "May it never sling its barbed coils around either of us, eh?"

Tegan gave him a wry look, but at the moment he was fully in agreement with the cynical sentiment. He came off the last step and saw Reichen's gaze travel to the hand that rested on the butt of a loaded, holstered Beretta. Raw scrapes and traces of blood marred Tegan's knuckles from where his fist had chewed up the marble of the shower.

The German arched a dark brow.

"Had a little incident upstairs," Tegan said. "I'll pay you back for the damage."

Reichen dismissed the offer with a cut of his hand. "I would be insulted if you tried. By my account, I am the one still in debt to you."

"Forget it," Tegan said, only slightly less uncomfortable with the gratitude than he was itchy to be out of the house where Elise was likely hating him now. "I need to go check things out in the city. We've had word of some activity coming out of Boston, which probably means trouble on the way over here."

Reichen's expression sobered. "I've heard there have been increased Rogue problems in your city. Is it true that there were dozens of them housed at the location the Order destroyed last summer?"

"We didn't stop to count, but yeah. It was a large lair."

The Darkhaven male swore softly. "Breed vampires gone Rogue aren't exactly social creatures. To have so many in one place is troubling to say the least. You don't suppose they were attempting to organize?"

"It's possible," Tegan said, knowing full well that was exactly what Marek was orchestrating. That is, before the Order had rolled out a C-4 welcome mat at the abandoned asylum where the bulk of Marek's suckhead army had been headquartered.

"Tegan." Reichen cleared his throat. "If you—or the Order—need anything at all from me, you have only to ask. I hope you know that. I would require no explanations whatsoever, and I assure you the Order would have my complete cooperation. And my trust."

Tegan saw frank honesty in the Darkhaven male's eyes, and a keen intelligence that seemed to say that for all his reckless charm and bravado, Andreas Reichen was not one to make frivolous gestures of alliance. If he offered his friendship, he offered his honor too.

"Consider my resources your own," Reichen added, lowering his voice to a confidential, deadly serious level. "Men, money, arms, subterfuge, or intelligence . . . you name it. Whatever tools I have in my reach are available to you and the rest of the warriors."

Tegan nodded his thanks. "You have to know, aligning yourself with the Order isn't going to make you very popular among your Darkhaven peers, Reichen."

"Perhaps not. But then who can stand the self-righteous bastards, anyway?" The German clapped Tegan on the shoulder. "Let me take you into town to meet someone. If you need information about any shady dealings, or movement taking place in Berlin's underbelly, then you really must talk to Helene."

"The female you were with earlier tonight?"

"Yes. She is a dear friend . . . with certain other benefits." Reichen grinned. "She's human, not Breedmate, in case you wondered."

Tegan had been wondering, in fact. He hadn't missed the healing bite mark on the woman's throat as Reichen had kissed her good-bye at the curb, but he hadn't detected any kind of blood scent on her. Nothing beyond the bland, coppery tang of basic *Homo sapiens* red cells.

And it hadn't appeared that Reichen had scrubbed the woman's mind after feeding from her either.

"She knows about you—about the Breed?"

Reichen nodded. "She can be trusted, I assure you. I've known her for many years, and we are business partners in her club as well. She has never betrayed my trust. She won't betray yours either."

Reichen smoothed his hair back at his temples, then gestured for the mansion's front door. "Come. Let me make some introductions for you."

A short while later, Tegan found himself seated in a plush red velvet booth inside a high-end brothel called Aphrodite. The place was swank and expensive, an adult playground filled with beautiful women, sumptuous furnishings, and a host of assorted pleasures to be had at a price firmly negotiated up front. Tegan watched with mild disinterest as more than one small orgy was under way in full public view.

The clientele at the club was almost exclusively human,

with the exception of Reichen, who was evidently no stranger to the establishment. He sat across from Tegan in the large booth, his fingers toying idly along the shapely arm of Aphrodite's proprieter, the stunning Helene. More than one of her girls had come around to have a look at Tegan. He'd been offered drinks, food, company, and quite a few temptations not found on the club's general menu.

As the last beautiful prostitute sashayed away from them on her teetering high heels, Helene shot him a slight frown. "If you have specific personal tastes, I'm sure I can make arrangements to accommodate you."

Tegan shifted on the soft velvet seat. His personal tastes had narrowed down to one female alone, and she was back at Reichen's estate, probably wishing she'd never met him. "I appreciate the offer," he told Helene, "but I didn't come here to get laid."

"We were hoping you might be willing to help keep us informed of any . . . unusual activity taking place in the city," Reichen added. "It would require your total confidence, of course."

"Naturally," she said, nodding in shrewd agreement. "Are we talking about keeping an eye on unusual human activity or something else?"

"Both," Tegan said. Since Reichen had obviously made her aware of the vampire nation and trusted her to keep the secret, Tegan didn't see any point in mincing words. "We've been seeing an increase in our Rogue population back in the States. We think we know where it's coming from, but there's a good chance some of those problems may come to roost here in Berlin. If you hear anything out of the ordinary at all, you need to make us aware."

The human female inclined her chin. "You have my word."

She held out her hand to Tegan and he took the opportunity to read the woman's emotions. His touch told him instantly that there was nothing dishonest in her intent. She meant what she'd said, and her word was good.

Tegan released her and leaned back as one of her employees came up to the table. "One of my clients has had too much to drink," the young woman complained. "He's getting loud and unruly."

Helene's smile was serene, but her eyes were as sharp as laser beams locking on to a target. "Will you excuse me? Duty calls."

She got up from the booth and smoothly motioned for one of the many bouncers to accompany her. When she had gone, Reichen lifted a brow at Tegan. "She's charming, don't you think?"

Tegan grunted. "She has her appeal, I suppose."

Reichen narrowed his gaze on him now. "I'm curious. Is celibacy something all of the Order adheres to?"

The question drew Tegan's head up sharply. "What the hell are you talking about?"

"I've just watched you turn away about a dozen flawless women who would have prostrated themselves at your feet for the chance to please you. No man has that kind of control. Unless—" The Darkhaven male chuckled. "Unless the rumors circulating at the reception the other night are actually true. Is there something going on between you and the lovely Elise Chase? Something beyond the business that brought both of you to my city?"

"There's nothing going on between us." Or at least there shouldn't be. And wouldn't be, after the way things had gone tonight. "I have no claim on the female what-soever."

"Ah. I was out of line. Forgive me for suggesting," Reichen said, obviously taking the hint from Tegan's clipped tone that the matter was not open for discussion.

Tegan rose to his feet. "I'm out of here."

He was suddenly itching to be outdoors on patrol, away from the open carnality of the club. And he didn't trust himself to return to the estate with Reichen when all that would do was put him back in close proximity with Elise.

"Don't wait up," he growled, then stalked out of the place and into the night outside.

CHAPTER
Twenty-three

Elise awoke just after dawn that next morning, following a fitful night of little sleep. Somewhere during the night, her survival instincts had kicked in and she realized that she could not stay any longer here with Tegan and hope to emerge with her heart intact. She had to leave Berlin and return home to Boston. The few belongings she had with her were packed into a small bag that sat near the door. She was showered and dressed, and had already called a taxi to come and take her to the airport.

She'd insisted on coming here with Tegan in the first place because of her vow to Camden primarily, and because she wanted to do her part to uncover whatever secrets might have been hidden in the old book that Marek had been so eager to have. But she was failing Camden—failing herself—every second she wasted on thoughts of Tegan and the hopelessness in imagining any sort of future with him.

She had accomplished what she'd come to Berlin to do: Petrov Odolf would be questioned, and the containment facility would be expecting Tegan again today, with or without Elise's personal escort. Now her time would be better spent back home, where the Rogues and their leader still posed an immediate, deadly threat.

A knock sounded on her door, followed by the soft female voice of one of Reichen's kin who lived in the Darkhaven. "Hello? I don't mean to disturb you . . . "

"It's all right. I'm awake. Come in."

Elise crossed the room from the window, where she'd been pacing a track for the past several minutes. She opened the door, expecting to hear that her car had arrived. The young Breedmate waiting there smiled shyly and held out a cordless telephone.

"A call for you," she said. "Will you take it?"

"Of course." Elise put the phone to her ear as the other female retreated down the hall. "Hello? This is Elise Chase."

There was a moment of silence before Petrov Odolf's mate spoke. "It's Irina—we met yesterday at the containment facility?"

"Yes, of course. Is anything wrong?"

"No. No, nothing is wrong. I hope you don't mind that I called. Director Kuhn told me where to find you . . ."

"Not at all." Elise moved back inside her guest room and sat down on the edge of the bed. "What can I do for you, Irina?"

"I found something today, and I am wondering if it might be of use to you."

"What is it?"

"Well, I was putting some of Petrov's things in storage and I found a shoebox containing some of his deceased brother's personal effects. They're mostly mundane . . . photographs, jewelry, some monogrammed desk items, that sort of thing. But at the bottom, I found some old handwritten letters wrapped in a folded piece of embroidery. Elise, these letters that Petrov's brother was keeping . . . he must have spent weeks writing them, but they're filled with nonsensical ramblings. I can't be sure, but I think it might be the same odd things Petrov had begun writing in the time before he went Rogue."

"Oh, my God."

"Do you suppose the writings might be of some help to you?"

"I'd really like to see them to find out." Excitement shot through Elise as she fished a pen and some paper out of her purse. "Would you be willing to let me have them?"

"Yes, of course. That's why I called."

Elise glanced at her packed bag, biting her lower lip. She could leave for the States anytime. This potential new information was more important. "I can be in a taxi in just a few minutes, Irina. Give me your address and I'll leave as soon as I can."

A cream-colored Mercedes taxi idled at the end of the gated drive, which had been under Minion surveillance since dawn. From his vantage point several hundred yards away, concealed by the thick green of the surrounding forest and peering through high-powered binoculars, the Minion watched as a slender blond woman hurried out to meet the waiting car.

The bitch appeared to be a perfect match for the video image he'd gotten via e-mail from his Master. To be certain, he pulled the picture out of his jacket pocket and took another look. Yes, that was her all right.

The Minion smiled as the woman got into the taxi.

"Showtime," he murmured, letting the binocs swing from the cord around his neck as he clambered down out of the tree where he'd been hiding.

He jogged over to his car, ditched on a narrow private lane nearby. He hopped in, turned the key, and rolled out after his quarry.

Irina Odolf lived in a small, tidy town house on a tree-lined residential street on the outskirts of Berlin's west end. Elise was surprised, though not shocked, that the woman had decided to make her home outside the Darkhavens after losing her mate to Bloodlust. She likely would have done the same in her situation.

"There were just so many reminders of what I was missing after he was sent away," Irina explained as she and Elise sat down for coffee in the sun-filled dining area. Glass doors shaded by vertical blinds overlooked the community's snow-patched common courtyard that ran along the backs of the houses. "Petrov and I have many friends in our Darkhaven, but living there without him was too difficult. I suppose if he comes home—*when* he comes home," she amended, idly smoothing the lacy edge of the tablecloth. "When he comes home, then we'll return there and start our life over again."

"I hope that day comes soon for you both, Irina."

The Breedmate looked up with a teary-eyed smile. "So do I."

Elise took a sip of her coffee, dimly aware of a slow pound building in her temples. It had been present since she got into the taxi that brought her here, a trip that had taken her through the center of the city, where the din of human thoughts had battered her through the metal and glass of the car. But she used the focus that Tegan had shown her, and the worst of her psychic pain had faded to a manageable level.

Being this close to a lot of humanity was certainly a test. Irina's neighborhood was a tightly packed cluster of homes, with a steady stream of cars traveling up and down the street outside, bringing even more noise to the chatter filling her head.

And underneath the general rumble of discontent she was receiving, Elise detected something darker . . . just out of her reach.

"Would you like to see the letters?"

Irina's voice snapped Elise back to attention. "Yes, of course."

She followed the woman out of the dining room and into a cozy little den at the end of the hall. A man's desk sat across from an inviting reading nook, the masculine furnishings impeccably polished and organized, as though awaiting the imminent arrival of their owner.

Irina motioned Elise over to the desk, where an open shoebox sat next to an old weaving that had been laid flat. A stack of folded papers rested on top. "Here they are."

"May I?" Elise asked, reaching to pick up the collection of letters.

At Irina's nod, she unfolded the first one and glanced

at the page. It was filled with a hasty, violently uneven scrawl. The words were barely legible, written in what appeared to be Latin, by a hand that seemed guided by madness. Elise fanned through the other papers, finding more of the same on them.

"Do you think it means anything?"

Elise shook her head. "I can't be sure. I'd like to show it to someone, though. You're sure you don't mind if I take these?"

"Do what you'd like. I have no use for them myself."

"Thank you."

Elise glanced at the weaving that lay on the desk. It was incredibly beautiful and obviously very old. She couldn't resist tracing her finger over the intricate stitches of the medieval garden design. "This is lovely. The detail is incredible, like a painting done with a needle."

"Yes, it is." Irina smiled. "And whoever made it had an interesting sense of whimsy too."

"How so?"

"I noticed it when the piece was wrapped around the stack of letters. Let me show you."

She folded the square cloth diagonally, turning up one edge so that the designs on the lower left and upper right corners touched. At the place where they met, the delicate embroidery revealed the hidden shape of a teardrop falling into the basin of a crescent moon.

Elise laughed, delighted by the clever artistry of the work.

"The woman who made this was a Breedmate?"

"Apparently so." Irina carefully smoothed it out again. "It must be from the Middle Ages, don't you think?"

Elise couldn't answer, even if she had a guess. At that instant, a lancing blast of pain sliced into her mind. It was pure menace, something deathly evil . . . and it was suddenly very close.

Inside the house.

"Irina," she whispered. "Someone's here."

"What? What do you mean someone—"

She held up her hand to silence the woman, fighting through the mental assault as her mind filled with the violent thoughts of the intruder.

It was a Minion, sent on a mission to kill.

"We have to get out of here right now."

"Get out of here? But I don't—"

"You have to trust me. He'll kill us both if he finds us."

Irina's eyes went wild with fright. She shook her head. "There's no way out from back here. Only the window—"

"Yes. Hurry! Open it and get yourself out of here. I'll be right behind you."

Elise silently closed the room's door, then dragged the bulky leather chair in front of it while Irina worked on opening the ground floor window. The Minion was quiet in his stealth as he prowled farther into the town house looking for his prey, but the savagery of his thoughts betrayed him as loudly as a screaming alarm.

He'd been sent by his Master to kill her, but he meant to drag things out. Make her bleed. Make her scream. That's what he enjoyed the most about his job.

And he was almost giddy with the idea that he'd get to exercise his perversions on two women instead of just the one.

Oh, God, Elise thought, revulsion surging up the back of her throat.

She called upon the power of Tegan's blood inside her and her own determination, working furiously to focus through the chilling knowledge of what was stalking toward her up the hallway.

"The window lock is stuck," Irina gasped, struggling in her panic. "It won't open!"

That worried shriek drew the Minion like a beacon. Heavy footsteps pounded toward the end of the hallway now. Elise grabbed a thick book from a shelf and ran to Irina's side, smashing the heavy binding against the window casement to loosen the sticky lock.

"There it goes," Elise said as the mechanism finally gave way. She dropped the book and pushed the glass aside, then knocked out the screen and let it fall to the ground below. "Climb out, Irina. Go now!"

She felt the Minion bearing down on the room where they hid. His thoughts were malicious, black with menace. She heard his guttural roar the instant before he threw himself at the door. He came at it again, then again. The hinges screamed with the impact, the frame splitting as he came at the thing again with the force of a battering ram.

"Elise!" Irina shrieked. "Oh, my God! What's going on?"

She didn't answer. There was no time. Elise lunged for the letters, but as she pivoted with them toward the window and her only hope of escape, the Minion shoved the door open wide enough for him to heave into the room. He threw the obstructing chair out of his way and came at her, brandishing a dreadful-looking hunting blade in his hand. He snarled, and the stretch of his features gave prominence to a vicious scar that cut down his forehead and onto his right cheek. The cloudy eye in the path of that scar was gleaming with malice.

"Don't run away so soon, ladies. We're going to have a little fun."

Hard fingers clamped around Elise's neck before she could dodge the Minion's reach. He shoved her onto the surface of the desk and leaned over her. Slapped her so hard with the back of his big hand that her vision swam and the whole side of her face rang with pain. With a powerful drive of his arm, he planted the tip of the blade into the wood next to her head, missing her by a deliberate, scant inch.

His grin was full of sadistic humor as his fingers closed tighter on her neck. "Play nice and maybe I'll let you live," he lied.

Elise kicked and twisted, but his grip was unrelenting. With her free hand, she cast about for anything to use as a weapon. The shoebox tipped on the desk, spilling its odd collection of cuff links, pictures . . . and a pearl-handled letter opener. Elise tried not to call attention to her find, but she was determined to get hold of it.

"Let her go!" Irina shouted.

"You'd better not move," the Minion growled, glancing up at her in warning. "That's right, bitch. You stay put, or your friend here is going to eat steel."

Elise closed her eyes as Irina sobbed at the window, paralyzed by terror. But in the moment the Minion was distracted, Elise's fingers closed around the hilt of the letter opener. She knew it would be a sorry match against the knife her attacker had, but it was better than nothing at all.

The second she got a firm grip, Elise brought the makeshift weapon up in a sweeping arc. It struck the Minion in the side of his neck.

The deep puncture sent him rearing up off her with a

howl, his fingers clutching at the bleeding wound. Elise didn't realize he had gone for his own knife until he drove it toward her. She rolled away, narrowly escaping his clumsy, irate strike.

The Minion stumbled a bit, pressing his hand to his neck and looking dazed as the front of his shirt went red with spilled blood.

"You fucking bitch!"

He barreled toward her again, throwing his weight at her and knocking her to the floor. Elise thrashed in an effort to get out from under him, but he was a big man and he was furious now. She managed to roll over onto her back, the letter opener still clutched hard in her hand, trapped between the Minion's arm and ribs.

She saw his knife come up near her face.

"No," she gasped, sick with the weight of him and the acrid stench of his spilling blood. "Damn it, no!"

With a blind stab, she stuck the Minion with the letter opener. It went into his ribs, another deep wound that sent him yowling in pain. He reared back, choking and wheezing, giving Elise the chance to get away from him.

"Oh, God," Irina gasped, staring in abject horror. "What's going on? Who is that man? What does he want with us?"

"Irina, get out now!" Elise cried, grabbing the letters and shoving the other woman toward the open window.

They both hurried out, landing on the frozen grass below. Elise saw the Minion sitting on the floor inside, pale with shock and going nowhere fast. But she didn't dare relax for a second.

"We have to get out of here, Irina. Do you have a car?"

The woman said nothing, her face going as pale as the

snow outside. Elise took her shoulders and met her stricken gaze.

"Do you have a car, Irina? Can you drive?"

A glimmer of focus came back into her eyes. "What? Oh . . . yes . . . my car is parked over there. Next to the alley."

"Then come on now. We have to go."

CHAPTER
Twenty-four

Commotion in the foyer of the Darkhaven woke Tegan from a light doze in his guest room. Something was wrong. Really wrong. He heard Elise's voice—heard the elevated pitch in her usually calm tone—and vaulted to his bare feet in an instant, all of his senses tripped to full alert.

Naked except for the pair of blue jeans he pulled on as he headed for the hall outside, he registered the muffled sounds of a female crying. Not Elise, thank God, but she was down there too, talking fast and clearly upset.

Tegan got to the staircase and glanced down to the open entryway of the estate. What he saw just about leveled him where he stood.

Elise, having just returned from somewhere outside, covered in blood.

Holy hell.

He rocked back on his heels, his stomach dropping like a stone to a vicinity somewhere around his knees. Elise was drenched in scarlet. The front of her clothes were stained deep red, as if someone had opened up her jugular.

Except it wasn't her blood, he realized as the metallic odor of it drifted up to fill his nostrils. It was someone else's blood—a human.

The relief he felt in that moment was profound.

Until a desperate brand of anger set in.

He put his fists on the railing and swung his legs over, dropping to the floor of the foyer on a tight-bitten curse. Elise hardly glanced at him as he stalked toward her, his body shaking with the depth of his fury. But all her focus was on stricken, incoherent Irina Odolf, who had collapsed onto an upholstered bench near the front door.

Reichen came in from the kitchen carrying a glass of water. He handed it to Elise.

"Thank you, Andreas." She turned and offered the drink to the sobbing Breedmate. "Here you go, Irina. Drink a little of this if you can. It will make you feel better."

Tegan couldn't see anything wrong with the other woman aside from shock. Elise, however, looked like she'd just come in from the front lines. A livid bruise ran along her jaw and up the side of her cheek. "What the hell happened? And what the fuck were you doing outside of this Darkhaven?"

"Drink," Elise coaxed her charge, all but ignoring Tegan. "Andreas, do you have a quiet room where Irina can lie down for a while?"

"Yes, of course," Reichen replied. "There's a sitting room here on the first floor."

"Thank you. That should be fine."

Tegan watched Elise taking control with a gentle command that came so easily to her. He had to admire her strength in the midst of obvious crisis, but damn it, he was fuming. "You want to explain why you're standing here bruised and bathed in blood?"

"I went to see Irina this morning," Elise replied, still not troubling herself to meet his angry gaze. "A Minion must have followed me—"

"Jesus Christ."

"He broke into Irina's town house and attacked us. I took care of it."

"You took care of it," Tegan said darkly. "What happened? Did you fight with the son of a bitch? Did you kill him?"

"I don't know. We didn't wait around to find out."

She took the glass of water away from Irina, who wasn't drinking much anyway, and set it down on the floor. "Are you able to stand up now?" she asked the woman, her voice caring and concerned. When the Breedmate nodded, Elise took her under the arm and helped her to her feet. "We're going to walk you to another room where you can rest, all right?"

"Allow me," Reichen said, smoothly moving in and taking Irina's slack weight onto himself. He gingerly guided her out of the foyer, toward a pair of open double doors off the grand entrance.

When Elise started to follow them, Tegan reached out and caught her by the hand. "Elise. Wait."

Given little choice, she paused. Then she blew out a slow sigh and turned to face him. "I really don't need your disapproval right now, Tegan. I'm exhausted, and I want to get out of these awful clothes. So, if you plan on lecturing me, it's going to have to wait—"

He pulled her to him and she fell silent as his arms went around her in a fierce embrace.

He couldn't let go. He couldn't speak. His chest was constricted with an emotion he didn't want to acknowledge, but could hardly deny. It wrenched him, pressing like a vise around his heart.

Ah, fuck.

Elise might have been killed today. She'd managed to get away, sure, but she'd been in serious danger with that Minion and there was always the very good chance that things would end badly.

He might have lost her while he slept. When she'd been out of his reach, and he'd been unable to protect her.

The thought hit him hard.

So unexpectedly deep.

All he could do right now was hold on to her. Like he never wanted to let her go.

Elise had expected anger from Tegan. Perhaps arrogant male censure. She couldn't have been more shocked to feel his arms holding her tight.

Good Lord, was he actually trembling?

She stood in the warm, strong cage of his embrace, and felt some of her edgy tension begin to break. The bone-deep fear she'd refused to let herself feel until now started to pour into her limbs. She leaned into Tegan's welcome strength, bringing her hands up to rest against the hard muscles of his bare back, her unhurt cheek lying on the smooth plane of his chest.

"There are some papers," she finally managed to say. "Petrov Odolf's brother wrote a bunch of letters. I thought they might be important. That's why I went out to see Irina."

"I don't care about that." Tegan's voice was thick, vibrating against her ear. His fingertips pressed into her shoulders as he brought her away from him and stared down into her eyes. That gem-green gaze was penetrating, so intensely serious. "Jesus Christ, I don't care about any of that right now."

"It could mean something, Tegan. There are some strange verses . . . "

He shook his head, scowling now. "It can wait."

He reached out and wiped at an apparent smudge on her chin. Then he tilted her face up to his. He stared at her for a long moment before he kissed her.

It was brief and tender, filled with a sweetness that robbed Elise of her breath.

"Everything else can wait for now," he said quietly, a dark ferocity in his voice. "Come with me, Elise. I want to take care of you now."

He led her by the hand, out of the foyer and up the main staircase to her guest room on the second floor. She walked inside with him, paused as he turned to close the door behind them. He glanced down to where her packed bag sat on the floor. When he looked back at her, there was a question in his eyes.

"I had been planning to leave Berlin today. I was going to go back to Boston."

"Because of me?"

She shook her head. "Because of me. Because I'm confused about a lot of things, and I'm losing focus on what matters. The only thing that should matter—"

"Your vengeance."

"My promise, yes."

Tegan came to stand in front of her, his broad chest filling her vision, radiating a warmth she wanted so badly to feel against her again. She closed her eyes as he began carefully unbuttoning her bloodstained blouse. He peeled the sticky silk off her body and let it drop to the floor.

Maybe she should have felt awkward or at least resistant, allowing him to undress her after the awful way things had gone between them last night. But she was sickened by the gore on her clothes, and there was a shaking, distressed part of her that welcomed Tegan's care. His touch was protective, not sexual, all steady strength now. Capable and compassionate.

Her ruined pants went next, along with her socks and shoes. And then she was standing before him in just her bra and panties.

"The Minion's blood soaked through to your skin," he said, frowning as he ran his hand over her marred shoulder and down along the line of her arm. In the adjoining bathroom, the shower turned on. "I'll wash it off you."

She walked with him into the spacious bath suite, saying nothing as he gingerly removed the last of her clothing.

"Come on," he said, guiding her around the wall of mottled glass bricks that separated the large shower area from the rest of the room.

Warm steam rolled around them as they neared the spray.

"You're getting all wet," Elise said when Tegan strolled in ahead of her without taking off his jeans.

He merely shrugged. Water sluiced all over him, into his tawny hair and down the thick, banded muscles of his shoulders and arms. Cascading rivulets ran over the beautiful lines of his *dermaglyphs*, and onto the darkening denim that covered his long, powerful legs.

She looked at him and felt as if she were seeing him with fresh eyes . . . seeing him for the first time. There was no mistaking what he was—a solitary, deadly male, trained to kill and nearly perfect in his apathy. But there was a stunning vulnerability about him as he stood in front of her now, soaking wet, his hand extended out to her in kindness.

And if the warrior in him gave her pause before, this new vision of him was even more unnerving.

It made her want to run into his arms and stay there, forever if she could.

"Step under the water with me, Elise. I'll do the rest."

She felt her feet moving beneath her, her fingers coming to rest in the warm center of Tegan's palm. He brought her into the soft rain of the shower. Smoothed her hair back from her face as they both became drenched together.

Elise melted into the warm water and the even greater heat of Tegan's body brushing against hers. She let him soap her skin and shampoo her hair, glad for his comforting touch after the ugliness of her day.

"Feel good?" he asked as he rinsed her off, the low vibration of his voice traveling through his fingertips and into her skin and bones.

"It feels wonderful."

Too much so, she thought. When she was with Tegan, especially like this, he made her forget about her pain. He made it all too easy to accept the void that had existed for so long in her heart. His tenderness could make her feel so full, pushing away all the darkness. Right now, as he caressed her and held her so safely in his arms, he made her feel loved.

He made it far too tempting to imagine a future where she could be happy again. Whole again, with him.

"I'm failing in my promise to my son," she said, forcing herself to draw away from the comfort of Tegan's touch. "All I should be concerned about is making sure Camden's death wasn't in vain."

Something flashed in his eyes, only to be shuttered an instant later by the fall of his spiked, wet lashes. He reached behind her and shut off the water. "You can't spend your life living for the dead, Elise."

Reaching above her, he grabbed a folded towel from the supply stacked on a high shelf built into the marble of the shower. When he passed the towel to her, Elise met his gaze. The hauntedness reflecting there took her aback.

There was a bleakness staring back at her. The pain of an old wound, not yet healed.

She'd never noticed it before . . . because he'd never allowed her to see it.

"You blame yourself for what happened to your mate, don't you?"

He stared at her for a long, quiet minute, and she was certain he would give her an aloof denial. But then he exhaled a hushed curse, ran his fingers through the wet hair at his scalp. "I couldn't save her. She depended on me to keep her safe, but I failed her."

Elise's heart stumbled a beat in her chest. "You must have loved her very much."

"Sorcha was a sweet girl, the most innocent person I've ever known. She didn't deserve the death she was given."

Elise wrapped the towel around herself as Tegan sat down on the marble bench that ran the length of the shower stall. His thighs were spread, his elbows resting on his knees.

"What happened, Tegan?"

"After her abduction, some two weeks later, her captors sent her back to me. She'd been raped, tortured. As if that hadn't been cruel enough, whoever held her also fed on her. She came back to me a Minion of the one who brutalized her."

"Oh, God. Tegan."

"Sending her back like that was worse than killing her, but I guess they left that task to me. I couldn't do it. In my heart, I knew she was gone, but I couldn't end her life."

"Of course not," she assured him gently, her heart breaking for him.

Elise closed her eyes on a softly whispered prayer as she eased down onto the bench next to him. She didn't care if he rejected her compassion; she needed to be close to him. He had to know that he wasn't alone.

When she put her hand on his bare shoulder, he didn't flinch away. He pivoted his head to the side, meeting her sympathetic gaze. "I tried to make her better. I thought if I drew enough of her blood away and gave her my own in return—if I could feed her from my veins and siphon off the poison in hers—maybe by some miracle she'd revive. So, I fed to feed her. I went on a blood rampage that lasted for weeks. I had no control. I was so consumed by guilt and the need to make Sorcha better that I didn't even notice how quickly I was slipping toward Bloodlust."

"But you didn't slip, did you? I mean, you must not have, to be sitting here now."

He laughed sharply, a coarse, bitter sound. "Oh, I slipped all right. I fell, like all addicts do. Bloodlust would have turned me Rogue if it hadn't been for Lucan. He stepped in, and put me in a stone cell to wait the disease out. For several months, I nearly starved, feeding in only the smallest quantities needed to keep me breathing. Most of those days, I prayed for death."

"But you survived."

"Yeah."

"And Sorcha?"

He shook his head. "Lucan did for her what I wasn't man enough to do. He freed her from her suffering."

Elise's heart lurched with understanding. "He killed her?"

"It was an act of mercy," Tegan answered tightly. "Even though I hated him for it all these past five hundred years since. In the end, Lucan showed her far more compassion than I was able to. I would have kept her alive only to save myself from suffering the guilt of her death."

Elise smoothed her palm over Tegan's strong back, moved by his confession and by the love that had been taken from him so long ago. She had thought him cold and unfeeling, but it was only because he hid his emotions well. His wounds went deeper than she could ever have guessed. "I'm sorry for everything you've been through, Tegan. I understand now. I understand . . . so much now."

"Do you?"

The bleak, narrowed gaze that met her eyes was penetrating in its intensity.

"When I saw you downstairs, covered in blood—" He broke off abruptly, as if unable to form the words. "Ah, fuck . . . I never wanted to feel that kind of fear and pain again, do you understand? I didn't want to let myself get that close to anyone again."

Elise looked at him in silence, hearing his words, yet uncertain he could actually mean them. Did he really mean to say that he cared for her?

His fingers were a feather-light brush against the dull throb of her bruised cheek. "I do care," he said, a quiet reply in answer to the question he'd read with his touch. He brought her under the shelter of his arm, just holding her, his thumb idly stroking her arm. "With you, I think it would be very easy to care too much, Elise. I'm not sure that's a risk I can afford to take."

"You can't . . . or you won't?"

"There's no difference. Just semantics."

Elise leaned her head against his shoulder. She didn't want to hear this now. Didn't want to let him go. "So, where does that leave us now? Where do we go from here, Tegan?"

He didn't say anything one way or the other, just held her close and pressed a tender kiss to her brow.

CHAPTER
Twenty-five

The rest of that day passed in a blur of tactics and information gathering. At sundown, Reichen had sent a couple of his associates out to Irina Odolf's residence. The report had come back that the Minion was gone, evidently on his own motor, even though Elise had certainly slowed the bastard down based on the amount of blood he'd left at the scene.

Armed with her description of him, Reichen was already in town looking for possible leads. Tegan hoped like hell they located the Minion son of a bitch because he was looking forward to finishing what Elise had started.

As for her, as much as Tegan might have liked to have

kept Elise in his arms—or, better still, naked in his bed—
he knew it was a path that would only lead him deeper
into complicated territory. Instead, he had turned his attention to the journal they'd intercepted from Marek,
and the stash of letters Elise had recovered from Petrov
Odolf's belongings.

Both contained instances of the same peculiar
phrases:

> *castle and croft shall come together under the crescent moon*
> *to the borderlands east turn your eye*
> *at the cross lies truth*

It was a riddle of some sort, but what it meant—if it
meant anything at all—remained to be seen.

Petrov Odolf didn't seem to understand it either, despite the fact that his Breedmate said he'd been scribbling
those very words compulsively in the time leading up
to his turning Rogue. Like his brother before him had
as well.

And like who it was that once owned the old journal
with Dragos's *dermaglyphic* symbol scribbled onto its pages.

Now Tegan stood across the containment cell from
Petrov Odolf, eyeing the restrained Rogue with precious
little patience. He and Elise had been at the facility for
the past hour, getting exactly nowhere in their continued
round of questioning with Odolf.

His medication had been reduced, so at least the
Rogue was conscious, but he was far from lucid.
Strapped into a free-standing, vertical steel-mesh body
cage, his muscular arms bound down at his sides, feet
shackled together, Petrov Odolf looked every bit the dangerous beast he was. His big head sagged down on his

chest, glowing amber eyes shifting back and forth across the cell without focus. He snorted and grunted through his elongated fangs, then began another round of futile struggle against his restraints.

"Tell us what it means," Tegan said, talking over the racket of clanging metal and mindless animal snuffling. "Why were you and your brother both writing these phrases?"

Odolf didn't answer, just kept fighting his bonds.

" 'Castle and croft shall come together under the crescent moon,' " Tegan recited. " 'To the borderlands east turn your eye.' Is this a location? What does it mean to you, Odolf? What did it mean to your brother? Does the name Dragos mean anything to you?"

The Rogue shook and strained until his face looked like it was going to explode. He tossed his head back and forth, snarling furiously.

Tegan blew out a frustrated sigh and turned to face Elise. "This is a fucking waste of time. He's not going to be any use to us."

"Let me try," she said.

When she moved forward, Tegan didn't miss the fact that Odolf's feral gaze tracked her across the room. The Rogue's nostrils flared as his blood-addicted body worked to get her scent.

"Don't go near him," Tegan warned her, regretting the fact that he'd promised Elise he wouldn't use his weapons on the Rogue except as a last resort. His first line of attack was an emergency syringe of sedative given to him by Director Kuhn. "That's far enough, Elise."

She paused several feet away from the Rogue. When she spoke, her voice was soft with patience and compassion.

"Hello, Petrov. My name is Elise."

Elliptical pupils narrowed even farther in the center of Odolf's amber eyes. He was still panting from exertion, but some of his struggling eased as his focus locked on to Elise.

"I met Irina. She's very nice. And she loves you very much. She told me how much you mean to her, Petrov."

Odolf went still in his tight cage. Elise took a step closer. Tegan growled a warning, and although she stopped, she didn't acknowledge his concern.

"Irina's worried about you."

"Not safe," Odolf murmured, almost imperceptibly.

"What's not safe?" Elise asked gently. "Is Irina not safe?"

"Nobody's safe." The big head shook back and forth as if caught in a seizure. When it passed, Odolf peeled his lips back off his huge fangs and dragged in a deep breath of air. "At the cross lies truth," he muttered on the exhale. "'Turn your eye . . . turn your eye."

"What does it mean, Petrov?" Elise read the entire passage back to him. "Can you explain it to us? Where did you hear this? Did you read it somewhere?"

" 'Castle and croft shall come together,' " he repeated. " 'To the borderlands east, turn your eye . . .' "

Elise moved forward another half-pace. "We're trying to understand, Petrov. Tell us what you know. It could be very important."

He grunted, his head going back on his shoulders, tendons stretching tight in his neck. " 'Castle and croft shall come together under the crescent moon . . . To the borderlands east turn your eye . . . At the cross lies truth.' "

"Petrov, please," Elise said. "We need you to help us. Why isn't it safe? Why do you think nobody is safe?"

But the Rogue wasn't hearing her now. With his eyes squeezed shut, head tipped back, he whispered the non-sensical phrases over and over again, a rapid, breathless stream of insanity.

Elise glanced back at Tegan. "Maybe you're right. Maybe this is a waste of time."

He was about to agree when Odolf suddenly began to snicker. His mouth spread wide, he dropped his head down and started whispering in a voice so small Tegan could barely hear it. He caught bits and pieces of the riddle, then Odolf blinked and it was as if a crystal clarity settled in his mind.

In a completely rational, coherent voice, he said: "That's where he's hiding."

Tegan's blood ran cold. "What did you say? That's where who's hiding—Marek?"

"Hiding away." Odolf chuckled, already slipping back into his madness. "Hiding, hiding . . . 'at the cross lies truth.' "

Once again, Tegan considered the *glyph* they'd found in the journal. The Breed line it belonged to was long extinct. But then again, maybe Marek wasn't the only one to come back from what had been merely a presumed death. "Is this about Dragos? Is he alive?"

Odolf shook his head, eyes falling serenely closed. He launched into another chorus of the riddle, murmuring it in a maddening, singsong voice.

"Goddamn it!" Tegan growled, stalking right up next to the cage. "Is Dragos in hiding somewhere? Are he and Marek allied in some way? Have they been plotting something together?"

Odolf kept chanting, unresponsive now. Not even when Tegan grabbed hold of the metal box he was in and gave it a hard shake did Odolf show any indication of awareness. The Rogue had mentally checked out.

"Shit." Tegan raked a hand through his hair. In his coat pocket, his cell phone vibrated with an incoming call. He flipped it open and barked into the receiver: "Yeah."

"Any progress?" It was Reichen.

"Not much."

Behind him in the cage, Petrov Odolf was snapping at the air, growling and cursing. No point in lingering any longer. Tegan gestured for Elise to follow him out of the Rogue's holding cell and into the adjacent observation room.

"We're just wrapping up," he told Reichen. "Did you get anything on the Minion?"

"Yes, we have something. I'm at Aphrodite with Helene. She's seen the man in here before once or twice. Had some trouble with him, in fact." Reichen cleared his throat, hesitating. "He, ah, apparently works for a blood club here in the city, Tegan. Probably supplies women for it."

"Jesus." He looked at Elise, his veins going tight at the thought of her being anywhere near trafficking scum like that. Blood clubs among the Breed, while illegal, had once been the preferred entertainment of a certain class of vampire. They catered to the bored and affluent, and those with appetites that tended to run toward the cruel. "Any idea where I might find this place?"

"Naturally, to avoid unwanted attention, the clubs seldom meet in the same location. Helene has already put out feelers for you. She'll probably have something back within the hour."

"I'm on the way now."

"What's going on?" Elise asked as he snapped the cell phone closed and slid it back into his coat.

"I have to meet one of Reichen's contacts in the city. She has some intel on the Minion who attacked you today."

Elise's fine brow arched. "She?"

"Helene," Tegan said. "She's a human friend of Reichen's. You saw her last night when we picked him up outside her club, Aphrodite."

Elise's look said she remembered very well the half-naked woman who walked Reichen to the curb. "All right, then," she said with a quick nod. "Let's go talk to her."

Tegan reached out to catch her arm as she started to walk out to the corridor. "I'm not taking you to Helene's club, Elise. I could drop you back at the Darkhaven—"

"Why?" Elise shrugged, unconcerned. "I'm not afraid to go to a nightclub."

Raw images of what Tegan had seen at Aphrodite the night before came back to him in vivid detail. "It's, uh, not that kind of club. You wouldn't be comfortable there. Trust me."

Her eyes widened in understanding. "Are you telling me it's a brothel?"

He didn't answer right away, not that she needed him to spell anything out for her. He watched her absorb the idea, her brow creasing in a slight frown. "Have you been there?"

Tegan lifted his shoulder slightly, wondering why the hell he felt bad about admitting it. "Reichen took me there to meet Helene last night."

"Last night," she said, her pale purple eyes narrowing on him. "Last night, you went out to a brothel . . . after we . . . *oh*. Okay. I see."

"It's not what you think, Elise."

He had the sudden absurd impulse to assure her that nothing had happened while he was at Aphrodite, but Elise didn't seem interested in hearing any excuses. With brisk movements, she put on her coat and started buttoning it up.

"I think I'm ready to go now, Tegan."

He fell in step beside her as she headed up the corridor. "I shouldn't be long with Reichen. Once I finish up, I'll come back to the Darkhaven and we can try to make sense out of what little we got from Odolf tonight."

Elise turned a level look on him. "We can talk about that on the way to Aphrodite," she said. "I'm going with you."

He met her unwavering stare and exhaled a defeated chuckle. "Suit yourself then. But don't say I didn't warn you."

Despite living a sheltered existence in the Darkhavens, Elise had never considered herself a prude. But walking with Tegan into the private back entrance of Aphrodite gave her an instant education in eroticism.

They were let in by a huge, muscle-bound man in a dark, tailored suit. He wore a wireless communication device on his ear, with a small microphone that extended near his goatee-rimmed mouth. He spoke into the mic, presumably advising his employer that her guests had arrived, as he escorted Tegan and Elise through the main floor of the club.

Festooned in bright carnival colors, with polished brass fixtures and sumptuously appointed furnishings, the lounge and bar area was a visual feast. Beautiful nude women re-

clined on animal-print sofas, some of them entertaining a
male client or two in full view of all. Still others performed
together, kissing and caressing one another as men wearing
silk robes or sauna towels watched with rapt, heated stares.

On another cushioned nest near the bar, a man was
being serviced by four women at once. Elise could hardly
keep from gaping at the erotic tangle of tanned arms and
legs. Even over the soft, pumping beat of the music pouring in through the overhead speakers, she could hear the
slap of skin meeting skin, and the pleasured moans and
hoarse shouts of release coming from practically every
corner of the lounge.

Surrounded by so much humankind, Elise weathered
the low drone of her talent, which stirred to life as soon as
they entered the club. Fortunately, most of the input hitting her was of a lustful nature, some of it graphically so,
but nothing disturbing enough to cause true pain.

She remembered Tegan's coaching and reached with
her mind for one of the least offensive voices that was filling her head. She brought it forward, using it to damper
the others as she made her way through the place.

When she braved a glance at Tegan, she found him
staring at her. If he noticed any of the public couplings
taking place all around them, he didn't seem fazed in the
least. No, he seemed to be more interested in measuring
her reaction. His gaze was hard, penetrating. His jaw
seemed clamped tight enough to shatter his teeth.

The intensity of his look made her too warm inside.
Elise blinked, glancing away. But glancing away from
him meant seeing more of the club. More raw, pulsing
sexuality, which only made her all the more aware of
Tegan and the very vivid knowledge of how good their
bodies felt together.

She couldn't have been more relieved when their escort paused in front of an elevator bank and led them inside a waiting car.

They rode up to the fourth floor. The elevator opened into a glass-walled suite outfitted as both office and bedroom. Reichen stood up to greet them, rising from an elegant sprawl on the luxurious round bed. His white dress shirt was unbuttoned and hanging loose, his finely cut gray trousers showcasing his trim waist and smooth, muscular chest. The vampire's *dermaglyphs* swirled over his pecs in winglike flourishes, drawing the eye to the masculine beauty of his form.

He seemed accustomed to being admired and merely smiled as Elise and Tegan strode into the room.

"I didn't realize you would be accompanying Tegan here," he said, gallantly taking Elise's hand. "I hope you aren't too shocked."

"Not at all," she said, hoping her discomfiture didn't show.

Reichen brought her in front of the tall brunette Elise had seen him with the other night. The woman wore a simple yet sophisticated ivory sweater and pants outfit that looked like it belonged in a boardroom more than a brothel. Tonight her long raven-dark hair was swept up in a loose chignon, secured with a pair of gleaming, tortoiseshell chopsticks.

She was the picture of professionalism, a curious contrast to the live video feeds playing on flat-screen monitors mounted behind her on the wall of the office. While images of people on the main floor of the club writhed and bucked on-screen, the woman merely smiled pleasantly as Reichen and Elise paused in front of her.

"This is Helene," Reichen said. "She owns the club, and she is also a trusted friend of mine."

"Hello," Elise said, offering her hand. "A pleasure to meet you."

"Likewise," came the accented purr in reply. Elise's fingers were gripped in a firm yet feminine hold that echoed the confidence gleaming in Helene's dark eyes. That self-assured gaze slid in Tegan's direction and politely feigned unfamiliarity, a gesture that seemed for Elise's benefit. "Hello and welcome to Aphrodite. Both of you."

"Good to see you again, Helene," Tegan said, his tone cutting through all pretense. "Reichen tells me you have some intel."

"Yes, I do."

The woman picked up on Tegan's all-business tone and reached for a laptop computer that sat on her desk. She opened it and typed something on the keyboard. Behind her, one of the wall-mounted video screens went black, then came back on with a freeze-framed surveillance image of a man seated at the club's bar downstairs. The scar down the Minion's face identified him instantly.

"That's him," Elise said. She could still feel his punishing hands on her, could still hear his ugly thoughts ringing in her ears.

"He came here only a few times. He was a prick, very nasty to the girls. I banned him a couple of months ago. It wasn't until later that I heard rumors of his involvement in the blood clubs." Helene glanced over at Elise. "You were lucky today. I'm glad you gave him some pain."

Elise didn't feel any pride in what she'd done. But more than that, she inwardly shuddered at the mention of blood clubs. They were all but unheard of in Boston for many decades, due mostly to the Enforcement

Agency's crackdown on the illegal operations. Quentin had especially despised them as little better than organized sport where humans were the captive playthings of twisted members of the Breed. To think that she and Irina had been in arm's reach of one of the suppliers for that kind of activity put a chill in her marrow.

Tegan's hard gaze on her now told her that he didn't like the idea any more than she did. "Do you have any leads on the area's clubs? Anything on this guy's associates, or someone who might know his name or where to find him?"

Helene nodded and typed something else into the laptop. "I have cultivated a few close friends among the police. Not surprisingly, this Minion is no stranger to the law." She walked over to a laser printer behind her desk and retrieved a sheet of paper as it came out of the machine. "I was able to get his most recent arrest record, which contains his name and last known address."

"Beautiful *and* resourceful," Reichen said approvingly as Helene passed the report to Tegan.

Elise watched Tegan drink in every detail of the report, his eyes narrowed, calculating. He glanced over at Reichen. "Will you see Elise back to the Darkhaven?"

"Of course. It will be my pleasure."

"What are you going to do, Tegan?" Even as she asked the question, she knew his intentions. He was going out to kill the Minion who'd attacked her. She could see the warrior side of him locking in to place, its sights fixed on the target with deadly focus. "Tegan, just . . . be careful."

He met her gaze for a long moment, then looked again to Reichen. "Get her out of here. I'll meet you back at the Darkhaven when it's finished."

Elise wanted to throw her arms around him, but Tegan was already stalking toward the elevator, a solitary warrior with a single purpose. This was who he was, who he would always be.

She closed her eyes as he stepped inside the waiting car and the polished brass doors closed behind him. Her senses tracked him as he descended, her blood link to him warm and alive in her veins. It was the only part of him she could truly hold on to; she wasn't sure he would ever let her close enough to have anything more.

CHAPTER
Twenty-six

Tegan crouched low on a rooftop, his eyes trained on a light-filled, curtainless window in the building next to him. The Minion had been on his cell phone for the past fifteen minutes. Judging from the speed his lips were moving and the look of worry on his distorted face, it appeared he was in the process of trying to talk his way out of some pretty serious shit. No doubt his Master was on the other end of the line, getting the unhappy news that his orders hadn't been executed quite as planned.

Tegan's mouth quirked as he watched the Minion squirm and pace his filthy, rathole apartment. The human's neck was bound with thick gauze, a spot of blood coming through the white bandage where Elise had stuck the bastard. His bare chest was similarly doctored up and from the way he was clutching at his ribs as he spoke, Tegan guessed he was probably sporting a perforated lung as well.

Next to him, on a coffee table cluttered with porn magazines and empty beer bottles, was a blood-soaked shirt and open boxes of medical supplies. More cotton gauze, white surgical tape, even a used roll of suture filament and a bent sewing needle. Evidently he'd been busy with a little do-it-yourself first aid after he fled Irina Odolf's place that day.

Wasted effort, Tegan thought with grim satisfaction as the Minion abruptly ended his call and threw the cell phone down onto the table.

He disappeared into another room, then came out a second later, gingerly shrugging into a flannel shirt. He buttoned up, shoved the phone into the pocket of his jeans, then grabbed his coat and headed for the door.

Tegan was already on the pavement below by the time the Minion exited his building. He stepped into the human's path and shoved the guy back with a sharp mental command.

"What the hell!" The Minion's look of annoyance quickly bled into one of alarm when Tegan flashed him his fangs. "Oh, shit!"

He pivoted to run back into the building, but Tegan blocked him faster than the human's eyes could follow. He reached out and grabbed the Minion by the throat, closing his fingers around the thick neck.

"Aagh!" the Minion cried, struggling and wheezing against the sudden choke hold.

"Yeah, that probably hurts," Tegan said coolly. He squeezed harder, increasing pressure to allow only the smallest bit of air to pass into the Minion's lungs. "Had a little trouble in town today, did you?"

"Let . . . go . . . "

Tegan's touch told him of the Minion's recollection of what happened at Irina Odolf's place. He read the Minion's anger, his surprise at Elise's retaliation, his disgusting intent to make her suffer for it deeply, had she not been able to get away from him.

"Who sent you after her?" Tegan demanded, all but certain on his own, but needing to hear it. "Who's your Master, you sick fuck?"

"Piss off, vampire," the Minion gasped, but inside he was panicking and in a great deal of pain. His mind surrendered the name to Tegan's touch, even though his tongue refused to speak it.

Marek.

It came as little surprise to Tegan that Lucan's brother owned this one. He wouldn't doubt that the powerful vampire had a far-reaching network of human mind slaves at his disposal. God knew he'd had many long years to covertly lay the groundwork for whatever dark plan the deceptive son of a bitch was working on.

But it wasn't anger at Marek that tightened Tegan's grip on the Minion's injured throat, as much as he wanted to tell himself he was just crippling one more leg of his enemy's army. What filled Tegan's mind as he choked the life out of the sorry excuse for a man was the cold knowledge that the human had put his hands on Elise.

For the fact that the Minion had enjoyed hurting her, Tegan intended to take his sweet time ending the bastard.

• • •

"Was the lamb not to your liking?"

Elise snapped back to attention and met Reichen's gaze across the intimate restaurant table. "No, it's delicious. Everything was just incredible, Andreas. You really didn't have to do this."

He made a casually dismissive gesture with his hand, but his smile was full of pride. "What kind of host would I be to let you go all day without a proper meal? It seemed only fitting that I treat you to one of the city's finest dinners."

They were seated together in a top-floor restaurant in one of Berlin's most exclusive hotels. After learning Elise hadn't eaten for several hours, Reichen had insisted they detour there after they'd left Helene's club.

He wasn't having anything, of course. Those of the Breed could only consume prepared food in the smallest quantities—a practice reserved for rare moments when a vampire found it necessary in order to pretend to be human.

Elise had hardly eaten either, despite the fact that the food and wine in front of her was nothing short of amazing. As hungry as she was, she had little appetite. She could hardly think of eating when Tegan was out there somewhere, fighting her battles.

Outside the window at her left, the nighttime city twinkled with life below. She looked out, letting her gaze wander over the tangle of milling pedestrians, rushing traffic, and the illuminated beauty of Brandenburg Gate.

None of the humans out there had the first clue about the war that was rising within the Breed. Few in the Darkhavens knew either. Those who were in a position to know of Rogue conflicts chose to turn a blind eye, trusting politics and protocol to keep things in their proper place. Everyone went about their lives, oblivious, comfortably ignorant, while Tegan and the other members of the Order dirtied their hands and risked their lives to maintain the fragile peace within the Breed and its dependent link to humankind.

She had been one of those sheltered many. When she looked across the table at handsome, sophisticated Reichen, she was reminded how easy her life had been before. She had lived in the cushioned lap of wealth and privilege as Quentin Chase's mate. A part of her realized how easy it would be to return to that kind of existence, to pretend she'd never seen the terrible things she'd witnessed outside the Darkhavens these past several months, or done the terrible things she'd convinced herself she had to do in vengeance for Camden's death.

A cowardly part of her wondered if it might not be too late to go back to her old life and forget she'd ever met the warrior called Tegan.

The answer came in the quickening of her pulse, a stirring that flared at just the thought of him.

Her blood would never forget him, no matter how far she ran. And neither would her heart.

"Would you prefer to try another dish?" Reichen asked, leaning over the table to touch her hand. "I can call the waiter over if you—"

"No. No, there's no need for that," she assured him, feeling rude and unappreciative of his kindness. Tegan probably didn't need her concern. He certainly wouldn't want it. She couldn't turn off her feelings for him, but that didn't mean she had to let them consume her. "Thank you for bringing me here, Andreas. I can't remember the last time I had such wonderful food and wine. Quentin and I enjoyed nice dinners together, but since his death, I guess I never really saw any reason to go to the effort."

Reichen gave her a mock scowl, as if he'd never heard a more preposterous thing. "There is always a reason to enjoy all of life's pleasures, Elise. I personally do not believe in deprivation. Not in any shape or form."

Elise smiled, knowing he was deliberately putting on the charm now. "With that kind of life philosophy, I'm betting that you have broken a lot of hearts in your time."

"Only a few," he admitted, grinning.

He lounged back in his seat, one arm slung over the back of the chair, his aristocratic profile etched in light by the warm glow of the candle flickering on the table. With his dark hair slipping loose of its queue, his tailored white shirt unbuttoned one more notch than was decent, Andreas Reichen had the look of an indulgent king surveying his subjects from atop his tower keep.

But there was a restless undercurrent to his practiced air of nonchalance, perhaps a trace of boredom. There was a cynical wisdom in his eyes that indicated for all his easy charm, the male had seen more darkness than he would ever let on.

Elise wondered if, despite his privilege and his obviously libertine ways, Andreas Reichen might have a bit of the warrior in him as well.

"What about Helene?" Elise couldn't resist asking about the stunning female who wasn't a Breedmate, yet seemed to know a great deal about the vampire nation due to her apparent relationship with Reichen. "Have you and she . . . known each other for a long time?"

"A few years. Helene is a friend. She is my blood Host on occasion, and we enjoy each other's company, but it's primarily a physical arrangement."

"You're not in love with her?"

He chuckled. "Helene would probably say that I love no one more than myself. Not altogether untrue, I suppose. I've just never met a woman who tempted me to want anything permanent. Then again, who would be mad enough to put up with me?" he asked, turning a dazzling smile on her that would have made any other woman leap up to volunteer for the task.

Elise took a sip of her wine. "I think you are a very dangerous man, Andreas Reichen. A woman would be well advised to guard her heart around you."

He arched a brow at her, looking rakish and serious at the same time. "I would never want to break your heart, Elise."

"Ah," she said, tilting her glass at him in mock salute. "And now you have just further proved my point."

Tegan arrived back at Reichen's estate in a foul mood. The Minion who would have killed Elise was dead, and that was good enough news. But as he'd squeezed the last breath out of the human, Tegan had come away with two critical pieces of information.

The first, that Marek had given kill orders on Elise to several of his Minion contacts in and around Berlin. Which meant Tegan needed to get her the hell out of the city as soon as possible.

He was already putting that plan into motion. He'd just hung up with Gideon, who was going to see that the Order's private jet was fueled and cleared for departure out of Tegel Airport in one hour.

The second thing he came away with tonight was that no matter how much he wanted to deny it, Elise mattered to him. She mattered in a way he could hardly fathom. He cared for her like his own kin—more than that, in fact—a truth that had been driven home pretty clearly when she'd come back after the Minion attack covered in blood. He respected her, not only for her courage, but for her strength. She was an extraordinary woman, far better than he could ever hope to deserve.

He wouldn't even try to pretend that he could resist her. Walking with her into Helene's club had nearly wrung him out. All he'd been able to think of was what he wanted to do with Elise. He'd caught her uncomfortable glance as they strolled through the place, and he hadn't missed the fact that her breathing had kicked into a rapid beat, her pulse drumming loud enough for him to feel it as a vibration in his own body.

She couldn't have known how badly he'd wanted to pull her into one of Aphrodite's plush alcoves, strip her naked, and drive himself deep inside her soft, moist heat. Just thinking about it now gave him a massive hard-on.

And then there was the matter of their blood bond. That was easily the worst of it. As offended as he should be by the whole idea, he found himself looking forward to the next time Elise would take his vein to her mouth. He actually liked knowing that it was his blood making her strong, helping her cope with the psychic gift that had been slowly destroying her before.

His blood that would keep her alive close to forever if they completed their bond. All he'd have to do is drink from her, and they would be linked to each other inextricably.

Yeah, that was exactly what he wanted.

And what the fuck, he might as well admit it—to himself, at least.

He loved her.

Which brought him back to his current state of aggravation. He entered the Darkhaven, which was quiet except for the handful of residents who hadn't gone out for the night. Tegan stood outside Elise's guest room and knocked on the closed door. No response. He tried again, feeling like an idiot as one of the younger females approached from up the hallway.

"Good evening," the woman said, smiling pleasantly.

Tegan nodded curtly and waited until she sauntered down the stairs to the main level of the mansion. He knocked one last time, then opened the door and went inside the empty room.

Where the hell was she? And where was Reichen? Why wouldn't they have returned by now?

A tremor of dread snaked up Tegan's spine.

Ah, Christ. If anything had happened to her . . .

He stalked to the pair of French doors that opened onto a small balcony overlooking the estate's front grounds, intending what, he didn't know. The blast of cold air braced him as he stepped outside and listened to the surrounding night.

If one of Marek's human assassins had managed to find Elise while he was away—

Just then, Reichen's sleek black Rolls-Royce limo came gently up the drive, making an elegant sweep as it came to rest outside the mansion's main entrance.

Relief washed over Tegan as the driver came around and opened the rear passenger door. He helped Elise out, Reichen exiting directly behind her.

"Thank you again for dinner," Elise said as Reichen strolled in front of her and offered his hand to help her up the mansion's steps.

"It was my great pleasure. Truly."

Something primitive and possessively male rose to attention at the intimate tone Reichen was using on Elise.

"Perhaps I could entice you to extend your stay in Berlin," said the Darkhaven lord as he inched closer to her, his large frame towering over Elise and obscuring her from Tegan's view. "I would very much like to get to know you better, Elise."

Tegan could hardly contain his growl as Reichen reached out to touch her, then leaned down to deliver what was unmistakably a more than friendly kiss.

She didn't draw back. She didn't slap him or run away in outrage.

And why should she?

Tegan hadn't given her any reason not to consider other males. No, he'd practically shoved her into Reichen's arms. He should be relieved that she might look elsewhere for a mate. He sure as hell was no prize.

Elise deserved far better than him—or Reichen, for that matter. And Tegan was going to tell her as much, damn it.

His foul mood heading farther south every second she remained out there with the Darkhaven male, Tegan stalked back into her room to wait for her.

CHAPTER
Twenty-seven

Elise drew out of the very unexpected kiss, her fingers pressed to her lips. It had been a pleasant, if brief, contact but she felt absolutely nothing for the handsome man who was now looking at her in awkward, yet understanding, silence.

"I'm sorry, Andreas. I shouldn't have let you do that."

When she glanced down, embarrassed, he gently lifted her chin so that she was looking at him again. "The fault is mine. I should have asked you first. No," he said, correcting himself. "I should have recognized that your heart is already spoken for. I did, actually, but I suppose I wanted to be certain that I stood no chance. I don't . . . stand any chance, do I, Elise?"

She smiled up at him apologetically and slowly shook her head.

"Ah. I feared not. The lucky bastard." Reichen exhaled, stripping the thin leather thong from his queued hair and raking his hand into the loose, dark waves. "I think I've finally run out of charity when it comes to that warrior. After this forfeit to him, Tegan will have no choice but to accept that my debt to him is paid in full."

Elise warmed to his praise, even though she wasn't sure it was valid. Tegan had made no claims on her, despite her feelings for him. In fact he seemed intent on keeping her at arm's length. He would probably be relieved if she were to suddenly develop an affection for another male.

But that wasn't going to happen. Reichen was right; her heart was no longer hers to give. Tegan had it, whether he wanted it or not.

She looked up into Reichen's striking dark eyes. "You're a good man, Andreas. A very kind man."

He gasped dramatically. "Stop, I beg you! You have thrashed my pride enough for one night. I'm a devil and a cad, and don't you forget it."

Elise laughed, and went up on her toes to kiss his cheek. "Thank you for dinner. Thank you for everything, Andreas."

He nodded, then strode ahead to open the mansion door for her.

"Good night, beauty," he said, then waited in the foyer as she made the climb upstairs to her guest room.

Tegan heard her light footsteps pause outside her room door. He waited silently, stealthily, as the crystal knob turned and the panel swung inward. Elise took only a step inside, then she paused, listening. Her blood link to him instantly gave him away; she could feel his presence. He knew it by the softly indrawn breath she took, her eyes searching the dark room.

"Tegan?"

She flipped the light switch. Walked farther into the room. He stayed still, watching her rub a chill from her arms as she crossed the thick rug and went to the open French doors. She looked out onto the balcony, her movements cautious, uncertain.

"Tegan . . . are you out here?"

The sweet scent of her drifted up to him as a chill night breeze swept in from outside. Reichen's scent was on her too—a dark, musky undertone that set Tegan's teeth on edge. Jealousy spiked in him, raw and feral.

Instinctively male.

As she drew back to close the doors, Tegan came down from the corner of the room where he'd been suspended spiderlike. He dropped soundlessly behind her, his body blocking her as she pivoted around and gasped.

Startled, her eyes went wide. "Tegan! Where were y—"

He pulled her to him in a hard, unyielding embrace and slanted his mouth over hers. His kiss was forceful, deliberate. An animal male putting his stamp on what he meant to be his, and his alone.

Elise didn't fight him. He felt her hands come up around his neck, her fingers linking together at his nape and holding him close. She kissed him back, sighing into his mouth as he pushed her lips apart and plunged his tongue between them, needing to taste her.

Needing to claim her.

Christ, she inflamed him. Every cell in his body was lit

with heat, with hunger for her. He couldn't be gentle, not when everything primal in him was fully awake, fully aroused. All that was Breed in him responded as well, lust thinning his pupils and stretching his fangs. He ground his pelvis against the tender curves of Elise's body, letting her feel the hard ridge of his cock. She moaned as they pressed together, her heartbeat banging like a little drum in his ears.

"Oh, God, Tegan," she said, her voice a breathless rush of warm air when he finally withdrew from the lush sweetness of her mouth. "I'm so glad you're here. I was worried about you tonight."

He grunted, low in his throat. "Yeah, I noticed. I saw how concerned you were, down there in Reichen's arms."

"You saw us . . ."

He smirked, baring his fangs. "I can still taste him on your lips."

"Then you must also taste the fact that he isn't the one I want," she said, not flinching at all as he let his mouth travel along her soft cheek, down to the tender skin below her ear. "It's you, Tegan. I want to be with you. In case you hadn't noticed, I've fallen in love with you."

He snarled, pulling back to hold her in a narrowed glare. They were the words he wanted to hear—the words he'd been prepared to force out of her after seeing her caught up in another man's arms. Still, it leveled him. His mouth went suddenly dry.

She was so beautiful, so courageously open.

All his aggression leaked out of him as he gazed into the deep amethyst pools of her eyes. He ran his fingers along the delicate line of her jaw, hardly able to draw breath as she tilted her head to the side for him, exposing the vulnerable column of her throat. He couldn't resist touching the place where her pulse beat the strongest. The ticking flutter beneath his fingertips was like a brand searing into his skin. He let his thumb trace over the soft skin, then gently bent to place his mouth atop the tender, beating artery that carried Elise's lifeblood.

Saliva surged into his mouth, swamping him with the need to taste her now and seal their bond completely.

But Tegan only kissed her.

With reverent hands, he lifted the hem of her sweater and carefully peeled it off her. Tenderly, he caressed her soft skin. She sighed as he stroked her breasts, the nipples peaking like dusky rosebuds beneath the thin satin of her bra. He unfastened the front clasp and bared her to his appreciative gaze.

"So beautiful," he said thickly, letting his fingers skate along the soft underside of the creamy swells.

He knelt down before her and took one dark pink nipple into his mouth. His fangs were huge now, and it took great care not to graze the sharp edge of them against her tender skin as he suckled the pebbled flesh with his tongue. But he was careful. He held her as though she were made of glass, every inch of her precious and breakable. A treasure he was unworthy of, yet determined to cherish.

Elise's arms came down around his shoulders. She held fast, arching into him as he lavished the same attention on the other breast. He let his mouth travel down her belly while his hands worked to free her of her slacks and panties. The skin of her hips was like velvet against his palm. He kissed the lean curve of her pelvis, then trailed lower, into the trim thatch of blond curls between her thighs.

He spread her legs and put his mouth to her sex, cleaving his tongue into the wet heat of her core. She quivered as he feasted on her, her body feeling limp and boneless in his arms as he picked her up and carried her to the bed. She lay back and watched him under heavy lids as he undressed for her, the hunger in her gaze like a physical heat on his skin.

Naked and painfully aroused, Tegan stood at the edge of the mattress and let her take her fill of him with her eyes. He held his breath as she sat up then came toward him on her hands and knees. Her hands were curious and questing, soft but firm, as she took his engorged shaft and stroked it from tip to balls and back again. She licked her lips, eyes flicking up to his in question.

His low exhalation must have been permission enough. Tegan watched her descend on him, those moist lips parting as she took the head of his cock into her mouth. He moaned, reaching down to bury his fingers in her short blond hair as she sucked him deep, torturing him with the slow, steady slide of her tongue against his sensitive flesh.

She increased her rhythm and he spun quickly toward the edge of his control. With a pleasured snarl, he pulled away from her devastatingly sweet mouth and pushed her down onto the mattress. He climbed over her and kissed her deeply, feeling the ferocity of her desire in every place their bodies touched.

"Do you want me inside you, Elise?"

"Yes," she gasped, arching up to meet his body. "I need you inside me, Tegan. Now."

He was only too willing to oblige. Thrusting in one long stroke, he filled her tight channel, swallowing her soft cry. Her body milked him, the walls of her sex gripping him like a moist, hot fist. Tegan pumped his hips, watching emotion play over Elise's beautiful face.

"You feel so good," he told her, wanting only to please her.

His woman.

His mate.

His love.

He could feel her orgasm building along with his own. She was panting now, writhing to meet every hard flex of his hips and moaning in protest with every slight withdrawal. She turned her head to the side, where his arm was bracing him up. With a deliciously animal sound, she nipped at his wrist, closing her pretty white teeth down onto his skin. The pinch of her blunt little bite was an erotic pain that went through him like an arrow.

"Yeah?" he said, looking down into her hungry gaze. "You want to drink from me as I make you come?"

She nodded weakly and gave him another small bite in reply.

"You got it, sweetheart. But not the wrist this time." Holding her against him, he rolled onto his back and brought her up astride him. "I want to feel you at my neck, Elise. I want to hold you while you drink from me. I want to feel you bite into me."

Touching her, he felt her uncertainty. "I've never done it that way before."

"Good," he said, entirely too pleased to hear it. "I've never asked anyone to do it that way before. So, will you, Elise?"

She frowned, but her eyes were rooted on his throat. "I don't want to hurt you . . ."

He chuckled, adoring her all the more for her concern. "Come here," he said, wrapping his hand around her nape and guiding her down to the exposed column of his neck. "Sink your teeth into me, Elise. Take your fill."

She bent over him, their bodies still intimately joined, eyes locked together. Her breath skated hotly across his cheek as she descended. Warm lips pressed below his ear and parted. He felt her wet tongue, then the hard line of her teeth as she positioned her mouth over his vein.

The instant she bit down, Tegan nearly exploded inside her. She broke his skin in a sharp, delicious flare of pain that sent his hips bucking up off the mattress. He gripped her ass and drove into her as she suckled from the wound she'd made. She began to ride him, plunging hard, then rising up slowly on the length of his shaft. The wet sounds of her drinking so close to his ear was erotic in the extreme, her pleasured moans and wet lapping the sexiest thing he'd ever heard.

When she threw her head back and screamed with her breaking orgasm, Tegan lost all hope of control. He sat up with her, hooking her legs around him as he continued to rock into her. She clung to him as her body shuddered around his sex, wave after wave of release rippling against him. Tegan ran his palm over her glistening skin, bending down to taste the enticing curve of flesh where her neck and shoulder met.

He should have known better.

Ah, hell. Maybe he did know better and had to do it anyway.

The drum of her heartbeat pulsated against his mouth. Tegan followed it, moving up Elise's throat until his mouth hovered at the tender patch of skin beneath her ear. She whimpered as he hesitated there, his tongue licking along the line of her artery.

His fangs throbbed in time with her pulse, every Breed

instinct in him rising to the temptation that lay just a breath away from completion.

Elise's hands came up around his head. "Tegan . . . Oh, God . . . *do it.*"

He nipped at her, just a small test of her mettle. In answer, she impaled herself deeper on his cock, grinding against him as another orgasm shuddered through her.

It was too much for him to bear.

Tegan held her head to the side in one hand and lowered his mouth to her neck. His fangs sank in easily, sharp points penetrating her tender skin like a warm knife through butter. She cried out as he took the first long pull from her vein. Her body arched catlike in his arms, then eased into a languid calm as he began to drink.

And oh, God, she was sweet. His mouth filled with a sudden rush of her blood, the heather-and-roses scent of it saturating his senses. He was greedy for it, could not recall ever knowing anything as exquisite as the taste of Elise on his tongue, the vibrant essence of her blood coursing into his body, lighting him from within.

With each quenching, binding swallow from her vein, Tegan's hunger for her rose. The lust he'd known for Elise before was just a pale hint of the desire he knew now.

Possession rolled over him like a storm. He roared with need for this woman—his woman now, irreversibly.

Irrevocably.

He pushed her down beneath him and let the awakened beast in him have its head.

Elise could only hold on to Tegan as he covered her with his body and drove her toward another shattering orgasm. She reveled in the feel of his long fangs penetrating deeply into her neck, in the hard suction of his mouth as he drew her blood down his throat and completed their bond.

There was nothing gentle about him now. His unbreakable self-control had snapped, and she had never known anything quite so arousing as Tegan gripped in the wildness that had overcome him the moment he took his first taste of her blood.

He spun her out on an endless wave of pleasure, making love to her until they were both sated and panting, lying boneless in each other's arms. When it was over, he ran his tongue over the punctures he'd given her, sealing the wound with a tender lover's kiss.

"Are you all right?" he asked her, smoothing his fingers through her hair.

"Mm-hmm." Elise nodded, groggy but enlivened at the same time. "I'm very all right."

She'd never been better, in fact. Although it hadn't escaped her notice that when she told Tegan she loved him, he hadn't returned the sentiment. A little late to be worrying about that, perhaps, but now that the worst of her hungers had been dealt with, reality was edging in again to spoil things.

"I haven't said those words in a very long time, Elise. I didn't think I ever would again."

"Don't do that." She sat up and drew out of his reach, embarrassed that he'd invaded her emotions with his touch. "And don't feel that you have to say anything kind because of what just happened here."

"I don't feel that I have to say anything."

"Good. Please don't. I don't think I could stand your charity right now."

He reached out and took her hand in his. "If I tell you

that it pissed me off to see you kissing Reichen, and that I never want to see you kissing any other male ever again, it's not because I feel I have to tell you that."

Elise stared at him, hardly daring to breathe. His amber-tinged eyes were intense as he held her gaze, his pupils still thinned from desire. When he spoke, his voice was rough, the tips of his fangs gleaming.

"I don't feel I have to be kind because of what we just did here, so that's not why I'm telling you that you are unlike any woman I've ever met before. I wasn't prepared for you, Elise. Holy hell . . . not even close."

She glanced down to where their hands were linked together, his strong fingers firm and protective, always so gentle with her even though they were trained for war and combat.

"It wouldn't be charitable of me at all to tell you that I hope you never want another male as much as you want me." He exhaled a wry laugh. "Do I love you? Yeah, God help you, but I do."

"Tegan," she whispered, bringing her hand up to rest against his cheek. The bite she'd given him was already healing over, his skin knitting together. She touched the red mark tenderly, then looked up into his eyes. "Kiss me again."

His mouth quirked at the corner as he pulled her into his arms. They had barely gotten started before a low buzzing sound drew Tegan's head up with a groan.

"What is it?" she asked as he vaulted out of the bed and grabbed his cell phone from his discarded pants.

"It's our ride back to Boston. I've arranged a flight out tonight."

He answered the call, his tone clipped and serious—

back to warrior mode in an instant. "Yeah. Right. Tegel Airport. Corporate terminal. Departure in one hour."

Elise slid off the mattress and padded over to where Tegan stood, naked and gorgeous. She wrapped her arms around him, pressing the front of her body against the hard muscles of his backside. She nipped his shoulder blade, smiling as goose bumps rose along the beautiful *dermaglyphs* on his arms. She heard his low growl of interest and couldn't help but smile as he cast a heated look at her.

"You'd better make it two hours from now," he instructed the person on the other end of the line. "Something's just come up."

Elise glanced down as he turned to face her. Something had indeed come up—quite impressively, in fact. She backed away, her lip caught in her teeth as Tegan disconnected the call, his hooded eyes rooted on her.

He tossed the phone aside.

Then he pounced.

CHAPTER
Twenty-eight

They slept most of the trip back to Boston, Elise contentedly curled up in Tegan's arms. He'd told her that the Minion who attacked her at Irina's was dead. He'd also informed her that the human mind slave was just one of several in Berlin who'd been given orders by Marek to hunt her down. Elise had accepted the news with her usual calm understanding, but Tegan couldn't help holding her a bit tighter as she dozed across his lap.

Marek was a treacherous enemy. He'd been a formidable warrior, ruthless in battle, often unnecessarily cruel. Tegan had known Lucan's elder brother well, had trusted him with his life more than once on the field. They'd fought side by side in the Old Times, when the Breed was young and trouble with Rogues was commonplace. Marek had been one of the original members of the Order, but he'd always been the renegade. He balked at his younger brother's command—Lucan was founder of the warrior class and a natural-born leader, two things Marek seemed unable to accept. Impatience and arrogance were Marek's strongest traits, and the two things that prevented him from getting the respect he felt he deserved.

The fact that he'd been presumed dead for so long—some six centuries—only to resurface in Boston with obvious plans to target the Order, seemed to indicate that Marek had somehow learned to bide his time. He'd shown great patience in staying hidden as long as he had, and Tegan had no doubt that the vampire had been using those years to his benefit. He had a plan, and he was slowly but surely putting it into motion. That the name Dragos was suddenly in the mix, along with the Odolfs' cryptic ramblings, hinted at trouble of a very old nature.

Tegan flipped open the journal and read the strange passages again. It had to be a location, but where? And what did it signify?

That's where he's hiding, Odolf had blurted.

Tegan didn't think it referred to Marek. But could it possibly be Dragos? Or might it be someone else who wasn't even on the Order's radar yet?

Whatever Marek was after, and whatever secret it was that haunted Petrov Odolf and his kin, it did not bode well for anyone.

As the jet touched down in Boston, Tegan phoned the compound and told Gideon to assemble the others for a meeting. They were going to have to rout out Marek, wherever he'd run to, and make sure that the Order stayed one step ahead of him.

One of his Minions was dead, according to the latest report out of Berlin. Marek was enraged to lose another of his pawns, but since the human had failed to carry out his task, Marek could only hope that the Minion was made to suffer in his final moments of life. The savagery of the killing left little doubt that he had suffered greatly, his body broken and bloodied almost beyond recognition. And that fact was surprising in itself, considering the Minion's executioner had most certainly been Tegan.

He had killed the Minion that Marek had dispatched to get rid of the Darkhaven female—not with the immaculate, cold efficiency the warrior was known for, but with a clearly evidenced rage.

Tegan had killed with a vengeance.

That he'd acted in retaliation over the female could mean only one thing: Tegan cared for her.

Marek could hardly wait for the chance to exploit that weakness in the warrior. He'd nearly destroyed Tegan once through his love of a woman; how gratifying it would be to use this new affection to finally finish him off for good.

How satisfying it would be to finish off all the Order, and to assume his rightful place as the ruler of all the Breed. It was what he'd been working toward all along, a plan that had required more patience than Marek had thought himself capable of.

He'd been dreaming of his crowning moment for centuries—ever since the warrior Dragos had confided in him a powerful, damning secret.

Marek got up from his desk and paced to the tall window that overlooked a moonlit Berkshires valley in the distance. The woods were thick out here, as dense as any medieval forest. The landscape reminded him of the Old Times, his thoughts returning to the Order's long-ago past.

Back then, a war had been raging within the vampire nation. It pitted father against son, except the fathers in this scenario were the band of vicious otherworlders—the Ancients, alien creatures who arrived on Earth thousands of years ago and preyed on human blood for their survival. Their eventual sons, the hybrid progeny born of alien seed carried by human mothers, formed the first generation of the Breed.

Marek, Lucan, and Tegan were among those rare Gen One sons. They saw firsthand the savagery perpetrated by the Ancients on humankind, the wholesale slaughter of entire villages at times, lives lost to ravenous vampire appetites. The carnage had never disturbed Marek the way it did his younger brother.

While Lucan despised the terror the Ancients delivered, Marek often indulged in it himself. The power to stir panic and kill without recourse was heady stuff, and more than once he wondered why the Breed shouldn't simply enslave their human Hosts and claim the planet for their own. Marek had been feeding those seeds of discontent to the Ancients for some time when all of his plans were thrown into a tailspin.

In a fit of Bloodlust, his alien sire took the life of Marek and Lucan's mother. The creature slaughtered her, and Lucan, claiming justice, took the vampire's head in exchange. With that killing of an Ancient, Lucan declared war on the remaining few like him and any who served them. Lucan formed the Order, pulling Marek into the fold as well, along with Tegan and five other Gen One vampires all pledged to end the mass carnage and start a new way of life for the Breed.

Such noble, lofty intentions.

Marek could hardly contain his derisive chuckle, even now. He hadn't been the only one of the Order to bristle at Lucan's vision of a peaceful coexistence with humankind. Another warrior, Dragos, eventually confided in Marek that he had different ideas for the future of the Breed.

And even more intriguing, he'd actually taken steps to ensure that future.

While the Order waged war on the surviving Ancients, hunting them down one by one in a battle that took years to complete, one of those deadly creatures remained.

Dragos and his alien sire had made a pact. Instead of killing the vampire, Dragos had helped to hide him away.

It wasn't until sometime later, after Dragos was mortally injured in combat, that he chose to spill his secret to Marek. But the bastard wouldn't surrender all of it. Dragos refused to give Marek the location of the crypt where the Ancient slept in a state of prolonged hibernation.

Marek's rage over that omission had been uncontrollable. He put a blade to Dragos's neck, and with one furious blow, he sent the vampire—and that crucial bit of information—to the grave.

Marek had gone after the only other person who might have been of use to him: Dragos's Breedmate Kassia. But the female was shrewd, and in the moment her mate perished at Marek's hand, she must have known the same danger would soon be coming to her doorstep.

By the time Marek arrived at Dragos's castle to drain

the secret out of her—literally, as it were—Kassia had thwarted him by taking her own life.

In the time since, Marek had been on a single-minded quest to find Dragos's secret. He'd willingly tortured and killed for it. He'd long ago tossed away his honor, pretended his own death, and betrayed his kin, all for the chance to be the one to unleash the ancient terror and use it to serve his own whims.

Finally, after an endless time of searching, he'd recently come upon the first truly useful clue: it was the name of Odolf, a Breed family from the Old Times who'd had ties with Dragos's mate, Kassia. She had given them something of great worth all those centuries ago, but not even torture had given Marek the answers he needed.

And now the Order was getting closer to the truth every moment. Marek's jaw clamped tight at the thought. He hadn't worked this hard, waited this long, just to let everything slip through his fingers. He refused to consider it might even be a possibility.

He was going to win.

The real battle was only beginning.

A few minutes after they arrived at the compound, Tegan showed Elise to his quarters so she could shower and relax while he headed for the tech lab, where the Order had assembled at his request. As he walked in, Lucan gave him a knowing nod from where he stood next to Gideon at the bank of computers. Niko, Kade, and Brock sat around the table at the center of the room, the two newbies fitting right in as they traded gibes with

Dante and Chase about the week's Rogue tallies and which of them had the sharper eye.

But it was the sight of Rio that made Tegan's mouth lift in surprise and satisfaction. The Spaniard leaned against the back wall of the lab, apart from the others, broody but alert. Determination rolled off him like an electrical charge. He lifted his chin to acknowledge Tegan's arrival, the scarred side of his face stretching taut with his grim smile.

The once-lively topaz eyes were flinty now, sober as the grave.

Tegan looked at his brethren, some of whom had fought at his side for centuries, others who had yet to be truly tested, and he couldn't help feeling a sense of pride to be included among their ranks. For a long time, he'd thought of himself as being alone in this war. Sure, Lucan and the others always had his back, as he had theirs, but Tegan fought every battle as if it belonged to him alone.

He'd lived every day wallowing in his own dark isolation . . . until a courageous beauty taught him not to fear the light. Now that he'd found her, he wanted to make sure the darkness he'd known would never touch her.

And that meant keeping her safe from Marek.

"What's the word out of Petrov Odolf?" Lucan asked as Tegan set his duffel bag of gear down on the table.

"Most of the time, the word is crazy. The rest of the time, he's catatonic." Tegan pulled out the handwritten pages they'd gotten from Irina. He handed them to Lucan. "Before he went Rogue, Odolf had been writing compulsively and in secret. Evidently his brother, who also went Rogue sometime before him, had been obsessed with a similar habit. Look familiar?"

"Shit. The same thing we found in the journal Marek was after."

Tegan nodded. "Odolf said something odd in one of his rare moments of clarity. When Elise and I asked him what the riddle meant, he said, 'That's where he's hiding.'"

"That's where who's hiding?" Gideon asked, taking the pages from Lucan and giving them a quick visual scan. He read one of the verses aloud. "Does this reference some kind of location?"

"Maybe. Odolf wouldn't say. Maybe he doesn't know." Tegan shrugged. "That's all he gave us, just started rambling after that. We didn't get any further with him."

Dante came out of his loose recline at the table, putting his feet down on the floor with a thump. "Whatever it means, it's big enough to get Marek's interest. No good ever came out of that."

"And he's willing to kill anyone who gets in his way," Tegan added. "After he found out we were in Berlin, Marek put out orders to some of his Minions in the city to kill Elise. One of them got damn close."

"Son of a bitch," Lucan hissed, his features hardening in anger.

"She injured the bastard and thankfully managed to get away. That night I went out and finished him off." Tegan felt Chase's stare from across the room, and he turned a sincere look on the male. "Elise has become . . . very precious to me. I'm not about to let anything happen to her. I'd give my life to keep her safe."

Chase looked at him for a long while, then he nodded tightly. "What about the *glyph* you found in the journal? That symbol belonged to one of the first warriors, didn't it—a Gen One male called Dragos?"

"Yeah," Tegan said. "There's got to be a connection, but I'm not sure what it is. I know Dragos is dead. Lucan can vouch for that since he saw the body."

The Order's leader inclined his head in agreement. "His Breedmate saw it too. Evidently seeing her mate dead must have been too much for Kassia. That same night, she took her own life."

Nikolai grunted. "So, what have we got to work with here? Our own Romeo and Juliet scenario, a batshit Rogue talking riddles, a dead-end *glyph* scribbled into the margin of a musty old book, and Marek somehow in the middle of it all."

"Get to Marek, and you'll start getting answers," Dante put in, his voice low and deadly.

Tegan nodded. "Right. But first we need to find him."

"No hard leads there," Gideon said. "He's gone deep underground since we ran up against him last summer."

"So we hunt him down like the vermin he is," Rio snarled. "We root him out and smoke the son of a bitch."

Tegan glanced over at Lucan, who was absorbing the conversation in stoic silence. Amid the talk of enemies and battles to come, it was sometimes easy to forget that Lucan and Marek were blood kin. "You cool with all this?"

The silver stare that held Tegan's eyes was unwavering. "Whatever Marek is up to, he has to be stopped. The question isn't if, but when. And by any means."

CHAPTER
Twenty-nine

Elise heard women's voices as she strolled the corridor on her way out of Tegan's quarters. The muffled laughter and easy conversation drew her, reminding her of the friendships she had enjoyed in the Darkhaven, when her life had seemed so full. Although she didn't feel as empty as she had in recent months, there was still a space in her heart that was open—a small void that made her miss being part of a community.

She didn't know what the other females would think of her. Although it seemed years ago to her, it was only a handful of days since the confrontation she'd had with Tegan in front of the Order—when he'd publicly suggested she find a willing male to be her blood Host without the sanctity of a vow. He'd only done it to push her away, but if the Breedmates here at the compound had heard about it, she was probably a subject of pity with them, if not scorn. There were few females in the Darkhavens who would be able to look her in the eye after something like that.

As she neared the open door of the room where the warriors' mates had gathered, Elise prepared herself for cautious greetings and the quiet whispers that were sure to begin once she had passed.

"Elise, welcome back!" Gabrielle exclaimed the instant her kind brown eyes lit on her. "We heard you and Tegan had just come back. I was actually about to go and find you. Do you want to join us?"

The women had a nice little repast of fruits and cheeses spread out on the coffee table in the center of the cozy library. Tess was putting down small plates and there was already an extra one waiting for Elise. Savannah stood in front of a dark cherry sideboard, pulling a cork from a bottle of chilled white wine. She looked over at Elise and smiled as she began pouring into several long-stemmed glasses.

"Want some?" she asked.

"Okay." Elise walked into the inviting chamber and accepted the glass from Savannah's outstretched hand. "Thank you."

The awkwardness she expected didn't happen. As soon as she settled in with the women, Elise was bombarded with questions about the trip, about what she and Tegan were able to uncover, and about where things stood with regard to Petrov Odolf and the journal Marek had been so determined to get his hands on.

They weren't interested in gossip or scandal, and Elise

found herself falling into an easy conversation with all three of the intelligent, savvy women. She told them all she knew, relating the details of Tegan's and her visits to the containment facility.

She had just begun to tell them about the writings Irina had given her when Tess put down her wineglass, her brows knit in a frown.

"What happened to your face? You're bruised."

Elise nodded, idly touching the tenderness that still lingered in her cheek and jaw. "Oh. A Minion did that."

"My God," Savannah gasped, her concern echoed by Gabrielle and Tess as well.

"Does it hurt?" Tess asked, moving around the table and kneeling next to Elise.

"It did at first. It's not so bad now."

"Let me see." She carefully tilted Elise's head. When her hand came to rest on the bruise, Elise felt a warm tingle spreading from the female's palm to the tips of her fingers. Dante's mate had worked her healing touch on Elise before, but that didn't make her marvel at Tess's talent any less. The trauma of the injury faded away, muting until not even the slightest twinge of discomfort remained.

Elise let herself sink into the peaceful sensation that swept over her as Tess drew her hand away. "Your skill is amazing."

The pretty female shrugged her shoulder as if uncomfortable with the praise. "There are some things that are beyond my ability. I can't take away scars or correct wounds that have already healed on their own. Some damage is irreversible. I'm learning that with Rio."

Savannah reached over to squeeze Tess's hand. "He's doing a lot better since you've been working with him.

The fact that he's even out of bed at all is due mostly to you."

"No, it's pure rage that drives him," Tess said. "My being able to heal some of his physical wounds is only incidental."

"Rio was injured in a Rogue ambush last summer," Gabrielle explained to Elise. "He got pretty messed up from exploding shrapnel, but the worst of it was when he found out that his Breedmate had set the Order up for the attack."

Elise's heart twisted at the very idea. "How awful."

"Yeah, it was. Eva betrayed Rio and the others to Marek. In exchange, Lucan was to be the primary target of the explosion. Lucan was supposed to die that night, but the bomb only injured him. He and Rio were hit, but Rio took the worst of the impact." Gabrielle took a sip of her wine, her gaze sober, reflective. "I was there when Eva confessed what she'd done . . . and when she proceeded to take her own life."

"Those were some dark days," Savannah said. "It was really hard losing Eva like that. I thought she was a friend. What she did to Rio and to the others is unforgivable."

"Rio certainly won't let it go," Tess added. "Dante and I are really concerned about him. I wonder sometimes if he's too far gone—you know, on the inside. When I work with him, there are times I feel like I'm looking at an armed grenade that's just waiting for an excuse to go off."

Savannah exhaled a wry laugh. "Pretty bad when Rio makes Tegan look like a poster boy for normal and well-adjusted."

Elise glanced down, feeling her cheeks heat up at the

mention of Tegan. When she looked up again, it was to find Gabrielle watching her. "He wasn't too terrifying in Berlin, was he? Tegan doesn't make it easy for anyone to be around him."

"No. No, he was fine, actually," Elise said, rising to his defense. "He was kind and protective . . . well, and frustratingly complicated. He's the most intense man I've ever known. And he is . . . so much more than people might think."

She felt the room go quiet. Three pairs of female eyes were rooted on her now, each of the warriors' mates staring at her as fire shot into her face.

"Elise," Gabrielle said slowly, her eyes brightening with understanding. "You and Tegan . . . really?"

Before she could stammer out an admission, she was pulled into the female's happy embrace. The two other Breedmates took turns congratulating her as well, making her tear up at the instant circle of sisterhood that they were so willing to accept her into.

It was through a moist, bleary gaze that Elise got her first glimpse of the tapestry that hung on the far corner wall of the library. The colors of the medieval setting were dazzling, depicting a knight on horseback as richly as if it were paint on canvas.

The intricacy of the needlework was extraordinary . . . familiar.

And unmistakable.

She'd seen a similarly intricate piece when she'd met with Irina Odolf. The embroidery that had been wrapped around the stack of letters Irina had found.

"That weaving," she said, hardly able to breathe. "Where did it come from?"

"It's Lucan's," Gabrielle said. "It was made for him

in the 1300s. A long time ago, when the Order was still new."

Elise's pulse kicked into an excited tempo. "Who made it, do you know?"

"Um, a woman named Kassia," Gabrielle said. "She was a Breedmate to one of the Order's original members. Lucan says her talent with needle and thread was unmatched, which you can see from the detail in this piece alone. According to him, this was the last weaving Kassia made, and her most stunning work. That's Lucan on the warhorse—"

"May I look at it?" Elise asked, standing up and walking over to see it up close.

On a distant hill behind the knight on the rearing stallion, a castle smoldered under a thin sliver of a moon. A crescent moon.

And beneath the horse's hooves lay a trampled field, rutted with deep tracts of earth.

castle and croft shall come together under the crescent moon

The strange riddle played through her mind, carried there in Petrov Odolf's tormented voice.

It couldn't be . . . could it?

Elise ran her hand over the delicate stitches of the tapestry's detailed border. All of it had been woven with such deliberate care. And in the lower right corner was the weaver's mark—a Breedmate symbol, just like the one she'd seen on the embroidery Irina showed her—sewn into the design.

Was there a message hidden somewhere in here?

Hidden here all this time?

"What is it, Elise?" Gabrielle came up behind her. "Is something wrong?"

Elise's heart was racing. "Would it be all right if we took this down from the wall?"

"I guess so . . . yeah, sure." She got up on the cushioned chair situated next to the tapestry and reached up to lift the piece from its hanging mount on the wall. Gabrielle held the tapestry gingerly in her hands. "What do you want me to do with it?"

"Lay it flat, please."

"I'll clear the table," Savannah said, and she and Tess went to work quickly removing the food and dishes to make space. "Okay, here you go."

Elise trailed Gabrielle as she spread the tapestry out. She studied the piece in silence for a moment, remembering the rest of the cryptic verse:

> *to the borderlands east turn your eye*
> *at the cross lies truth*

"I'd like to try something. I will need to fold the cloth, but I promise I'll be very careful."

At Gabrielle's agreeing nod, Elise brought the top of the tapestry toward the center of the design, then lifted the bottom of the piece and folded them so that the castle and the field below Lucan's mount met.

" 'Castle and croft shall come together under the crescent moon,' " she murmured, watching as the two meeting portions of the design formed a new picture.

"It looks like some kind of mountain range," Tess said, as a distinctly shaped rock formation became visible within the stitches. "How did you know to do that?"

"The Odolf journal contained odd scribblings—the

same weird phrases that Petrov Odolf became obsessed with in the weeks before he went mad with Bloodlust and turned Rogue. The same phrases that his brother had written before he went Rogue. My God . . . it seemed like a puzzle we were never going to solve."

Gabrielle's eyes were wide. "You mean this tapestry is somehow linked to all of that?"

"I think it must be," Elise whispered. She looked back down at the folded design. " 'To the borderlands east turn your eye . . .' Maybe if we turn the tapestry to the left?"

She pivoted the weaving ninety degrees, so that the top border was facing east. The folded center was running vertical now. And within the design emerged another—one that hadn't been obviously visible until held at this new angle. The faint outline of a cross was stitched into the tapestry, and in the center of it was a single word spelled out in the threads.

" 'Praha,' " Elise read aloud, astonished that a voice from so long ago was suddenly speaking through the silk and canvas of her work. "The secret, whatever it is, is in Prague."

"That's incredible," Savannah gasped.

She reached out and ran her fingertips over the hidden text. No sooner had they skimmed the stitches when the female drew her hand back as if she'd been burned.

"Oh, my God." Her dark brown eyes were stricken and wide. She pressed her hand down onto the fabric again, holding it there in grave silence.

"Savannah, what do you feel?"

When she finally spoke, her voice was airless with dread. "This tapestry has a few more secrets to tell."

CHAPTER
Thirty

$\sim$

The warriors were gearing up for patrol when the glass doors to the tech lab whisked open and four beautiful women rushed inside. Elise and Gabrielle were carrying the tapestry from Lucan's library; Tess and Savannah walked behind them with serious looks on their faces. Savannah seemed especially grim, her mouth drawn into a flat line, her hands flexing and fisting at her sides as she walked.

Tegan met Elise's anxious gaze. "What's going on?"

"The tapestry," she said as she and Gabrielle spread it out on the meeting table. "I think we've figured out what the Odolf riddle refers to."

"You serious?"

"Yeah." Her sober expression told him that it wasn't going to be good news.

Tegan and the other warriors gathered around the women. "Okay. Let's see what you have."

He watched, astonished and proud, as she recited each puzzling verse and folded the design accordingly. It was incredible, and so obvious now that Elise was putting it together for them. The tapestry correlated exactly to each seemingly nonsensical phrase. When Elise was finished, she stepped back and revealed an entirely new design—one that Kassia had hidden in the threads as she sewed the piece all those years ago.

Elise met Tegan's curious look. "When I was at Irina's place, she showed me some needlework that was incredibly detailed. It also had a secret design woven into it. When I saw this tapestry on the wall just now, I knew it had to have been made by the same hand. The more I looked at it, I wondered if there might be something more to it."

Tegan smiled. He didn't care one bit that everyone saw him bring her under his arm and lovingly kiss her brow. "Good work."

"I know that mountain range," Lucan said as he inspected the weaving.

Tegan nodded, also recognizing the distinctive formation that lay northeast of Prague. "It's not far from the region where most of the Breed was living at the time."

"So, this is meant to be some kind of map?" Rio asked. "If so, what are we looking for?"

"It's not what, but who." Savannah's soft voice drew everyone's attention. "The tapestry points to a location where Dragos helped hide someone. The vampire who fathered him."

"Jesus Christ."

Tegan didn't know which of the warriors muttered the curse, but each one of them had to understand the weight of what Savannah had just said.

"Dragos's Breedmate wove this piece specifically for me," Lucan put in with a dark scowl. "Are you saying Kassia deliberately hid this message in here? Why? And why the hell wouldn't she come to me and tell me about this?"

"Because she was afraid," Savannah said. "She'd been entrusted with a terrible secret, and she feared what might happen if she let it out."

Gideon glanced over at his mate. "You felt all that in the cloth, babe?"

Savannah nodded. "There's more too. And it's not good."

"Tell us," Lucan said grimly. "Whatever you can read in this thing, we need to know."

The room went still as Savannah reached out and put her hands on the tapestry. The Breedmate's unique gift of psychometry had been useful to the Order in the past, but everyone watching as she began to absorb the emotional history of the piece fell into total silence, well aware that they'd never needed Savannah's special talent more than now.

"Kassia was tormented by what she knew, but Dragos kept a close eye on her and she knew that if she told the secret, her mate would find out. He might move what he was hiding, and then there would be no hope of fixing what he had done." Savannah closed her eyes in concentration. "Kassia had no one to share her burden with—not even her dearest friend, Sorcha."

Tegan felt his jaw go rigid at the mention of the sweet

girl who met such a terrible end because of his failings. As if to say she understood what he was feeling, Elise's hand came to rest gently on his arm. Her touch was caring and compassionate, her soft gaze tender.

Savannah went on. "When Lucan asked Kassia to make this tapestry, she realized that maybe there was a way to warn him of what Dragos had done. So, as she stitched the remembrance for Lucan, she added clues and prayed one day he'd discover them before it was too late."

"What did Dragos do?" Lucan asked, his deep voice booming in the quiet of the lab. "How the hell did he begin this deception?"

For a long time, Savannah didn't speak. She slowly withdrew her hands, and when she turned to face the Order's leader, her pretty features were bleak.

"When you declared war on the last of the Ancients—only a few months before this tapestry was made—Dragos and the alien creature who fathered him forged a pact. Dragos helped his father escape into the mountains rather than stand and fight you and the rest of the Order."

Lucan's scowl was dark, anger building in his tense stance. "Dragos and several others battled the one who sired him. Dragos was the only one to come out of the skirmish alive. He was severely wounded—"

"All part of his ruse," Savannah said. "After they killed the others, Dragos helped hide his father in a protective crypt he'd built specifically for him in the mountains outside Prague. Dragos's wounds were from his father, but only to help conceal the truth of what actually happened. The plan had been to leave the Ancient in a state of hibernation until things settled down with the Order. Then the Ancient would be awakened to feed again, and to start a new generation of his Breed offspring."

"Holy hell," Gideon muttered, ripping off his pale-blue glasses and rubbing his eyes. "Did Kassia know if Dragos ever got the chance to go back and free the bastard?"

Savannah shook her head. "I don't think so. I'm not picking up anything to indicate that she knew the outcome. Dragos told her where the crypt was located, and that's what she stitched into the tapestry. She wanted Lucan to have the clues in case anything were to happen to her."

"Oh, Lucan," Gabrielle said, wrapping her arms around him.

"There is . . . something more," Savannah said. "There was a child. Kassia was pregnant when she made this tapestry. Dragos was away on a mission for nearly a year—so long that she had her son in secret and sent him away to live with another Breed family before Dragos returned. She refused to let her only child be a victim of her mate's dangerous alliance, so she took steps to protect the baby and give him a safer future."

"Let me take a wild-ass guess about the name of the family Kassia turned to," Gideon drawled.

Savannah nodded. "Odolf."

"You know," Kade interjected, "I've heard that under the right conditions, the Ancients were capable of hibernating for generations."

"Try centuries," Tegan said, reflecting on the savage otherworlders who spawned him and the rest of the Breed's first generation progeny. "For all we know, that last remaining Ancient is still out there, holed up near Prague and waiting to be unleashed."

"Christ," Dante hissed. "The world would be a very different place if an evil like that was turned loose again."

Niko clucked his tongue. "And if someone thought to ally himself with that kind of deadly power? Somebody like Marek . . ."

"We can't afford that risk," Lucan said. "So, it looks like we need to haul ass to Prague and see what we can find."

"Reichen's only a few hours away from there in Berlin," Tegan said. "He's offered us his help in whatever way we can use him."

Lucan narrowed his eyes, considering the idea. "Can he be trusted?"

"Yeah," Tegan said, nodding in certainty. "I can vouch for him."

"Give him a call then. But keep the details to a minimum. Let him know we're on the way and we're going to need transportation. We can rendezvous with him on arrival at Tegel Airport."

"Shouldn't we head straight for Prague instead and meet up with him there?" Brock asked.

Tegan shook his head, picking up on Lucan's tactic. "Reichen may be trustworthy, but we don't know about anyone else around him. Marek's already aware that we've got an interest in Berlin. No sense tipping our hand about Prague."

Lucan nodded. "We'll fill Reichen in once we arrive."

"Right," Gideon said. "I'll get clearance for a flight out tonight."

There was none of the usual bravado as the lab emptied out and the warriors each went to prepare for the mission ahead of them. Tegan normally would have gone off to suit up by himself and think in peace. He thought he probably should now, but then Elise linked

her fingers through his as the two of them paused in the
vacant corridor.

"Are you all right?" she asked, her gaze as sober as his
must have been. "If you want to be alone, or if you have
something you need to do . . ."

"No. I don't."

He thought about calling the denial back and feeding
her some line of bullshit that he was needed somewhere
else right then, but the words wouldn't come. And he
found he couldn't let go of her hand.

He'd be leaving in a few hours, and the odds were
pretty damn good that he wasn't coming back.

He was going in this time with one goal: to personally
take out Marek. Even if he had to take himself out in the
process. Tegan was more than ready to bring the war to
Marek, and, one way or another, that son of a bitch was
going down.

"Come on," he said to Elise, tipping her chin up to
meet his kiss. "There's only one place I want to be
right now."

Elise and Tegan spent the rest of the day in his quarters,
making love, and, it seemed, avoiding talk of what the future might bring them. She knew the secrets the tapestry
had revealed weighed heavily on him—on all of the
Order—but Tegan seemed especially remote as dusk
drew near and the group of them prepared to head out.
He had withdrawn in some way, as if he were already
gone, fighting the ghost of an enemy that had haunted
him for too long and had to finally be exorcised.

His call to Reichen earlier that day had brought
troubling news: Petrov Odolf had slipped further into

Bloodlust and was not doing well. The word out of the containment facility was that the Rogue had become increasingly unstable in the hours after Tegan and Elise left him that last time. At some point overnight, he lapsed into violent seizures and attacked one of his handlers, nearly killing the attendant in a fit of rage.

As for Tegan, he seemed skeptical of Director Kuhn's report to Reichen. He didn't trust the facility director, and, as he hung up with Reichen, he left the Darkhaven male with a mission to get more answers about the Rogue's condition.

"Be careful," Elise told him as they walked out of his quarters to meet the others who were gathering in the main area of the compound.

Tegan paused and kissed her passionately, but there was a distance in his eyes.

"I love you," she said, stroking his strong jaw and trying to tamp down the worry that was beating like a caged bird in her chest. "You'd better come back to me soon, you understand? Promise me."

The sounds of the other warriors talking in the hallway up ahead drew his attention. Weapons and gear jangled, deep male voices rumbling against the marble walls. That was his world calling him, the duty he'd been sworn into for longer than she'd been alive.

"Tegan, promise me," she said, forcing him to look at her. "Don't do anything heroic."

The corner of his mouth quirked into a wry grin. "Me, heroic? Not a chance."

She smiled with him, but her feet felt leaden as they walked the rest of the way up the corridor to where the Order, and Tegan's role among them, waited.

Everyone else was already gathered. Elise met the

serious faces of the other Breedmates, Tess and Gabrielle holding on to their mates as the departure time drew near. It had been agreed that Gideon would stay behind at the compound where he could monitor the operation from base and be a touch point for the others while they were in the field.

The biggest surprise was Rio. The recuperating warrior was dressed in combat gear and waiting with the rest of them, the look in his topaz eyes nothing short of fury. His muscled body radiated pure malice—white-hot and volatile—and Elise suddenly understood Tess's concerns about him. He was terrifying, even simply standing still.

Elise resisted the urge to hold on a little tighter to Tegan's hand when she felt his arm flex as he prepared to join his brethren.

God, but she didn't want to let him go.

Not when they'd just found each other.

"All right," Lucan said, his gaze steady as it lit on each of the warriors in turn. "Let's do this."

CHAPTER
Thirty-one

Andreas Reichen was waiting with two Mercedes SUVs on the tarmac at Tegel Airport as the Order arrived in Berlin. Tegan made quick introductions while the warriors threw their gear into the vehicles and got situated for the ride out to Reichen's Darkhaven estate, which was to serve as the operation's temporary base.

"I'm honored to assist," Reichen told Lucan and Tegan as the three men loaded the last of the bags and weaponry. "I've often wondered what it might be like to stand among the Order as one of your own."

"Be careful what you wish for," Lucan drawled. "Depending how things go, there's a good chance we could end up knighting you on the field."

"Try not to look so enthused," Tegan said, catching the glint of eagerness in the civilian's eyes. "What's the word out of the containment facility?"

Reichen shook his head. "Dead end, literally, I'm afraid. Odolf went from bad to worse as it turns out. He slid further into Bloodlust—went into violent convulsions. He even started foaming at the mouth. The attendant I spoke with said it was very strange, as if Odolf had gone rabid. A few hours later, they were wheeling him down to the morgue."

"Shit." Tegan exchanged a glance with Lucan, his hackles rising. The report had Marek written all over it. "What about this foam Odolf was spitting? Was it pinkish, foul smelling?"

Reichen frowned. "I don't know. I could make some more inquiries, do some more investigating—"

"No, forget it. I'll take it from here," Tegan said.

Lucan knew exactly where this was heading. "You don't suppose that Rogue was fed Crimson . . ."

"Only one way to find out. I'll be back in a couple of hours."

"It will be dawn in about that long," Lucan warned.

Tegan glanced up at the still-dark sky, the moon well into its westward slide. "Then we better stop yakking about it so I can get out of here. I'll catch you all back at the Darkhaven."

"Tegan. Goddamn it—"

He heard Lucan's terse oath behind him, but he was already across the blacktop and moving through the airport complex to the streets outside.

• • •

Director Heinrich Kuhn was in his office at the containment facility, writing up disposal documents for the body of his recently deceased patient, when the frantic call came in from security. There had been a perimeter breach. A Breed male—Gen One warrior, by the size and power of him—had infiltrated both the exterior and interior gates and was now somewhere loose in the facility.

"Shoot to kill, sir?" asked the head of security, anxiety edging his voice.

"No," Kuhn replied. "No, he is not to be killed. But apprehend him by any means, then bring him to me."

Kuhn hung up the phone. He had no doubt as to who the intruder might be. He'd been warned that the Order would not be far behind once word of Petrov Odolf's death began to circulate. He regretted that he'd permitted the warrior called Tegan into the facility in the first place—him and the Enforcement Agency female both. It was his job to protect his patients, from distress outside and from within themselves. In that, he'd failed Petrov Odolf, though no more than when he'd permitted the final visitor in to see him.

It was fear of that last individual that set the director to pacing his office now. Somehow, against everything he knew to be right, he'd let himself be recruited into a collusion that had ended with Petrov Odolf's hideous suffering and eventual death. Kuhn had been promised a similar personal experience if he didn't prove useful to his new, lethal acquaintance.

Maybe he would be wise to slip out before the situation escalated any further. It was perilously close to dawn, after all, and he really had no wish to sit around waiting for more trouble to land on his doorstep.

Too late, he thought, not a second later.

Kuhn wasn't sure precisely when he felt the first stir of the air around him, but as he turned to face the closed doors of his office, he found himself staring into cold, deadly green eyes.

"Guten morgen, Herr Kuhn." The warrior's smile was chilling. "I hear we've had a few problems here in your little Bedlam."

Kuhn inched back behind his desk. "I-I'm not sure what you mean."

In a fluid, instant motion, the warrior leaped across the room and landed in a crouch on top of the desk. "Petrov Odolf is dead. That slip your mind?"

"No," Kuhn replied, realizing he had just as much to fear from this male as he did the one who killed Odolf. "It was unfortunate, but he was very ill. Worse than I suspected."

The director carefully slid his hand along under the edge of his desk, searching for the button that would sound a silent alarm. He'd hardly had the thought before a sharp blade lifted his chin.

"I wouldn't do that if I were you."

"What do you want?"

"I want to see the body."

"What for?"

"So I will know whether or not you need to die."

"Oh, God!" Kuhn wailed. "Please don't hurt me! I had no choice—I swear to you!"

"You swear."

The answering scoff was crisp with contempt. The dagger at Kuhn's throat eased up, only to be replaced by the clamp of hard fingers. There was a heat that traveled through him from that punishing connection—a draining sense of invasion that buzzed like gnats in his brain.

The cold green eyes boring into his wide gaze went narrow. "You lying son of a bitch. You and Marek—"

The crack of Kuhn's office door being smashed off its hinges split the air. There was a sudden report of gunfire, staccato blasts that came from no less than four armed security guards as they poured inside and opened fire on Kuhn's assailant.

The warrior roared as the guards hit their mark all at once. As soon as the grip on Kuhn's throat began to ease, he backed away—as far as he could get out of the massive vampire's reach. He watched in stricken relief as the warrior slumped, then rolled off the desk onto the floor.

A wordless snarl curled out of the slack mouth, the ruthless eyes rolling back into the warrior's skull. Kuhn gathered his courage now and approached the fallen beast. He stared down at the collection of tranquilizer darts that protruded from his body.

"Are you all right, sir?" one of the guards asked.

"Yes," Kuhn replied, even though he was still trembling from the altercation. "That will be all for now. I don't want this incident recorded in any way, do you understand? As far as anyone here is concerned, it didn't happen. I will see that the intruder is removed from the premises."

When the guards had gone, Heinrich Kuhn took out the cell phone he'd been given and dialed the sole number that was programmed into the device. When the low voice answered on the other end, Kuhn told him, "Something interesting just arrived. Where would you like me to deliver it?"

• • •

Lucan knew something was wrong even before the night gave way to dawn. Now, a couple of hours toward noon, he could only assume the worst. It wasn't unusual for Tegan to go solo on his own personal missions, but this time he was off grid completely. He hadn't returned from the containment facility. He hadn't reported in, and there wasn't even so much as a cell phone signal to indicate where he was or what kind of shit he might be into.

Calls to the facility had been useless. According to everyone Lucan spoke with, Tegan had never arrived. As for getting some intel on Odolf's death, all inquiries were being personally handled by the director of the place, one Heinrich Kuhn, who would not be reachable until he reported back to work at nightfall.

Lucan didn't appreciate the bureaucratic stalemate, particularly when he was getting a very bad feeling that Tegan was in trouble.

"Still nothing?" Dante came out of the room where the rest of the Order and Reichen were covering the night's upcoming trip to Prague. The warrior exhaled a low sigh when Lucan gave a shake of his head. "I know this mission is critical, Lucan, but damn. I don't feel good about leaving Tegan behind."

"We're not." Lucan met the serious stare of his brethren. "I need you and Chase to head up the mission. I'm going to stay behind and locate Tegan."

"How are you gonna go about doing that? We've got no idea where he is, or if he's even still in the city. It'll take you forever if you're planning to go door-to-door."

Lucan shook his head. "I think I know of a better way to find him."

CHAPTER
Thirty-two

Tegan's mind came awake before the rest of his body. His throat burned, still raw and coated with the residue of whatever drug had been shot into him by Kuhn's guards. He was no longer in the containment facility; his nose told him that much. Instead of the clinical stench of that place, he smelled old wood and brick, a hint of fresh paint as well, coming from somewhere overhead . . .

And nearby, the odor of a recent death. The cloying scent of spilled, coagulating Breed blood—a lot of it— hung like a thick shroud.

He didn't have to attempt to move his limbs to know that he was restrained. The weight of heavy manacles and chains hung from his wrists and ankles, his body drawn spread-eagle between two large wooden beams.

Overhead, coming from outside whatever structure it was that imprisoned him, he heard the chatter of crows as they flew by. Even though it was dark where he was being held, it was daylight outside, his brain reasoned as the cawing grew distant. He must have been here—wherever here was—for hours.

He cracked one eyelid open, hardly able to lift it. His vision swam, instant vertigo making him sag deeper into his restraints.

"Awake at last," mused a voice Tegan recognized, even in his half-drugged state. "Those idiots employed by Kuhn almost killed you with their tranquilizer darts. And that is a privilege I intend to save for myself."

Tegan didn't respond. He wouldn't have, even if he'd been able to make his sluggish tongue form words. Marek deserved no respect whatsoever.

"Wake up," came the terse command. "Wake the fuck up, Tegan, and tell me where he is!"

Hard fingers gripped a handful of his hair, lifted his head roughly when he didn't have the strength to do it on his own. A heavy, closed-fisted blow landed on the side of his face, but he barely registered it through the fog of his sedation.

"Need a little convincing, do you?"

Footsteps sounded across a creaking, plank wood floor as Marek left him to slump and walked a few paces away. He came back a moment later. Tegan's head was yanked back. Something was pressed beneath his nose. When the fist connected with his gut, he sucked in his breath.

The involuntary reaction brought the sting of fine powder traveling up his nostrils and in through his open mouth. He coughed, choking on the foul substance, and knew at once what Marek had just fed him.

"There we are. A little Crimson ought to speed things up."

Marek backed away as Tegan tried to spit the drug out. It was no use. He could feel the Crimson seeping into his sinus passages, clinging to the back of his throat. Like an electrical current shot straight into his brain, the drug made him spasm and shudder. He felt it absorbing into his bloodstream, heat traveling along his strung-up limbs. When the initial quake subsided, Tegan opened his eyes and fixed a murderous stare on his captor.

Marek crossed his arms over his chest, grinning. "Back online already, eh?"

"Fuck you." He tried to bring his arms down, but the chains held fast. His head was clearing, but his physical strength was still subpar at best. It was going to take time—or a stronger, riskier hit of Crimson—to shake off the effects of the tranqs.

"Where is he, Tegan? Have you found the hiding place yet?" Marek's eyes were hidden behind dark sunglasses, but Tegan felt the furious heat of his stare. "I know the Order has the journal. I know you've seen the riddle. And I know you spoke with Petrov Odolf. What did he tell you about it?"

"He's dead."

"Yes," Marek agreed civilly. "Overdosed on Crimson, as you no doubt suspected when you went to see Herr Kuhn over here."

Tegan's gaze followed Marek's casual gesture to the source of the death stench in the room. Director Kuhn's headless torso lay on the floor next to a broad-bladed, blood-soaked sword.

Marek shrugged. "He outserved his purpose. All of the quivering, hapless sheep inhabiting the Darkhavens have outserved their purpose, wouldn't you agree? They've forgotten their roots, if they really ever understood them. How many generations have been spawned since the illustrious first that you and I are both a part of? Too many, and each generation has grown weaker, their blood diluted with feeble *homo sapiens* genes. It's time to start fresh, Tegan. The Breed needs to sever its atrophied branches and begin a new reign of Gen One power. I want to see the Breed thrive. I want us to be kings—the way it should be."

"You're insane," Tegan growled. "And you only want power for yourself. You always did."

Marek scoffed. "I deserved to rule. I was eldest, not Lucan. I had the clearer vision for how our race should evolve. The humans should be hiding from us, living to please us, not the other way around. Lucan didn't see it that way. He still doesn't. His humanity is his greatest weakness."

"And yours has always been your arrogance."

Marek grunted. "What was yours, Tegan?" His tone was a bit too light, too taunting in its casualness. "I remember her, you know . . . Sorcha."

Tegan hated like hell to hear that innocent girl's name on his enemy's lips, but he swallowed the rage that was building inside him. Sorcha was gone. He'd finally let her go, and Marek would not be able to goad him with her memory.

"Yes, she was your weakness. I knew that when I went to her that night. You remember, don't you? The night she was abducted from your home while you were out on patrol with my brother on one of his endless missions?"

Tegan lifted his gaze to Marek. "You . . ."

The vampire's smile was cruel, full of amusement. "Yes, me. She and Dragos's Breedmate bitch were thick as thieves, so I'd really hoped Sorcha might be able to tell me the secret Dragos took to his grave and what Kassia sought to cheat me out of when she took her own life before I could wrench the truth out of her. But Sorcha didn't know anything. Well, not quite. She knew about a son Kassia had delivered in secret and sent away—an heir that Dragos himself had known nothing about."

Ah, Christ. Tegan closed his eyes, understanding only just now what Sorcha must have endured—and at Marek's hand.

"She broke easily, but then I knew she would. She was never strong. Just a sweet girl who trusted you to keep her safe." Marek paused, as though reflecting. "It almost seemed a waste to turn her Minion since she'd given up all her secrets at the first bit of pain."

"You son of a bitch," Tegan snarled. "You sick, goddamn son of a bitch! Why, then? Why did you do it to her?"

"Because I could," Marek replied.

Tegan's roar echoed up into the rafters of the place, rattling the black-washed windows that were set high into the roof. He fought his bonds but the momentary burst of spent adrenaline only left him coughing and exhausted. The shackles cut into his wrists as his weight sagged once more, his thighs too weak to hold him.

"And because I can, Tegan," Marek added, "I'm going to kill you and everyone you care about if you don't tell me what that goddamn riddle means. Tell me where to find the Ancient!"

Tegan panted, suspended helplessly from his chains. The sedatives were pulling him under again, making his head spin. Marek watched with detached calm, yet standing well out of reach. Very casually, he walked to the door and motioned two of his Minion guards inside. He pointed to Kuhn's desecrated body.

"Take that rotting corpse out of here and let it burn."

With his servants rushing to carry out his orders, Marek turned his attention back to Tegan. "You look like you need some time to think about what I've asked you. So, you think, Tegan. You think hard. And we'll chat some more when I get back."

Elise took one look at Gideon's face when he came to find her in Tegan's quarters, and she knew something was terribly wrong.

"It's Lucan," he said. "He needs to talk to you."

She took the cell phone and swallowed hard before answering. "What's happened to him?" she said into the receiver, not bothering with a greeting when every cell in her body went suddenly still. "Lucan, tell me he's okay."

"I'm, ah . . . not sure about that, Elise. Something's gone down over here."

She listened woodenly as Lucan explained Tegan's disappearance. They hadn't seen him, hadn't heard from him, for several hours. Lucan was going to send the rest of the Order out to Prague with Reichen at dusk, but he was staying behind to begin searching for Tegan. He wasn't sure where to begin, or even how long it might take to scour the city for any sign of where he might be. Suspecting that she and Tegan shared a blood bond, their best means of tracking him would be Elise.

"We can't be certain," Lucan said, "but it's a fair guess

that Marek might have him. If that's the case, there won't be a lot of time before—"

"I'm on the way." She glanced at Gideon, who was waiting just outside. "Can you get me a flight out right away?"

"The Order's jet is still in Berlin, but I can see about chartering another one."

"There's no time," she said. "What about commercial air?"

He frowned, concerned. "You really want to sit on a plane for half a day with a couple hundred humans? You think you're up for that?"

She wasn't sure, actually, but she damn well wasn't going to let that stop her. If she had to hitch a ride with a plane full of convicted killers, she'd do it, if that's what it would take to make sure Tegan was all right.

"Just do it, Gideon. Please. The first flight you can get me on."

He nodded and took off at a jog up the corridor to handle the details.

"I'll be there as soon as I can, Lucan."

She heard his low exhalation, and the caution in his voice. Lucan wasn't convinced that they would be able to do anything for Tegan, even if they managed to find him.

"Okay," he said. "A car will be there to pick you up and bring you to Reichen's estate. We'll start searching as soon as you get here."

CHAPTER
Thirty-three

The flight to Berlin was long and taxing. Elise took each hard minute, every hour, as it came, determined that she would be stronger than the ability that had owned her for so long. She had Tegan to thank for helping her overcome the worst of it—not only his showing her how to manage the psychic talent, but also the love she had for him, which drove her forward even as the familiar, vicious migraine began to pound in her temples barely an hour into the flight.

Elise got through it because she had to. Because Tegan's life might very well depend on her now.

God, she could not fail in this.

She could handle anything except losing him.

As soon as the jet's wheels touched ground that evening, Elise's determination to find Tegan—and bring him home safely—redoubled. She ran out of the terminal and met Lucan outside at the curb, where he waited with one of Reichen's vehicles.

"You realize that if we do find him, Tegan's going to kill me for bringing you in on this," Lucan said as she approached the car. He said it kind of jokingly, but she didn't miss the fact that there was no humor at all in his gray eyes.

"*When* we find him, Lucan. There can't be any ifs." She tossed her carry-on bag into the back and climbed into the passenger seat. "Let's get started. I don't want to rest tonight until we cover every street in this city."

Dante, Reichen, and the rest of the Order pulled the two SUVs to a stop just off a moonlit, wooded stretch of road an hour outside Prague. The forest was thick here, only the smallest light from a few remote homes glowing in the darkness. They got out, all seven of them garbed in black fatigues and armed to the teeth with guns, thousands of titanium rounds, and a healthy cache of C-4 explosives.

Each Breed male also carried a sheathed broadsword strapped on his back—unconventional weaponry for modern warfare, but totally necessary hardware when you were dealing with something as nasty and powerful as the creature they were intending to rouse out of its slumber.

"That's got be the place," Dante said, pointing to the jagged silhouette of the mountains ahead of them. "The outline is a perfect match for the design in Kassia's tapestry."

"Probably take us a couple of hours to make the hike up there," Niko put in. His cheeks dimpled with his eager grin, the white glint of his teeth bright against the cover of night. "What are we waiting for? Let's go bag the motherfucker."

Dante held him back with a firm hand, scowling at the young warrior's zeal. "Hold up, all of you. This is not a fucking game. It's not like any other mission we've done. That thing that was sealed away in this mountain is not your garden-variety vampire. You take Lucan and Tegan and put them together—shit, throw Marek in there too—and you still aren't coming close to what this creature can do. He's Gen One times a hundred."

"But his head can be separated from his body, same as any one of us," Rio pointed out in a low, deadly voice. "The fastest way to kill a vampire."

Dante nodded. "And we're gonna have one shot at him, no more. Once we find the crypt and get inside, first priority is putting three feet of razor-sharp steel through the bastard's neck."

"And we'll need to do it before it has a chance to get up," Chase added. "If we let this thing rouse before we're in place and ready to kill it, there's very good odds we won't all make it out of there."

"Someone remind me why I didn't want to be an accountant when I grew up," Brock drawled.

Niko chuckled. "Because accountants don't get to make things go boom."

"They don't get to smoke many suckheads either," Kade added, sharing in the joke.

Brock's answering grin was big and bright white. "Oh, yeah. Now I remember."

Dante let everyone settle in to the plan, the younger

males blowing off nervous energy with humor and smack-talk. But as the team of them started up the wooded side of the rocky incline, they fell silent and serious. None of them were certain what lay at the end of this journey, but they were all prepared to meet it together.

Elise wasn't sure how long they'd been driving. Easily hours. They navigated through each section of the city, the affluent and the derelict, stopping at regular intervals to let her listen to the darkened streets and alleyways. Waiting for her veins to prickle with the awareness—the fervent hope—that Tegan was near.

She didn't want to give up.

Not even as the night began to wane toward dawn.

"We can make another circuit through town," Lucan said, the Gen One warrior no more inclined to abandon Tegan than she was. Even though the coming daylight was as much a threat as any deadly enemy.

Elise reached over and touched the large hand that turned the steering wheel onto yet another street. "Thank you, Lucan."

He nodded. "You love him a great deal, do you?"

"Yes, I do. He is . . . everything to me."

"Then we'd better not lose him, eh?"

She smiled and shook her head. "No, we'd better not . . . *oh, my God . . . Lucan.* Slow down. Stop the car!"

He braked at once, and pulled over near a tree-lined, elegant residential street. As the vehicle came to a halt, Elise put down her window. A cold February breeze rushed inside.

"Down here," she said, her veins tingling.

She focused on the sensation, pulling it into her, trying

to divine its source. It was Tegan; she had no doubt. And the heat that traveled her bloodstream was not a pleasant warmth, but an acid burn.

The searing heat of pain.

"Oh, God. Lucan, he's being held somewhere on this street—I'm sure of it. And he's hurting. He's hurting . . . very badly." She closed her eyes, feeling it even more now that the car was turning onto the pleasant drive. "Hurry, Lucan. He's being tortured."

She felt queasy, both with the idea of Tegan being abused, and with the twisting anguish coursing through every cell in her body. But she held on, searching for any sign that they were getting close. The white-hot spike of pain that hit her as they drew up on an old stone-and-timber manor house told her they had found him.

The house was set back from the street, quiet, but well tended. Obviously lived in. A white Audi sedan was parked at the carriage house garage. There was birdseed in the feeder hanging from a pine bough in the center of the yard. A kid's sled lay on the snowy front walk.

"Right here," she told Lucan. "He's in that house."

Lucan frowned as he took in the same details she had, but he cut the headlights and killed the engine. "You're certain?"

"Yes. Tegan is being held inside."

She watched as Lucan armed himself. He was already wearing an arsenal of weapons—two large handguns and a pair of sheathed daggers—but he grabbed a leather satchel from behind the passenger seat and un-zipped the bag to reveal even more.

He glanced up at her and muttered a ripe curse. "I'm not sure it would be safe for you to wait—"

"That's good," she said, "because I don't plan to. I can help you find him once we get in."

"No way, Elise. It's too fucking dangerous. I can't take you in there. I won't." He slapped a clip into one of his guns and holstered it. Then he pulled another knife and a coil of wire from the duffel and stuffed both into a pocket of his combat jacket. "As soon as I head for the house, I want you to slide over and take the wheel. Drive out to the—"

"Lucan." Elise met his stern gray gaze and held it firmly. "Four months ago I thought my life had ended. My heart was ripped out by Marek and the Rogues who serve him. Now, by some miracle of fate, I'm happy again. I never dreamed I could be. I've never known this kind of love—the love I have for Tegan. So, if you think I'm going to sit out here and wait, or run out of harm's way when I know he's in trouble—when I know he's in pain—well, I'm sorry, but you can forget it."

"If my brother is the one holding him—and let's be goddamn clear about this, we both know it's got to be Marek—then there's no telling what we're going to find in there. Or what might come out of there when the dust finally settles. Tegan could already be lost."

"I need to know, Lucan. I'd rather die trying to help him than stand by or walk away."

A slow grin spread over the face of the Order's fear-some leader. "Anyone ever tell you that you're one stub-born female?"

"Tegan might have said so once or twice," she admitted wryly.

"Then I guess he'll have to understand what I was up against when he sees you with me." He handed her a sheathed dagger attached to a leather belt.

Elise strapped the weapon around her waist and cinched the buckle. "I'm ready when you are, Lucan."

"Okay," he said, shaking his head in defeat. "Let's go get our boy."

They exited the car and swiftly, cautiously approached the human residence. As they neared the place, Elise was assaulted with both the pain of Tegan's suffering and the growing awareness of Minions on the property. Her mind filled with a concert of corrupt thoughts, ugly voices pounding into her consciousness.

"Lucan," she whispered, mouthing a warning to him. "Minions inside—more than one."

He nodded, and motioned for her to come up near him. He gripped a wooden trellis that climbed up the side of the house, testing its strength. "Can you climb it?"

She took hold of the makeshift ladder and started pulling herself up. Lucan met her at the top; all it took for him to reach the level roof of the second-floor terrace was a powerful flex of his legs. He landed soundlessly from his fluid leap and thrust his hand down to help pull her up the rest of the way.

A pair of French doors were open onto the tiled patio, the wispy white curtains riffling out like ghosts. Elise could see a woman in a nightgown lying motionless on the floor inside the room. Her arm was outstretched, unmoving, the wrist savaged and resting in a pool of spilled blood.

"Marek," Lucan said softly, in explanation of the carnage. "Will you be all right walking through there?"

Elise nodded. She followed him in through the scene of recent violence, past the dead human woman and the husband who had evidently tried without success to fend off the vicious vampire attack. Bile rose in Elise's throat

as they stepped out into the hallway and found the body
of a young boy.

Oh, God.

Marek had broken in and killed them all.

Lucan ushered her past the child, taking her wrist and
holding her behind him as he made a quick visual check
of the hallway. She felt the sudden blast of mental pain,
but had not seen the Minion coming until he was on
them, having come out of another room just as they approached. Lucan silenced Marek's mind slave before the
human had a chance to scream a warning. With a dagger
slicing deeply across the Minion's throat, it sputtered in
shock, then dropped in a lifeless heap to the floor. Lucan
gave it no pause at all. He stepped over the corpse, waiting for Elise to do the same.

As they neared a stairwell that led to an upper floor of
the house, Elise's veins lit up with an electric kind of intu-
ition. She could almost feel Tegan's heart beating inside
her own body, his labored breath a constriction in her
own lungs.

"Lucan," she whispered, pointing to the open door.
"It's Tegan. Up there."

He moved into the unlit well and peered up the stairs.
"Stay close, and stay behind me."

Together they climbed the steep, narrow steps. At the
top was a barred door. Lucan lifted the metal lock. He
glanced back at her, and even in the darkness she could
see the expression that seemed to caution her to brace
herself for whatever they might find on the other side.

Tegan was alive behind that closed door—that much
she was sure of—and that's all she needed to know. "Do
it, Lucan," she whispered.

He pushed the door open and barreled through like a

freight train, drawing a large blade and burying it into the Minion guard who pounded toward them in attack. Elise held back her scream as another one moved in and got like reward, going down in a bleeding, heavy crumble to the wood-planked floor.

But it was the sight of Tegan that nearly ripped a keening howl from her throat. Shackled to a pair of thick beams with irons on both wrists and ankles, his body bowed out, hanging limply from its restraints. His beautiful face was nearly concealed by the lank droop of his sweat-soaked, blood-coated hair, but Elise could still see the damage there. He was bloodied and beaten all over from a recent bout of torture, his body not yet having the time to speed healing to the abused tissue and bones.

She thought him unconscious until a visible tension suddenly crept over his muscles. He knew she was there. He felt her presence just as she would know his anywhere.

"Tegan . . . " She started to run to him, but drew back sharply when he lifted his head and she saw the razor-edged glint of fury in his eyes. "Oh, God . . . Tegan."

"Get out of here!" His voice was raw gravel. The amber eyes glaring at her from under the bruised brow were filled with animal rage and pain. His fangs were enormous, more deadly than she'd ever seen them. He railed against the chains that held him. "Goddamn it! Get the fuck out of here now!"

"Tegan." Lucan stepped up now, approaching warily but without hesitation. He reached out to take hold of one of the manacles fastened to Tegan's wrist. "We're taking you out of this place."

"Get back," he growled.

Lucan sniffed at the air. "What the fuck?" He wiped

his thumb under Tegan's nose, where a faint pink crust had collected. "Ah, Christ, Tegan. Crimson?"

"Marek . . . he gave me a lot of the shit, Lucan . . . " Tegan grunted, the slits of his pupils going thinner in the middle of all that glowing amber. "You get it now? It's Bloodlust. I'm too far gone."

"No, you're not," Elise told him.

"Jesus," he hissed through the huge fangs. "Leave me—both of you! If you want to help me, Lucan, get her the hell out of here. Get her far away from here."

Elise walked up to him and gently touched his matted hair. "I'm not going anywhere. I love you."

As she tried to soothe Tegan, Lucan tore the shackle and chain free from the post with a mighty yank of his arm. Tegan's right arm dropped down loosely, metal clanking. When he reached for the other, it was Tegan who growled a warning.

"Lucan—"

Too late.

The gun blast cracked sharply in the dim room, an orange explosion coming from near the stairwell. Lucan took the hit in his back and went down on one knee. Another shot rang out, but the reporting ping said it missed the target and hit stone instead.

More gunfire erupted as two Minions and a Rogue—Marek's henchman, all of them armed with semiautomatic weapons—poured in and started squeezing off rounds. Elise felt a heavy weight curl down around her, pulling her into the shelter of hard muscle. Tegan's breath sawed roughly in her ear, but his free arm was wrapped around her, his body arched over her to protect her from the fray.

She felt helpless, watching Lucan battle three opponents while she cowered in the cage of Tegan's body. Lucan dodged many of the rapid-fire rounds, but a good lot of them hit their mark. The Gen One warrior weathered the assault, returning fire as the dance of combat put the room in a smoke-filled, ear-splitting chaos. The Rogue went down in the fray, killed by Lucan's titanium-laced bullets. The body sizzled and convulsed on the floor, writhing as death swiftly claimed it.

When one of the Minions came in closer, his sights trained on Lucan, who was eluding the gunfire of another and sending back more of the same, Elise reached down to feel for the hilt of her dagger. She pulled it loose of the sheath, knowing she would have to throw it, and she would have only one shot.

Tegan growled her name in warning as she rolled free of his arms. She came up to her feet and took quick aim, then brought her hand back and let the blade fly.

The Minion roared as the dagger embedded deep under his arm. He fell back with his weapon still firing, sending a spray of bullets high into the rafters. Some of them hit the black ceiling, the sound of shattering glass an ominous counterpoint to the battle taking place below.

"Oh, God," Elise gasped as painted shards dropped from the broken skylights.

The ceiling was glass—recently coated with black paint to blot out the sun. Marek must have taken that immediate precaution when he set up camp in the humans' house.

Now, as another large piece of glass broke away and fell to the floor, Elise stared up at the sky overhead.

A sky that was slowly pinkening with the first early light of dawn.

CHAPTER
Thirty-four

They'd been scouring the steep, jagged crag for some hours and still no trace of the crypt. Night was starting to fade. None of the warriors scaling the rocks had any real affection for the sun—particularly Dante, after a nasty UV tangle a few months ago—but as later generation Breed, they could each withstand daylight for a short amount of time. With the aid of their solar-protection gear, they might be able to double that exposure.

But not so for the Ancient they hunted now. If the Gen One offspring of that alien being began to blister and burn in under ten minutes, the Ancient's UV-allergic skin and eyes would incinerate in seconds. That made for a decent backup plan, if the Order somehow failed to take the creature's head.

Assuming they could even find the suckhead's hiding place amid all this inhospitable rock.

Dante shot an assessing glance up at the sky. "If we don't get a hit on something in the next half hour or so, we'd better start heading back down."

Chase nodded. He stood beside Dante in the mouth of a shallow cave that had yielded nothing but some discarded beer bottles and the days-old remnants of an extinguished campfire. "Maybe we're off somehow. Some of us could branch out along the farther ridge and check closer to the summit."

"It's got to be here," Dante said. "You saw the tapestry. That range Kassia sewed into the design is this one, right where we're standing. We're close, I'm telling you—"

"Hey, D." Nikolai was perched on a rocky promontory several yards above the mouth of the cave. "Rio and Reichen just found another opening up here. It's pretty tight, but it goes deep into the mountain. You might wanna have a look."

Dante and Chase made a quick scramble up to where the others had gathered. The mouth of the cave—if you could even call it that—was a vertical slit in the rock. Small enough to be concealed unless you were right on top of it, yet wide enough for a man to sidle through with care.

"Chisel marks," Dante observed, running his hand along the edge of the opening. "Based on the weathering, they've been here for a while. This could be the place."

Six sober gazes held his as he drew the sword he carried and quietly gave the operation's commands. He would go in first, see how far the opening went and if there was anything on the other side. The others would wait for his orders—two on guard outside the mouth of the cave, and the rest ready to move in behind him on his signal if they had in fact found the crypt.

He squeezed between the vertical plates of rock, his head turned toward the pitch blackness ahead of him. The smell of bat dung and mold offended his senses the deeper he crept inside. The air in here was cold, damp. There was no sound at all, only the soft scrape of his movement as he progressed.

Somewhere along the way, he noticed that the crush of stone was easing. The walls began to widen incrementally, then, at last, they opened up onto a cavernous space deep within the mountain.

Dante stepped on something that crunched beneath his boot.

His eyes were keenest in the dark, and what he saw made the blood drain from his head.

Holy hell.

They'd found Dragos's secret. No doubt about it. Dante was standing in the middle of the Ancient's hibernation chamber, a crypt carved into the side of a mountain, just like Kassia's tapestry had said it would be.

Dante didn't recall speaking—hell, he wasn't even sure he was drawing breath in that moment—but within moments he was joined by his brethren.

"Jesus Christ," one of them murmured, hardly audible.

Rio's whispered prayer in Spanish spoke for everyone: "God help us all."

Tegan lifted his head, turning a fleeting, uncertain gaze up to the broken skylights above their heads.

Fuck.

He didn't dare look long. Even dawn's early, filtered wash of light was like acid pouring over his retinas. Lucan was feeling the effects too. He took a hit in the thigh, the remaining Minion's shot driving him down to the floor. As a Gen One vampire, he could absorb more damage than others of their race, and he had, his body expelling the rounds he hadn't been able to dodge, the wounds bleeding but already beginning to heal over.

But he was under the open ceiling now, and thin tendrils of smoke began to rise up off his exposed skin. He bellowed, transforming in his rage. His lips peeled back as his fangs ripped out of his gums and his eyes went bright amber.

The Minion started to retreat now, realizing what he was up against. Lucan rolled out of the light and pulled the trigger of his 9mm. A single shot rang out. The Minion dropped, but he wasn't dead yet. Lucan squeezed off another round, finishing the bastard.

Then, silence.

The hollow click of an empty cartridge.

At the same time, Tegan's own Gen One abilities were slowly coming back to life. But he couldn't yet physically break the bonds that held him. He wasn't at all sure he should. The Crimson he'd been made to ingest was thrumming through every cell in his body, corrupting him like the poison it was.

He felt his Bloodlust rising, compelling him to feed the thirst that wanted to rule him.

He snarled as Elise came over to him and tried to work one of his manacles free. "Get away, damn it! I don't want you here. Get out of here while you still can."

She kept tugging on the cuff, ignoring him completely. "There's got to be a way to get these off you."

He saw her eyes sweep the room, searching for a tool. "Elise, goddamn it!"

She scurried over to one of the dead Minions and pulled the semiauto out from under the heavy bulk of the body. "Take this," she ordered him, slapping the weapon into his free hand. "Shoot the chains, Tegan. Do it now!"

He hesitated, and she made a hasty grab for the gun.

"Damn it, if you don't, I will!"

She didn't have the chance. The gun clattered to the floor, and, in a blur of movement, Elise was yanked off her feet by invisible hands and thrown several yards away. She crashed down, landing hard in the litter of broken glass. The scent of heather and roses swamped the room.

Marek stood in the open doorway, a sword in one hand, his other raised and pointed in Elise's direction, holding her there with the power of his mind. His mental grasp closed around her throat, cutting off precious air. She choked and clawed at the tight band of energy that was strangling her.

"She bleeds, warrior," he taunted Tegan. "And how your Rogue eyes thirst for it."

Lucan drew a blade from his hip and sent it flying. In that instant, Marek's focus switched, flicking to the airborne dagger and deflecting it with a thought. Undaunted, Marek strode forward, chuckling as he came up on Lucan's bloodied, UV-scorched face. "Ah, my brother. Your death will be particularly sweet after all these years of waiting. I only wish you could live to see my rule come to pass before we say good-bye."

Marek raised his sword and swung it hard. Lucan rolled at the last second, leaving only hard wood planks in the way of his brother's weapon. The blade bit deep into the floor, momentarily frozen there.

In a flash of movement, Lucan was up on his feet. He grabbed the nearest thing he could find—his hands closing on a length of copper utility pipe that ran up the wall. He wrenched it loose. Water spurted from the severed connection like a small fountain.

"Lucan!" Tegan called out as Marek yanked his sword free and spun to bring it down on his brother.

Lucan met the blow, blocking the downward arc with the long tube of copper. It bent under the strain, but Lucan held fast, fury blazing in his amber eyes. Marek's dark glasses were knocked askew in the scuffle, revealing still more amber as brother met brother in a murderous bid for control. Marek tried to drive the sword harder, leaning into the blade with all the considerable strength of his right arm. Lucan didn't give an inch. The two Gen One warriors grunted as they held each other at an impasse.

Above them, the sky was growing brighter, hotter, singeing both where the light touched open skin.

Released of Marek's hold, Elise coughed and gasped, struggling to breathe. Her pain lanced across Tegan like a physical blow. And the sight of her bleeding—the bright red lacerations on her hands, on her face—sent a jolt of adrenaline arrowing through Tegan's veins. He ripped his other arm loose of its bonds, roaring up into the rafters.

And across the space from him, Marek and Lucan's stalemate was taking a treacherous turn. It happened in an instant, Marek's hissed oath was vicious, the only hint of what was to come. Bearing down on Lucan with his right arm, he reached into his shirt with his free hand and withdrew a small vial of red powder.

With a quick slash of his wrist, the Crimson flew at Lucan's face, coating his eyes and cheeks in the fine dust. He lost his hold on the pipe.

Ah, Christ.

Lucan.

Marek drew back with a smile as his brother heaved forward. He raised the sword high above his head. And as he began to swing it down, a sudden flash of light cut across Marek's face, hovering in his eyes. It was piercingly bright, the sun reflected in a powerful ray that burned Marek's eyes and nearly blinded Tegan where he stood.

He averted his gaze and found Elise on her knees in the broken glass. In her hands was a large shard, which she held steady and unflinching, throwing the light in a deliberate beam into Marek's face.

It was all the chance Tegan needed.

Crossing the room in long strides, he swung the chains that hung from his wrists. He caught Marek around the neck with one, coiling the thick links and wrenching the vampire off his feet. The other snaked around his sword arm, losing Marek his weapon. Marek fought Tegan with his mind, but every attempt was blocked by Tegan's rage. He pinned the bastard under his foot, ignoring the sudden pleas for mercy and forgiveness.

"It ends here," Tegan snarled. "You end here."

Tegan unslung the chains from Marek's arm and reached down to retrieve the sword. He saw Lucan's somber nod as he raised the blade over Marek's neck. Marek howled a curse, then fell silent as Tegan brought the sword down in a swift, lethal swing.

"Tegan!" Elise cried, racing over to him as soon as it was over.

She threw her arms around him, helping to unwind his chains from Marek's lifeless body. She was at Lucan's side next, helping Tegan to move him into a shaded corner of the room.

Tegan saw her glance anxiously up at the open ceiling. "Come on. We have to get you both out of here right away."

She led them down the stairs, then disappeared into one of the bedrooms. She came out carrying a large duvet and a thick wool blanket. "Take these," she said, helping to drape the shrouds over both of them. "Stay under there. I'll help you out of the house and into the car."

Neither of the two warriors had any argument. They let this petite female—Tegan's mate, he thought with a swelling surge of pride—guide them into full-on daylight, then into the back of Reichen's car.

"Keep your heads down and stay covered," Elise ordered them. She closed the back door, then ran around to the driver's seat and hopped in. The engine fired up, tires squealing a bit as she hit the gas. "I'm getting us the hell out of here."

And, by God, so she did.

CHAPTER
Thirty-five

Elise watched Tegan sleep, relieved that his ordeal was over. With Marek's death, there would be much healing to come, not only for Tegan and her as well, but for Lucan and the rest of the Order. A dark chapter of their past had closed at last, the secrets aired. Now they could all look ahead to the future, and whatever tests the new dawn would bring.

Elise had thought she'd feel some sense of triumph over Marek's death: the one ultimately responsible for Camden's suffering was no more. She'd made good on her promise, with Tegan's help.

But she didn't feel victorious as she smoothed a strand of soft, tawny hair off Tegan's brow. She felt anxious and concerned. Desperate that he be all right. The Crimson that Marek had given him was slow to wear off. He'd been sleeping fitfully since they arrived back at Reichen's Darkhaven estate. Bouts of convulsions had wracked him, and his skin was still clammy to the touch.

"Oh, Tegan," she whispered, leaning over him to press her lips to his. "Don't leave me."

God, if she lost him to that hideous drug too, after everything they'd been through . . .

The tears slid down her cheeks, the first time she'd allowed herself to break down in the hours since they'd been back. The first time she'd actually let herself consider what would be the worst scenario.

What if Tegan didn't fully revive? He'd been so close to Rogue once before—what would it take for him to slide into that pit of hopelessness? And if he did, would he be able to climb back out?

"You won't get rid of me that easily."

She wasn't sure if she heard the words spoken out loud, or merely as a wish in her heart. But when Elise drew back, she was looking into Tegan's eyes. His gorgeous, gem-green eyes. Only the barest trace of amber remained.

His name was a sigh on her lips, a thankful prayer. She kissed him hard, and wrapped her arms around his broad shoulders on the bed. His answering growl of interest made her smile against his mouth.

"You're back," she murmured, so relieved.

"Mmm," he grunted, his hands coming up to caress her. "I'm back, Breedmate. Thanks to you."

"So, you finally admit it—you need me."

His smile was wicked. "Come up here with me. I want to show you just how much."

She got up on the bed with him, straddling his hips and fully expecting him to pull her down on top of him and begin the seduction he was so skilled at. But he only looked at her. When he stroked her cheek, his fingers were tender, reverent.

"I admit it," he said, his gaze so sincere it made her heart clench. "I'll admit it to you now, and to anyone, anytime. I need you, Elise. I love you. You are mine. My woman, my mate, my beloved. My everything."

Her vision swam with watery happiness. "Tegan . . . I love you so much. Tell me this is real. That this is forever."

"You think I'm the type of male to settle for anything less?"

She shook her head, bleary-eyed with joy as she leaned down and kissed him.

The staccato rap on the door went ignored for a couple of seconds, but then Lucan's deep voice sounded on the other side. There was a tense edge to the warrior's tone. "How we doing in here?"

"Come in, Lucan," Elise called to the Order's leader—after what they went through together today, her dear, trusted friend.

She got up from Tegan's body despite his groan of protest and walked over to meet Lucan as he came inside. He was cleaned up and healing, but it would take some time before his body was completely restored. He gave Tegan a weary smile as Tegan swung his legs over the edge of the bed and sat up.

"What is it?" Tegan asked, snapping back into warrior mode despite the fact that he'd been leveled for the past few hours. "What's happened?"

Lucan didn't mince words. "Dante and the others just called in from Prague. They found the crypt up in the mountains, just like Kassia's clues said they would. It was all there, T. A cave carved into the rock, a hibernation chamber full of *dermaglyphic* symbols and the bones of the humans Dragos fed his father in preparation of his long sleep."

"But," Tegan prompted, pulling Elise toward him like he wanted something firm to hold on to.

"But it was empty." Lucan shook his head, ran his hand through his dark hair. "The goddamn crypt had already been opened. Someone freed the bastard. We can only guess how long ago, but it appears to have been years. Decades, even."

"Then . . . he's out there somewhere?" Elise asked, dreading confirmation of that terrible fact. "What are we going to do?"

"We start looking," Tegan said. "Christ, assuming the Ancient is alive, he could be anywhere. A needle in a haystack."

Lucan nodded. "And we're going to need all the resources we can get. Rest up, both of you. We won't be heading back to Boston until the others return from Prague tonight."

With that, Lucan turned and started for the door. Halfway there, he paused. He came back to Tegan's bedside, his expression serious. "From the beginning, Tegan, you were more brother to me than any kin by blood. You still are."

Tegan felt likewise, in spite of all they'd been through. Maybe because of it. "I'll always have your back, Lucan. You can count on it."

Lucan held out his hand to him. As the two warriors clasped their palms together, Tegan felt the warmth of friendship—of brotherhood—flowing between them. It

surprised him, how welcome that affection actually was
to him. And how much he'd missed it.

Lucan nodded. The powerful Gen One vampire's eyes
warmed with unmistakable respect as he turned to Elise.

"The Order is in your debt," he told her, now holding
his hand out to her. "For what you did to bring us
Dragos's secret, and for what you did here today for
Tegan and me . . . I am personally in your debt. Thank
you, Elise."

She gave a little shake of her head as she placed her
fingers in his broad palm. "No thanks are necessary. I'm
happy to do whatever I can to help the Order. And
Tegan."

Lucan smiled as he carried her hand to his lips. His
kiss of gratitude was chaste and sincere, but it still made
Tegan growl a little.

"You are well mated," he said, that sage look shifting
to Tegan.

"Yes, I am," Tegan agreed without the slightest hesitation. He grinned at Elise, desire sparking as always just to
look at her and know that by some miracle of fate, she
was his. "I am very well mated."

Lucan nodded. "Rest up. I won't bother you again until we're ready to move out and head back to Boston."

As soon as he was gone, Elise wrapped Tegan in a lov-
ing embrace, her lips warm with promise as she kissed
him. He felt the strength of her love surrounding him,
and he knew that no matter how dark the coming days
might be, he would always have this light to hold him. He
kissed her back, interest stirring rigidly to life.

"You heard Lucan," she murmured against his mouth,
a smile in her voice. "You need to get some rest."

"So?" he growled, playfully nipping her supple lower lip.

Elise laughed. "So, maybe we should wait to do this until we get home."

Tegan rolled her onto the bed with him, smoothly pinning her under his awakening body. He looked down into her wide lavender eyes, which held him with so much love it staggered him.

He kissed her slowly, tenderly, sincerely.

"I am home," he said, his voice rough with emotion as he pressed her down beneath him. "This is the only home I'll ever need."

About the Author

With family roots stretching back to the *Mayflower*, author
LARA ADRIAN lives with her husband in coastal New
England, surrounded by centuries-old graveyards, hip ur-
ban comforts, and the endless inspiration of the broody
Atlantic Ocean. To learn more about Lara and her nov-
els, please visit www.LaraAdrian.com.

Read on
for a sneak peek of

Midnight Rising

by

LARA ADRIAN

Coming from Dell
in spring 2008

"Evocative, enticing, erotic…"
—J. R. Ward, *New York Times* bestselling author of *Lover Unbound*

Midnight Rising

LARA ADRIAN

Nationally Bestselling Author of *MIDNIGHT AWAKENING*

Midnight Rising
On Sale spring 2008

Chapter One

The woman looked completely out of place in her pristine white blouse and tailored ivory pants. Long, coffee-dark hair cascaded over her shoulders in thick waves, not a single strand disturbed by the moist haze that hung in the air of the forest. She was wearing tall elegant heels, which hadn't seemed to keep her from climbing up a wooded path that had the other hikers around her huffing in the humid July heat.

At the crest of the steep incline, she waited in the shade of a bulky, moss-covered rock formation, unblinking as half a dozen tourists passed her by, some of them snapping pictures of the overlook beyond. They didn't notice her. But then, most people couldn't see the dead.

Dylan Alexander didn't want to see her either.

She hadn't encountered a dead woman since she was twelve years old. That she would see one now, twenty years later and in the middle of the Czech

Republic, was more than a little startling. She tried to ignore the apparition, but as Dylan and her three traveling companions made their way up the path, the woman's dark eyes found her and rooted on her.

You see me.

Dylan pretended not to hear the static-filled whisper that came from the ghost's unmoving lips. She didn't want to acknowledge the connection. She'd gone so long without one of these weird encounters that she'd all but forgotten what it was like.

Dylan had never understood her strange ability to see the dead. She'd never been able to trust it or control it. She could stand in the middle of a cemetery and see nothing, then suddenly find herself up close and personal with one of the departed, as she was here in the mountains about an hour outside Prague.

The ghosts were always female. Always youthful-looking and vibrant, like the one who stared at her now with an unmistakable desperation in her exotic, deep brown gaze.

You must hear me.

The statement was tinged with a rich, Hispanic accent, the tone pleading.

"Hey, Dylan. Come here and let me get a picture of you next to this rock."

The sound of a true, earthly voice jolted Dylan's attention away from the beautiful dead woman standing in the nearby arch of weathered sandstone. Janet, a friend of Dylan's mother, Sharon, dug into her backpack and pulled out a camera. The summer tour to Europe was Sharon's idea; it would have been her last great adventure, but the cancer came back in March and this time the chemotherapy wasn't making so much as a dent in the disease. Sharon was still in the hospital, and at her insistence, Dylan had taken the trip in her place.

"Gotcha," Janet said, clicking off a shot of Dylan and the towering pillars of rock in the wooded valley below. "Your mom sure would love this place, honey. Isn't it breathtaking?"

Dylan nodded. "We'll e-mail her the pictures tonight when we get back to the hostel."

She led her group away from the rock, eager to leave the whispering otherworldly presence behind. They walked down a sloping ridge, into a stand of thin-trunked pines growing in tight formation. Russet leaves and conifer needles crushed on the damp path underfoot. It had rained that morning, topped off with a sweltering heat that kept many of the area's tourists away.

The forest was quiet, peaceful . . . except for the awareness of ghostly eyes following Dylan's every step deeper into the woods.

"I'm so glad your boss let you have the time off to come with us," said one of the women from behind her on the path. "I know how hard you work at the paper, making up all those stories—"

"She doesn't make them up, Marie," Janet chided gently. "There's got to be some truth in Dylan's articles or they couldn't print them. Isn't that right, honey?"

Dylan scoffed. "Well, considering that our front page usually runs at least one alien abduction or demonic possession story, we don't tend to let facts get in the way of a good story. We publish entertainment pieces, not hard-hitting journalism."

"Your mom says you're going to be a famous reporter one day," Marie said. "A budding Woodward or Bernstein, that's what she says."

"That's right," Janet put in. "You know, she showed me an article you wrote during your first newspaper job, fresh out of college—you were covering some nasty murder case upstate. You remember, don't you, honey?"

"Yeah," Dylan said, navigating them toward another massive cluster of soaring sandstone towers that rose out of the trees. "I remember. But that was a long time ago."

"Well, no matter what you do, I know that your mom is very proud of you," Marie said. "You've brought a lot of joy into her life."

Dylan nodded, struggling to find her voice. "Thanks."

Both Janet and Marie worked with her mother at the women's center in Brooklyn. Nancy, the other member of their travel group, had been Sharon's best friend since high school. All three of the women had become like extended family to Dylan in the past few months. Three extra pairs of comforting arms, which she was really going to need if she ever lost her mom.

In her heart, Dylan knew it was more a matter of *when* than *if*. The relapse had come on fast, the cancer proving even more relentless than the first time.

Nancy came up and gave Dylan a warm, if sad, smile. "It means the world to Sharon that you would experience the trip for her. You're living it for her, you know?"

"I know. I wouldn't have missed it for anything."

Dylan hadn't told her travel companions—or her

mother—that taking off for two weeks on such short notice was probably going to cost her her job. Part of her didn't really care. She hated working for the cut-rate tabloid anyway. She'd attempted to sell her boss on the idea that she was sure to return from Europe with some decent material—maybe a Bohemian big-foot story, or a Dracula sighting out of Romania.

But selling bullshit to a guy who peddled it for a living was no easy task. Her boss had been pretty clear about his expectations: If Dylan left on this trip, she'd better come back with something big, or she didn't need to come back at all.

"Whoo, it's hot up here," Janet said, sweeping her baseball cap off her short silver curls and running her palm over her brow. "Am I the only wimp in this crowd, or would anyone else like to rest for a little bit?"

"I could use a break," Nancy agreed.

She shrugged off her backpack and set it down on the ground beneath a tall pine tree. Marie joined them, moving off the path and taking a long pull from her water bottle.

Dylan wasn't the least bit tired. She wanted to keep moving. The most impressive climbs and rock forma-tions were still ahead of them. They had only sched-uled one day for this part of the trip, and Dylan wanted to cover as much ground as she could.

And then there was the matter of the beautiful dead woman who now stood ahead of them on the path. She stared at Dylan, her energy fading in and out of visible form.

See me.

Dylan glanced away. Janet, Marie and Nancy were

seated on the ground, nibbling on protein bars and trail mix.

"Want some?" Janet asked, holding out a baggie of dried fruit, nuts, and seeds.

Dylan shook her head. "I'm too antsy to rest or eat right now. If you don't mind, I think I'm going to take a quick look around on my own while you all hang out here. I'll come right back."

"Sure, honey. Your legs are younger than ours, after all. Just be careful."

"I will. Be back soon."

Dylan avoided the spot where the dead woman's image flickered up ahead. Instead, she cut off the established trail and onto the densely wooded hillside. She walked for a few minutes, simply enjoying the tranquility of the place. There was an ancient, wildly mysterious quality to the jutting peaks of sandstone and basalt. Dylan paused to take pictures, hoping she could capture some of the beauty for her mother to enjoy.

Hear me.

At first Dylan didn't see the woman, only heard the broken-static sound of her spectral voice. But then, a flash of white caught her eye. She was farther up the incline, standing on a ridge of stone halfway up one of the steep crags.

Follow me.

"Bad idea," Dylan murmured, eyeing the tricky slope. The grade was fierce, the path uncertain at best. And even though the view from up there was probably spectacular, she really had no desire to join her ghostly new friend on the Other Side.

Please . . . help him.

Help him?

"Help who?" she asked, knowing the spirit couldn't hear her.

They never could. Communication with her kind was always a one-way street. They simply appeared when they wished, and said what they wished—if they spoke at all. Then, when it became too hard for them to hold their visible form, they just faded away.

Help him.

The woman in white started going transparent up on the mountainside. Dylan shielded her eyes from the hazy light pouring down through the trees, trying to keep her in sight. With a bit of apprehension, she began the trudge upward, using the tight growth of pines and beech to help her over the roughest of the terrain.

By the time she clambered up onto the ridge where the apparition had been standing, the woman was gone. Dylan carefully walked the ledge of rock, and found that it was wider than it appeared from below. The sandstone was weathered dark from the elements, dark enough that a deep vertical slit in the rock had been invisible to her until now.

It was from within that narrow wedge of lightless space that Dylan heard the detached, ghostly whisper once again.

Save him.

She looked around her and saw only wilderness and rock. There was no one up here. Now not even a trace of the ethereal figure, who lured her this far up the mountain alone.

Dylan turned her head to look into the gloom of

the rock's crevice. She put her hand into the space and felt cool, damp air skate over her skin.

Inside that deep black cleft, it was still and quiet.

As quiet as a tomb.

If Dylan was the type to believe in creepy folklore monsters, she might have imagined one could live in a hidden spot like this. But she didn't believe in monsters, never had. Aside from seeing the occasional dead person, who'd never caused her any harm, Dylan was about as practical—even cynical—as could be.

It was the reporter in her that made her curious to know what she might truly find inside the rock. Assuming you could trust the word of a dead woman, who did she think needed help? Was someone injured in there? Could someone have gotten lost way up here on this steep crag?

Dylan grabbed a small flashlight from an outer pocket of her backpack. She shined it into the opening, noticing just then that there were vague chisel marks around and within the crevice, as if someone had worked to widen it. Although not anytime recently, based on the weathered edges of the tool marks.

"Hello?" she called into the darkness. "Is anyone in here?"

Nothing but silence answered.

Dylan pulled off her backpack and carried it in one hand, her other hand wrapped around the slim barrel of her flashlight. Walking forward she could barely fit through the crevice; anyone larger would have been forced to go in sideways.

The tight squeeze only lasted a short distance before the space angled around and began to open up. Suddenly she was inside the thick rock of the mountain, her light beam bouncing off smooth, rounded walls. It was a cave—an empty one, except for some bats rustling out of a disturbed sleep overhead.

And from the look of it, the space was mostly man-made. The ceiling rose at least twenty feet over Dylan's head. Interesting symbols were painted on each wall of the small cavern. They looked like some odd sort of hieroglyphics: a cross between bold, tribal markings and gracefully geometric patterns.

Dylan walked closer to one of the walls, mesmerized by the beauty of the strange artwork. She panned the small beam of her flashlight to the right, breathtaken to find the elaborate decoration continuing all around her. She took a step toward the center of the cave. The toe of her hiking boot knocked into something on the earthen floor. Whatever it was clattered hollowly as it rolled away. Dylan swept her light over the ground and gasped.

Oh, shit.

It was a skull. White bone glowed against the darkness, the human head staring up at her with sightless, vacant sockets.

If this was the *him* the dead woman wanted Dylan to help out, it looked like she got there about a few hundred years too late.

Dylan moved the light farther into the gloom, unsure what she was searching for, but too fascinated to leave just yet. The beam skidded over another set of bones—Jesus, more human remains scattered on the floor of the cave.

Goose bumps prickled on Dylan's arms from a draft that seemed to rise out of nowhere.

And that's when she saw it.

A large rectangular block of stone sat on the other side of the darkness. More markings like the ones covering the walls were painted onto the carved bulk of the object.

Dylan didn't have to move closer to realize that what she was looking at was a crypt. A thick slab had been placed over the top of the tomb. It was moved aside, skewed slightly off the stone crypt as if pushed away by incredibly strong hands.

Was someone—or something—laid to rest in there?

Dylan had to know.

She crept forward, flashlight gripped in suddenly perspiring fingers. A few paces away now, Dylan angled the beam into the opening of the tomb.

It was empty.

And for reasons she couldn't explain, that thought chilled her even more than if she'd found some hideous corpse turning to dust inside.

Over her head, the cave's nocturnal residents were getting restless. The bats stirred, then bolted past her in a hurried rush of motion. Dylan ducked to let them pass, figuring she'd better get the hell out of there too.

As she pivoted to find the crevice exit, she heard another rustle of movement. This one was bigger than bats, a low snarl of sound followed by a disturbance of loose rock somewhere in the cave.

Oh, God.

Maybe she wasn't alone in here after all.

The hairs at the back of her neck tingled and before she could remind herself that she didn't believe in monsters, her heart started beating in overdrive.

She fumbled around for the way out of the cave, her pulse jackhammering in her ears. By the time she found daylight, she was gasping for air. Her legs felt rubbery as she scrambled back down the ridge, then raced to rejoin her friends in the safety of the bright midday sun below.

He'd been dreaming of Eva again.

It wasn't enough that the female had betrayed him in life—now, in her death, she invaded his mind while he slept. Still beautiful, still treacherous, she spoke to him of regret and how she wanted to make things right.

All lies.

Eva's visiting ghost was only a part of Rio's long slide into madness.

His dead mate wept in his dreams, begging him to forgive her for the deception she'd orchestrated a year ago. She was sorry. She still loved him, and always would.

She wasn't real. Just a taunting reminder of a past he would be glad to leave behind.

Trusting the female had cost him much. His face had been ruined in the warehouse explosion. His body was broken in places, still recovering from injuries that would have killed a mortal man.

And his mind . . . ?

Rio's sanity had been fracturing apart bit by bit,

worsening in the time he'd been holed up alone on this Bohemian mountainside.

He could bring it all to a halt. As one of the Breed—a hybrid race of humans bearing vampiric, alien genes—he could drag himself into the sunlight and let the UV rays devour him. He'd considered doing just that, but there remained the task of closing the cave and destroying the damning evidence it contained.

He didn't know how long he'd been there. The days and nights, weeks and months, had at some point merged into an endless suspension of time. He wasn't sure how it had happened. He'd arrived there with his brethren of the Order. The warriors had been on a mission to locate and destroy an old evil secreted away in the rocks centuries ago.

But they were too late.

The crypt was empty; the evil had already been freed.

It was Rio who volunteered to stay behind and seal the cave while the others returned home to Boston. He couldn't go back with them. He didn't know where he belonged. He'd intended to find his own way—maybe go back to Spain, his homeland.

That's what he'd told the warriors who'd long been like brothers to him. But he hadn't carried out any of his plans.

Now, easily months later, he lurked in the darkness of the cave like the bats that inhabited the dank space with him. He no longer hunted, no longer had the desire to feed. He merely existed, conscious of his steady descent into a hell of his own making.

For Rio, that descent had finally proven too much.

Beside him on a hollowed-out ledge of rock ten feet up from the floor of the cave rested a detonator and a small cache of C-4. It was enough boom to seal up the hidden crypt forever. Rio intended to set it off that night . . . from the inside.

Tonight, he would finish it.

When his lethargic senses roused him from a heavy sleep to warn him of an intruder, he thought it to be just another tormenting phantom. He caught the scent of a human—a young female, judging by the musky warmth that clung to her skin. His eyes peeled open in the dark, nostrils flaring to pull more of her fragrance into his lungs.

She was no trick of his madness.

She was flesh and blood, the first human to venture anywhere near the obscure mouth of the cave in all the time he'd been there. The woman shined a bright light around the cave, temporarily blinding him, even from his concealed position above her head. He heard her footsteps scuffing on the sandstone floor of the cavern. Heard her sudden gasp as she knocked into some of the skeletal litter left behind by the original occupant of the place.

Rio shifted himself on the ledge, testing his limbs in preparation of a leap to the floor below. The stirring of the air disturbed the bats clinging to the ceiling. They flew out, but the woman remained. Her light traveled more of the cave, then came to rest on the tomb that lay open.

Rio felt her curiosity chill toward fear as she neared the crypt. Even her human instincts picked up on the evil that had once slept in that block of stone.

But she shouldn't be there.

Rio couldn't let her see any more than she already had. He heard himself snarl as he moved on the rocky jut overhead. The woman heard it too. She tensed with alarm. The beam of her flashlight ricocheted crazily off the walls as she made a panicked search for the cave's exit.

Before Rio could command his limbs to move, she was already slipping away.

She was gone.

She'd seen too much, but soon it wouldn't matter.

Once night fell, there would be no further trace of the crypt, the cave, or of Rio himself.

HE HAS RESISTED TEMPTATION FOR
CENTURIES, A STONE-COLD WARRIOR
WHOSE FROZEN HEART REFUSES TO
THAW—UNTIL HER. . . .

With a dagger in her hand and vengeance on her mind,
Darkhaven beauty Elise Chase prowls Boston's streets
in search of retribution against the Rogue vampires
who took from her everything she cherished. Using an
extraordinary psychic gift, she tracks her prey, well
aware that the power she possesses is destroying her.
She must learn to harness this gift, and for that she
can turn to only one man—the deadliest of the
Breed warriors, Tegan.

No stranger to loss, Tegan knows Elise's pain. He
knows fury, but when he slays his enemies it is with ice
in his veins. He is perfect in his self-control, until Elise
seeks his aid in her personal war. An unholy alliance is
forged—a bond that will link them by blood and
vow—and plunge them into a tempest of danger,
desire, and the darkest passions of the heart. . . .

Visit our website at www.bantamdell.com.

US $6.99/ $9.99 CAN

ISBN 978-0-553-58939-9

5 0 6 9 9

9 780553 589399